"A masterful debut."   *Edmonton Journal*

"Haunting. . . . By shining her writer's penlight into the shadows of another dark era, Lambert reveals that there is still much to be learned about ourselves."

The Globe and Mail

"Beautifully written. . . . [Lambert's] work has an echo of those other great Canadian writers, Alice Munro and Carol Shields."   *The Daily Mail* (UK)

"Readers are sure to applaud."   *The Vancouver Sun*

"Lambert's book is elegant, evocative and absorbing, full of the aftershocks of sorrow its narrative demands. It is fine work from a writer on the cusp of high accomplishment."

The London Free Press

"*Radiance* is a sublime meditation on the consequences of battle. The subject could not be more topical and her insights could not be more penetrating. A magnificent novel."

Kevin Patterson, author of *Consumption*

"An extraordinarily moving novel. . . . With each turning of the page, my admiration for Shaena Lambert grew: she is a marvellous writer!"

Isabel Huggan, author of *Belonging*

RADI

SHAENA LAMBERT

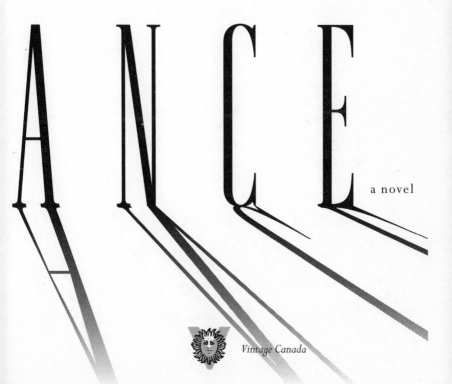

ANCE

a novel

Vintage Canada

VINTAGE CANADA EDITION, 2007

Published in Canada by Vintage Canada, a division of Random House of
Canada Limited, Toronto, in 2007. Originally published in hardcover in
Canada by Random House Canada, a division of Random House of
Canada Limited, Toronto, in 2007. Distributed by Random House of
Canada Limited, Toronto.

Vintage Canada and colophon are registered trademarks of Random
House of Canada Limited.

www.randomhouse.ca

Library and Archives Canada Cataloguing in Publication

Lambert, Shaena
Radiance : a novel / Shaena Lambert.

ISBN 978-0-679-31379-3

I. Title.

PS8573.A3885R23 2007A   C813'.6   C2007-903609-0

Cover design: LBBG – Rachael Ludbrook
Text design: Andrew Roberts

Printed and bound in Canada

2 4 6 8 9 7 5 3 1

For my parents
and my parents-in-law

—*Barbara, Douglas, Norma, Norman*—

with love

ASH MAID

WHEN THE HIROSHIMA PROJECT WAS LONG OVER and all the dust had settled, Daisy discovered that she could close her eyes anywhere, in a crowded room or doing the dishes, and see the girl getting off the plane. She would always think of Keiko as "the girl," though she had been eighteen when she came to stay, old enough to be called a woman. The press seized upon the name Hiroshima Maiden—such an odd way to describe an A-bomb survivor: as though Keiko might have stepped out of an Arthurian legend, wearing a cone-shaped princess hat; as though being ravaged by the bomb might have transformed the girl, giving her, along with a history of suffering, some fairy-tale virtues. Purity perhaps. Or maidenly goodness.

Daisy Lawrence had stood in a small roped-off area on the tarmac of Mitchell Air Force Base, waiting for the airplane to land. Irene Day, one of the Hiroshima Project's principal organizers, stood beside her. The rain was stiff that day— stinging pellets that flew at them sideways out of the gauzy marsh east of the air base. A few feet away a dozen journalists huddled in a grey group, hats pulled low.

Irene Day had dressed appropriately—she always did—in a mannish little fedora and matching kid gloves. She was the sort of woman, Daisy thought, who would choose the right outfit for a hurricane. Next to her Daisy felt dowdy—blond hair frizzing in the wet, feet aching in tight patent-leather pumps.

Of course she knew better than to be thinking about her shoes at a time like this. This was an important moment in history, this chill March day of 1952: she was about to greet a Hiroshima survivor, the first ever to set foot on American soil. Daisy pulled in her stomach, already held tightly in place by her girdle, and did her best to adopt a look of calm expectancy. She moved closer to a freckle-faced young photographer, so that his broad back blocked the rain, which seemed to come from all directions now—stinging her chin and cheeks and the backs of her knees.

At last the gleaming plane hove into view above their heads. It headed out to sea, then banked and came in low, bouncing at the end of the runway, rising like a bird, landing, hissing, skipping. It hung poised for several seconds on one wheel before righting itself with a bump and coming to a stop, emitting black exhaust in a rather alarming fashion. For what seemed an inordinately long time the airplane engine thudded and the propellers churned and thumped. But at last the propellers stilled, the plane gave a final shudder and several air force cadets rolled the steel stairs into place.

The airplane door, massive and unyielding, seemed to need some battering knocks from the inside before it swung open. The pilot, a wing commander in a navy uniform complete with epaulettes, stepped jauntily down the steps, shook hands with the cadets, then walked across the runway. He was followed by two stewards and twenty tanned, robust soldiers—the plane seemed endlessly to disgorge them—men returning from military duty in Hawaii, where the plane had touched down for refuelling.

Then at last Keiko stepped onto the platform. She lifted one gloved hand to straighten her hat. How strangely it glowed in the overcast air, whiter than white. Even from this distance Daisy could see the mottled rhubarb stain on her cheek. The famous atomic scar. She tottered on the platform, looking as though the hard rain might blow her away. The purse Keiko clasped—Daisy learned later—had been picked up in a Honolulu gift shop. It was encrusted with tiny iridescent nautiluses.

Daisy felt an urge to say something to mark the magnitude of the occasion. She turned to Irene, but she was already up ahead, arguing with one of the cadets guarding the gate. He clicked the metal latch with his thumb in an irritating manner, then shook his head severely.

"But I'm the *chief* organizer of this project," Irene was saying. She wasn't, but how was the cadet to know? He shrugged. Irene raised her hand, as though intending to knock the boy's cap off. "Let me by," she hissed, but all at once the freckle-faced photographer, the one whose broad back had sheltered Daisy from the rain, strode forward and leapt the rope. The cadet cried out for him to stop, but the photographer had an agenda of his own: he dashed towards the plane, leaping puddles, soaking his trouser legs, letting his hat blow off, not even turning to see it roll wildly away. And now the rest of them followed suit, and Irene and Daisy were picked up and blown, or so it felt, over the trampled rope and across the runway. They were no longer the official welcoming delegation, not by a long shot: they were part of a mob.

That was Keiko Kitigawa's welcome to America.

The girl turned towards the advancing stampede. With one hand she groped behind her for the banister. The other hand she held up, fingers spread in an ineffectual fan, attempting to

shield her face, with its bubbled scar, from the repeated flash of
the cameras.

2.

IMAGINE A GIRL to whom you can attach any stereotype.

Imagine her stepping off a plane, holding up a hand to keep
her prim round hat in place.

Imagine her as inscrutable.

Imagine her as incomparably damaged.

Imagine her as carrying the seeds of something entirely new—
radioactive seeds—lodged in her bones, skin, hair.

Imagine her as the first of her kind to come to America: children of the atomic bomb. Children who are asked, repeatedly, in
letters that arrive each spring, to donate their bodies to science,
so that when they die—six years later, or forty—their hearts
can be examined, their cells studied, their kidneys filled with
turquoise dye, placed in a Petri dish.

Now imagine what it would take to shake these multiple iden-
tities. To stand up, under that weight, and launch yourself out of
Tokyo on a Boeing 747, to sleep and wake and find yourself over
a huge grey sea—far below you there are the ragged shapes of
waves, like ice floes on the tundra.

Whatever occurs down there is invisible. Some species of fish
that live in those waters have never been discovered.

Keiko had come to America to have her face operated on. She
had pulled herself forward to this place, urged by her mother,
whose spirit she prayed to before leaving Hiroshima. She had
risen early, before her Aunt Yoshiko could hear her, and she

had dressed in the smart outfit she wore for the first leg of her journey, a herringbone skirt and matching jacket with a cream satin lining. She had crept down the hall to the ugly little parlour decorated in the western way, all her uncle's bad taste. She had knelt before the shelf that held the *ihai,* the little placards that represented the spirits of the dead. Grandfather's placard was more august than Mama's, though they were both quite simple markers, made of white wood with names inscribed in ink and the word *Matsumi* at the bottom. *Spirit.*

During the night the oil light had guttered and gone out. Keiko relit the flame and then made her prayers. Always a tiny part of her asked for forgiveness. Always her mother's spirit was quick to say yes—too quick. She had been prone to indulgences, always giving Keiko two of the red rice cakes at festival time, taking none for herself.

You have been greedy, Keiko addressed herself silently. *And you will pay the price.*

"Forgive me," she said out loud—and what she meant was for living when so many others had died. When Mama died. When Grandfather died. And not only must she ask forgiveness for living, but for wanting to live; for receiving the highest marks in her graduating class at Hiroshima Prefectural High School; for rejoicing over things that ought not to bring so much happiness, like the breezes that come up from the Inland Sea, or a cascade of plum blossoms, only yesterday, falling around her, a young man—an American in uniform—smiling at her as she crossed the street. He had seen only one side of her face.

Her interview, four months before, had taken place at the Atomic Bomb Casualty Commission in the building where *hibakusha,* atomic-bomb survivors, were routinely examined. She had sat up very properly in the small room, on the thin high bed covered in white cloth. She had let the American doctor study her face, moving her chin back and forth, pushing back her hair, touching the round keloid behind her left ear. The handsome doctor, his name was Dr. Carney, murmured, "Exceptionally pretty," not expecting Keiko to understand.

"Thank you." Her English was polished, almost perfect. Her first surprise for them.

"Tell us a little about yourself," the kind one had said. His name was Mr. Atchity, the head of the whole project—and because some instinct told her what it took to excel, the words had flowed out. *I believe we must work together to outlaw atomic weapons. Goodwill. Friendship.* And then—when that did not seem to be enough—she had begun to speak of the day of the bombing. Words she had never before spoken came from her mouth, as though guided by a spirit beyond her, like a singer finding, at last, a song in her exact range, a strange song she didn't know she could sing until that moment.

"There was a bright light."

Ah.

The two men stopped leafing through their notes, stopped looking to see the name of the next girl.

"I remember it so clearly. A bright, terrible light."

They listened. Transfixed by what she might say next.

"I was standing on a rock in our garden and I raised my hand—like this, you see—to block the blast."

The kind one put his papers down. He took off his glasses, wiped them on a handkerchief, put them back on his nose. The other one, the handsome doctor who smelled sweaty, jumped from his chair and took Keiko's hands and pressed the palms with his thumbs—an excited gesture for which he didn't seem responsible.

"Miss Kitigawa—we need a girl who is prepared to speak to the American people."

"I can describe what I remember."

"And in return we will remove the scar. I believe we can. It looks *eminently* removable."

They asked her more questions. They took notes. She told them things she had not spoken, ever. She told them about Grandfather, and Mama, and Mr. Takahura, all dead. She didn't tell them everything, but it was enough.

After the interview Keiko returned to her surrogate family: to her uncle who did not love her; to her aunt who was jealous of her. She told them that she had been chosen to go to America. Yoshiko decided to make a fuss. "Keiko-chan—when will we see you again?"

"Perhaps never," Keiko said coldly—thinking this thought for the first time, realizing how much she wanted it to be true.

Now she knelt before the shelf of her ancestors. This was the last chance she would have, perhaps ever, to kneel like this. She knew that the dead were blaming her, that her mother was pinching her lips together, even as she offered up every excuse for her daughter's conduct. It was wrong to hold on to life as she had. She knew this.

She prayed for a long time, then stood up, put out the wick and turned her back on the shelf that held her mother's spirit.

Keiko stared from her airplane window at the frozen sea, its tiny, immaculate pattern of waves. For a while, she thought, she would not be herself. She would have to be what she had said she was to the doctors; to the kind Mr. Atchity, the head of the Hiroshima Project; to the handsome but foul-smelling Dr. Carney, with his plump, hairy knuckles. She would have to be everything they wanted her to be. She would have to be nothing. But that was all right. She had received the highest marks ever on graduating from the Hiroshima Prefectural High School. She was good at what she attempted. Now she would hold her breath and count on her instinct—that instinct she must always ask forgiveness for—to tell her how to survive.

That was Keiko on the day of her arrival.

3.

THEY DROVE FROM THE AIRPORT in Daisy's sky-blue Chevrolet, Keiko up front, Irene in the back, leaning forward to talk. Keiko sat up very straight in a dress with layers of tulle beneath black and mauve seersucker. It crunched when she moved. She wore the hat, the gloves. In the trunk was her small but impressive collection of luggage. Daisy had imagined that the girl might arrive with a straw basket, a birdcage and a beaten leather trunk—immigrant luggage—but she came with a pearly set of matching Samsonite cases, a gift from the Japanese end of the Hiroshima Project. Daisy herself owned nothing so chic in the way of luggage.

How strange things must have looked to the girl, Daisy thought. Everything so glancing and bright, yet overprinted by extreme fatigue. Irene pointed out some Jersey cows in a field, their hindquarters bony, and Daisy assured Keiko that most American cows were fatter, a patriotism that embarrassed her immediately; this was the sort of thing that Walter, her husband, always mocked her for.

How unpleasant, too, to have to keep answering Irene's questions, what an effort to draw aside, with each response, the curtain of exhaustion. That was why she chose to say little, beyond introducing herself as Keiko's host. "Homestay mother" was how the Project liked to describe her. Meanwhile, Irene ploughed ahead with her welcoming comments, pointing out the shape of the city in the distance, explaining the next week's worth of activities.

"Eleanor Roosevelt. You know who she is, of course. Remarkable woman. She wants to meet you. I've made those arrangements, but not tonight. Tonight there's to be a party at my apartment, just the editors of the *Sunday Review,* and Daisy Lawrence here—you'll be staying with her next week, right after your first operation. Oh, and Dr. Carney will be at the party, of course—you've met him—and Dean Atchity, our fearless leader." She continued relentlessly. It seemed to Daisy that if Irene hesitated, even for a second, she would be forced to take in the reality: this quiet girl in the front seat who, turning slightly to acknowledge Irene, had no choice but to present her left cheek, with its massive atomic scar.

The only reason Daisy was in the car at that moment, hurtling towards the overcast city, doing something so bright and shocking that she felt dizzy, the only reason she was there at all was because she had run into Irene on Fifth Avenue five months before.

"Daisy Parker—not really!" Irene had leaned forward and kissed Daisy's cheek, a dry, papery touch that for some reason had made Daisy feel homesick.

"You haven't changed at all," Daisy said.

"Oh, I'm infinitely older. Ancient. But look at you. *Margaret Mary Parker.* We used to call you that, didn't we?"

Yes, her college friends had, spurred on by Irene, who had delighted in the arcane sound of Daisy's full name—the toning of church bells, the smell of incense. Daisy's gentle father had chosen it in a moment of religious enthusiasm following her birth, one of the rare moments he had put his foot down; Daisy's mother had shortened it immediately. Only one or two of the sisters at Sacred Heart, where Daisy went to school, had insisted on using the full name—and Irene, of course.

They had been quite close in college and then fallen away during the long war years, when they had little in common. Daisy had become a stenographer at Porter and Peck, while Irene had married and divorced twice. The second marriage had ended disastrously two weeks into the honeymoon. "He kept making passes at the ship's steward," Irene had told Daisy. "Imagine my discomfort. I had to bunk in with friends to give them time to be alone." Sometimes Irene made her life seem like a series of glittering events that had happened to somebody else.

"But look at you, Daisy," she said. "The suburbs must suit you. And how's that dishy husband of yours? Still writing?"

When Daisy mentioned that Walter was writing for radio, Irene rolled the word around in her mouth, as though to detect, by mouth feel, whether it was glamorous or outdated. "How wonderful! Shows I know?"

Daisy mentioned a few.

"A clever man, your Walter. And of course I think *Fall from Grace* has a seminal—absolutely seminal—place in American theatre." *Fall from Grace* was the play Walter had written many years before, before Daisy had met him. It had had a decent run off Broadway; one reviewer had even said that it was as good as something Clifford Odets would write. Then the war had come, and Walter had broken ties with all his old progressive friends, and come back changed. He had married Daisy, moved to the suburbs and written nothing important since.

"I was sorry—" Irene stopped.

Daisy had forgotten this side of Irene: how she could lower her voice, look you in the eyes, come gently to the point. In college, Daisy had sometimes felt that Irene represented the exact centre of the universe.

"Thank you."

"You told me about it last time we met. I wondered, you know, if I had listened properly."

They were talking about Daisy's miscarriage, her first one (Irene didn't know about the second), and the discussion they had had about it almost three years before. No, Irene had not listened properly. She had given herself over to the subject with rapt enthusiasm, offering condolences, providing theories—too many theories, some of them Freudian—about Daisy's depression.

"You were fine. You were wonderful."

Then all at once Irene looked sharply at Daisy, really looked at her. She took her by the arm, pinching her skin—such was her enthusiasm. "I have an idea," she had said. They walked up Forty-second Street to Schraffts, in the Chrysler Building, and ordered cheeseburgers and Coke. There, amid the hubbub of shoppers eating their creamed soup and burgers and hot fudge sundaes, Irene told her about the Hiroshima Project. It was backed by the *Sunday Review,* Irene's magazine, and it had all been going swimmingly until the Quaker woman chosen to be Keiko's host had backed out, afraid of the effect of atomic radiation on her children.

"Quakers are awfully difficult to work with," Irene sighed. "So passive. So *silent.* A most trying people."

Daisy glanced across the table at her friend, taking in the flat chest, French-manicured nails, thin nose that twitched as she spoke, a foxy mannerism that Daisy had briefly attempted to imitate in college. Irene's dark hair was pulled back into a chignon; her pale face was powdered; her lips were fire-engine red; a highly becoming veiled hat covered one eye, green beads sewn onto it, gleaming like flies' wings.

"What do you think, Daisy?"

"I don't know. I'm not sure."

"It's so seldom"—Irene leaned forward, holding the last nibble of cheeseburger in her hand— "so very seldom, in these terrible times, that any of us gets to play a role in history."

And Daisy had met her friend's eyes and said yes—just like that, on the spot—because the very idea of playing a role in history had made her feel electric.

4.

DAISY WAS UNDERDRESSED for the party at Irene's apartment; she hadn't brought a change of clothing, and so she had on the same gabardine suit she had worn to the airport. She was worried that she smelled, ever so slightly, of wet dog. In the bathroom she combed her sandy hair and applied powder to her soft, freckled cheeks, then stepped back to take a look. She still had a good figure, though it was a far cry from the one she had had in college. Nor was her face quite what it had been. Back then some of the girls had said she looked like a china doll, because she was sweet-faced and compact and blond. Now, at thirty-four years of age, if she was a china doll, she was a swollen one, plumped out so that she had barely been able to fit into last fall's cinch-waisted fashions. She was still pretty, but bigger, wobblier, and prone to tilting her head and smiling too brightly when pictures were taken—an eager show of normalcy that made her seem afraid.

She came out of the bathroom and looked around. The apartment was just beginning to fill, with journalists from the *Sunday Review,* Hiroshima Project organizers and some others ("notables," Irene had called them): funders, senators, people from city hall.

The apartment was part of Irene's first divorce settlement. She had ruthlessly sold off the contents—Louis Quinze mirrors, leather-bound books, collections of rare blue butterflies—and redecorated with a stark boxy sofa, zebra rug and black leather and chrome folding chairs. In tribute to her Village days, or perhaps because old habits die hard, she had stuffed a wine jug full of bulrushes and set it by the entrance to the kitchen.

Daisy went to the window and looked out over the filigree of wrought-iron palings, with their repeating pattern of pine cones, over window boxes in which Irene, characteristically, had placed nothing. Looking west she glimpsed Central Park, the flash of taxis between limbs of black trees. She took a deep breath, then turned, preparing to socialize. Keiko seemed to be managing. She sat on the white sofa, wearing a cobalt-blue dress with a stiff piqué collar and a pair of gloves with petal scallops at the cuff. On her head was a blue velvet cocktail hat, a teensy bit of a thing with two blue feathers poked into the top. Two young men sat with her—one on a low, tufted ottoman—and they were both asking questions, nodding every time she spoke.

And how do you like America so far?

Will you be going up the Empire State Building?

They ignored Keiko's scar. But there it was, Daisy could see it clearly now—the left side of the girl's face was towards her. *Don't look into my eyes*, that scar seemed to scream. *Don't look at my pretty cobalt-blue dress, or speculate on the immense effort it took to make this hat—look, instead, at the exact surface of my skin, the bubbles, the ridges, the bulbous keloid behind my ear.*

The scar covered the left side of her face, fat at the top, tapering to a point near her chin, like the outline of South America. It even had bubbles and gritty rifts resembling the ridges and chasms of mountains and canyons. And there, dangling behind her left ear like a strange adornment, was a shiny bauble of red-brown flesh: the keloid. No flesh should grow hard and round like that, Daisy thought, and a feeling of fascination, almost of desire, moved inside her—a muddy slurping inside the skin and bones of civility.

The girl was so young, that was the thing. Beneath her hat her hair looked soft, like baby bird's down, and it was cut around her face in a fey pixie style. Her beauty, if you could call it that (even with the scar she was very attractive), was of the gamine, boyish variety, so different from the blowsy women popular at the moment—the Jane Russells and the Marilyn Monroes. So different from Daisy herself. But the most startling thing about Keiko was her eyes. Daisy had noticed them at the airport. They were light brown, very clear, without any noticeable marks or striations. A milky circle surrounded each iris. Keiko looked up—a flash of those eyes—and Daisy quickly turned away. She didn't want to be caught staring like some rube at a carnival.

The room was certainly full of interesting people, just as Irene had said. Dean Atchity stood by the baby grand, hands shoved deep into his jacket pockets, talking in a low voice to one of his colleagues. The mutter of professionals. He was the senior editor and founder of the *Sunday Review,* and the head of the Hiroshima Project. More like the king, actually, that was how people treated him, a benign potentate. He certainly looked aristocratic, with his high polished forehead and intelligent, long-fingered hands (saved from being too feminine by the hairs above each knuckle). When Daisy had joined the Project she had lunched with him and his wife, Bertha—soufflés at Voisin. Up close he smelled warmly and pleasantly of cherry pipe tobacco, as though, en route from Fairfield County, he had breezed through a smokehouse.

By the punch bowl was the chief surgeon, Dr. Raymond Carney. Daisy hadn't yet met him; he had been in Japan when she joined the Project. Dr. Carney was a minor celebrity: for several years he had been on the radio with a show, highly rated in the Five Boroughs, called *Ask a Doctor*. Daisy had heard that he had plans with NBC to move the show to television. He was handsome, short, with bushy hair, and his radio voice was certainly attractive, though he seemed to be a bit of a showman. He had donated his surgical talents to the Project, pro bono.

There were also some congressmen in the room, a senator and a lot of junior-type female staff from the *Sunday Review*. The women dressed in stovepipe skirts that hobbled their knees, their faces powdered like vampires, their lips painted chilling shades of maroon and crimson.

For a moment Daisy felt a surge of her old jealousy. Here she was, in this glittering company, and all she could say for herself was that she was a housewife. And not just any kind of housewife: she was that most pitiable of God's creations, a housewife without children. Meanwhile, in the years since college, Irene had sailed into the stratosphere with her own column in the *Sunday Review*. It was called "The Women's Circle," perhaps not the most glamorous name, but it had a large readership. Daisy always leafed to Irene's page first, read her article top to bottom, then derided it meanly. "Oh, God," she would say to Walter, throwing the magazine down on the table. "Just listen to Irene. She's going on about the price of butter again." Or "Who could have guessed that gelatine was such a versatile substance?" But the truth was that given the stiff limitations imposed on her, Irene often managed to broaden her themes— exposing the plight of the grape-pickers, for instance, while explaining what wine to serve for dinner; exploring the changed world of the Chinese peasant while giving recipes for deep-frying egg rolls. She did everything, in short, that Daisy might have dreamed of doing if she had had the job. Which she didn't. Not by a long shot.

In college, and since living in Riverside Meadows, Daisy had harboured a secret wish to write. She wanted to write quite desperately at times, with lust and indignity and shame attached to the desire. Perhaps that was why she had married Walter: sublimated desire, as people loved to say. Yet whenever Daisy tried—sneaking in to sit at Walter's greasy old typewriter, typing out her story ideas—she felt humiliated by how tiny her observations turned out to be. By the time she had written and rewritten a single paragraph, it was just terribly filigreed and dead, as though she had applied layers of Byzantine gilding to a corpse.

Irene swooped down on her now. Her cocktail pyjamas were made of a clinging, draping duplon-type material; they could have gone through the apocalypse without a wrinkle. She wore an interesting and, to Daisy's mind, extremely unbecoming turban.

"I do hope I'm doing everything right," she whispered, a whiff of crab pastry on her breath. "We don't have much of a precedent, do we?"

"Everything looks beautiful."

"Well, I hope so. One must do one's best." She leaned close and Daisy had the impression of lightweight undergarments beneath her rustling pyjama suit, perhaps nothing more than a silk chemise. "I want you to see something. Look out the window. There." Irene pushed up the sash and both women put their heads out. Four floors down, on the sidewalk beside the green awning, Daisy saw a figure foreshortened—bare red head, overcoat, polished brown shoes. "It's that photographer from the airport—the one who started our stampede. He wanted to come up, and I rather thought it might be a good idea, but Dean said no. He doesn't want the press here tonight—all that's to start after the first operation. Still, one must admire the man's tenacity."

They peered below, and the man glanced up, freckle-faced and rosy-cheeked. He beamed when he saw them, and seemed about to wave, or call up even, but Irene pulled Daisy back and shut the window. "He's wasting his time tonight. Still, she'll be good with the press. Her English is wonderful, isn't it? So there won't be a language barrier." They were facing the room again. Irene lowered her voice still further. "Of course, her story is harrowing, Daisy."

Daisy felt her heart beat faster. "I'm sure it must be."

"When Raymond and Dean interviewed her in Hiroshima, Dean wept, that's what I heard."

"I can't imagine."

Irene shook her head. "Neither can I. Neither can anyone. That's why we need to hear her tell it, in her own words."

Daisy nodded. They stood for a moment in silence, listening to the hubbub around them, the girl at the centre—so poised— eye of the storm. Daisy remembered the feel of her palm, dry and papery, when they shook hands at the airport.

"So the first press conference is scheduled for a week today," Irene continued, "the day she gets out of the hospital. I'd like her to share the stage with Oppenheimer—you must know that he's come out against the Superbomb?"

"Yes, I've heard."

"But even he, with all his connections, doesn't know when they'll test the thing. Though he suspects it's nearly ready—they really are a set of bastards."

It was hard to tell exactly to whom she was referring, but Daisy knew it was the bastards in the Joint Committee on Atomic Energy, the ones secretly advocating the development of the hydrogen bomb, refusing to respond to public calls for a ban on the weapon. A ban on *testing*—that was what the Hiroshima Project advocated, a wise distinction that Dean Atchity had written about at length. For it was not conceivable that the nation, at this dangerous juncture, could or even should stop development of a fusion bomb, not with the Soviet Union at work on one. But if there were a complete ban on testing, the Project suggested, then neither side could successfully develop new bombs. So a ban on testing was really just as good as a ban on creation. As for the Superbomb itself, it was rumoured to be terrible. Daisy got confused by kilotonnage and megatonnage, but the Superbomb was supposed to be a hundred, or two hundred, or even three hundred times more powerful than the bomb dropped on Hiroshima.

"Of course, I'm keen to get moving, the support for a test ban is growing like mad. But I think that Dean is right. One step at a time." At that moment, Atchity beckoned to Irene, and with a kiss on Daisy's cheek she rushed away.

Daisy let herself take in the strangeness of the situation. There was Dean Atchity, senior editor of the *Sunday Review,* waving Keiko's empty punch glass at Irene, while Irene fairly blew across the room to take it from him. All of this for a girl who seven years before had been their sworn enemy. Seven years was not such a long time, and yet in other ways it was an eon. At that time, in that other world, the newspapers had been full of horrifying stories about the Japanese. They had killed American boys in horrid, fetid jungles. They had imprisoned and tortured them, then sent them back, after the war was over, scrawny and malnourished, ravaged by yellow fever and malaria. They had broken every article of the Geneva Convention. And in retaliation they had been bombed into defeat and submission. Yet here everyone was, gathered in Irene's apartment, attempting with all the goodwill in the world to atone for what had happened.

She could hear more polite questions being put to Keiko, while she sat looking picturesque and almost varnished, ankles crossed, gloved hands holding her glass. Daisy heard the girl's voice, oddly pure: *Thank you, yes, my flight was pleasant. Long, yes, but pleasant.* Daisy marvelled at her poise—though it was more than poise, it had to be. It was, at the root, a deep self-confidence. How else could she do all this? Be picked from among so many girls, all eager to come to America. Daisy remembered what she'd read: top marks at high school, an interest in fashion, dress designing, languages. Keiko was from a wealthy, established family—the memo had said "ancient." Daisy wasn't sure what ancientness meant in Japanese terms. She pictured a samurai grandfather, a grandmother wearing a flowing silk kimono, squatting on a tatami mat, serving tea. She set these images against the pattern of her mother's old willowware platter, remembering the curious collection of items in her mother's lacquered cabinet. "My chinoiserie," her mother used to call these things—fans and wooden dolls with bobbing heads, a porcelain tea set with crackled glaze.

Daisy made her way to the punch bowl and scooped some of the cherry liquid into her glass, spilling a drop onto a white stripe of the zebra carpet, where it spread like watery blood. The patter of voices was all around her: names of writers she didn't recognize, writers who had eschewed first names in favour of initials; the language of Freudian psychology: neuroses, psychoses; "What do you do when the fellow living right next to you has a nervous breakdown?" Nervous breakdowns were increasingly common, Daisy had noticed with some alarm. Joan Palmer, her neighbour, talked in dire and knowing terms about an old school friend who had attached a vacuum cleaner hose to the exhaust pipe of her car and asphyxiated herself in her garage while her children watched *Howdy Doody.* Daisy prided herself on never having come close to a nervous breakdown. The only time she had felt near to one at all was after her miscarriages. Then she had let herself go terribly, into a place that it hurt to think about now. For a long time, a very long time, she had felt sealed behind glass.

She added a second splash of punch then took a sip. It was better not to think about such things, marooned among people she didn't know, or the ache could open up again, as though it were a hole in the fabric of the world, a hole she couldn't see, because it was tilted up on one edge. Sometimes it opened up at the oddest moments, blossoming with darkness.

People beside her were talking about the McCarthy Hearings. "A charlatan," she heard. "A blackguard."

"And yet," a girl with red lips was saying, "there are Reds in the State Department. Not two hundred and five. Not fifty-four—but some. We *know* this." Whatever else she said was lost in a mumble of voices. This was why Walter hadn't come: he hated people who talked like they knew everything. Blatherers, he called them. Poseurs. Only he didn't pronounce it in the French way. He said *posers*, with the accent on the first syllable. Like it was a solid word from the western United States—a word from Puget Sound, perhaps, from the woods where he had grown up, where men had no truck with French pronunciation.

5.

DR. CARNEY SLID NEXT TO DAISY as she stood beside the punch bowl. Up close the skin beneath his eyes was puffy. Now that he stood next to her, she had the impression that Carney might be a heavy drinker: he had the flamboyant flush, the wet eye.

"You must be the host mother." His tone was light, disparaging.

Daisy straightened her back. "No," she said, "as a matter of fact, I'm a journalist with the *Sunday Review.*"

He laughed.

"What?"

"Not in a million years."

"Perhaps I write for 'The Women's Circle.'"

He shook his head and offered her a cigarette, which she took. He lit a match and Daisy, bending, breathed in the smell of his hands. He had clean nails and stubby, unsurgeonlike fingers. There was a plumpness at the base of his thumb that she found erotic.

"*She* writes for the *Sunday Review,*" he said, gesturing with his chin at Irene, who had thrown back her head to laugh at something Dean Atchity had said. "And *she*—" He pointed to a woman dressed in a black turtleneck, leaning against a wall, talking to a man in grey. "But you–" He looked her up and down, at her pointed breasts in her gabardine suit jacket, at her tightly cinched waist (when she took off her girdle later that night, her stomach was imprinted with leaves and flowers). "You put on your best suit," he said, "nothing too showy, but flattering, and you drove here. Commuted."

"Couldn't I have taken the train?"

"Unlikely," he said. "Got yourself a car, a station wagon, I'd guess. And you like to use it."

"And where did I commute from?"

"Long Island," he said promptly. "Or possibly New Jersey."

"And how do you know all this?"

He bent so close that she could feel his lips against her hair. She half expected him to bite her earlobe, or thrust his tongue suddenly and thickly into the whorl of her ear, but he merely said, in a hot voice: "It shows." Then he stood back and laughed. "But there's nothing wrong with that. You lovely ladies are what keep the world turning."

Daisy placed her glass on the table. "You happen to have misread me completely."

He dipped into the punch bowl. "As a matter of fact, Irene has told me quite a bit about you. Said you were just right to host our visitor. Please don't take offence."

"I wouldn't dream of it."

She nodded goodbye to Dr. Carney and made her way through the crowd to the bathroom, where she locked the door and splashed cold water on her face. In the mirror she looked blurry—and bloated too, from eating too much at night after Walter had shuffled away from the supper table, his slippers on the hall floor sibilant and gritty. She would stand in the cool of the Frigidaire, eating beef stroganoff, using up precious energy—energy that was badly needed in Germany or Japan, in restructuring France or still-conserving Britain. She took her spoon, or even Walter's spoon if it was close, and shovelled the creamy wine-flavoured noodles into her mouth. She hardly chewed, just took the food in as snakes do. She had read some-where that they could swallow an animal three times their size by relaxing a muscle deep in their throats.

When Daisy returned to the living room, Irene was calling for everyone's attention. "Dean would like to say a few words," she said. "Nobody move!"

Atchity had taken up a position by the front door, where he could address everyone. His ears were backlit by one of the sconce lights on the wall behind him, to unfortunate affect: they shone pink in a rather distracting way. "I do have a few words," he said in his thin, practical voice. "Possibly more than a few words." He cleared his throat and then began to speak.

"For the past year," he said, "I have had the honour to work with a team of dedicated doctors and philanthropists, both here and in Hiroshima. Our goal has been nothing less than to bring victims of the atomic bomb to New York City, to Mount Sinai

Hospital, so that their faces can be operated on by the best plastic surgeons in the world. Sometimes it looked as if this project might not even get off the ground. At other times we were full of hope and anticipation. Tonight, we see the first fruits of our labours. We welcome you, Keiko Kitigawa, to Manhattan and to the Hiroshima Project. It is our dear hope that you will be only the first of many visitors from Hiroshima to come to our city for restorative surgery. This is the beginning—only the beginning."

There was applause.

Atchity rocked back on his heels. "Even as we stand here," he said, "united by this humanitarian cause, we must be mindful of the dangers we face. Last month, Senator McMahon, the chairman of the Joint Senate-House Atomic Energy Committee, told us for the first time, without equivocation, that the United States is indeed developing a new Superbomb. All of civilized humanity cannot help but be appalled. And as we know, the Soviet Union has also announced plans to build its own thermonuclear weapon.

"Never, in the long road civilization has travelled, have we so badly needed human voices—voices raised in protest, voices raised to condemn, voices, like Miss Kitigawa's, that can describe, from personal experience, the devastation caused by the atomic bomb."

A murmur of approval went around the room. Daisy, standing near the bedroom door, was only a few feet from Keiko. Her eyes were lowered, studying her punch glass. Atchity emphasized the devastating story she would soon tell, beginning immediately after her hospitalization. A surge of pity passed through Daisy. People had surrounded the girl since she had arrived at the apartment; every important person had been introduced to her. How insensitive they had been, squeezing her like an accordion, no thought to how tired she must be. If Daisy could have, she would have sidled up to the girl now—she was, after all, hardly more than a child—and looked her right in the eye, past that disfiguring scar. *I know how it is with you.* That was what Daisy's look might say. *I know how overwhelmed you are. Yes, I can see into you— a little, just a little.* Throughout the party, and even in the car from the airport, had she been waiting for this opportunity? It certainly felt that way now.

Dean was describing how a fusion bomb would alter the course of civilization. "We are on the brink," he said, "and soon we will pitch forward into the dark unknown." A buzz went through the crowd. They liked those words, *the dark unknown.* And it was true, Daisy thought. They were, every one of them, staring into the future, trying to make out its dread shape. The very taste of nuclear weapons was in the room—their ashen dust, their radioactive itch.

She was just a small stone's throw from Keiko. This was Daisy's opportunity and she decided to take it, as kind, gentle Dean began to wrap up.

"We are the children of the atomic bomb," he was saying. "All of us, in this room. It is our dark mother. We live now and forever in its shadow. People in the world are divided in many ways—particularly in the Soviet East and the freedom-loving West—but, if I might paraphrase the words of that great thinker Bertrand Russell—whose name you will see on the Project letterhead— 'Let us but remember our humanity—and forget all the rest.'"

There were calls of *hear, hear,* and Keiko, perhaps sensing Daisy's stare, glanced her way. Daisy smiled. It was the smile that had always done the trick in college: a tender, sweet, girlish smile that said, *I am a person of goodwill. I won't hurt you.* In fact, when Daisy was a girl of ten she used to ride the bus smiling at complete strangers in just that way, trying to brighten their day.

Oh that scar—the large, bubbled territory—and those amber

eyes. The girl took in Daisy's smile, the frightened edges of it, and then she frowned, just like that, and looked away. As though Daisy's smile were a gift she had no use for. As though refusing a glass of punch.

Daisy stood frozen, blushing deeply. She had an awful complexion for showing her feelings. The room seemed to thrum, that particular thrum of birds beating their wings against a window. She must have been mistaken. Why would this girl, whom they had brought to New York at such expense, be refusing her smile?

Later she would think about that moment many times. In the spring and summer, after Keiko came to live with her, she would think about it, telling herself she must have imagined that glance of malevolence, the goosebumps rising on the girl's arms. But later still, when Keiko was gone, she knew it was the realest image she carried of the girl. Never lose sight of your first impressions, she told herself then—they act as guides.

But now Dean was urging everybody to raise their glasses high and drink to a shared future.

To the pilot project, to the pilot project.

For a moment the air was thick with the general murmur, then they touched their glasses together—a musical tinkle, low and high, like wind chimes.

6.

DAISY WASN'T ONE TO THINK about history—capital H—or progress, or even politics very much. It would have felt pretentious to start any sentence, as Irene so often did, with *Here we are, on the brink.* Or *This terrible time that we live in.* Even the word *postwar* was laden, carrying a freight load of something-or-other that seemed clearer to everyone else than to her. Yet driving home that night, she had Dean Atchity's words in her head: how he had called the bomb "our dark mother." She hadn't paid full attention, but now the words, associated as they were with the coolness of Keiko's frown, sounded in her mind—dire and appalling, yet foreign and exciting too.

They were poised, all the men and women in the room, and soon they would pitch forward into the unknown. That was what Atchity had said. But they weren't blind instruments of fate; they could alter the unknown, bring light into the darkness, even such a small band of people as they were. Atchity seemed to have nothing less in mind than the elimination of atomic weapons. And why not? The A-bomb had only been invented seven years before. It was a new thing. Certainly all the best minds—Dean Atchity, Albert Schweitzer, Bertrand Russell, even the A-bomb's inventor, Robert Oppenheimer—were writing in *Life* and the *Sunday Review* that it would be utter madness to develop a hydrogen bomb. They used calm, reasonable tones, the way you might talk to a toddler who had picked up a gun. They seemed to believe that the world might still bring these weapons under the control of the United Nations. Then, working as one civilized mass, humanity could lock every thermonuclear and atomic blueprint in a vault and bury it at the bottom of the sea.

The rain had stopped and the moon was full. In the city the buildings had obscured it, but when Daisy had driven over the bridge and through the outskirts of Brooklyn, with its jumble of auto-parts shops and high-rise housing projects, each topped with its stubby water tower, there it was, large and poker-faced, smoky at the edges. Once she was well along the Northern State Parkway, she kept glimpsing it behind the stone bridges that spanned the highway, or flashing between the scrubby hemlocks, glimpsing it and then losing it again.

The twinkling lights of housing tracts broke the emptiness of fields. Occasionally she passed an abandoned farmhouse, windows bleakly facing the four lanes of parkway, where once they had stared, probably with equal bleakness, into acres of potatoes, fields of corn. The subdivisions in Nassau County were so new that by daylight they looked outlandish, newly seeded. At the red light near Levittown, she could hear the train in the distance, heaving and screeching.

You do something, Daisy was thinking, and then you do something else, and all at once you discover you have altered the course of your life. *My friends, there is a choice.* Weren't those Atchity's words? In the back of her mind was a fairy tale she had read as a child. In it a Russian prince, the youngest brother, of course, is asked to find a rare and beautiful bird with wings of fire. On the way he stops on the road to feed an old woman. It is a small act, quite natural for this youngest son who, like youngest sons in all fairy tales, is blessed with an easy kindness. Later the old woman helps him with certain magical tasks: rescuing the princess, opening the cage of the firebird.

Before her miscarriage, the summer she and Walter had moved to Riverside Meadows, she had made many happy and foolish plans. They usually featured Walter, lean and distinguished, sitting beside their neighbour, Gerald Strickland's pool, while Daisy waded with her toddler in the shallow end; Walter heading out the door, looking handsome and clever, off to the city to deliver his radio scripts while Daisy fed the baby or vacuumed or even found time to bake bread. Walter, Walter, Walter. He was at the heart of everything. He and the baby. After the first miscarriage, her family doctor said there was still lots of hope. She had a good chance of giving birth to a perfectly healthy baby. The important thing was not to wallow in grief. He had used that word, *wallow,* and Daisy had seen herself up to her ears in mud, lavishly despairing. *Be strong, be bold*—her family doctor had said. *Take the bull by the horn,* by which she assumed he must mean Walter. This type of miscarriage—caused by a malformation in the growth of the fetus—was not uncommon.

"Thank you," Daisy had said. "I know you're right."

"I am right. You'll see."

"Thank you."

She had gathered herself together and left his office, feeling that she had gathered not just her purse, her gloves, but the sly, criminal side of herself that refused to budge. How could she possibly explain what she felt in her core? Something had happened to her, and she had crossed over. There was glass between herself and the gorgeous, plain streets of Riverside Meadows.

Walter had been wonderful at first—comforting her as she wept onto his tartan shirt breast. But after weeks of this he began to hint that there was something unseemly in her suffering. Something overdone. The neighbourhood wives—Joan and Evelyn and Fran—had comforted her as well, but they soon grew tired of her sorrow. Daisy had hardly been showing, and she could always try again—in the hierarchy of misfortune, hers didn't rate particularly high. Now, getting tortured in an enemy prison for six months, as Fran's husband, Ed Warburgh, had been—tortured so severely that you still felt terrible shooting pains in your feet and had to soak them every night in seltzer—that was misfortune. Or losing a twin brother, as Joan Palmer had done (her brother had fallen from the monkey bars and snapped his neck when she was eight)— that was sorrow. Up against these tragedies, there was no room for Daisy's hard little ball of grief.

Eventually she did what everyone urged her to do. She tried again, becoming pregnant right away. She told no one but Walter. Shyly, despite herself, she felt a bright bubble of hope take root. As she did the dishes, as she took out the trash, there it was—an idea that made her hold her breath, burn for an instant, with wanting. This went on for a month—no more: one night she dreamed of being rocked by a huge creaking boat. When she woke and groped between her thighs, her fingers came back wet.

Her worst mistake—in her dry, indefatigable sorrow—was believing she could speak to Irene. It still made her ashamed, remembering how Irene had leaned across the tabletop at Rumpelmeyer's, taking in every word, consoling, sighing, avid for more. When their drinks arrived she had applied herself, with equal fervour, to her strawberry float.

"Here's the number of my shrink." She had pressed a card into Daisy's hand as they stood on the sidewalk, preparing to depart. But Daisy knew better. Never would she see Irene's shrink. He would jot down his notes, pencil scratching mightily with every word she uttered, recording the darkness before it had even taken form. He would have a thousand reasons to explain what was wrong with her, and it wouldn't just be the miscarriages. He would want her to talk about her childhood, of course—the death of her beloved father, her disinterested and noisy mother, now living in California with her second husband. He would want to know how Daisy had *really* felt, being uprooted from her home in Syracuse at the tender age of nine and sent off to boarding school. And there would be no point trying to explain that she and her mother had always been somewhat distant, and that by far her favourite memories were from those days at Sacred Heart, curtsying in chapel when Jesus' name was sung, or reading her Who-Dun-It at lunchtime, curled up in a hole in the cypress hedge.

Not to mention what a shrink would make of Walter—Walter, ten years older than Daisy, a father figure if you ever saw one. Or of Irene, Daisy's oldest and most detested friend. It could easily be a life's work trying to get to the bottom of who Daisy was, and there was no way they could afford it.

Yet driving home that night she felt optimistic. The vibrations from the road rose through the steering wheel, jiggling her gloved palms, her forearms, her cheeks. The moon was full. The night smelled good. She pulled off the parkway and drove up the newly tarred face of Old Middle Road. The field to her left was tilled but unplanted. It had been corn for the last two years now, but the year before that, the year Walter and she had moved to Riverside Meadows, it had been planted with pumpkins. When Daisy rolled down the window she smelled a fertile undercurrent that reminded her of the tops of carrots. There was also the bitter whiff of dusty cement after rain. The moon hung to her left, pocked and scarred, its mouth clawed to one side. But it was luminous—white and full and luminous—floating above the line of poplars at the edge of the field, coming in and out of sight, like a signal she couldn't read.

7.

Riverside Meadows was situated between the Northern State Parkway and the Jericho Turnpike, on a mile-square tract of land that had once been a farmstead owned by the Willard family. Despite its name, it wasn't built on a river at all, just a muddy stream called Willard's Creek. But that hadn't stopped two New Jersey businessmen, brothers with a taste for the picturesque. As for the meadow part—the meadow was what had been ploughed under when they built the streets and houses.

All of the homes were of two styles: Cape Cods, like Daisy's, with fake shutters and peaked roofs, or modified ranch styles, with stone cladding and adjoining carports. Each house, whether ranch or Cape Cod, had a colonial lamp post at the edge of the lawn, a brick walkway and a raised garden bed, also brick, running beneath the front windows.

The streets had been named after trees: Cypress, Poplar, Linden. Heading east, they ran parallel for a quarter-mile, past the site of the yet-to-be-built high school, then met the fields and petered out without warning, like the abrupt changes that take place in dreams. In the other direction they met in a crescent before straightening out to a single road that intersected Old Middle Road, with its drainage pipe that children liked to crawl through. Beyond Old Middle Road was the new elementary school, and beyond that a footpath wound down a scraggly slope, past a marsh, through two fields to Strickland's grocery store, which was out on the turnpike. This was the path the women of Riverside Meadows took to get their groceries if their husbands had the car. A half-mile down the road from Strickland's stood the village of Stoney Creek.

Everything seemed new. Any time of day or evening you could step outside and smell the churned dirt. Still, when you looked closely, there were traces of an older world beneath the newness of Riverside Meadows: traces in the dogwood, sticky with honey-pollen, which grew beside the creek; traces in the rank clusters of skunk cabbages in the marsh beyond the school. Snakeroot and goldenrod sprang up in the prim boulevards, as though all the growth and construction didn't matter at all in the end, not compared to another current that flowed beneath the suburb, fertilizing the grasses and the weeds.

❋

Daisy turned onto Linden Street and parked in front of her house. Next door, Fran Warburgh's place was lit up like a Christmas tree. Junie was bouncing a rubber ball in the carport, practising O'Larrys even now, in the dark. She did it for hours. Other noises came from the Warburghs'—dishes being washed, loops of clarinet (Ed, Fran's husband, loved Benny Goodman). Often Daisy heard Ed and Fran fighting, the baby crying, Junie screaming at her twin brother, Jimmy Jr., but tonight domestic peace reigned.

Keiko was coming to stay right after her first operation, and Daisy had purposefully not told the Residents' Committee. She imagined the women of Riverside Meadows approaching the house, demanding to know why they hadn't been consulted. *What have you brought into our midst? What heavy dose of reality? What blast from the outside world?* Well, let them be furious. They would be in the wrong; Daisy would be in the right. She would stand on her front steps and when they said, *How dare you?* she would shrug, as though to say, *My actions speak for themselves. I will not demean them with speech.* But the neighbours probably wouldn't storm her house, that was too overt, not Joan Palmer's style at all. More likely they would start a whisper campaign from house to house. *Have you heard what Daisy Lawrence has done? This is what happens when you have too much time on your hands.*

But suppose that the neighbourhood women did appear at her door, whisks and rolling pins in hand. And suppose they didn't accept Daisy's beatific silence. All right then, she would talk. She would tell them about the new and dangerous time they had entered. That would surprise them, because Daisy was pretty sure they didn't think she had a clue about politics. She would use elements from Dean Atchity's speech, but in her own words, and talk to them about brotherhood and the shadow of the bomb, how it covered everyone like a dark mother.

We are on the cusp, she would say, light streaming from her fingertips, her eye sockets. That was how it might feel, standing on the doorstep, as though she, Daisy Lawrence, had stepped onto a geyser of bright water and it was flooding her with liquid righteousness. She had joined a fight that included Einstein, and Bertrand Russell, and Dean Atchity, so who was Joan Palmer, with her snarky tongue and gins at three in the afternoon, to try to stop her? She couldn't, that was all. She didn't have a prayer.

All the lights in Daisy's house were off, which meant that Walter had gone out walking, something he did most nights. After dinner he pulled on his rubber boots and his corduroy jacket and slipped his tobacco into his pocket. If they had had a dog he would have whistled for it; instead, he simply stepped out the back door and let the screen door hiss closed. Then he walked for miles. Daisy imagined him smoking, muttering to himself, trying out lines from scripts, shaking his head, carrying on imaginary disputes. When he came back his trouser cuffs were coated in mud and grass stains, which meant that he had left the streets and wandered though the fields, and even broken away from the fields and walked trails north of the turnpike. For all she knew he may have left those trails behind too, and followed the streambeds, letting his ankles sink deep into the ooze. She wanted to know where he went, but something in how Walter was when he came home, a bruised meanness that surfaced on his walks, stopped her from asking.

I am the Whistler, and I know many things, for I walk by night . . .

That was the beginning of the radio show Walter wrote for, *The Whistler*. It was originally broadcast out of California, sponsored by the Signal Oil Company, but three years before it had gone national. Parts of the show may have leaked into Walter's system, because he acted like the main character—slipping off in the night, lurking in backyards, smoking and walking and muttering to himself. To make ends meet, Walter also sold occasional scripts to other nighttime programs, including *The Inner Sanctum,* which always began and ended with a creaking door, or *Lights Out,* which started with a gong, then the ominous words, darkly and evenly spaced: *It. Is. Later. Than. You. Think.* Occasionally he also wrote for soaps, *Our Gal Sunday* and *The Guiding Light.* It wasn't too hard to sell a script to a show like that—you just had to have an in with some of the other scriptwriters, who then commissioned you to take some of their work, taking a cut along the way. But Walter's dialogue always sounded more suited to a show like *The Whistler,* even when he was writing for *The Guiding Light:*

But I love you, Sal.

I know you do, kid. Now, can you turn off the lights? I need my beauty sleep.

Daisy got some leftover stew from the fridge and ate it sitting on the kitchen stool, listening to the General Motors news hour. Lots about the House Committee on Un-American Activities, which had recently visited Baltimore to expose Communist infiltration of the education system. Some teachers had been "friendly," confessing their role, while others had been unfriendly. She was glad when the newscaster began talking about a tarantula found by a New Jersey housewife; apparently it had stowed away in a shipment of bananas. Daisy didn't know the whole story about Walter's left-wing days—he had shared stories at first, but not lately, not for years. They did seem to have been quite left wing indeed. The fact that he now hated his old colleagues with a pure anger that sometimes frightened her might not help very much, though maybe it would. Still, the idea of Walter being called up to testify was unthinkable. It was like imagining Irene Day being called up (she also had had her time in the United Front, during her last year in college). And what was unthinkable, Daisy chose not to think about. She switched the radio off.

The kitchen looked ready for Keiko's visit, though it wasn't anything grand. The countertop was turquoise Formica. The ivory linoleum had already begun to yellow in patches, and by the back door the seam had separated, so that going outside Daisy often caught her toe. The wallpaper, which Daisy had put up when they moved in and now disliked, was a pattern of cherry clusters against a background of silver and beige stripes.

Outside, a dog in Stoney Creek howled, noticing the full moon.

She put her bowl in the sink and stood at the back door, looking into the Warburghs' backyard. Ed was in his greenhouse. She could see his watery shape through the windows, toiling under two light bulbs. When he retreated to one end, his shadow shrank, and when he stood up it shot across the glassed roof. Through the fogged glass he held up something that looked like the bloodied head of Medusa, snakes flopping and hissing. It took a moment to realize that he was shaking dirt from a mass of lily tubers. What would he say to all of this? Ed had been locked in a cell in a place none of the neighbours could pronounce. Shamshuipo. A prisoner-of-war camp. The prisoners had been so badly malnourished they'd stolen vitamins from the Red Cross boxes in the storeroom. They'd been discovered and one of them had been kicked to death—kicked to death for stealing vitamins.

Ed wasn't going to be pleased about Keiko. At a picnic once, eating a cob of corn, Daisy had seen him reach into his mouth and pull out an incisor before continuing to eat.

But if he made a fuss he would be wrong, and every rational being, every person in the Project, would say so.

A light flicked on in the hallway.

"Walter?"

"Yes'm."

"I thought you were out walking."

"I thought you thought that."

"What were you doing?"

"Working."

"With the light off?"

"Thinking. I was thinking."

"Are you hungry?"

He shuffled down the hall into the kitchen, tall and gaunt. "Don't worry about me, Daisy," he said. He was wearing what he usually wore when he did his writing: a pale blue cardigan, cuffs dirty and faded, which stunk of smoke. Underneath he had on flannel pyjamas printed with a repeating pattern of cowboy hats. Where had those pyjamas come from? Daisy certainly hadn't bought them for him. He must have picked them out for himself one day at Macy's perhaps, because his old pyjamas were in rags. Sitting at the kitchen table, rolling a cigarette, he was a discouraging sight.

"You know," Daisy said, settling across from him. "I've heard that many writers get dressed to work, even if their desks are in their bedrooms."

"You've heard that, have you?"

"Murray Kesselman gets dressed every day, puts on his hat, and goes to his office. And he works there, nine to five."

"Murray Kesselman!" Walter said with an ugly laugh. He was given to ugly laughs these days. "Murray Kesselman is like one of those damn monkeys you put in front of a typewriter. Sooner or later, if you're lucky, something comes out, but believe me, it's pure accident. Murray Kesselman!" Murray Kesselman got top dollar working exclusively for *The Inner Sanctum.* Daisy had known his wife in college. When Walter sold to *The Inner Sanctum,* he did it through Murray, and Murray took ten per cent.

Walter laid a rolling paper on the tabletop, with its constellations of gold flecks, then pinched a small mound of tobacco onto it. The ring finger on his left hand had been cut off at the knuckle by a sawmill blade many years before, back when he worked in the woods of Puget Sound. Daisy had always loved that stump finger: she had even slipped it into her mouth once, when they were making love. It was soft at the top, like the soft spot on a baby's head. She could tell he hadn't liked her doing that, though he didn't pull it away.

That stump finger reminded her of what he had been, way back when: a Walter of the western woods. He had worn a lumberjack sweater and cleated boots, and read Shakespeare at night in his bunk. When he'd been taunted by the other loggers, called The Scholar, he had been forced to bang a few heads together. It seemed that that was how debates were settled in the woods of Puget Sound. This was all years ago, before Walter had come east, become a writer, a radio man. Before the war. Before Riverside Meadows. Before Daisy.

"Anyway," she said now, "you can't stay in your pyjamas when Keiko comes."

He gave her one of his looks, but all he said was, "You don't think she's seen worse?"

"Look, Walter, I know you don't approve of this whole—experiment—as you call it."

He lit his cigarette, then leaned back in his chair so that it was balanced on its two back legs.

"You know that wrecks the chairs."

"I reckon I do by now, Miss Daisy." He let the chair fall to rest with a thump, then sat and smoked, snapping his jaw, blowing smoke rings.

"Look," she said. "I just want you to be nice."

"Nice like Dean Atchity?"

"Sure. That would be a start."

"He's a noble guy, right?"

"I think he is."

"Well, it's funny, Daisy. I've been doing some reading about your Dean Atchity in the newspapers. You know what Dean Atchity did when he was called in front of the House Committee on Un-American Activities?"

"I've heard the stories. It doesn't change a thing."

"They didn't have stenographers who could write fast enough."

"What does that have to do with anything?"

"He practically broke the goddamned machine." Walter blew another smoke ring.

"You can't hate everybody forever."

"No?" Walter said, looking up. "Just watch me."

It was true what he'd said, Daisy thought. He could hate everyone forever. It had become his gift: hating his old friends, shaking his head at their lies. Recently she had found a newspaper article in his study with the name of a friendly witness circled, the word *Liar* written above it in pencil. It wasn't that the fellow had told what he knew. Walter hated them all—the ones who were friendly and the ones who weren't.

Now he made eye contact, a rare thing these days. "As far as I'm concerned, this project is just so much fakery. *New faces, Daisy,*" he said. "Think about it. That's what your project is promising. My God, I could write a neat little radio pitch to promote what you're doing: 'Gong—now listen, young ladies, maybe it's time to try plastic surgery. It's Dean Atchity's all-American solution to that pesky atom bomb.'"

"Oh for Christ's sake, Walter!" When he got heated up like this, Daisy often ended up agreeing with him, but she really didn't want to hear this tonight. She took a hard look at him: he was, after all, a man wearing cowboy pyjamas; a man with salt-and-pepper bristle covering his cheeks; a man who had worked for years on a play, never produced, which had turned into two plays, which had morphed into an enormous novel. *The Dark Night of David Greenberg,* it was called, in honour of his friend—a man whose diabolically sexy smile Daisy knew intimately, though only from a photograph in Walter's wallet. Greenberg had hopped on the SS *Batory* in 1936, off to Moscow to help with the Great Experiment, as people liked to call it back then, and had never been heard from since.

The novel was eight hundred pages long, written in tiny, obsessive notes on the backs of envelopes, and in many typewritten drafts, on yellow paper, which, as far as Daisy could see, did not differ at all from draft to draft. Writing a novel was like starting a small business: numbered boxes filled Walter's study, all labelled in his tight handwriting, *Dark Night, Dark Night, Dark Night.*

Daisy looked at him now, this husband of hers. He was a man whose eyesight had become so bad that he needed a magnifying glass to read the fine print in newspapers; a man who might lie on the bed for two hours, blowing smoke at the ceiling, claiming he was composing dialogue in his head (*decomposing,* Daisy called it). Sometimes it broke her heart to hear the shushing of his slippers on the linoleum, or to see the small leavings in the kitchen sink from one of his snacks.

"If you'd been there tonight," she said, "you would have seen for yourself how sincere this project is. But you didn't come."

He shrugged.

"So now I'm just asking you one thing, Walter. All that matters is that you and I are good to Keiko. I want you to be kind. Can you promise me that?"

"Kind?" He laughed when he said it. "Sure, Daisy. I'll be kind."

He tucked his tobacco into the pocket of his sweater, took a banana from the fruit bowl and tucked it into his other pocket, and then he stood up and went down the hallway towards the bedroom. She caught a brief glimpse of his face, pouched and ashen, split by the mirrored panels of the telephone alcove.

8.

THAT NIGHT DAISY FOUND IT DIFFICULT to sleep. She was thinking about Keiko, everything she knew about her, which wasn't much—a few bits of information Irene had passed on in her memos. A girl who had lost her mother and grandfather in the bombing. Her father had already died—a soldier killed in Manchuria. Irene's memo had suggested that the mother was a woman of refinement and elegance. She and Keiko had moved from Tokyo to Hiroshima after the father was drafted into the Imperial Army. The mother spoke a variety of languages, which explained Keiko's skill with English.

After the bombing, Keiko lived with her uncle and aunt, attending high school. In the afternoons she worked in her aunt's hair salon, sweeping up the wet strands of hair left by clients. Daisy imagined her aunt speaking loudly up front: *Yes, that is poor Keiko. She comes to work here after school. We keep her in the back, because her scar might frighten customers.* Hiroshima victims were sometimes treated like untouchables. Daisy had read that. She saw Keiko tossing her sweepings into an incinerator in the cobbled back alley, watching them pop and fizzle. This was what Daisy could construct from the odd bits of information she'd been given. She saw a Cinderella, an ash child, someone the Project hoped to lift to grace.

But she had to leave a few facts out, to make this picture come together. Keiko must be intensely driven, for instance—not the usual image of Cinderella. After all, she had received the highest marks at Hiroshima Prefectural High School. Daisy had never been given the highest marks in anything, and for a second she felt the intensity of the girl, not as a victim, but as someone who got high marks. When Daisy was a student at Sacred Heart Academy, the nuns put the girls in rows according to how smart they were. Daisy had been placed midway back in the second row. Keiko would have been the first girl in the first row. If she had gone to Sacred Heart, that is. Daisy couldn't put this thought in the same pocket as the other image: the blasted girl. The victim.

Although she lay beside Walter, he didn't touch her, and she didn't touch him. If he rolled towards her, she would roll onto her side, and he would snuggle against her back, pulling close. But that was all. She liked the feel of his body, as long as he was neutrally tucked against her in this brotherly way. It had been a long time since they had made love, and as she lay in bed, she imagined how cold she would have to get—the sheets thrown back, moving on top of him, looking down at his bare chest, which in the pale light from the moon would be as erotic as a winter vegetable. His long legs, fleshy at the thighs, reminded her of parsnips.

Anyway, Walter no longer seemed to find her desirable. She was sure she must feel moist, unpleasant—her neck thickened, her waist thickened, a fug of female unpleasantness rising from the folds of her underwear. To make love successfully you have to see yourself as erotic. If you don't, you're done for. Imagining Walter stroking her arm, her thigh, was as arousing as imagining him stroking a piece of cheese, she thought, picturing a yellow slab of Gouda.

Despite all this, he still made a yeoman's effort, now and then. At first, it always felt like play acting to Daisy. Then, temporarily heated by a flood of dark oil, which filled her joints, her breasts, between her legs, she would—in accordance with some ancient memory—groan and part her thighs, touch Walter, make him groan, while another part of herself, chaste and pale and appalled, stared down at them from the ceiling, wanting it to end.

Why do this? she asked herself.

To what end?

For what?

That night she had a dream.

A light was shining through the window. It was like an ambulance or police car light, blinking on and off, blue and red. She opened the door and rested her face against the cool screen, which left crosshatch marks on her cheek. The night was dark; no stars or moon in the sky. Then Joan Palmer appeared on the brick walkway carrying a soft bundle wrapped in flannel.

"What happened?" Daisy asked.

"The school blew up." Joan's face was pocked, like the moon's. "But look, I saved this." She handed Daisy the bundle and together they unwrapped it. Inside was a piglet. But something was wrong with it. Its flesh was dusty, caked in talcum. Looking closely, she saw minuscule craters covering its skin, each ringed with a hard, fleshy edge. She dropped the pig and it trotted across the lawn, then down the street.

When Daisy woke it was still night. Even before she opened her eyes she could feel those cratered marks, so like ringworm, covering the skin of her forearms.

9.

IN OTHER PARTS OF THE CITY, the men and women involved in the Project were asleep or awake, and Daisy couldn't

imagine any of them, caught as she was in the box of her bedroom, rimmed by her frosty lawn, then the houses of Riverside
Meadows, the bare fields, the dog barking at the moon. But
already it must have been happening, as each of them lay in bed,
or finished their last drink, or switched off the television set: the
city felt heavier because Keiko was there—more real, darker.

On her palatial bed in her Upper East Side apartment, Irene Day
lay beside Raymond Carney, who was, in fact, her lover. Irene was
touching his arm in the way he liked, the tip of her index finger
barely grazing the hairs. When he did this to her, she couldn't stand
it—she preferred to have her skin scratched mightily so that she
could feel the red streaks like lightning bolts under her eyelids.

They were talking about Daisy.

"She always had such limited ambitions in college—house,
babies, normalcy. Funny how wanting normalcy somehow
makes it harder to achieve."

Raymond laughed.

"Everyone thought she'd marry right out of college, plucked
by one her amiable boyfriends. She had plenty of them. But then
there were the long years at Porter and Peck—and now, here she
is—shipwrecked in that awful suburb."

A pause as Irene moved the pads of her fingers over the inside
of his wrist.

"Do you think she's attractive?" she asked.

"She's soft."

"Men like women to have a kind of fuzzy softness, don't they?
It gives them something to pierce."

A pause.

"Do you think she's sexy?"

"Do you, Irene?"

"Yes," Irene said shortly. "I suppose she is."Then she added that
there wasn't much going on underneath. To which Raymond

replied, "Ah, well, perhaps that's more pleasant, in the end." A jab at her. Though perhaps he actually believed it. God, it made her groan with agony, a moaning like the moaning of a ship's sodden flooring, at what men could think about women, especially after reading Robert Graves. This dreadful concept that women should be muses; that simply by standing still in a grove of trees they could be in touch with their deepest nature; while men, who lacked this insentient connection, needed to go out and act. Slay a few strangers. Write an epic.

"You know," Raymond said, drawing his arm away, "Descartes believed that women don't have souls. Women and cats." She knew he was trying to hurt her, in a tender, loverly way (because wasn't finding out what hurt another person, and then prying and poking at those places, part of what lovers did—an extension of the act of sex itself?). He did this sometimes as they lay in bed, or even when they were in the throes of sex, murmuring her name: *Irene,* then *Irene Podborsky*—making her laugh, despite herself, at the ridiculous humbling cadence of her maiden name.

She got up now and went to the window, closing the blinds to block out the streetlights and the moon. "I'll check with my shrink," she said lightly. "He'll know if I have a soul."

"He'll say you have an id."

"I don't think I need more than an id. It causes enough trouble on its own."

"Yes, imagine what would happen if your soul and your id were in cahoots—angels and devils wrestling for control."

She came back to bed and covered herself with the sheets. "But that won't happen, because—as you say—I don't have a soul."

"Does that bother you, Irene?"

She shrugged. "I don't need one. It would be different if we were talking about something really useful."

"Like a pair of shoes?"

"Or a hat."

He laughed.

A few ribs of light fell across the wall. Irene stared at the ceiling. Did she have a soul? She had never felt that she had one—and perhaps that was what she lacked. Years of money spent on therapy and this was her problem! No soul. But what was a soul? All she seemed to have were needs and wants and thoughts. She wondered briefly what it was like for other people, but saw nothing in her mind's eye but dark blue space.

Raymond lay beside her, satin sheets soft on his body. Irene's bedroom always smelled of Eau de Joy. He had been needling her, but in truth he liked how sealed off Irene often seemed, how impervious. He was always guessing, trying to open her up, to stare into her core, which he imagined to be seeded and white-fleshed, like an apple's.

He stopped thinking about Irene and pictured the girl instead.

He planned, very soon, to write a memorandum about the girl's condition. It would be for the Hiroshima Project, but he would circulate it to a few important people in the Atomic Energy Commission. They were watching the Project with interest.

Underlying facial structure intact.

No apparent loss of subcutaneous tissue.

Scar tissue has the colouring of a port wine stain (naevus vinosus), and is heavily bubbled and hypertrophic.

Mandibles well drained.

She was beautiful. He would not say that. Indeed, he knew he shouldn't even think that. She was eighteen, after all: a vulnerable child. He felt a stirring of compassion, quickly superseded by other feelings. She was slight, like a boy. He had not yet done a full physical examination, but he imagined her breasts, the areolae darkly shaded, like eggplant. The scar was a mass of bubbles, like the slow spread of lava across her cheek. The keloid behind her ear was hard, round, purple-red, with a softness where it attached to the skin behind the earlobe.

> From what I've tasted of desire
> I hold with those who favour fire—

Words by Robert Frost. Not bad, he thought. Appropriate.

He imagined himself sitting at the edge of the bed while the girl knelt between his knees, wearing a sky-blue silk kimono, something that had been in her family for generations. She undid the belt, the *obi* he had heard it called, but it seemed to take forever to unwind. Her fingers were small and her palms parched, like monkey's paws.

Then she was naked between his knees.

What part of her will he touch first? The small breasts he can't look at? The rounded belly? The thin thighs? There was no question. Dr. Carney reached out to cup the dangling keloid, its weight brushing his palm.

And in another part of the city, Tom Orley—the freckled young wire-service photographer who at two o'clock had started the stampede at the airport, and at five o'clock had stood outside Irene's apartment for the better part of an hour—now bent over a small desk, chewing the end of his pencil, composing a letter.

That afternoon, after the trip to Mitchell Air Force Base, he had developed his photographs in silence, dipping them in solvent, hanging them to dry, watching in the purple-lit basement as the girl appeared—white hat, white teeth, a face both new and deeply familiar.

He took the photographs to the Associated Press office, and his boss paid him six dollars, part of which he spent at the automat for coffee and pie with cheese. He drove a cab for what was left of the day—stopping for an hour to see if he could get a last photo of Keiko leaving the party. At nightfall, driving back to Brooklyn, her face still glowed in his mind, lit by the purple light, emerging out of shadow.

When he got home, his landlady, Mrs. Gordienko, was sitting in the back room watching *Winner Takes All*. She had carpeted the back room, once a sunroom, and put in a brown couch and folding metal TV table. The tray showed two Indian wigwams on a sandspit, in front of a mauve lake. The air smelled of sauerkraut and sausage— Mrs. Gordienko's dinner. She patted the sofa, inviting him to sit, but he shook his head. He asked for a pencil and a piece of paper, and she said to check the hall drawer. There was a stub of a pencil in there, and some stationery from a motor hotel in Atlantic City.

Tom's attic room contained a single bed with a green chenille bedspread and a small desk, which had belonged to the landlady's son. You could still see where he had gouged his pen into the groove of the wood. He had died in Okinawa, shot dead instantly in shallow water as his division landed on the beach.

Tom wrote:

Dear Miss Kitigawa,

I saw you get off the airplane, and in fact I took a picture that you'll see printed in the newspaper. I am a photographer, at least that's one thing I do. I also drive cab for the Dial-a-Cab Company and I used to be a farmer, or at least I worked on a farm, because that's where I grew up (in Iowa) and when I was in the war I took aerial photographs of enemy territory. So I guess you could say I've done a lot of everything, or not much in particular, depending on what you think of farming, or aerial photographs.

Miss Kitigawa, I'm sorry if I keep straying off topic.

The topic of my letter is that although I saw you get off the plane, and took your picture, it wasn't until later, when I was developing it in my dark room, which is actually my landlady's basement room, which she has kindly let me convert into a dark room, that I saw that you look like my sister Emmy.

I thought it was a bit of a coincidence, as not many people look like Emmy.

I am sorry to have to mention this, but my sister Emmy isn't alive. She is dead, and that is a fact I still have trouble with, but there you go, the Lord works in mysterious ways and we must bear up under his Might. That is what my mother says. She is a great Believer, and I guess in some ways I take after her, though in fact I have a lot of trouble believing in God. Though I am told I look like my mother, and I do like the sound of the scriptures.

If you want to know what happened to Emmy, I will tell you. She had poliomyelitis.

Please just rip up this letter if you mind me writing to you, but maybe you won't do that. Something made me think today that you may be looking for a friend. We could have coffee or go see a movie. I feel like I might be able to say just about anything to you and you would understand. I haven't felt like this since Emmy died, and of course Emmy didn't understand all that much really, because she was eleven when I left the farm and when I came back she was in the iron lung.

Please write back to me at the address above if you think you would like to meet me. I hope you say yes. I haven't told you much about myself yet, so I'll just say that I love Gene Tierney and Clark Gable. My favourite food is beef on toast with gravy. I go to the movies a lot, also I like listening to the soaps and I am hoping to buy a television soon.

                        With sincere good wishes,
                        Tom Orley

II   FOX CHILD

10.

KEIKO'S GRANDFATHER TOLD HER STORIES about foxes: foxes in graveyards, foxes that turned into women, foxes with licorice lips, nothing faces. There were names for different colours of fox, different potencies. Kitsune—common fox; yako—field fox; genko—black fox; shakko—red fox; reiko—ghost fox. Then there was the bakemono. Keiko told Daisy about the bakemono towards the end of her stay. It took human form, and looked and seemed like a woman, though it was from the spirit world. This fox frightened Keiko, and by the time she left it frightened Daisy as well.

Keiko's grandfather once told a story about a bakemono who married a farmer. They lived happily for seven years. But one day the farmer looked out the window and caught a glimpse of his wife crossing the yard. Something was strange. At first he thought it was the way she moved, but then he realized that she wasn't casting a shadow. He knew at once that she was a bakemono, and so she had to flee, back to the world of ghosts.

Keiko told this story to Daisy as though it explained things.

There was a twist to the ending. The farmer had been a good husband—easily frightened but good—and so the fox wife had left a kerchief full of money on his pillow. Spirit creatures often had access to secret riches and, according to Keiko's grandfather, they weren't afraid to share.

When Keiko first told her about the fox women, Daisy pictured prints of the floating world, which she had seen in an art book at the library: women of Edo with long white faces, fingers strangely plump at the knuckle, feet erotically swollen, tiny passive mouths, eyes that gave nothing away. But Keiko, who had heard these stories as a child, saw the women differently, with wild hair down to their knees, ululations like wind passing through darkened teeth.

Little one, her grandfather said. *I met a woman in the graveyard the other day. Would you like to hear the story?*

Oh, the chill Keiko got hearing those words, remembering the graveyards they had passed on the train from Tokyo, the graves on the steeply raked hillside like rows of teeth, like the *ihai* markers in the family shrine. They passed graveyard after graveyard at the entrance to every village, and between the villages the bamboo forests flashed by, green and yellow rain. So many of the ancient dead had been forgotten, which was why they were so dangerous, their names never whispered, their gravestones fallen over. *I passed through such a graveyard,* Grandfather said. *Keiko, I walked so quietly.*

Go on, Ojii-chan.

People needed the old stories, her grandfather thought, just as they needed the ancient shrines, though government officials had dismantled many. Still, a wrong turn down a cobbled alley, a set of stone steps, would still lead to a secret Inari shrine, or a weather-beaten statue of Jizo, surrounded by stones, each set there by a grieving parent to ease a dead child's passage. Yes, the shrines were still there, in shadowy back streets, squeezed between noodle houses, in overgrown thickets along the river, behind the great military warehouses.

The two of them sat on the veranda together, his prized *shoji* screens of cypress wood opened to the garden, where it rained. He could hear the frogs singing, and the ringing of the oyster sellers' bells as they poled their way upriver, selling to the houses that faced onto the Ota. On a clear day he could see the black walls of Hiroshima castle rising above the trees on the other side of the river. He could smell the tatami, and the rain on the gravel pathway, and also the vague bathroom smells from the back of the house.

Go on, Ojii-chan.

Give me a second to remember.

Tell me about the ghost. The ghost in the graveyard.

And get in trouble with your mother and Yoshiko?

Tell me.

She pulled his sleeve.

He took a moment and then he began his story, and as he spoke, the child grew silent, frowning, her beautiful eyes narrowing. She looked as though she was hoping to detect an error, but Keiko's grandfather knew better: people looking for errors in stories listened from their heads, but Keiko was listening from deep inside. Her heart was listening.

This time he set his story beneath the bridge that spanned the river a hundred yards from their house. It was an eerie place, close to the Inari shrine, which he knew his granddaughter loved and feared—its vermilion gates opening to a tiny grotto, inside of which, on a small altar, gifts of sake had been left, and fried tofu in little bowls. Mothers came to this place to pray for their children. On the branches of a pine tree in the grotto they attached slips of fortune paper, *omikuji,* on which were written blessings for their sick children, their unborn children. Other coils of paper shook on the sacred ropes stretched taut above the shrine—so many pieces of paper flapping dryly, like the wings of small insects. To the right and left of the gate, two stone foxes stood guard on their haunches. It stunk in the grotto, a fuggy smell of sweat. Sometimes beggars walked up the riverbank and entered the temple and ate the food. For this reason, Keiko's mother had forbidden her to go there, though she often went herself, like most mothers, to pray for her daughter's well-being.

"I was walking across the bridge," he said. "And I heard a whispered voice calling from the fox shrine. I went to investigate. It was an old fisherwoman. She pointed at me as though she knew me. 'You are the man who likes stories,' she said. 'I know many stories—and they all happened.' To my astonishment, her eyes rolled back in her head. She flapped her hands wildly about her and sat down in the mud."

"Why?"

"She was remembering."

When the woman came to herself, she said that her husband had once been married to another woman. He was happy with this wife, and she was happy with him. Every day he came to the bridge to fish, and every day he came home with a good catch. The only bad part was that to reach home again, he had to walk by the Inari shrine. By day he didn't mind, and even left food there, but at night the place frightened him.

But one night he was late for his young wife, and rather than circling the shrine, he cut through the grotto. He was almost out, just making his way up the stone stairs on the far end, when he heard the strumming of a beautiful instrument. He turned to see a woman sitting on a stone beside the fox statue, her head bent over the strings of a koto. She was slender. Her long hair was done up in combs.

"Oh, most beautiful creature," he cried out (forgetting his wife at home). "Let me come nearer."

"Come as near as you want," she called over her shoulder.

"Then I will come close."

He took three steps towards her.

"Come nearer still," she whispered. "Undo my hair."

He reached out and slipped the combs from her hair.

"Unwrap my robes." At that moment she turned to face him, and lo and behold she had no face at all: she was blank as the moon. Then she was on top of him, holding him down with great force, her breath foul and bloody. With all of his strength he pushed her away and ran—between the stone foxes, out the gate, losing his sandals in the process, running until at last he reached his house. Only at the sight of his wife seated by the fire did he slow down. She was bent over, cooking their dinner.

"Oh, wife! I have been accosted by a terrible creature!"

"I have never seen a terrible creature," his wife said, stirring the pot. "Tell me what she looked like."

"Beyond description. When I got close she was a monster."

"And why did you go so close, husband?"

"She made me. She lured me."

"She must have been very powerful."

"Oh, she was."

"I would never want to meet such a woman." His wife looked up calmly. Her face was wiped clean of features, blank as the moon. He screamed and turned to run, but tripped over his own feet and fell to the ground. When he opened his eyes, the wind was blowing through the house, and everything was gone.

That—the old woman said—was the unfortunate end to her husband's first marriage.

11.

AFTER THAT NIGHT AT IRENE'S, Daisy did not see Keiko again for more than a week. The excision of the keloid had been uncomplicated, just as Dr. Carney had promised in his memo to committee members. "A triumph," Irene enthused, speaking a little too loudly into the telephone so that Daisy had to hold the receiver away from her ear. "A triumph. Raymond is a very skilful surgeon."

Daisy detected an edge in her voice. Irene was miffed, but at what Daisy couldn't say.

The Monday that Keiko came to stay, Daisy rose early. The sky was neither dark nor light yet, the grass still wet from dew. She pushed open the back door, feeling the cool air against her skin. Fran Warburgh's house was quiet. Daisy couldn't see it from this angle—exactly parallel to her own, it was visible only from the side windows—but she could feel the lack of fret and business.

Standing still, she heard whistling in the laurel bush, and something calling from the maple tree across the back alley. Another bird answered from behind the house. Then they were everywhere, peeping and crying, crowing and cheeping. Robins pulled worms from the grass, looking picturesque. Daisy closed the door and put on coffee.

At seven-thirty she woke Walter and told him that he'd better shower and dress if he was going to get downtown on time. Mondays were the day he delivered his scripts, catching the 9:03 from Stoney Creek. To catch this late a train was almost disreputable: it was the train of the unemployed, women shoppers and the occasional person, like Walter, who made his money from the arts. Most husbands caught the 7:23 or, at the latest, the 8:03. On Tuesdays, which were rehearsal days for *The Whistler,* Walter left for work even later, but then he took the car and stayed away until after Daisy was in bed. Anyway, today of all days she didn't want him lazing around. And she certainly did not want him standing on the front stoop in his cowboy pyjamas when Dean Atchity and Irene arrived with Keiko.

When Daisy opened the curtains, Walter covered his face like a vampire. She started to go through his clothes.

"Don't do that." He didn't move an inch, not even his head.

"I want to make sure your wool suit is clean."

"Don't." He felt for his cigarettes and stuck one in his mouth.

She went into his small office—originally a walk-in cupboard adjoining the bedroom—and opened the tiny window a crack. Not much light came in, as this window, too, faced the Warburghs' house. His study was a shambles, and stunk of cigarette butts and old bananas. Daisy was pretty sure a peel must have dropped behind the desk. On the wall he'd taped a magazine picture of the Rockies, a train whistling out of a tunnel. She looked at the clippings on his desk—a picture of Alger Hiss, looking bleak and distinguished. An article about perjured testimony. Another about Ethel Rosenberg. "WHAT WILL HAPPEN TO MY BOYS?" the headline asked. A good question.

Why had he clipped these from the newspaper? How did they fit with his novel? He seemed to be putting everything he could think of into his book—all of modern history—though it was supposed to take place mostly in Russia, and follow two generations of the Greenberg family. Early on he had given her parts to read–she remembered a sister chased through the corn, raped by laughing Cossacks; an old man—David Greenberg's rabbi father—who accosted David and his friends on a street in the Bronx, holding them with his glittering eye like the old mariner, warning them not to mess with politics. Some of these scenes Daisy had loved. Some had seemed far-fetched, peculiar, the characters stock: bloated apparatchiks and Comintern bureaucrats, with names like Georgi and Sergei. In fact, much of this stuff, especially the second part of the book where David returns to Russia, read like *The Whistler*—good and evil pitted against each other in a dark alleyway. The women either good as gold, or femme fatales with pencilled eyebrows and nasty hearts.

She looked over her shoulder, but he was still in bed—she could see his long legs, corpselike, beneath the sheets. She straightened the clippings, then came out and shut the study door.

"You really must get up," she said to his reclining shape.

She went to check Keiko's room, something she'd done a hundred times in the last week. It had a dresser, a full-length mirror and a small desk. Depressing brown carpet, tacked down and permanent, covered the floor, but that was the room's only real blemish. She had spread a sky-blue blanket on the single bed beneath the window. On the nightstand, beside a lamp with a pink pleated shade, Daisy had fanned out a selection of magazines—*Seventeen, Good Housekeeping.* This was the room she had planned to turn into the baby's room. Well, now it had another purpose.

As a finishing touch, Daisy got the cut-glass vase down from a high shelf in the kitchen, then went outside in bare feet and dressing gown, a pair of kitchen scissors in her hand, to cut some laurel from the bush by the fence, create a bit of cheerful greenery. Fran was in her yard, taking down the laundry she had left out overnight, red hair shining ferociously in the morning light. It was natural, but it was also so bright, particularly against the white of her face, that it looked like something out of a dye bottle. She wore a green-and-gold duster, the amorphous housecoat women of Riverside Meadows usually donned for housework, though this one had been jollied up with a mandarin collar. Daisy wanted to turn around and go back in, but Fran had seen her, so she came down the steps and began clipping laurel from the bush.

Fran had done a white wash the day before, underwear, brassieres, blouses, a shirt of Ed's, and most of it looked damp from the dew. She shook her head. "Ed needs this shirt."

"Can't he wear another one?"

"He wants this one." .

"Why don't you iron it?"

"He won't wear damp."

"Maybe it won't be damp after you iron it."

Fran set her laundry basket down, as though all at once the weight was too much. "Patti spat up on the first shirt Ed put on this morning. This is the only other one that's clean." She fingered the shirt, still on the line, and looked as though she might start to cry. She was young, just twenty-four, but already she had three children—Patti, the baby, and Junie and Jimmy Jr., the twins—and another on the way. Little things overwhelmed her. Her house was a jumble of teething rings, baseball gloves and cut-out dolls, and Ed was forever telling her to get it into shape. "He says I'm a *slattern*," she said to Daisy once, tasting the unfamiliar word in her mouth, slyly proud that Ed had come up with it.

Now she focused on Daisy. "You've done something strange, haven't you?" She said it in that blank way of hers, and at first Daisy didn't know what she meant. "Ed read it in the papers. There's a girl coming here. Someone Japanese." She let go of the shirt and came to the fence, pushing a piece of hair from her face. "I was just thinking things were getting better. We were going to buy a TV." This was the kind of illogical statement that Fran always came out with. "Everyone's furious at you," she added.

To have everyone furious at her was new. Daisy had always, at least until recently, been the person everyone liked. The morning light reflected off the greenhouse roof, bright, unambiguous. Daisy shut her eyes.

"Are you all right?" Fran asked.

"So what is everyone saying?" Daisy opened her eyes again. Cool, pretty spring, as far as the eye could see. Fran was watching her with interest.

"You know how Ed is. He can't get over things."

She meant that he couldn't get over the place where he had been a POW. "I know everybody's had bad things happen to them, but he's different. He gets so mad sometimes. When he holds his breath, I think he's going to have a heart attack. But he never hits me, if that's what you're thinking."

That wasn't true. Everyone knew that he hit her sometimes. Daisy felt a pull of guilt, as though what she had started, inviting Keiko, might squirm out of her control and ignite a brush fire.

"He's gone to the Residents' Committee," Fran said.

"I haven't broken any rules. Not one."

"That's not what he says. What were you thinking?" Fran gestured towards the fences, the neighbours. "They all fought."

"I know that. That shouldn't matter."

"The meetings next month. Joan's going. And Evelyn."

"I'm sure Joan has some awful theory about me—like it's Oedipal."

Fran was about to speak, then bit her tongue, and Daisy knew this meant yes, that Joan Palmer had a dozen theories about her behaviour, awful theories that got at her underside, that pushed around in the cracks and crannies.

Daisy thought about the oration she had been planning: the frightening world they had entered, and how small acts, such as the taking in of a scarred stranger, were the acts that might save them. But her skin felt icy. Besides, the idea of actually speaking such words seemed ludicrous. She was talking to Fran Warburgh across a fence, not delivering a speech at the United Nations. That was the problem with daydreams, they set up a parallel world, where people didn't say things like: *He never hits me, if that's what you're thinking.* And where Joan Palmer didn't control the hearts and minds of the women. Stalin could learn a thing or two, studying Joan's tactics.

A child started to scream inside Fran's house, repeating the word *pig* until it rose to a piercing crescendo. Junie, Fran's daughter, appeared at the door. She was red-headed. Blue veins showed at her temple. She seemed quite composed, considering the screaming. "Jimmy Jr. hit me—he hit me in the mouth."

"I did not." Jimmy Jr. appeared at the door. "She made that up." His hair was strawberry blond; Junie's closer to auburn. They had named him "Jimmy Jr." even though his father's name was Ed, a fact that had confused Daisy at first. It seemed his grandfather, Ed's father—a conductor on the Fifth Avenue bus— was the Jimmy for whom he had been named.

"He hit me in the mouth!" Junie repeated.

"Jimmy Jr.—that wasn't kind." Fran's voice was weary, though it was still early morning. Whenever one of her children wanted anything, Daisy had noticed—discipline, a Popsicle, a ride to the store—she grew instantly listless, as though the blood had poured out of her body. "Now go and wash up."

Junie made a face and turned to go inside, giving her brother a kick in the shins as she passed.

"See?" Jimmy Jr. said. "See what she does?" But Fran had turned from him. After another moment he too went inside. When the door closed, Fran leaned across the fence.

"Just be careful, Daisy."

"I am being careful."

"But is it true? It said in the paper she was hit by the bomb."

"She's a Hiroshima survivor, if that's what you mean."

Fran began to shake her head, thinking this information over. "That's really something, Daisy Lawrence."

There was more screaming from her house. Fran unpegged Ed's shirt from the line and put it on top of the basket.

"I'm going to iron it," she said. "I really think he may not notice the damp."

12.

APPARENTLY, ROBERT OPPENHEIMER QUOTED a few lines from *The Bagavad Gita* as the first-ever atomic bomb exploded above the white sands of Alamogordo. Daisy sometimes wondered how he had managed to have such an appropriate verse on the tip of his tongue. Had he memorized it beforehand so he could whisper it at that perfect instant? Or was it possible that he had lied, telling people that this was what he had been thinking. Maybe, like Daisy, he had let his mind wander to his shoes.

This is what he was rumoured to have whispered:

I am become death, the destroyer of worlds.

And as if that weren't good enough, he had added:

If a radiance of a thousand suns were to burst at once into the sky, that would be like the splendour of The Mighty One.

His quote was thoroughly famous in the spring of 1952, and, like a piece of perfectly appropriate music, it swam into Daisy's head as Keiko came across the front lawn. There she was, the scar on her cheek like the electric mauling of some terrible

beast; there she was in her gleaming patent-leath
petite hat with its two small feathers. A disturbing
been with Daisy all morning, ever since Fran had sai
something strange. Keiko had been exposed to a ghastly, bright
substance that had altered her skin, her bones, her blood. As she
crossed the lawn, Daisy wondered if the radiation in the girl's
skin cells could leach out, pour into her own body, affect the
marrow of her bones, her womb even. Such a sick, uncharitable
thought, but there it was. The breeze blew the girl's skirt. She
seemed small, yet massively potent.

Daisy stood at the picture window for one more second,
half-concealed by the curtains, watching Atchity and Irene and
Keiko come up the walkway. The row of plum trees on the
boulevard looked itchy with new growth—hard balls of
blossom that in another week or two would unfurl in the sun.
She was not lurking, but if anyone had seen her behind the curtains, they would have been forgiven for thinking that she was
lurking. She left the window, threw open the front door, came
down the brick steps, smiling gaily, parodying a housewife
greeting long-awaited guests. Being herself but also acting the
part. Behind her the house gleamed with normalcy—enticing
in its way, like the gingerbread house in the fairy story.

Keiko did not bow in that Japanese way they had all been
expecting; she did not look up the street or down the street. She
did not murmur something appreciative about the house.
Instead, as they watched, Joey Palmer's three-legged cat crossed
the lawn, meowed, and rubbed itself against Keiko's skinny leg.
She bent and scratched it behind the ear, digging her fingers into
its fur in exactly the spot where her own bauble-shaped keloid
had been. A bandage now covered her ear.

"Well, Keiko," Irene said. "Here it is. Home, sweet home."

Next door the curtains fluttered. The women of Riverside

Meadows, like animals in a jungle habitat, were camouflaged except to the expert eye. Daisy took Keiko by the arm and led her along the walkway, up the steps and into her house. She sat Keiko and Atchity down in the kitchen, and then she and Irene went to collect Keiko's things.

"I'm very angry with Dean," Irene said as soon as they were outside again.

"What did he do?"

"If I say, you'll just tell me I'm not nice."

"Is that what I do?"

"I don't know. Perhaps not."

"Go on."

They were standing on the brick walkway. Irene looked down, studying the herringbone pattern. "We did the press conference this morning, at the Barbazon," she said. "Such a good spot. Everybody came. But just when things became heated, I mean at the point where the reporters were getting useable material, Dean shut it down." She looked up. A tiny ridge of foundation rested on her upper lip, like icing. It wasn't really unattractive; a highly attentive lover might lick it away. "It's difficult for everyone," Irene said, shaking her head. "But it doesn't help just to shut things down. Where will we be then?"

Daisy asked her to explain what had happened.

There had been fifty journalists in the room, all clicking and shoving. First they asked about the hydrogen bomb, and these questions Keiko had answered nicely. "She's got the anti-Superbomb stuff down pat," Irene said. "She understands that our only real hope is for a test ban." But then the questions had grown more personal.

Can you tell us where you were at the time of the bombing?

Were you knocked unconscious?

What was the explosion like?

The girl had glanced at Dean Atchity like a frightened colt.

"What then?" Daisy asked softly. The scene had a prurient appeal, she had to admit: the girl cornered by the bright lights, all those men asking what everyone wanted to know. *Describe what happened.*

"He cut it off. Made a joke. 'Now, gentlemen, no need to cross-examine her—this isn't a House Committee.'"

Daisy felt obscurely disappointed, but all she said was that the girl must need to rest.

"But, Daisy, she's rested since she arrived. And we need the press's interest: we can't fundraise without them. And without money, we can't bring more A-bomb victims here for surgery. I know it sounds harsh, but Keiko has an obligation."

"Perhaps Dean wants her to settle in, which might be wise—"

"Of course, it's wise. Dean's always wise, but no amount of wisdom is going to stop the hydrogen bomb. Wisdom only goes so far." Irene opened the trunk of Dean's Oldsmobile.

"What do we need then?" Daisy had never heard wisdom held in such low regard.

Irene took out two pieces of luggage, pearly grey with white stitchwork and solid leather handles, and set them on the ground. Daisy gathered up the rest—a leather carry case, also pearly grey, and two large hat boxes. "Seventy per cent of Americans oppose the H-bomb," Irene said. "You know that."

"Yes."

"Well, Keiko could make that number rise to eighty per cent. Or ninety. She could speak nationally, internationally even. We don't need wisdom, Daisy, we need a political fire." Irene closed the trunk with her elbow and they made their way back up the walk.

"I'm sure she'll tell her story," Daisy said. "She'll do it when it's time."

Irene stopped and looked at her friend shrewdly for a second, then she put the bags down on the grass. "Daisy," she said softly, "encourage her to speak."

"I hardly know her."

"That will change. She's going to like you. Everyone does."

Daisy muttered that she hoped so, but she was remembering the look Keiko had given her at Irene's party.

"You will speak to her?"

"What would I say?" Daisy whispered.

"Encourage her to talk about herself. Draw her out. You're a wonderful listener, that's one of your skills."

Daisy felt a softening inside her. At Sacred Heart she had always volunteered to take the blackboard brushes outside and bat them against the wall. She liked to help.

"Let her know—gently, in your way—that she has an obligation."

"To the Project?"

"Even to the world, if you like. As soon as she's had that scar removed, we'll need to start planning the tour. It will be big news—especially with Bertrand Russell and Albert Schweitzer and Dean Atchity all pushing for a test ban too. But the heart of it must be Keiko."

"And supposing she won't."

Irene smiled at Daisy, then leaned across and kissed her cheek. "She'll tell you her story. You're the sort of person everyone talks to. Now let's go inside, shall we? They'll wonder what's holding us up."

Their conversation was over. Irene carried the two suitcases to the front door. Daisy, equally laden, came up the stairs behind her. "What was the question that frightened her?" she asked before Irene could open the door. "At the press conference, I mean."

Irene stopped and turned, a small frozen smile on her lips.

"The last question? It had to do with her mother. Why her mother died and she didn't. You see, Keiko had confessed to Dr. Carney in Hiroshima that she told a fib to her mother on the day of the bombing, saying she was sick and couldn't go to school. It seems that Keiko's lie may have saved her—her classmates were doing civilian work close to the centre of the explosion. I said as much to a journalist or two, and so a reporter asked a question about it. It's terrible, I know, but you can't blame the reporters for asking. It's what they do."

They went inside and set the luggage down. In the kitchen, Dean was ready to go. As he made his goodbyes, he took Daisy's hand in both of his, shaking it earnestly. He was leaving Keiko in competent hands, he said, and Daisy did feel competent under his benevolent gaze.

Then at last, with a kiss on both cheeks from Irene (Daisy could smell her powdery Eau de Joy), the two went down the path, slammed the doors of Dean's Oldsmobile, negotiated a wide, three-point turn and drove away down Linden Street.

13.

THERE WERE TO BE MANY SURPRISES as Keiko settled into the routines of Riverside Meadows, but the largest had to do with Walter. Daisy loved him, and she wanted him to be the man that she loved, but sometimes she felt as though their marriage took an act of will, like sucking in her stomach. She had gone into it admiring Walter so much. He had seemed like a puzzle she couldn't figure out; a foreigner who always sounds mysterious because one doesn't know the language. But now that she could decipher the words and phrases, they often seemed to hold less than she had imagined, not more—to be ideas that anybody might have had.

When Keiko moved in, Daisy didn't know what to expect: Walter might be charming, or he might be brutal—taking out his anger about the Project on Keiko herself, revealing a pettiness that sealed him, once and for all, into a diminished category in Daisy's head. It was a test, and it was only looking back, after the Project was over, that Daisy realized that she might have set it up on purpose, that cagey dark side of hers crafting a situation that would force both of them to be their true selves.

The first night she bustled around the kitchen, preparing fried chicken and biscuit dough. She had made a jellied Waldorf salad the day before, a recipe she had never tried, and there was chocolate cake for dessert. Daisy felt watched, though not by Keiko (at Daisy's suggestion she had retired to the bathroom to have a long soak in the tub), but by Irene and Dean, and the whole Hiroshima Project committee. To create a congenial atmosphere, that oft-maligned yet coveted atmosphere of the American suburb, was Daisy's job. She wanted to do it impeccably. She wanted it sung from the rooftops: *Daisy Lawrence is a wonderful hostess.*

She dredged the chicken, then poured a cup of oil into the electric fry pan. That moment stuck in her head for days afterwards, covering the white, goosebumped chicken skin in flour, tiny hairs sticking up, human almost. There were layers of feeling in that one moment. She was worried that her efforts wouldn't pay off, and also that something about their house wasn't right, had never been right, and that Keiko would sense this. But sense what? A darkness at the edge of Daisy's vision, a feeling in her stomach. Then there were more simple feelings: she wanted Keiko to be happy—but would she be? Could she be? She was also surprised that Keiko was taking such a long bath, and now—could this be possible?—following it with a shower. She would use up the hot water, and Daisy would need to boil water for the dishes. Somehow, tactfully, Daisy would have to let her know that the hot water was limited.

She wished that the committee had given her a primer on Japanese habits. She had heard that long baths were the custom of the people: a clean society, that was what one heard, never wearing their shoes in the house, bathing every day. Because of their water problems, and old habits learned in their youth, Walter and Daisy bathed three times a week and felt that to be sufficient. Growing up on Puget Sound, Walter had bathed once a week in a tub in the kitchen, his mother heating pots of water on the wood-burning stove.

Daisy stood looking out the kitchen window at Ed's greenhouse. The window was quickly steaming up, the chicken spattering and frying, the biscuits sat in buttery dollops on a cookie tray, ready for baking. In another few minutes, Keiko came out of the bathroom dressed for supper. She had taken care, looking formal and uncomfortable in a burgundy cotton dress with a white bolero jacket overtop. Her skirt had a crinoline under it, and it rustled as she moved.

"Refreshed?"

"Yes, Mrs. Lawrence."

"Oh, don't call me Mrs. Lawrence—it makes me feel so old. Daisy is fine."

Keiko nodded. Her scar was brightly washed, the ridges shining. Her voice when she spoke was curiously without undertones. It had no burrs or thorns in it, nothing to catch you. "You are very kind," she said.

"Come. Let's make you comfortable until Walter gets home. He won't be long—then we'll have a *lovely* dinner." Oh, she sounded like the advertisement, often played on the radio, for Uncle Ben's Converted Rice. We'll have a *lovely* dinner.

She gestured for Keiko to sit at the kitchen table.

"May I help prepare the dinner?"

But there was nothing left to do except slide the biscuit tray into the oven. Daisy wished she had had the foresight to leave more undone, so that they could have worked industriously together. Nothing to do. Daisy checked the chicken, then turned to see the girl watching her, freakishly quiet, scrubbed, well dressed. How long had they been alone together? A minute. If they were to spend six months together, would each minute be this agonizing?

Daisy took a bunch of carrots from the refrigerator, cut away the tops and rinsed them under water.

"Let's prepare these together."

Keiko sat in one chair, Daisy in the other, a bowl between them, and they peeled the carrots. Keiko had not seen this kind of peeler, but Daisy showed her how it was done and she mastered it immediately, letting the translucent orange shavings fall into the blue bowl. There now. That wasn't so bad—each of them caught in their task, doing something with their hands. Keiko's fingers were slender with moonlike nails, the cuticles exposed. No hangnails. She obviously took care of them. Daisy could hear the ticking of the clock stove; the ticking of the linoleum floor, which contracted after the sun went down, a series of hurried clicks, like a voice tsk-tsking. The peeled carrots glowed naked under the fluorescent light. *Draw her out. That's your skill,* that was what Irene had said. If only she could see them now, bathed in such awkwardness, such silence. It occurred to Daisy that if she had had children, she would have known what to do. She had felt awkward in just this way with the frightful twins, Junie and Jimmy Warburgh, the time that Fran had left them in Daisy's care. The girl had curled up beneath the kitchen table and refused to come out, saying something about being a bear, while Jimmy Jr. had sat out on the front step picking a scab, wiping blood on his face, then had run inside screaming that he'd been hit by a car. Even the Warburghs' baby, Patti, seemed to hate Daisy: she never shushed or calmed in her arms, but squirmed and writhed as though about to eject a massive amount of spit-up. She was a terrible baby for spitting up, always had a spatter of yellow stuff on her bib.

Daisy glanced at the clock.

Walter would be back on the 6:06 train—another ten minutes. But filling that time felt like its own form of hell, this particular circle being saved for charitable American women who didn't have the knack of making their foreign guests comfortable. Daisy drew a deep breath and began to speak, a patter of goodwill. *I do hope you'll like it here. Bedroom faces south. Comfort. Riverside Meadows pleasant in spring. Calm out here, in the suburbs.* Perhaps it was the mention of "calm," but all at once Keiko looked up, as though deciding to take a risk.

"Are we far from Manhattan, Mrs. Lawrence?"

"Not far. Not far. Easy as pie to get on the train. An hour's ride."

Keiko nodded.

"Are you—I mean, is that all right?"

"I am very pleased to be here. But I was told I would be in Manhattan. I didn't think this was Manhattan."

"Oh my, no, not by a long shot!" Daisy got up and found a pot in which to boil the carrots. "I mean, everyone thought you'd like it here. An American suburb and all that."

Keiko lowered her head—at last, at last, that standard Japanese gesture. But it didn't seem to be an answer.

There was a long pause, and then Keiko spoke. "Do you not have a television set, Mrs. Lawrence?"

Her voice was so feathery and soft that Daisy wasn't sure she'd heard her.

"A television set?"

"Yes."

Well, this was a surprise, and a bit of a sore point. Walter refused to buy one, being a radio man. "Oh dear, I'm afraid we don't. Not yet—the new ones are so expensive. I hope you don't mind."

"You are very kind. Of course not."

"Are you used to television then?"

"I never watched television in Japan. But Miss Day had a television set, and when I stayed there before the operation, we watched several interesting shows."

"Ah, so you're a TV fan already. Well, don't tell Walter, my husband, he hates the thing. Writes for radio. That's his style."

"I enjoy radio too, Mrs. Lawrence."

"Well, you're in luck. We have one of those."

At that moment Walter opened the front door. Daisy sped down the hall to greet him, wiping her hands on her apron, miming delight. In about one second she must have signalled her alarm, because he gave her what Daisy thought of as his Walter look, raising an eyebrow as he kissed her cheek.

"All this excitement for me?"

When he entered the kitchen, Keiko stood up, and Walter made a most civil bow. Keiko bowed back.

"We were just discussing our lack of a television set," Daisy said.

"Ah. My wife's sore point. So, you're Keiko," he said. "Well, I'm Walter. I don't suppose that's a tremendously hard name to remember. You got many Walters in Japan?"

"I have met two Walters."

"So many—now tell me how you've managed to do that."

"One was the husband of a customer at my aunt's hair salon. The other Walter taught English at my old school." Her face had brightened at his entry. She had been waiting for him, perhaps, just as Daisy had—both of them like actors sitting in their places, ready for the lights to go up. Daisy looked at Keiko curiously: yes, the girl was definitely brighter. Coquettish even.

Walter put his hands in his pockets, rocked back on his heels and looked her straight in the eye, a long cool look, then he muttered something about leaving the two of them to get better acquainted.

"No, don't," Daisy practically shouted. "Keiko and I have spent lots of time together. You stay. I'll mix you a drink."

"Daisy's always trying to get me drunk."

"He's joking. Stay, Walter—" But he was gone, down the hall, past the porcelain shepherdess in the telephone alcove. They heard the click of the bedroom door. Daisy smiled, more of a flinch really, then turned to check the biscuits. They were almost done. Keiko was watching her, waiting to see what would happen next. Her expression remained unaltered, but Daisy was pretty sure she detected a ripple of alarm beneath the surface.

She turned down the chicken, then excused herself and went down the hallway to the bedroom. She stood for a moment listening: no typing, or scribbling of pencil on paper; but there was not, on the other hand, that most depressing of sounds, the shifting of bed springs. She knocked lightly, then went through the bedroom to Walter's study. He had already changed into a tartan shirt and his pale blue cardigan, and he was leaning back on his chair. The metal ashtray on the desk was full to overflowing with the butts of rolled cigarettes. Sometimes when he ran out of tobacco, he smoked them. She felt a dry despair looking at him.

"Dinner is ready. Please come. And please behave."

"Behave like what?"

"Like someone nice. Like my husband."

He laughed.

Daisy was prickly with anxiety. "Won't you be a nice host?" she said, hating the tone in her voice. She was hearing the hum of dark wings: one part of her was standing in the doorway, pleading; the other part was watching to see if he could, in fact, turn from her, and from the girl in the kitchen, resume the sorting of papers and clipping of articles that constituted so much of his writing life. They were standing on a bridge, and if he turned away she would know who Walter was once and for all. She would see his shrunken heart.

He leaned back in his chair, bounced a couple of times.

"Don't do that."

He lit a cigarette, blew out. He never smoked with his left hand; it drew attention to the stub.

"She's out there now. I'm sure she finds this very strange."

"Go then."

"I don't see how you can object to what we're doing. You're the one who's always been so sold on brotherhood."

He rested the tips of his fingers on the desktop, and Daisy thought he was going to push himself up and walk out through the front door, along Linden Street, towards Willard's Creek. Gone. Instead, he gave her one of his looks—as though if she didn't know what was happening, he wasn't going to explain: she'd just have to figure things out for herself.

"Don't give me this you-know-better-than-me crap," she said.

"I'm not giving you anything," he said. They both stared at the words, and then she went to take the biscuits out. They were hard. Keiko had brought out one of the magazines from the bedroom and was leafing through it at the table. She looked up briefly, then returned to the advertisement she was examining—a page-wide spread for Lux soap. A woman who looked like Myrna Loy floated like a genie above a pile of laundry.

Daisy went back to Walter's office. He was staring at the wall, leaning back in his chair. She resisted an urge to reach out and straighten it. After a second he let his weight bring the front legs forward. He stubbed his cigarette out, then picked up the ashtray and dumped it into the trash can under his desk, banging it twice to dislodge all the butts. A gum of tobacco held them to the bottom.

"You asked me why I don't like the Project, and I'm going to tell you, so you know, and you won't ask me again. Okay?"

"Okay."

"Well, here it is: I don't like using people as guinea pigs."

"But how am I doing that?"

"Maybe you're not."

"I'm not."

"You said I could finish. Maybe you're not. Maybe you're as innocent as spring." Daisy saw something she wasn't expecting: warmth in his blue eyes. "But I guess you'd say I have a new principle, Daisy, something I picked up after a few years bashing my head against a wall—and here's what it is. You don't use people to make political points."

"We're not."

He smiled, an upturn of the lips with no mirth in it at all. "You're not," he said. "But mark my words, they are. Atchity is. Ray Carney is. Your dear friend Irene Day certainly is: she's incapable of doing otherwise." He stood up. "But that's the Project. And as you point out, she's here now. So I'll be civil, and come for dinner, because that's what you want. That is what you want, isn't it?"

Daisy nodded, watching his eyes.

"Just don't fool yourself, Daisy," he said. "You're not like them—I'd never think that of you, but you and I both know why you're doing this."

"We do?"

"Sure we do. Sure we do." Then he did something surprising. He reached out to touch her hair. Daisy pulled back as though he meant to hurt her. "You've got a bit of ash there," was all he said.

The feel of his hand on her hair made her want to cry. "I didn't really mean to badger you," she said.

"Yes you did. But it doesn't matter."

"I was trying to be mean."

"I probably deserved it."

"Oh, Walter!"

He picked out the last bit of ash from her hair, and they went together into the kitchen.

14.

HER DREAM IS REOCCURRING. There is a train. Faces she cannot see. She travels towards the city, which is laid out on a grid, dark and light, the lit parts pulsing, the dark places thick and porous and mottled, as though saturated in syrup. Always the city comes to her like this—taking the form of a cross, with the northern edges, near Harlem, touched by snow; the Lower East Side filled with boxy rooming houses, where sometimes for hours, for days, she tries to find a place to live; the heavy mass of West Side brownstones weighs the city in place.

In her dream, children of ten, eleven, twelve run beside the train. She asks, first politely, but then with growing concern, if anybody has seen the conductor. She thinks he ought to stop for the children. It is unsafe, their bare feet close to the tracks, some of them running, jumping up, thumping their hands against the glass. It is a game at first, a child's game, though sometimes right from the beginning it is more serious: the children are sick, and in increasing desperation Daisy turns from passenger to passenger, trying to find someone who can share her alarm. Her voice comes from far away, or she has forgotten how to form words, or she describes what is happening and everybody turns to the window, but nobody can see the silent figures but Daisy herself. They are pale and skinny and green, their palms against the window as translucent as the inner sheaths of grass blades.

Once, just after she and Walter had moved to Riverside Meadows, she stayed up late, listening to the testimony of Treblinka survivors on the radio. That night she woke standing on the bed, trying to keep the ceiling from caving in. Walter took her hands from the ceiling, coaxing her to lie back down. That time there had been a long line of people waiting for the train: children and mothers. They rode towards the city for hours, everyone aboard, but at one steep curve the train ran off the rails and turned upside down, which was why she was pushing at the ceiling. She was trying to get out.

The testimony she had heard on the radio had been about children in the Warsaw ghetto. The SS stopped them on the street and offered them candy—*Close your eyes, open your mouths.* When each child did as he was told, opening wide, the SS officers had inserted their pistols and pulled the trigger.

After each nightmare Daisy reached for Walter. As she woke she knew, as she didn't at other times, that he understood her grief, its thickness and heat, the emptiness at her core. But when she woke up on the night of Keiko's arrival, Walter wasn't there.

She sat up. Daisy heard a door softly close. Now that was strange. It was the spare room door, Keiko's bedroom: she could tell by the way it brushed the carpeting. She heard the bathroom door close, the flushing of the toilet, then the shuffle of Walter's slippers down the hall. The bedroom door opened and clicked softly behind him. He pulled back the covers.

"What's up?" Her voice came out surprisingly loud.

"Nothing."

"Where were you?"

"Kitchen."

"But why?"

"I heard Keiko."

"Oh—you should have woken me. What happened?"

"She got up to go to the bathroom, and then I saw her bedroom light was on. I figured she might be hungry."

"But she ate dinner."

"Just a thought. I offered to fry her an egg sandwich."

"But she'd eaten."

"Look—I thought she might be hungry again. Anyway, she wasn't."

A pause.

"That was good of you."

"Do you think so? I was hungry myself."

"But the dinner was good, didn't you think? I mean, she seemed to like it."

"Really good, Daisy."

"I think this is going to work out." Daisy said this quietly.

He took his time before answering.

"Could be," was what he said.

15.

THE REMAINDER OF APRIL was a whirl of activities, or so it felt to Daisy. It was a swirl of busyness, a veritable blitzkrieg of appointments and outings, sightseeing and lunches. This was a campaign, after all, albeit one for peace, and Irene Day and Bertha Atchity and the other Hiroshima Project organizers intended to carry it out with the same unstinting effort with which they had organized rubber and tin drives during the war.

Keiko was already something of a celebrity: her picture getting off the plane—taken by that insistent photographer from the wire services—had appeared in almost every newspaper in America; and so the Project did its best to make sure that she got celebrity treatment.

Irene, Bertha and Daisy whisked Keiko here and whisked her there—to a cocktail party at the Japanese Cultural Association, to dinner at the Hawaiian room of the Hotel Lexington, where girls in grass skirts served them drinks in coconut shells. She lunched at the Rockefeller Center roof gardens, paddle-wheeled to Coney Island and shopped at Bergdorf's, where Daisy felt moved to spend far more than she could afford on a lambswool scarf for the girl. Keiko thanked her nicely, yet Daisy felt in retrospect that there had been something stilted in her response. Something ungenerous. Her thank you passed every rule of etiquette, but it lacked the spark at the core. Later, lying in bed, Daisy even wondered if perhaps Keiko had wanted the plum-coloured cashmere scarf she had been fingering. But surely she knew how much cashmere cost! Irene could afford it, and Bertha Atchity probably had a sweater set for every day of the week, but Daisy did not own a single article of cashmere.

The mystery of Keiko's response was solved the next morning when she appeared in the kitchen with a package wrapped in violet tissue paper, held in place by a bit of ornamental straw. Inside was a handkerchief embroidered with a small pink rose. Daisy exclaimed over it, while Keiko gave a closed-lipped smile: clearly, her sense of obligation had been removed.

As promised, Keiko was introduced to Eleanor Roosevelt in her offices at the newly opened United Nations building, where

Mrs. Roosevelt was the head of the International Human Rights Commission. It was an event to which Daisy was not invited. She understood why that had to be—not everybody could squeeze into Eleanor Roosevelt's small office—but still she was hugely disappointed. It didn't bother her that Keiko got to meet Mrs. Roosevelt (though she clearly had no idea who she was), but it did irritate Daisy to see Irene waltz across the United Nations plaza wearing a black beret and elbow-length gloves, looking like a French intellectual. The only thing missing was a copy of *Being and Nothingness* tucked under her arm. "I'll just scoop Keiko up and whisk her away," she said, and while Irene scooped and whisked, Daisy walked to Penn Station and took the train back to Riverside Meadows.

Keiko heard the Philharmonic at Carnegie Hall, rode a Circle Line steamer around Manhattan and saw Frank Sinatra on stage at Radio City Music Hall. (What she made of the besotted teens in saddle shoes and rolled-up jeans, screaming *Frankie, Frankie* and bursting into tears, Daisy could not say.) Keiko tasted borscht at the Russian Tea Room and rode through Central Park in a carriage with yellow spokes. She raised her eyes to look, with polite interest, at the terror of Picasso's *Guernica*, which filled an entire wall of the new Museum of Modern Art. Daisy felt a thrilled horror as the picture sank in to the full degree, and she waited, holding her breath, but she needn't have worried. After a minute or so, Keiko merely pulled down her glove to look at her small, blue-strapped watch. The crying mothers hadn't swooped from the wall, wailing and screaming; the multi-eyed babies hadn't caused her to flee in tears. She listened carefully as Bertha explained that the fat fingers and the many-sided faces were the Parisian method of showing emotions simultaneously. The girl was seamless. She gave nothing away.

They ended up seeing sights that Daisy hadn't seen in years, not since arriving in the city a decade before, to take her stenographer's job at Porter and Peck. Only once, for instance, had Daisy gone up the Empire State Building. Standing on the observation deck, Daisy wondered what it must be like for Keiko to look across the whole city, seeing both the Hudson and the East rivers, and the Statue of Liberty, and so many bridges, not to mention the black and gold and silver spires of downtown, the Singer Building and the Woolworth Building and others Daisy couldn't name, rising up all around them like enormous cliff faces. While every other major city in the world had been smashed up by the war—Berlin, Paris, London, Tokyo (and Hiroshima, of course)—here was New York, looking so finished, so monumental. Far beneath them, gliding soundlessly past the Flatiron Building, candy-coloured cars glinted in the afternoon sun.

Who is she, who is she, who is she? Daisy wondered as Keiko stood with one gloved hand on the limestone balustrade, her eyes raised politely to view the skyline. After a long moment, Daisy could bear it no longer.

"What do you think?" she asked.

"It is very nice." Keiko met Daisy's question with the usual cool façade, the blank look. Though it wasn't blank, not really. Daisy thought she could detect the tiniest amount of alarm on the girl's face, as though, quicker than quick, some deeper aspect of herself scurried for cover. Like a spider freezing in someone's shadow, the best disguise being to remain still. An idea, and not a bad one—Daisy had felt this way herself.

What did Keiko think of the Empire State Building, with its signage indicating *The Longest Uninterrupted Elevator Ride above the Earth's Surface*? What did she think of the gargoyles of the Sherry-Netherland Hotel, each dangling a massive street lamp in its teeth? Or the castle bulk of the Plaza, the Italian grocery stores brimming with wine barrels and pecorino cheese rounds? What did she think of the deep whistle of the *Queen Mary*, heard on every street corner, as it slid from its berth on the Hudson? What did she think of the lions guarding the library, the Camel cigarette man blowing fifteen-foot smoke rings across Times Square? Was she astounded? Was she glad to see it all? Or did she wish everyone dead?

Imagine travelling around Manhattan and trying to siphon that gargantuan, glittering experience through the eyes of an eighteen-year-old Hiroshima victim: it was like trying to fit a tidal wave through the eye of a needle. Daisy stole glances at the girl as they hopped into a carriage, or as they slid into a mahogany and velvet booth at Oscar's, but she couldn't penetrate the surface. Keiko's manner was civil and correct—but perfect civility, Daisy realized, wasn't precisely what was called for. Keiko had misjudged. A certain amount of innocent exuberance was needed to grease the Project's wheels.

Irene noticed.

In the pink-tiled bathroom at the Waldorf, she asked if Daisy had detected something "a bit off."

Daisy felt ruffled. Protective. She said she wasn't sure what Irene meant.

"Ah well, let's leave it then." Irene took a seat in a plush chair and dabbed at her eyeliner with the dampened corner of a tissue.

"But what do you mean?" Innocent little Daisy. In truth she knew very well.

"She doesn't strike you as a trifle blank?"

It was typical of their relationship that Irene could fearlessly name what Daisy pretended not to notice. Still, it felt wrong to be judgmental after the hell the girl had been through. Who were they to complain, especially about something so subtle as the girl's lack of enthusiasm? Besides, maybe this was how people showed enthusiasm in Japan.

"She doesn't seem to like us," Irene said. Another truth.

Daisy stammered that these things took time.

"Do they? I haven't found that. I usually know who I like right away."

"Then you don't like her?"

"Oh, I wouldn't say that. But she's cold, that I will say. Which makes our job all the more difficult."

Daisy refused to agree with her friend, but sliding back into their booth, she felt the girl's coolness, just as Irene had said: a small force field of hostility emanating from the top of her head. It would be good, Daisy thought, to take the girl aside—not now but at some point—and talk to her severely. Here's how we do things in America, Daisy could imagine saying: we say thank you like we mean it, we shake hands like we mean it and we evince a delighted interest in our surroundings, especially when taken on long sight-seeing cruises around Manhattan by Circle Line ferry.

But for now she kept these thoughts to herself.

16.

TOWARDS THE END OF APRIL—almost a month after Keiko had arrived in America, and ten days before she returned to hospital for the removal of her major scar—the State Department lifted the veil of secrecy surrounding atomic testing. It was a calculated move to prepare the public for the hydrogen bomb, at least that was what people in the Project said. Not only was each atomic test reported in detail in the newspapers, but for the first time the bomb blasts were televised as well. Not having TV, Daisy read the accounts in the newspaper—the reporter rhapsodizing about the mushroom cloud, its shades of fiery red and stormy black, and describing the surging winds that followed.

The paper said that flocks of "atomic tourists" set up deck chairs in the desert to watch the explosions. The Atomic Energy Commission condoned this. Daisy put the paper down and closed her eyes. She could imagine how these onlookers must have felt when that mysterious thing, the atom, was whacked in two before their eyes, creating an unearthly jag of light across the desert air, a mighty heaving in the molecules of earth and sky.

Dr. Carney called the bomb mass entertainment. Bread and circuses. "He thinks it's a brilliant ploy," Irene said. "He says the blast fills all the empty cracks left in people's souls from the misery and carnage of the war."

"Goodness."

They were on the telephone again, Irene and Daisy.

"It forces people to realize we're in a new world. That's what Raymond says."

As the advent of gaslight had shocked Victorians (so Carney had explained to Irene), illuminating the docks and fairgrounds, the back alleys and secret parks—so the atomic bomb was lighting up its own generation of men and women.

"He says it's thrown a new light on everything," Irene said. "It has changed the world utterly."

"But he wants to stop it." Daisy said this uncertainly, as Irene had spoken with such relish.

"Yes, of course—that goes without saying." Irene lit a cigarette. "But in the meantime we also have an opportunity for study. The bomb, and people's attitude towards the bomb, is fascinating. People want to get close to it. Like moths."

That was what Dr. Carney had said.

✳

When Keiko travelled around Manhattan, people often recognized her as the girl from the newspapers. Her scar made her stand out. People stared, edging closer, seeming to want a heady dose of that acidic thing, radiation. When Daisy was with Keiko, she often felt itchy, as though she had slept in a bed full of cracker crumbs. Was that an effect of the radiation, or was it just the power of suggestion? The bomb, radiation, the entire world of atomic weapons was so new, who could say what peculiar abreactions any of them could expect?

But one thing was clear. Keiko's scar was like a badge, marking her in the public's eye. It said, Here passes someone who has experienced the dread fire. *The dark mother,* Atchity had called it, words that haunted Daisy. And yet that expression was strange, because the bomb wasn't dark at all. It erased shadow. It illuminated what might have hidden. It was fire and light in uncountable measure.

To the men and women who watched Keiko as she fed the ducks in Central Park, or lined up for a hot dog, she might have been a visitor from a strange planet, touched by the dust of Mercury or Pluto, so odd did she seem, so tainted with something foreign. Briefly, Daisy imagined shooing them all away, her large bottom waggling as she scurried to and fro. *Get away,* she would hiss. *Don't stare.* But to no avail. There was something ancient at work here. It made Daisy think of conquering soldiers parading their shackled slaves through the streets of Babylon—a picture she'd seen once, in a book of Bible stories: rows of slender Hittite girls, dressed in white, chained together at the neck. The onlookers had gawked and laughed, but they had also desired them. That was why she remembered the picture so vividly. It had been arousing to lie in the sun on the parlour floor, looking at those slave girls all dressed in white. Now this was strange but true, she thought: victimhood seemed to fuel desire. Men, especially, seemed to want to taste Keiko's vulnerability, sidling near her on the subway ramp, staring at the tracks, pretending to be nonchalant, focusing on their erections. Dr. Carney too: he always stood close to Keiko, within the circle of all that, so that he could breath in the heady scent of antiseptic and dried blood and lemon bath splash. Daisy noticed this. She couldn't help it.

One afternoon Dr. Carney performed a pre-surgical examination on Keiko's facial scarring. Daisy and Irene waited downstairs in the lobby of Mount Sinai Hospital. It took longer than expected, and it was almost dark outside when Dr. Carney and Keiko rejoined the women. "All's fine—right, Keiko?" Carney said briskly. They stood together in the middle of the lobby—a place where the acoustics took on an odd resonance. Keiko gave him a closed-lipped smile, then lowered her eyes to study the granite floor.

At that moment, the wire-service photographer popped from behind a pillar.

"Miss Kitigawa."

He stopped them in their tracks with his flat Midwestern accent. A look of rare alarm passed across Keiko's face, and she blushed—a mulberry stain.

"I'm not here for a photo," the man said quickly. "Please don't worry about that, miss." He hunched his large frame, in order to meet Keiko's eyes. "My name's Tom Orley," he said softly. "Maybe you recognize it—I've sent two letters, and I saw you at the press conference. Had the feeling you saw me too."

"Who are you?" Dr. Carney stepped forward, looking ready to seize the fellow by his collar.

Tom Orley straightened, taller than Carney by a good eight inches. He glanced around at them amiably, then back at Keiko.

"I am very sorry if I've alarmed you, Miss Kitigawa. Here——" He reached into his inner jacket pocket and brought out a long, thin navy blue box.

"What is it?" Dr. Carney snapped. He reached for it, but the fellow pulled it back.

"It's for Miss Kitigawa, if you don't mind," he said. "For Keiko." She raised her face then and looked into his eyes—intense brown. Warm and bovine. "If I give you this, will you open it later?"

She held out a gloved hand and he put the box in it. Then he turned, walked across the lobby and exited through the revolving doors. Through the large window Daisy saw him get into the driver's seat of a cab.

There was a beat or two of stillness.

"Oh dear," Irene said softly. "What a dreadful man." When nobody said anything she shivered theatrically, then glanced at Carney, to gauge his reaction.

"What has he given you?" Carney asked.

Keiko opened her palm. There was the prettily hinged leather box.

"Open the latch, dear," Irene said.

Keiko pushed at the latch. It opened neatly on its two hinges. Inside, lying on a cushioned satin lining, was a gold watch. She lifted it up and held it out to them. It had a dainty face, tiny numerals; the gold band was constructed of inter-locking hearts.

Irene whistled. "A Lady Elgin watch. And from a complete stranger."

Keiko said nothing.

"It's not unexpected," Daisy heard Carney say, "for a young woman like Keiko to have admirers."

This elicited more exclamations from Irene, who agreed that it wasn't unexpected but still condemned the effrontery.

Carney put an arm around Keiko. "I'll give you a ride to the station," he said.

Keiko slid the box into her coat pocket.

That night Daisy watched the girl. She sat in the living room on the slippery green couch, with its vague pattern of leaves and roses, leafing through a magazine. She wasn't exactly ignoring Daisy as she bustled about, straightening up before Walter's arrival home, but she didn't bother to speak, either. When Walter came home there was the brightening—as though a curtain had been drawn. Now it was time to sit up straight, present herself. Walter entered the living room, having changed into his scruffy cardigan and tartan shirt. Daisy often wished she had the fortitude to hide them. He stood looking down at Keiko thoughtfully as she placed the magazine on top of another one on the polished side table, aligning their spines.

"How old are you, Keiko?"

"Eighteen."

He nodded, as though that explained a great deal. "Well, come into the kitchen," he said, "and I'll show you how to make a martini. Unless of course you know already."

Keiko giggled.

Now how was that possible? The girl had made no sound approaching a giggle in the three weeks that Daisy had been her companion. But when a nice-looking man offered her a martini, she giggled. In the kitchen Walter joked, saying that Daisy had never been able to mix a drink strong enough for him, not to save his life, but that he'd teach Keiko how to do it properly. Then he asked Keiko if she wanted one, and to Daisy's complete surprise she laughed outright and said she would try one, thank you, before she looked guiltily at Daisy. All at once an atmosphere of gaiety descended: measuring the vermouth, tasting the straight gin (which made Keiko choke), adding the olive— "This Important American Ritual," as Walter called it, broke the ice that night.

After dinner he pushed back his chair and got out his tobacco can and papers and took them out on the back steps. Daisy cleared the plates and cups, then carried the tablecloth outside and shook the crumbs over the back porch railing. She left the door open and Keiko came out to join them.

"Look," Walter pointed. They could see the Big Dipper clearly, even the two stars that circled round each other, which Walter explained were called Jack and his Wagon.

"We'll all have to walk down by the creek when the weather gets warmer," he said. "Right now the ground is too soggy, but in a few weeks, away from these lights, you'll be able to see a million stars."

"After the operation," Daisy added.

Keiko stiffened and Walter shot her a look—but it was all right. In another second Keiko raised her face and looked at the Dipper, and Walter pointed out Draco the Dragon, curling above and below the giant spoon.

17.

THE WEEK BEFORE Keiko was scheduled to return to the hospital, the weather changed. What had been a cold, rainy diffi-cult patch suddenly eased into a series of gorgeous blue-skied days. Linden Street, on which there was not a single linden in sight, came into blossom. Bees hummed. Robins chirped. Tulips, with a mad, invincible spirit, thrust their pointed leaves through the earth and unfurled their hot petals.

That afternoon Daisy took Keiko to the Éclair Bakery on First Avenue, thinking it would be nice to pick up a couple of pastries, then eat them in the sun in the United Nations plaza before meeting up with the others. She pictured the two of them sitting on a cement planter, licking cream from their fingers, looking comfortable with each other as Dean Atchity and Irene approached. If Daisy could create the outer look of ease, perhaps the inner feeling would spark into life as well.

As she and Keiko neared the front of the bakery line, a woman behind them—a portly East Side matron with grey-rinsed hair and a mink stole—tapped Keiko's arm vigorously with the handle of her umbrella.

"You're one of them, aren't you?" she said.

"One of whom?" Daisy said sharply.

"I don't see why your country deserves such charity. Look what you did to us."

"Shush now," Daisy said.

"Oh, don't you shush me!" The woman's eyes were watery and hard. "My son died in Saipan, and I think getting all misty-eyed because we dropped the atomic bomb is just—reprehensible." Her chest expanded like a robin's. "I'd drop that bomb again, any day, any second, if it would save my son."

"But it won't."

She shook her head. "I hate you people," was all she said, then she turned and left the shop.

Daisy turned to Keiko. She was looking down at the pastries behind the glass. Daisy was about to say all sorts of things— apologizing for the woman, apologizing for society, for America, for the bomb—when Keiko breathed out gently. "I have never tried a Napoleon," she said.

"Then I will buy you one."

That was how that incident was resolved. Keiko spoke with

extreme calm, and Daisy answered calmly. Only out in the street did Daisy allow her voice to rise, to carry a ring of indignation. "I can't imagine why that woman would say such things," she said. "You're not our enemy, Keiko." She *had* been outraged, but her voice now sounded false, even to herself, as though she were a cousin to the woman in the mink stole. Something stopped her from sounding genuine. And Keiko knew.

Daisy thought, She likes Walter because he's real. She does not like me, because I am not real, with my bright, cheerful smiles, my indignation. I am not real. And when she thought that, she blushed and felt judged.

They walked down First Avenue together. To their left was the East River, a quarter-mile of aching blue. In front of them a glass building shaped like an immense soapbox reflected the cloudless sky with blank, tropical splendour. This was the new United Nations building. It was too four-square for Daisy's taste, though she liked the idea of the six hundred delegates inside, turning the spanking new dials on their desks, selecting the languages of their choice. The building represented hope, and though it looked ugly and almost menacing, glinting in the afternoon sun, Daisy was attached to the idea of it.

In the UN plaza, they ate their pastries perched on the edge of a cement planter, beside a Henry Moore statue of a nude woman whose breasts seemed to protrude from her back. Across the pond flags from every country caught a breath of wind, straightened, flapped, then fell back against their poles. Daisy was tired of pussyfooting around, of being found wanting. It never seemed to end. *Margaret Mary Parker,* always trying to be a good person, but always ending up being a parody—a parody of goodness. That was how Irene made her feel, and that was how she felt now, having breathed her outrage to Keiko, only to be—as always— subtly rebuffed. It was pretty awful to be judged by Irene, but to be found wanting by Keiko—a Hiroshima victim, for God's sake, surely the paragon of victims—well, that was beyond anything Daisy had imagined. But then judging other people was obviously quite easy for Little Miss Was-Honoured-to-Get-Top-Marks.

"Keiko," Daisy took a last bite of her éclair, swallowing quickly. "I wish you'd tell me a little about yourself. I wish I could know you better."

Keiko breathed in and then she stopped breathing altogether—a signal that Daisy had cornered her. Daisy could have stopped, but a dark instinct told her to keep digging.

"I know it's painful to speak about the past. I feel that too. But perhaps you could tell me just a little. About your mother, for instance. Or your grandfather. You lived with him, I'm told—I mean, before . . ."

Keiko watched two ducks on the round pond. They looked out of place in the concrete plaza. One of them shook its feathers, then sailed on, the other following in its smooth wake. Daisy waited for her to speak, and then—after perhaps a minute—realized that Keiko simply did not intend to. There would be no answer. The girl watched the ducks until the question itself seemed to have stopped ringing in their ears, until its trail was gone. Then she lifted her wrist, that limp gesture Daisy knew profoundly, and checked her watch—not the new gold one, but the blue wristwatch with stitching, the one she always wore.

Keiko not answering seemed, all at once, to answer a number of questions. Daisy saw what she was up to. Keiko planned to get her face fixed, using the latest American surgical techniques, then ship out at the other end with not a [ ] to disturb things. It was hard to explain how Daisy saw [ ] the smooth surface of a pond, two ducks, the girl's [ ]ssive face, bandaged near the ear, but there it was—a small, dark revelation. There would be no press conferences, no anti-Superbomb speech, no fundraising efforts. The girl would not give much of herself. Not for any of them. And they—being the perpetrators of the bombing, the mighty victors—would accept whatever she did.

18.

THAT AFTERNOON, after Dean and Irene had arrived, and they had delivered Keiko to the office of the Norwegian representative (an elderly man keen on meeting a Hiroshima survivor), Daisy told them about the incident at the Éclair Bakery. She didn't mention her new theory about Keiko. Nor did she say what else she suspected—that men were taking an interest in Keiko because of her atomic disfigurement. This was just too morbid a subject to broach with Dean Atchity. He might think it was a product of Daisy's overactive imagination, a reactive sickness all her own. No, there were some people who were too kind and wholesome for what the world had to offer, and so you shielded them instinctively, the way you might shield children. Irene acted this way sometimes towards Daisy—but really it wasn't true. If anything, Daisy thought, she was picking up more than her share of disagreeable thoughts, and they were making her feel sticky all over, like a lint brush.

Meanwhile, she noticed, neither Carney nor Irene had told Dean about the fellow, Tom Orley, who had accosted them in the hospital lobby. Too strange, it had been, too *fantastical,* as Irene put it. "Such a queer intensity to the fellow."

They were standing in the plaza, preparing to part ways. As

Daisy finished describing the woman in her mink stole, Irene rolled her eyes in dismay. "The stupidity of mortals," she said.

"But not," Dean said, "altogether unforeseen or unexpected, given the circumstances."

"Not unexpected perhaps," Irene said, "but completely irrational."

"I wouldn't say *completely* irrational. Remember the circumstances."

"But unwarranted . . ."

"Definitely."

"And unwanted."

"Indubitably."

Irene looked relieved.

Dean propped a foot on the cement planter. He lit his pipe and threw the match into the newly turned dirt, between clusters of hyacinths. "We must remember that none of this is simple," he said. "I myself have been questioned by members of the press, even by my own daughters, about why I'm engaged in this project. And I'm often at a loss as to what to say. I know I want to help humanity, but that answer often sounds too altruistic, too superficial, though the desire to help humanity is anything but."

Daisy sat down on the planter near his foot. How good it would be to fall in line with Dean's judicious but slightly distant way of seeing things. He was the famous Father of the Project, after all, and his words seemed to possess an extra depth—to be letterpressed rather than hastily stamped. Daisy could almost see the mark they were making on history. For a moment she wished that she could tell him all the sorrows and self-recriminations that had preyed on her since the Project began.

"The war is only recently over," he continued. "So I think it is quite natural for people, especially those who have suffered huge losses, to take a while to understand that our terrible enemy is no longer there."

That made sense. Daisy remembered a poster she had seen on a street corner towards the end of the war, depicting Tojo as a worm, with crossed eyes, round glasses and many teeth in a fleshy-lipped mouth. He looked venomous—a crawling creature with a lethal sting, something you'd want to squish beneath your boot. Other times, in newspaper cartoons or in magazine ads, he had been drawn as a rat, or a snake, or even a tiny mouse with Oriental whiskers. Daisy had been sure that the man had huge ears, enormous buck teeth, a hideous squint; she was astonished, during the Japanese war crimes tribunal, to see pictures of a grave, good-looking gentleman. With their hate they had transformed him. And what had they done with that hate since? Daisy doubted that it had disappeared.

And what about the Japanese? What about the Rape of Nanking? What about bayoneting babies, shooting surrendering soldiers in the head? Where had all the other side's hatred gone? Was this something everyone could turn on and off like a light switch—or was it still all there? She remembered the chill she had felt at Irene's party, as Keiko turned away, aloofly dismissing her smile of goodwill.

Yes, it's still there, she thought. Buried, but still there.

Irene was surprisingly quiet through Dean's speech. But when she and Daisy were strolling down Forty-second Street (Dean had taken charge of Keiko for the afternoon), Irene got down to business.

"How go things with the girl?" she asked. "Have you managed to draw her out?"

"I've encouraged her," Daisy said.

They were at the corner of Third Avenue. Behind Irene, almost obscured by the criss-crossing shadows of the El, a bootblack was packing up his brushes, his back a wild diamond pattern of light and shade.

"What have you said?"

"Not much. But I've encouraged her."

Daisy described her hunches about Keiko, while Irene listened carefully. She took Daisy's arm and they crossed the street. "Carney will be interested to hear this—he's very keen on her psychology. Perhaps you've seen that. Dead keen. And he's quite sure others will be keen on it too." Daisy detected a note of bitterness.

They were silent for a while, except for the clicking of their heels on the sidewalk. "That journalist was strange, wasn't he?" Daisy ventured.

"He was fascinated by her. And not just because she's a pretty eighteen-year-old. I'm sure the scar has a lot to do with it."

"Yes," Daisy said—relieved to hear Irene voice it. "I thought so too."

They were nearing Grand Central Station and Daisy could feel the rumbling of the trains beneath her feet. "Why did you get involved in the Project?" she asked suddenly. She had never thought to wonder before. The Project seemed such a natural outgrowth of Irene's left-wing college enthusiasms, which had always felt charged with electricity. Charged but empty.

Irene took her time answering.

"Well," she said at last, "I suppose I have conscious reasons and unconscious ones, just like everyone. Consciously I want to make the world safer, and a large part of my motivation stems from that. I think it's a load of poppycock to believe we are only motivated by our ugliest repressions. A lot of people do things for quite simple, altruistic reasons—just as Atchity says—such as caring about the world, not wanting it to blow up."

Daisy looked at her friend. This was the side of Irene she

loved—how she could expand suddenly, showir
didn't expect.

"And the unconscious reasons?"

"Well, I think it's just the opposite, at least according to Freud. On an unconscious level I don't give a damn about humanity, and neither do you, for that matter. On that level it's all about our need to expiate our guilt, or some such thing."

This was nearer the heart. In another moment, if they followed this course, perhaps Daisy could bring up her itchy skin, and that atomic taste in her mouth, like pennies, which never seemed to go away. Then there were Keiko's silences, which seemed so potent. She wished she had paid more attention, in college, to the lectures in comparative literature. She was sure that Professor Campbell, in his dear way, had said something about silence in the Noh Theatre: how it got colder and more still until, at the climax, nothing at all happened. And then you just wept, or so she remembered, because the ghosts flooded out.

"On an unconscious level," Irene continued, "you and I—in fact all of us in the Project—are struggling to expiate our guilt for having used the bomb. We don't admit it, but there it is, or so Freud would have it. Though he'd probably throw in a dash of the death wish, for good measure."

"That sounds grisly."

"Grisly doesn't begin to describe it. We all want to die, according to Freud, or at least experience what death feels like, and what could be grislier than that? Except, perhaps, what he'd have us doing with our fathers in the meantime! Let me tell you, Daisy"—she took her friend's arm again—"my psychiatrist tells me there are nothing but *urges*. Obsessive, repressed, selfish urges." Her heels clipped cheerfully on the sidewalk. There would be no confiding in Irene today, Daisy thought. Just when you thought you were getting somewhere, she slipped blithely away, like water through a sieve.

They stopped to stare at a rubbery beige girdle in a store window. A sign above it read, *Ladies—This girdle will do all the work!*

"Heavens," Irene exclaimed. "How marvellous! You know I'm in favour of delegation."

19.

DEAN AND BERTHA ATCHITY'S HOUSE was an hour and thirty minutes northeast of the city, in Fairfield County, beyond the tight grid of suburbs that had recently devoured Rocklands and Westchester. The homes in the Atchitys' neighbourhood were much older than those in Riverside Meadows. Most had been built before the first war. Some were Cape Cod homes from the previous century, and a few old salt boxes dated from colonial times. Behind the Atchity house an acre of lawn and forest dropped to a small brook; in front another half-acre of lawn stretched invitingly, rimmed by a split-rail fence. Standing on the front porch, ringing the doorbell with Keiko beside her, Daisy could hear the mature birches shuffling their thousands of leaves in the wind. A Dalmatian ran around the house, barking.

This was the original prototype of the suburb, the Eden of suburbs. Everyone else was confined to the proverbial East, eking out their living in what seemed, comparatively, to be the dust. This was what they were all striving for: to live in gentle civility in a haven such as this, out of which you could make forays to express outrage (or rather civilized concern—Bertha would never express outrage) at the direction humanity was taking:

those *disturbing* hearings, that *concerning* H-bomb. Life would be so easy, Daisy thought, if everyone were given three acres of prime Connecticut real estate, a Dalmation and a split-rail fence.

Not far from where they were standing, the British had marched after landing in Bridgeport. Bertha had told her this the day they lunched at Voisin. The British had crossed this very property, wearing their curious spats and red jackets, bayonets in hand, torching barns, setting fire to fields. Brave deeds of independence had been enacted here—children bundled and carried to safety, homes defended from upper windows. One felt that goodness and freedom, albeit of a muted, civilized sort, had been victorious here, and that now the Atchitys were reaping the harvest.

Clumps of Virginia bluebells had seeded themselves around the bases of the birch trees, looking woodsy and natural. Why had nobody tried such a thing in Riverside Meadows? Was it that nobody knew how? Or would such an idea have seemed outlandish and showy in their little suburb, as though whoever did it intended to make a spectacle of their lawn. Of themselves.

Bertha came to the door, looking large-boned and encouraging. She was a force to be reckoned with, but not in the way that Irene was. Bertha was not a career woman. Instead, she poured her energy into charitable activities and was often written up in the newspaper's society pages. She lunched regularly at the Colony Club, with her middle-aged society set.

"Look who's here," Bertha called out as they entered the living room. Various people that Daisy recognized from the *Sunday Review* smiled and came to speak to them.

Dean's two teenaged girls, Stacey and Debbie, had come downstairs. They stood in the doorway looking faintly aggressive, their lips covered in coral lipstick. One wore a cheerleading skirt and a sweater with a big L appliquéd over her breasts. The other, a couple of years older, wore a pair of jeans and an untucked blouse. That was the way teenagers dressed these days, before they headed out to cheerlead, or just to neck with their boyfriends in parked cars.

Bertha took Keiko by the arm. "And now, my dear, you must—absolutely must—come say hello to someone special."

Keiko said something about being glad to visit such a nice home.

"I'm sure you're welcome wherever you go," Bertha smiled brightly at the girl. "This is a project of friendship, isn't it?"

At that moment Irene emerged from the kitchen, a martini in her hand, and gestured for Daisy to follow her. They went upstairs into a parody of a girl's bedroom: frilled coverlet, daisies painted on the dresser, a baby-pink vanity against the wall. Irene offered Daisy a cigarette and sat heavily on the bed. "So," she said. "Anything further?"

"No," Daisy said abruptly, surprising herself. "I said before. It's not easy."

"Don't I know it." Irene blew smoke into the pretty room. "Quite frankly, nothing's come out the way I thought it would. I told Carney about our conversation—your observations—"

"Oh." Daisy felt her heart sink.

Irene looked at her sharply. "You knew I intended to tell Raymond."

"I suppose I did."

"Well, don't look so surprised then. Anyway, Raymond says that if you can't persuade her to speak, he'll have to have a session with her himself, after the operation. But I hate the thought of that."

Daisy nodded. Thinking of Walter.

"I'd infinitely prefer it if you could get her talking. You have depths I don't have. You know that, Daisy. You always did."

A compliment. Daisy felt the pleasure of it.

Irene walked to the window. "Raymond bought her a kimono—did she show you? No, I suppose she wouldn't. A silky thing, from Saks. A kimono from Saks, for Christ sakes!" She stared out at the woods, the perfect vista of trees in new leaf, the brook hidden in the middle distance. Then she leaned her head against the frame. "He never bought me anything from Saks, not even at the beginning."

Cool, beautiful Irene. A dusting of powder from her forehead had come away on the window frame. Daisy went to her and put her arms around her, while Irene stood ramrod straight, hardly accepting the embrace.

"Next time she enters the hospital, he's going to sit with her, make her talk. He told me so. They all want him to do it—the folks at the AEC and the ABCC—all the men with their initials. So there's really nothing I can do, is there? Except that I feel, if someone else got her talking first, perhaps he wouldn't need to push and pry so much. Anyway, I've taken matters into my own hands. I've invited a reporter from the *Times* here tonight. He's probably talking to her right now—we should go see."

Irene turned from Daisy, firm but fragile.

Downstairs, the living room was full. And there Keiko was, with Bertha, being introduced to Peter Hoaring, a thin, sharp-faced reporter from the *New York Times*. Daisy saw him shake Keiko's limp hand, saw her hooded, silent, covert expression. What was Peter Hoaring saying? He had compassionate dark eyes, but the rest of his gaunt face reminded Daisy of a weasel. He would start with pleasantries, then move ahead in no time flat. Yes, he had put down his drink on the coffee table and was feeling in his jacket pocket for his notebook. Daisy edged towards them. She couldn't see Keiko's face, it was blocked by a small knot of women standing in the centre of the room, but she imagined it held its look of removed interest, almost haughtiness. Now Peter Hoaring leaned forward. What was his question? Daisy couldn't make it out, but it had troubled

Keiko: she was gazing away from him, across the top of the grand piano, at a small collection of Meissenware potpourri dishes. Keiko eyed a tiny salt dish painted with gold and purple pansies.

"A few words, if you might." Edging closer, Daisy at last could make this out. "About those devastating moments after the bomb dropped." Hoaring flipped open his notebook.

Keiko was cornered. They had her at last. She kept her eyes on the salt dish, the slender shaft of its minuscule silver spoon, perhaps gathering courage, and Daisy recognized the blank look on her face, as though her true self had rushed for cover, hidden in the bushes.

"One thing about those moments," Peter Hoaring said. "One memory."

From the bevy of women she heard the words *neutron bomb,* clear as a bell, and then Keiko's voice, so recognizable for its lack of depth.

"A single memory?"

"One."

"I have many."

"One will do."

A pause. Daisy stepped around the women. Now she could see the two of them perfectly: Keiko staring at the salt dish, Peter Hoaring holding his pad, waiting.

"When I think back to Hiroshima, I think of one thing."

Ah, now they were getting somewhere. Hoaring jotted eagerly, in shorthand. "Tell me what that one thing is."

"I think of a place my grandfather showed me."

"__rever?" He wrote this.

"__mple of Miyajima. It sits in the Inland Sea. It is con-

__be one of the seven wonders of Japan."

__v far from the epicentre of the bomb was it?"

"Quite far."

"And was it utterly destroyed."

"No."

There was a pause.

"Then why do you think of it?"

"It is considered very beautiful. Someday you may want to see it. There are many wild deer there. Pilgrims travel from all over Japan to view the famous red gate that stands in the water."

Peter Hoaring held his pencil between two fingers, then drummed it against his pad. Daisy felt him wanting to scream, *But what about the devastation?*

"Priests built the shrine on wooden docks that rise and sink with the tide." Now Keiko's eyes met Daisy's. Oh, what was there? The faintest wisp of a smile, as if confiding, *This is what I do. Now you know.*

Also something equally clear.

I cannot do this forever.

Hoaring would have kept at her, but Daisy obeyed her cue as neatly as if this were a double act. "Well, Keiko," she said brightly, stepping forward and taking her arm. "You're telling Mr. Hoaring about your home—I'm sure he's appreciative. But now I'm afraid you're desperately needed in the kitchen." Luck was with them, because Bertha Atchity stood up on the hearth and called for everyone's attention. She was about to serve cake, so everyone must gather.

Now you've seen.

That was what Keiko's eyes had said. Yet walking down the hall there was nothing complicit, no buzz of mutual recognition. Keiko's arm, as always, felt singularly limp.

In the large kitchen Bertha served the shortcake, ample slices topped with whipped cream. "No more Hiroshimas," she called out, licking whipped cream from her thumb.

No more Hiroshimas.

The cry was picked up by Bertha's daughter Stacey, and by one or two of the *Sunday Review* interns and then let drop. It was simply too difficult to eat strawberry shortcake and chant an anti-atomic slogan at the same time.

20.

KEIKO HAD NOW BEEN with Daisy and Walter for more than a month, and so far there hadn't been a peep from the neighbourhood women: Joan Palmer, or the terrible, shallow Evelyn Lithgow, or even from Fran Warburgh next door. They seemed to have retracted their claws and to be waiting, perhaps in aghast silence, perhaps plotting an attack. "I worry about it," Daisy said to Walter. "They said they had informed the Residents' Committee."

"Maybe we should have a party. A neighbourhood get-together."

"Nobody would come."

"You don't know that."

"I do."

They were happy, Keiko and Walter. They had found a routine where they listened to the Jack Benny show after supper, then the Lux Radio Theatre. Keiko's face relaxed, and when Walter spoke to her she smiled shyly, or laughed. This made Daisy feel restless. She cleared dishes, clattered them into the sink, breaking the china stem of her tomato-shaped relish dish. She cursed out loud at this—rare for her—but neither Keiko nor Walter heard her. They sat with soft smiles of identical appreciation on their faces, listening to Gracie Allen, who was guest-starring on the show.

"Her voice is squeaky," Keiko ventured.

"You can say that again."

Daisy watched for her neighbours, and though she didn't see them, she felt waves of hatred emanating from their silent houses. It was true that the Project wasn't going as she had hoped, but they didn't know that. It was just like Joan and the others to be hating her for having tried to do something halfway decent in this blasted heath of a suburb.

She did feel Ed coming and going—ostentatiously slamming his car door, glowering at her window, while his children dutifully chanted *Jap, Jap, Jap* during their games of war. *Jap* and *Kraut* were very much the words of ditch play on Saturdays on Linden Street. But perhaps this was not because of Keiko. Perhaps her presence hadn't even pierced the consciousness of the children. It was difficult to say. Since her miscarriages, Daisy had found children's minds almost impossible to decipher.

But then something did happen that was upsetting.

It began, late one afternoon, with a sound: a scraping of metal on stone, clear and hard, amplified by the cool, spring air. It seemed to emanate from the kitchen walls, that cherry-printed wallpaper, that was how loud it was, but then Daisy realized it was coming from outside. She stepped onto the back porch. Ed righted himself from his hunched position and wiped his brow on a red hankie. She could see his face over the fence. His body was reflected in the greenhouse, but even still she couldn't see what he was doing. He saw her standing on the porch, but let his glance slide past her, as though his real interest was in her garbage cans. Then he bent again to his task.

When Walter came home, an hour and a half later, Ed was still out there. The scraping of metal had given way to a gentle velvety sound, as dirt was piled on dirt. "I don't know what he's doing," Daisy whispered.

Walter put his hand in his suit pocket, found his tobacco and papers and began to roll himself a cigarette. Then he thrust open the back door. "Ed!" he called out.

Ed stood up. In the dusk his face looked purple. A thin coat of dirt clung to the sweat of his cheeks.

In his easy, loose-hipped way, as though he had all the time in the world, Walter walked down the steps and crossed the lawn to the fence. "What's up there, neighbour?" he said.

Ed seemed to be wiping his hands on his jeans. He must have reached into his pocket, because a moment later he held out a pamphlet. "Doing my civic duty."

Walter took the pamphlet. "You can survive," he read out loud. He flipped it over, read the back, then returned it to Ed. "Lots of digging to do yet?"

"Kids'll help."

"*Those* kids?" Walter pointed at the Warburghs' house. Junie had come onto the back porch, a tiny violin in her hands. "Jimmy Jr. busted one of my strings," she said. "I'm gonna slap him."

"Don't you slap your brother." That was Fran's listless voice from inside the house.

Ed laughed. "Yeah," he said, wiping his brow. "Those ones." He took the papers and tobacco from Walter and rolled himself a cigarette. They smoked together, then Ed flicked his butt into the hole.

"Not bad for a few hours' work," Walter said.

"It'll take weeks."

By the time Walter came back in, the smell of earth clung to his suit. Keiko was in the kitchen, and so Daisy had to follow Walter into the bedroom to get the news.

"Regulation bomb shelter."

"Oh, that's just like Ed. He's doing it to hurt us. To get at Keiko."

Walter shrugged.

"He thinks I put on airs—I know he does. He said as much to Fran."

Walter laughed. "Now that's something to take seriously." He gave her a little kiss on the cheek—a dry hit-or-miss affair, but better than nothing.

21.

THERE WERE ONLY THREE MORE DAYS before Keiko was to return to the hospital. Walter had caught the train to work. Keiko and Daisy were alone for the day.

"Why do you call Mr. Lawrence, Walter, but me Mrs. Lawrence?" Daisy said.

A pause. The girl was plainly startled.

"I am very sorry if I have offended you, Mrs. Lawrence. He asked me to call him by that name, and so I did."

"So did I!"

"I am very sorry, Mrs. Lawrence. I'll stop."

"Oh, call me Daisy, for heaven's sakes. That's how we do things here. We're less formal."

"Thank you."

But Daisy knew Keiko would never call her by her first name.

After breakfast the girl went to her bedroom.

The kitchen curtains moved in the breeze. Daisy thought about Keiko lying on her bed, rereading, for the tenth time, the copy of *Seventeen Magazine*. Daisy scratched her palms. They were itchy all the time now, red and hot, and so was the top of her head. What was this stuff, this radioactive stuff? Sometimes she was sure she could see it, glinting in the dust motes as the sun poured through the windows.

Daisy knocked on Keiko's door. She was sitting at the desk, looking through the magazine. Daisy told her she was going to walk across the fields to Strickland's Grocery to pick up some butter. Keiko could come along if she wanted. In all of her time here, all the comings and goings to Manhattan, Keiko had not once taken this little walk. If something had needed replenishing—soap, shampoo, butter—Daisy walked to the store alone. Keiko held back now, and so Daisy suggested that they pick up Popsicles, something she had heard Fran say, to bribe her children to come on the walk.

Keiko's face brightened, though Daisy suspected that she didn't know what a Popsicle was: maybe she thought it was something expensive. She said she would come, as soon as she was changed. She was a great one for picking out clothes, wanting on every occasion to wear what was appropriate.

When she came out of her bedroom, she had on a pair of pedal pushers and a short-sleeved blouse. She had wrapped a cashmere sweater around her shoulders. A gift, this one from Bertha Atchity. On her feet were clean white sneakers.

Daisy stood by the front door as Keiko came down the hall, past the telephone alcove, the little porcelain shepherdess in her nook. In three days she would be gone, off to the hospital, and then the scar would be removed. And what would she become next, Daisy heard herself thinking, the process all at once reminding her of a butterfly inside a cocoon. What would she emerge as? What final form would she take?

It seemed as though it might rain, and Keiko took a foldable plastic rain cap from her pocket, shook it out, and tied it under her chin. They passed Joan Palmer's house, and Daisy saw her at the window and waved. Joan stepped back. Who did she think she was—Mata Hari? Joan would be on the phone, calling Evelyn Lithgow. Sure enough, when they passed Evelyn's house, she was at the upstairs window, telephone in hand, watching them.

They crossed the elementary school playground and walked farther, through the field where the kids played baseball. It only took five minutes before they were in a different territory altogether. A dirt path ran beside the field for a hundred yards, then veered sharply down the slope. The path was worn and old. It must have been used for generations before the suburb was built, used by the Willards of Willard's Creek. Whenever Daisy took this path she pictured the ghosts of the Willard women walking in front or behind, the wet swish of their skirts in the long grass.

At the bottom of the hill was the marsh, a muddy bit of water that iced up in winter. Kids skated there, but there were so many grasses and bulrushes sticking up through the ice that Daisy had heard it wasn't much fun. In the summer they collected tadpoles in glass jars. At the edge of the pond was a bit of old fence, and then the path ran beside the creek. Joey Palmer's three-legged cat followed swiftly through the long grass. He didn't pull himself along, but moved with a muscular scrabble. The path narrowed and Daisy gestured for Keiko to take the lead. Her sneakers were muddy.

About a hundred yards along the creek path, there was an arched footbridge made of granite fieldstone. It was twice or three times as old as anything else in Riverside Meadows, even the barns and houses standing on the back roads. Its rough-hewn blocks of stone had been fitted together without mortar. Usually the creek was shallow, but today there was a lot of water rushing beneath the bridge, because of all the rain. Standing in the middle of it, they heard the poplars hissing. Daisy had a powerful sensation of another world beneath this one—a world of people, all dead now, who had settled this area, tilled these fields, grown tobacco and pumpkins. She could feel how sudden Riverside Meadows was, and that all the time another world was flowing underneath, like hidden groundwater.

They watched the wind bend the tips of grass blades. Keiko was panting, but when Daisy asked if she wanted to rest a little longer she said no, she wasn't tired. "I have not seen this bridge before," she said, breathing deeply. "It feels different than the other things here."

"It's older. Built before the suburbs. Built by a family called the Willards, who settled this area." With the tips of her fingers, Daisy felt along the crack where stone met stone. She added, "Perhaps it reminds you of the bridges from your home."

Keiko's chest was moving as she breathed. Her hands gripped the edge of the stone wall.

"Were there bridges like this, on the rivers of Hiroshima?"

Keiko looked into the water and said something. Daisy leaned over as well.

"Were there many?"

"Yes."

"Were they like this?"

"In some ways."

"Made of stone?"

"Mostly wood."

"But everything must have been destroyed . . ." Daisy knew she must be fast, or the blankness would descend.

But the girl merely shrugged. "The old bridges are gone, if that is what you mean. People built new ones. Now they use cement." She paused, then added, "It's stronger." Daisy saw no trace of irony in her eyes.

There they hung, Keiko and Daisy, not speaking, but not entirely silent either. It was as though they were both waiting for what might be said next, where the words might pull them. After a while, Keiko said, "They planted plum trees in my old district, the year after the war ended, and now they're big."

After all the hours, all the days, of waiting for the girl to speak, it didn't seem to cost her all that much. "Just like the ones on your street," Keiko said. "That size."

"Probably planted around the same time. This suburb was built in 1946."

Riverside Meadows and Hiroshima, both postwar constructions. After a while, to Daisy's amazement, Keiko spoke again. "Some people said they didn't want things to grow. My Aunt Yoshiko said that. She wanted things to be desolate forever. But I never liked it when she said that."

"But why did she want that?"

"So that nobody forgets." She said it so simply that Daisy was embarrassed.

"And what about you?" Daisy reached for her hand, and that was a mistake. The girl pushed herself away from the bridge and walked on. Her small head was swathed in the plastic cap, which had drops of moisture condensed in the inside pleats. Her shoulders were tiny, delicate, like the bones of a bird. Daisy imagined them hollow and porous, the consistency of pumice. The sun was behind the clouds, and the overcast light made her plastic hat shine. Her bare calves looked dark, almost purple. Her ankle socks, fluted red at the edges, glowed with a strange vibrancy.

Inside Strickland's Grocery, Daisy bought a pound of Land O' Lakes butter, then picked out two lime-green Popsicles. At the cash, Gerard Strickland sat on his stool doing a crossword, his yellow-white hair plastered to his scalp. He put the paper down and gestured to Keiko, who was near the front of the store, slowly turning a rack of comic books.

"So this is your Japanese guest. My we've been hearing a lot about you, miss." He used his habitual voice of professional courtesy, while he pressed the buttons on the register. He always made it seem like an esoteric and difficult skill: proclaiming the sale price from memory, then pressing at least five different buttons, pulling the cash lever. The cash drawer sprang open.

"You are the girl from Japan?" He winked at Daisy.

Keiko, studying a Captain Marvel comic, glanced up and nodded.

"We don't get the likes of you in these parts very often." He wrapped the butter in brown paper, tied it with butcher's string, then handed it to Daisy.

Back outside, they crossed the parking lot and walked along the edge of the cornfields, which were covered in lines of new shoots. In the first field they were six inches, but in the next field the shoots showed as stubble. When they reached the creek Daisy decided to speak again.

"Keiko, I understand, or at least I think I do." It was hard to say this, but she forged on. "What I mean to say is, I think I understand your wish to remain private about the bombing. About what happened. But you see, many people are depending on you . . ."

Keiko bypassed a puddle that blocked the path, reflecting wisps of cloud, then she stopped. "I think you are mistaken, Mrs. Lawrence. I have been very ashamed that I did not speak at the press conference. Or to Mr. Hoaring. I know that everyone expects this thing from me."

"Then why not try, at least a little? Tell your story. Then say a few words against the H-bomb. So many people are counting on you."

She looked at Daisy—oh, those remarkable eyes of hers. "I want to."

"Good, Keiko."

"Mrs. Lawrence, I can try, but I am not sure I can say what people want."

"I think a few words is all they want. Condemnation. And a few, you know, memories." This sounded so coarse. Daisy quickly added that it was for fundraising purposes mostly, to bring more girls over.

Keiko said something softly.

"I can't hear you."

"I do not remember," she said.

"Don't remember what?" For a moment Daisy was completely at sea. "What don't you remember?"

She didn't answer.

"Are you saying that you have forgotten the bombing?"

"I wish I could remember."

"But how could this be, Keiko? You told them about it in Hiroshima."

"I am very sorry. Please forgive me."

"What happened to your memory?"

"Please."

"But you *do* remember," Daisy said, despite herself. "You did, in Japan." She bent down and picked up a stick, a nonchalant gesture, but her heart was beating hard. There was a long silence; the girl standing beside the puddle.

At last Keiko said, "I don't think the things I would say could make any difference."

"Oh!" Daisy was glad to be on flat terrain again. "I think they would make a great difference. To everyday Americans. Just to hear, first-hand . . ." These words weren't right. They belonged to her false self. She shut her mouth.

They had reached the bridge, and they stopped in the middle again, looking down at the rush of muddy water beneath them.

"Come now, my dear," Daisy whispered. "Is it so terrible to say a few words?"

Keiko looked down at the gurgle of water breaking across a small logjam of twigs and old leaves.

"I'm sorry," Daisy said. "I couldn't hear you."

"After the bomb blast there was the bright light."

Daisy nodded.

"A bright light."

"It must have been terrible."

"I remember nothing else."

"You were unconscious, but then you woke up."

"I cannot say."

"But later still."

She shook her head.

"But the things you told Mr. Atchity in Hiroshima."

Keiko shook her head, then she looked at Daisy, eyes wilder than she had ever seen them. "I said what I *thought* I remembered. I am ashamed. I didn't tell the truth, Mrs. Lawrence."

Keiko was lying, Daisy was sure, lying about lying—but that didn't seem to matter so much. Daisy had a fleeting feeling that she understood this shadowy craft. What was hidden made sense. Keiko looked up again, eyes large and amber, the eyes of a deer. "I have done something bad coming here, when I cannot do what people wish of me." She spoke clearly and simply, and Daisy doubted every word she uttered, but still she wanted to say that she believed her. She didn't know what to do, so she took Keiko's hand. It was cold, and without thinking Daisy slipped it into her coat pocket. Daisy felt the girl's small fist clamped tight, her knuckles brushing something round—a chestnut picked up from the ground the autumn before. Keiko stood rigidly beside her, her hand in the older woman's pocket. Then gently, as though in a play, she let her rigid body relax, her cheek rest on Daisy's shoulder. Daisy put her arm round her. She seemed thinner to the touch than Daisy could have imagined.

"We'll figure something out," Daisy whispered.

22.

THE DAY BEFORE KEIKO LEAVES for her second opera-tion, Tom Orley sits in his landlady's kitchen, eating his two fried eggs in silence. Mrs. Gordienko leans in close, holding the enamel coffee pot, the better to smell his scalp, which in the morning smells so much like her son, Grigory's. She can see flakes of darkened skin along the part of his hair, very like the cradle cap Grigory used to get as a baby. She feels an urge, instantly sup-pressed, to pick at Tom's scalp. But even a genial young man like Tom would be offended at such a liberty. Mrs. Gordienko sighs heavily and turns off the frying pan.

Tom is thinking about you, Keiko. All the time, thinking about you.

Today, after he has eaten breakfast, he walks to the train sta-tion. He feels reckless and happy and hollow on the inside. Inside the hollow he carries a conductive fluid that lights him up, making him do things he doesn't normally do, like pat the silky ears of an Irish setter at the corner.

He gets on the Long Island Rail car and finds a seat easily. The train is deserted at this time of day, except for one fellow leaning his head against the glass. He looks like an ad man, some poor sucker who stayed out all night and now has to face his wife, head throbbing. His eyes are closed against the flashing as the train passes the iron girders of the station.

Back on the farm, Emmy, Tom's sister, came to him once and said that she heard voices. She was about eight at the time. He was fourteen. "Just a whole pile of people in my head," she had said. "I can't get them to stop." Turned out there was a father— she'd named him Baxter, and he was from Texas—and there was a mother with the sophisticated name of Eloise, and two children, whose names Tom never learned. At first Tom had gone along with it, but after a while she had become too serious and he had shouted at her to shut up. "They're not real," he had said. "They're made up." She had reached out and clawed his arms with her nails. It didn't hurt. It just surprised him.

"They're as real as you are," she had said, "probably realer. Eloise can speak French, and you can't."

French. That was rich.

"What does she say then?"

And before his startled eyes Emmy had leaned back, as though to yodel, and a wealth of French had poured from her lips.

During the war, he kept picturing her as that girl of eight, though in fact she'd been eleven when he left, taller and leaner. But upside down over Rouen and Dieppe, squeezed into the tail of a B-17, disoriented by the thudding of steel, which both surrounded him and came from the cavity of his torso, it was Emmy at eight whose face swam into view if he closed his eyes—bright pale eyes, pigtails, red knuckles. Her fury at the world for getting so much wrong!

In dreams he walks up the road towards the farmhouse. To his right is the ditch, full of oak leaves and mud. A fence post has been knocked down. The sight of barbed wire trailing on the ground, beside the ditch, makes him sick. His father is so careful with the fences. Beyond the ditch, the east field is dry and brown. No snow yet. The house ahead looks empty, though in his dream the border collie, Mitch, will soon come out wagging his whole body. He steps along the road towards home, but then, always, a woolly blankness like cotton batten invades the corner of his eyes. He tries to move but cannot swing his legs: he has forgotten how, or they grow limp, boneless and flabby. When he wakes, he is often sobbing.

In fact, the fence was intact the day he came home. He entered the farmhouse without incident, except that he surprised his mother at the stove, and she dropped a can of hot grease on her foot. She held him tight in her swallowing embrace, while Tom's father came down the steps behind them, the black jacket he wore on Sundays flapping at the arms. And where was Emmy? He looked over his mother's shoulder at his father—that gaunt, haunted face—and asked for his sister.

His father told him how Emmy had woken up one morning and called out, "I can't move my legs." This was the sort of highjinks she always used to be up to, and at first they thought it was a joke.

"*You* thought it was a joke," Tom's mother corrected. "*I* knew."

He tried to picture what they had lived through, the gradations of the disease—first hours, first days, the doctors, the specialists; the encroachment of the paralysis; poliomyelitis; until here they were—wiped clean by it.

All through the story, Tom kept expecting her to run downstairs, holding the rabbit.

They took him to the infirmary, a treed place, expensive, called Carling Memorial. The private room had green floors, yellow curtains in a plastic material, like shower curtains, that the nurses wiped down with sponges. Emmy at eighteen—that was a shock, almost as much as seeing her in the iron lung. She had become a plain girl, with sunken eyes close together, though she had the same overlapping front teeth. The machine expanded and contracted her chest, did her breathing for her.

He sat beside her and listened to the machine wheezing as it pushed her lungs in and out. Emmy's pale eyes looked back at him from the pillow, all resistance taken from her by the complications of breathing. Her braids had gotten messy, and that was upsetting because she always cared about their neatness. One of the things he had always liked was how she braided her hair right to the tip, so that they got thin as a rat's tail. "Real China Man braids," their father called them.

Emmy-Mae. Emily Mae.

What he had seen, as the girl got off the plane? What expression transmuted into the shadows and sepias and creams and opaque blacks of the photograph? Not Emmy at eighteen, or Emmy at eleven, or eight even—but Emmy as she had come to him upside down, the propellor of the B-17 thudding in his heart.

For a full thirty seconds before the lights and the darks took their solid forms, his sister had appeared in Keiko's place— bossy, determined face, wide forehead—before the photo showed someone else, another person. Only the flash of resistance the same—a glint of something so fast only he had caught it. He could imagine her grabbing the camera from his hands and smashing it on the ground. Or sitting beside him, teasing, provoking, as Emmy used to:

Look—you're holding the rabbit wrong.

You've put too much salt on the porridge.

That was the problem with everything now. Nobody could get inside him any more, tell him crazy things—things that made him laugh, or believe in French voices, or made him jealous of every wild idea that could pour out of a person's mouth. *I hear voices.* That was rich. He had hated her for it at the time, because it wasn't just any voices she heard, that wouldn't be enough for Emmy. It had to be French voices.

"I know how to breathe out of my eyelids," she had said another time, when she was about nine. That was during the period, for months, that she'd been afraid of the undead. Not the dead—not ghosts. The undead. Creatures half dead and half alive.

"What is it now?" Tom had said, exasperated, when she'd woken him by standing at the foot of his bed, just standing there, calling his name. He'd been cross as anything. For about the thirtieth time he had let her crawl into bed with him. "What is it now?" Course he didn't have to ask—he knew it was the undead again.

Now how was he supposed to live without those shadows? Nobody had mentioned the undead since. Without a word his little sister had taken them with her—all the shadow people, all the zombies, all the walking corpses, all the inhabitants of the half-light.

| | | STORYTELLER

23.

A scar line must follow the relaxed skin lines as much as possible.
The main factor in incision is direction.
With hypertrophic scarring we must debride the edges!

THESE WERE THE RULES Raymond Carney followed,
obvious once you knew them. *We must debride the edges!* In the
midst of the operation he had shouted that last instruction, as
though the unyielding thickness of the scarred skin was the
nurse's fault. Had he panicked? No—but he had had no way to
gauge, until after the actual excision of the tissue, just how
crusted the edges of the wound would be, how difficult to
pierce with skin hooks, almost impossible to undermine with
the scalpel. But that was over now—thank God.

"My dear girl," he had said when Keiko awoke. What words
to use? The atomic scar, the bubbled anguished flesh, the flesh
requiring debridement and filing, the toughest wound he had
ever excised— "The scar is gone," he had said to her. He saw
her eyes register this fact, and in another moment her lids
had closed.

Now Keiko lay in bed, her face completely bandaged with sterile gauze and a Tensor mask. Pressure on the skin after a graft must be above twenty hectograms for a full ninety days, to create a force greater than the intracapillary pressure. Hence the elastic garmenting over the sterile strips, the gauze, the peroxide cream. Against the white bandages, Keiko's eyes and mouth stood out like holes. To Raymond Carney she seemed immensely small and drained, as though she had been adrift on an ocean for years, then cast up here, in this bed.

He pitied her, he really did. What she was attempting was immensely difficult. And her evasions were admirable, almost like poetry. Such winged struggle. Such dark burrowing, all to avoid the one central question.

Where were you on August 6?

He must be careful, he told himself: the girl was tremendously delicate and had been more so since the operation. He must draw on deep and hidden reserves of gentleness. He must be very kind to her, even as he pushed her in the right direction.

Raymond sniffed deeply, checking beneath the high notes of antiseptic cream, the bleach used to wash the sky-blue tiles, for the lower tones of putridity. He smelled nothing, and that was good. The chances of infection in this early period were high.

Keiko was watching him now, but dully, dully; she might be in this world and might be in some other. That was good too, because it was time to check her bandages, and he did not wish (he checked his watch), seven hours and seven days after the operation, to have any repeat of The Unfortunate Incident. He had not yet found the best words in which to describe the Incident, which had occurred two nights before, though soon he would need to draft a memorandum alluding to it—a memorandum, addressed not to Dean Atchity and the Hiroshima Project, but to scientists of the Atomic Energy Commission. He was a man with two masters now: the Hiroshima Project organizers, who wanted to fix the girl's face, and the Atomic Energy Commission, with whom he was consulting on other aspects of the Project. They had agreed to fund his psychoanalytic sessions. They were eager to explore, just as he was, the effect of the bomb on the human psyche. They had masses of money too, which they siphoned through various universities. How people lived after the bomb, how they adjusted, remembered, resisted, set up defence mechanisms (or didn't)—this was crucial information for a country threatened daily by an armed and belligerent Soviet Union. What Dr. Carney was exploring was groundbreaking. The fellows from the AEC had said as much to him (after he had used those words himself, but still, groundbreaking was groundbreaking).

The Unfortunate Incident would have appalled Dean and the other Project organizers. No amount of calm explanation would have clarified Carney's position. This was one of the great pities about the Project and those who led it: they were, in the end, bleeding-heart liberals, with soft, mealy attitudes towards the future. They wanted to stop the Superbomb, and to create an international system of governance, and to abolish atomic weapons testing, but not one of them could look squarely at the thing they were attempting to abolish. They were like children, covering their eyes with blankets. In some ways Carney felt a deeper kinship with the soldiers at Yucca Flat, setting up their simulated towns, detonating all that atomic might, and then running into the blast, bayonets raised.

There were times when Carney actually felt he hated the Project organizers, especially Dean Atchity. They lacked that fine scientific impulse—the urge to know, the urge to look, simply to stare at what humanity had created. If you couldn't look at a thing, how on earth could you oppose it? How on this earth could you even begin? For a moment he saw them scurrying from the blast while he stood on the desert sand, successive waves of heat and light staining his skin, whipping his hair, turning his belt buckle red hot.

His attention shifted back to the bandaged girl in the bed. She was still watching him.

"Keiko," he said. "Can you hear me?" Her eyes stayed focused on him. The eyes of a listening child. Eighteen the girl was—half child, half adult. He remembered the lines of an anonymous poem from the Edo era, which he had read the night before. It was called, merely, "*Song.*"

> *I bathed my snow skin*
> *In pure Tamagawa River*
> *Our quarrel is loosened away*
> *And he loosens my hair.*
> *I am all uncombed.*
> *I will not remember him,*
> *I will not altogether forget him,*
> *I will wait for spring.*

24.

From: Dr. Raymond Carney
To: The Atomic Energy Commission
May 21, 1952

The following letter does not constitute a medical report, but rather rumination on the Hiroshima Project's surgical and psychoanalytical aspects. Please read it in that light. Medical reports have been filed at Mount Sinai (records 24–26/0001–May 21/Kitigawa) and delivered to the Hiroshima Peace Project.

Surgery: The subject had an atomic burn scar covering her left cheek from the hairline of her temple, running horizontally to her left eye, and diminishing to a point at her chin. Scar tissue had the colouring of a port wine stain (*naevus vinosus*), and was heavily bubbled and hypertrophic. Manual probing indicated a second-degree scar with intact subcutaneous tissue. In addition, the subject had a nodular keloid of 2.2 cm attached to the posterior portion of her left earlobe.

On March 30th the keloid was excised using standard excision surgery.

On May 12th the hypertrophic scar was removed. This operation required complete anaesthetization. Using No. 15 gradle scissors, a local flap of healthy skin from the subject's neck was undermined and stretched to cover a portion of the excised area. Where the subcutaneous area was damaged, near the left temple, and in all locations where the undermined flap could not be employed, a split thickness skin graft was utilized. A graft was rolled back from the subject's inner thigh, excess fat trimmed and the skin perforated to prevent haematomia. The edges of the wound were debrided and sutured with nylon thread. Pressure-gradient elastic garments will cover the face for no less than ninety days. Morphine, followed when appropriate by a standard pain relief formula, will be administered while she remains in hospital.

Post-surgery: As agreed, the long-term importance of this project lies less in the reconstructive surgery than in comprehending the mindset of an atomic-bomb victim.

the proliferation of atomic weapons, and the
...ipation of their future use, understanding the
psychological responses in a civilian population is vital
to national security.

Three analytic sessions have followed the subject's
surgery. These have taken place in her private room. I
sit near her in a chair while she lies comfortably in her
hospital bed.

I had made every effort to acquaint myself with the
subject's background, to the limited extent possible. The
grandfather was remarkable not only for his business
skills (a manager at Ujina Shipping), but for his studies
of folklore. Grandmother deceased, 1922. The mother,
Sumiko Kitigawa, had received a degree of education
unusual for a Japanese woman, attending Tokyo
University, where she majored in languages. After
Keiko's father, Kenji Kitigawa, enlisted in the Imperial
Army, she and Keiko took up residence in Hiroshima,
living with the subject's paternal grandfather. Also
residing in the grandfather's house at the time of the
blast were the subject's uncle, Taro Kitigawa and Taro's
wife, Yoshiko.

To open the first session, I tested the subject to
ensure that her mind was clear from the morphine,
which, though a useful pain inhibitor, can cause confu-
sion. When I had assured myself that her cognitive fac-
ulties were intact, I reminded the subject of aspects of
her story of survival. In Hiroshima she had mentioned
a fox shrine near a bridge within a short distance from
her grandfather's home. Obviously this shrine and the
superstitions attached to it had had a great impact on
the girl. To open the session, I had leafed through

Yanagita Kunio's little book *The Tales of Fox,* and I took it upon myself to read aloud a short story from the Hiroshima Prefecture. I then invited the subject to elaborate on its meaning. She immediately exhibited signs of alarm, and answered my questions evasively. For instance, she claimed to know personally all the characters in the small story—including the fox woman and the old man described. This sort of playful deception, masking the truth (even, to some extent, from oneself), may well be considered a primary aspect of the A-bomb temperament. The victim displays an obsessive desire for secrecy.

I find this aspect of her neurosis particularly fascinating. It is quite possible that Keiko's complex is typical of A-bomb neuroses, but a more lengthy study will be necessary to reveal the many layers of the mindset.

I must now speak of an unfortunate incident.

My attempt to bridge the divided aspects of her self caused a temporary heightening of the neurosis. On May 18th, 4:00 in the morning, after a particularly long evening session, Miss Kitigawa attempted to escape Mount Sinai Hospital. A nurse on duty spotted her as she made her way into the elevator. At first we were sure she had left the building, and, as you know, we spent several hours searching the neighbouring environment. In the end we found the subject in the basement of the hospital asleep beside the furnace. It appears from her own accounts (she remembers nothing of the incident) that she may in fact have performed these actions unconsciously; i.e., the subject may well have been "walking in her sleep."

25.

THERE IS SPEECH, and there is silence.

There is day, and there is night.

A long time ago there was the bomb blast, and then there were shadows lifting themselves from the wreckage, surging upwards. She can see what flickers between the burnt buildings, inside the flames. They are the souls of the dead, Mother and Grandfather and Mr. Takahura's daughter—but she can also see the flight of the household gods from their shelves in the burnt houses, the fleeing of the twin foxes from the Inari shrine beside the Ota River, the rising of the mountain *kami* from the pine groves on Miyajima. She wants to tell these spirits that she's sorry for everything. Sorry to have stolen Yoshiko's lipstick. Sorry because she had kept going, past the ones who begged for water. To the burnt woman on the bridge she had murmured, *I must find my mother.*

"I am sorry," she says. "Forgive me."

But it is too late. Everything that dwells in shadow has risen up, dislodged by the twelve-kiloton blast of uranium and plutonium. For a moment the flock of spirits hovers above the city.

Then they float free.

26.

MISS DAY IS THERE. Dr. Carney is there. One evening, for a long time, the red-haired man is in the room. He stands by the window, not feeling that he should sit, not until he is asked.

"You gave me a watch."

He cannot say a word. But this must be what he has waited for, because he sits down in the orange chair. She closes her eyes and then opens them again because she feels waves of heat coming from his body. He bends his head and she puts out her hand and touches his red hair. It is surprisingly full and springy against her fingertips.

This is the story Dr. Carney wants her to tell.

Harder to forget than to remember, in the end.

Here it is, she thinks. Here it is.

All night she lies in bed and tells herself the story. It is long and elaborate and involves her grandfather's foxes, and travelling north. *I left Hiroshima on April 1,* she says in the low, authoritative voice of her Ojii-chan. *All the plum trees were in blossom, but as I went north they were only in bud, and then eventually they were closed. When I reached the middle of Hokkaido—following the very road Basho took—the plum trees were covered in snow. At the edge of the orchard was a small village. Darkness had settled on this land.*

This is an interesting story, and she would like to tell it all the way through, but people keep interrupting her. Yoshiko is there, rebuking her as she tries to sleep. *Because of you, your mother went downtown. She said she had to give Ojii-chan his lunch box. But you could have delivered that lunch box yourself. And where is my lipstick?*

Kitsune-chan, her mother whispers. Fox child, little fox child.

In the night, her grandfather takes her on his knee. *There are so many stories,* he says. *Why do you keep coming back to this one?*

They want to know about the blast.

Let them tell it to themselves then.

This is so true she wants to cry. *Just tell me one story,* she begs him. *About going north, the plum trees—then the fox in the graveyard.*

You always ask for the same one. Yet I know a thousand. In Hiroshima, there are a thousand stories.

This is true—there are a thousand, or more. Stories people have told him, because he is the expert. They tell him strange stories about the foxes that live under the bridge, about badgers in the graveyard. Always these animals change faces, from animal to human. And then, just when they seem human, they turn into ghosts.

Tell me about the fox under the bridge.

And have your mother know I have frightened you? Don't think I am so foolish. I am in enough trouble with the womenfolk.

But you always tell me a story before I sleep.

Then it cannot be a frightening one.

She settles on his knee and he speaks. It is nice to be there: she can hear his voice both coming from his mouth and the rumbling of it in his chest. He will tell her the story of how all the animals got started. All the animals and the hills of Hiroshima. Long ago.

You know, he says, people say there was a time when there weren't any mountains here, or any rivers. The Ota River, huge as it seems to us, was just a drop of water on the ground, and not one of its seven branches existed.

But then the goddess Amaterasu came. She created the land and the rivers and filled the sky with sun. But no sooner was she done than a host of spirits swarmed up from the river and down from the mountains, claiming their right to control what she had made.

This is a story Keiko knows.

A huge battle ensued, but neither side could win. And at last they all sat down in the mud flats, out of breath. There is no way to win this, they said, and so it seemed, but at last a spirit suggested that whoever could first glimpse the sun on the following morning would reign supreme. A contest, the others cried. Yes, that was a fair way to decide how things should go.

All the spirits went to the water to wait for the sun, and every single one of them faced east, as it was only natural to do. All but the fox. He was the only one who turned his back towards the Inland Sea. The others taunted him, but he hummed a song.

"Did he ignore them?"

"He ignored them."

And just before dawn the fox, speaking softly and politely, said, "There it is, my friends. The sun."

The others turned, ready to taunt him further, but there it was: the first rays of the sun were reflected from a high peak of snow.

"And that is why," her grandfather said, "the fox guards the delta of Hiroshima."

"He was the smartest animal."

"He was the smartest."

Now that is a true story, Keiko thinks, coming out of sleep, trying to remember where she has seen the orange chair, the small rectangle of window, the thousand lights beyond.

27.

"HOW LONG HAVE I BEEN SLEEPING?"

"The operation was ten days ago. You are healing wonderfully. And you haven't been sleeping all this time. Don't you remember?"

"Where are the others?"

"Your scar is gone, Keiko." And then, after a while: "Can you speak?"

"A little."

"Do you want to sit up?"

"Yes, please."

"August 6. You were speaking of August 6 in our last session. The minutes before the bomb fell. You checked the hibachi."

"I was worried I would set the house on fire."

"Yes. You said that."

"Can I tell about the oyster boat?"

Behind her grandfather's garden, she can hear the sound of the oyster sellers rowing upstream in the morning.

She waits for Dr. Carney to write this down. She hears his pen moving, and she continues. She has decided to tell about the crickets—the *semi*. There are three kinds of *semi* that she hunts for in Ojii-chan's garden, including the fat ones with wrinkled wings, the *suzumushi,* that come out at dusk and ring like bells when you cup them in your hands.

The doctor wants her to focus on August 6, 1945. Eight-fifteen in the morning.

"Tell me about Hiroshima," he says. As though Hiroshima meant the bomb, the wind-lashed landscape full of the others crying out for water. She wants to tell him that Mr. Takahura next door grooms his pink and orange azalea bushes with scissors. He is fonder of his bushes than of his daughter. This is what Keiko hears Yoshi saying, and for once she thinks Yoshi has said something smart.

The year is 1945, the doctor reminds her.

It is the morning of August 6.

She can hear the plashing of the oyster sellers' oars. The veranda of her grandfather's house sits on stilts over blue pebbles that she imagines are the Ota River. The river itself is only a hundred yards away, beyond the mossy wall topped with broken tile. Here is where they live: Keiko's grandfather, her Uncle Taro and Aunt Yoshiko and Mama. Keiko's father ought to be with them as well, but he was drafted into the Imperial Army and died in Manchukuo.

At night Keiko and her mother walk over the bridge to the bathhouse. They watch the pleasure boats cruising up and down, breaking the tiered reflection of the castle into long shards, fins and eyes. By day the peddlers row upriver, selling wares from their bows.

Lying on the veranda in the afternoon, Keiko hears cars and hand-drawn carts thumping over the wooden bridge, a steady thud of tires, like a relative's voice, so familiar.

Her grandfather shows her the worn stone steps leading to the grotto of the Inari shrine where the foxes live. This is interesting. Leaning over the bridge, staring down at the dried mud and thick grasses, she asks him questions, all of which he takes seriously.

Why is four bad luck?

How many foxes live under the bridge, and what will they do if they catch us?

"He knew all about such things."

"What things?"

"Ghosts. *Kami*."

"Tell me about August 6."

Her mother is sewing a button onto her blouse. The heft of the thread—too thick for the cotton. The pearly button, two holes drilled in the centre.

"I don't mean the button."

He wants her to speak of later.

"Later I worried I had left the hibachi burning."

He writes this down.

One day her grandfather took Keiko by train north into the mountains of Chūgoku, collecting old stories. This was his interest, his vocation. The stories were disappearing, he said, like the old shrines, which were being knocked down every day to make way for the official Shinto shrines to the one sun deity, Amaterasu, an ancestor of the emperor.

Keiko clutched her grandfather's tattered briefcase while he slept, his head bumping against the window. Outside, graveyards flashed by on raked hillsides, green and yellow bamboo, a forest of water.

Hiroshima is a place of many stories.

During his lifetime, Ojii-chan collected 146 stories from around Hiroshima Prefecture. His proudest possession was a letter from Yanagita Kunio, to whom he sent these stories. In it, the famous folklorist thanked him kindly for his pains.

"Tell me about Hiroshima."

But she is. She is. It is a map she carries in her body, where north holds the hills and, beneath them, the wide suburban avenues, the streetcar rails dusted with snow. South is full of winding cobbled streets, smelling of fish. East beyond the castle is a flat plain that reminds her of her father. Here soldiers practice their drills and formations, carrying black bayonets. Once, a soldier gave Keiko a purple flower, a river flower, very common. He leant down and called her a pretty girl, and she felt ashamed.

"Why do you care so much about that old fox shrine?" Yoshiko said.

"I like to pray for the souls of the dead," she told her aunt, to see if she would be frightened.

"Better pray for yourself," Yoshiko answered tartly. "You're the one who stole my lipstick. Everyone knows."

"Speak about what you remember."

"I remember so much."

"Tell me about the bombing."

All right, she thinks. All right. She looks towards the window and sees Mama pinching her lips. She knows Keiko is about to do something bad, and she holds her breath, waiting.

❊

August is easy to remember.

As summer thickened around them, they sat on the veranda, the shape of the castle in the distance. Crickets buzzed like electricity in the garden wall. One night the rains poured down. But it is early morning now. August 6.

"Come inside," Keiko's mother says.

"I am happy here."

"I need your help."

"Why?"

"You ask too many questions, Keiko-chan. Come now."

Keiko goes sullenly.

She wears only her white undershirt and underpants. She has not dressed yet because she plans to tell her mother that she is sick, so that she will not have to go to school and yet again do the gruelling jobs schoolgirls have been allocated: the teachers give each of them a government-issued burlap bag, and send them to the town centre, where they have to fill the bags, again and again, with rubble from torn-down houses. They carry them to the middle of the roads and dump them, creating new mounds of rubble. These will act as windbreaks and firebreaks if the town is firebombed. Osaka has been firebombed. Tokyo has been firebombed.

"I am sick," Keiko says to her mother.

She stands in her underwear, her skin goosebumped. Her mother puts down her needle and looks at Keiko closely.

"I need your help," she says again. A needle with an eye too fine for her to thread. She is sewing the button onto her cotton blouse.

Keiko takes the thread and licks it, then tries to put it through the needle. She could do it easily, but if she is too quick, her eyesight as keen as ever, her mother will know she isn't sick.

But she cannot help herself; she must please her mother. And so she licks the thread, and finds the tiny hole and threads it through.

Already on the Ota River, there are beggars along the shore digging for edible weeds. It is early, yet so hot a rash is appearing behind Keiko's knees and beneath her mother's watch strap.

"I am sorry you are sick," Keiko's mother says, for it is her belief that if she pretends to believe her daughter, her daughter will grow more truthful with time. Keiko knows that sometimes her mother visits the Inari shrine and asks this exact thing, shaking the wooden box that holds the *omikuji,* hoping for a shred of paper that will answer her prayers, then attaching it with the others to the pine tree, so that it rattles in the wind. You can hear these wishes of mothers as you cross the bridge.

"If you are well enough, I want to ask you to do something, Keiko. I want you to deliver your grandfather's lunch to him when you go downtown with the other girls. He forgot it."

"My stomach feels bloated. I'm dizzy, Mama. I think I may fall down."

Mama sighs. "Then fetch me the lunch box from the kitchen and leave it on the foyer steps, so I don't forget it. I will take it to him myself. We cannot have your grandfather go hungry all day."

Keiko walks slowly down the hall. She is remembering the conversation she heard the day before: her grandfather talking to Yoshiko in the garden. Yoshiko said she could not bear the heat. She said it in a whining way; it was so like her to whine of heat when people were dying in the war, and Keiko knew that her grandfather thought so too, that Yoshiko's whining would make him think of his son, Keiko's father, dead in Manchukuo. Keiko strained her ears to hear Ojii-chan's reply.

"It is not so hot. Already one can feel the edge of winter, as the poem says." Keiko did not know which poem and she was sure Aunt Yoshiko didn't know either.

"Poems can indeed be fanciful," Yoshiko exclaimed. "But in truth the air is so hot, it feels as though it could catch fire."

"Yes, but underneath I smell the snow." Keiko imagines him raising his nose and sniffing.

More than once Keiko has heard Yoshiko telling Taro that Ojii-chan makes up stories and then ends up believing them himself. Keiko hates her for this, and so this morning walking along the quiet hallway in her underwear, Keiko sniffs for the snow. Later, when Grandfather returns from the town, she will tell him that she, too, has a good nose for winter. He will like that, especially as she is the one who gets heat rashes, not Yoshiko.

Last night her mother rubbed a pink ointment on Keiko's skin. It was cool, like milk. She had Keiko stand in the doorway to the garden, where the breeze was strongest, then she dabbed the lotion all over her skin with a kerchief. Keiko was not allowed to wriggle or drops would stain the tatami mat.

But now her mother is expecting Keiko to put the lunch box by the door, and then Mama will go downtown with it and find Ojii-chan and give him his forgotten meal. Keiko would have liked to be the one that handed it to him. Still, the lie was worth it. Keiko hates clearing rubble with the other schoolchildren. Perhaps she will tell her mother she is sick tomorrow too.

This is why her mother calls her Kitsune-chan, little fox child: it is the slyness in her. Also because she cried so much as a baby, nothing could soothe her. Keiko's mother said her real child must have been stolen away and replaced by a fox baby, and that was why Keiko had colic and couldn't sleep. Once Keiko asked her if this was really true, and Mama held her for a long time, and said of course not; but this morning, when Keiko lied about feeling dizzy, she saw the corners of her mother's lips bend in disapproval, as though her daughter were that fox child after all.

Now they have started—the crickets beside the stone wall that separates her grandfather's large garden from Takahura-san's. They are loud in the morning, singing *kana-kana-kana* just before the sun hits the wall. As soon as it slashes across the stone, they are silenced. But this is their hour now. Keiko slides open the hall screen, listening. She can hear tree frogs too, and her mother moving in their sleeping room, sliding open the cupboard where she stores their mattress.

If Grandfather were at home right now, he would have a story about why the crickets stop singing when sun hits the stones. He explains things, and not the way Taro explains things, painstakingly, until they are all dried out, and not the way Yoshiko explains, as though Keiko is in her way. Ojii-chan answers all her questions as though they are the most important questions anyone could think of: the real questions that sit in the shadows in the hall, and under the garden wall.

Perhaps she will be punished for her lie after all: her skin has started to really itch, and her head is filling with the sound of the crickets, rubbing their legs together. Her skin may itch all day long, and by the end of the day it will be as though Keiko is walking outside herself, looking at the girl with the patches of roughened skin. Then her mother will know she was really sick, and she will be sorry for doubting her. That will show them.

Keiko pads in her underwear and undershirt down the three steps to the kitchen. "Do make sure the hibachi is out," Yoshiko said this morning. "Yesterday you left for school and did not check, and the house could have burnt down. Luckily, your mother returned early and noticed. She does not need these extra worries." Yes, it is out. She picks up the black lacquered bento box sitting on the table in front of the hibachi. Returning to the hallway, which is suffused in soft light, she sees the low cupboard where the medicines are kept. She reaches in and brings out the bottle of pink lotion and pours it into her palm, rubbing it behind her knees. Then she reaches deep into the cupboard. Far at the back she finds a small wooden box: Burns Goldenloaf Cheese, the box says, in

English. There is a picture of a Dutch girl on the side of
which is neatly made, with dovetailed joints at the corne
where Keiko keeps the things she takes from Yoshiko, sma
that her aunt will want later. Not being able to find these things
is bound to bother Yoshiko immensely, and perhaps even make
her lose her mind. So far Keiko has her comb, and the blue cotton
sash of her *yukata,* and her cherry-red lipstick. Yoshiko asked Keiko
pointedly about the lipstick, but Keiko looked shocked: "Yoshiko-
san," she said. "You know I am not allowed to wear lipstick."

"You might have taken it anyway."

"Grandfather says that if many things go missing, evil spirits
are taking them."

Keiko was pleased to see that Yoshiko looked alarmed. "You
tell too many silly stories, Keiko," she said.

Now Keiko slides the Goldenloaf Cheese box to the back
corner of the cupboard, pulls the medicine bag into its place,
then slides the door closed. A final time she peeks into the
kitchen and checks the hibachi. Everyone is afraid of fire. The
enemies drop gasoline bombs because they know that Japanese
cities are made of wood. "We live in a matchbox," Yoshiko said
about Grandfather's house. "We are waiting to die."

Keiko hates her.

In fact, she has put a curse on Yoshiko. It wasn't hard—you do
it by making a bad wish while rubbing something that belongs to
the hated person. Keiko used Yoshiko's lipstick. She didn't wish
for her to die; she was afraid to do that. Instead, she wished for
her to break out in the rash that plagued Keiko, and also, while
she was at it, she wished for Yoshiko to become ugly.

Dr. Carney wrote down the words *Yoshiko's face,* then glanced up
at Keiko, lying in the bed.

"Does this issue feel important to you?"

"I don't know."

"Later her face wasn't burnt. But yours was."

That was true.

"As well, if you had told the truth, and gone downtown to clear rubble, and deliver your grandfather's lunch box, you would have died that day. You see that, don't you? Your dishonesty saved you."

She muttered something and Dr. Carney asked her to speak up. Her face was to the window. To encourage her to focus on the story, he rose and pulled down the blinds.

When she spoke, this is what she said:

Yako. Genko. Shakko.

"What is that?"

"Kinds of foxes. My grandfather knew them all."

"Ah."

"And then there are the *reiko*."

"What are those?"

"Ghost foxes."

"And what else?"

"Bakemono."

"Explain."

"He said they were real. Foxes that could turn into women. It happened all the time."

"Real?"

"Real."

This was funny for some reason, and they both laughed. "Have you met any foxes?" Dr. Carney asked.

A pause. She turned her face to the closed blinds.

"What are you thinking now?"

"I'm resting."

Keiko sits down in the foyer on the wooden step, cool against her bare legs, the bento box on her lap. She is still thinking about what

Yoshiko said: they do live in a matchbox. The floor is made of stone in the foyer, but the floors in the rest of the house are wood, covered in tatami matting. The walls are wood, covered in screens of fine paper, and the heavy doors leading into the front garden are made of the cypress from the Aomori Prefecture. They are Ojii-chan's pride and joy, with their striping in the grain that looks like women's hair. Sometimes he stands by the doors, absentmind-edly fingering the grain, taking pride in them with his fingertips. You might think that since his son's death he would stop caring about the grain of his doors, or about the depth of the moss in the garden, which is yellow now from lack of water, but which before the war was far deeper than Mr. Takahura's, but Grandfather cares more now, or talks about these things more, as though his son's death has made him want to fill his mind with the things he owns. It would be easy to hate him because of this. If it were Yoshiko being this way, Keiko would hate her. But instead, Keiko wishes that she could turn her grandfather's moss green, fill it until it sponged out, full of beads of water. But that would take a miracle; in Hiroshima right now, there is not enough fresh water for the people, let alone animals or plants.

Why did he forget his lunch box? She shakes it. He must have been sitting where Keiko is now sitting, lost in thought, putting on his shoes, not noticing that he didn't have the lunch box beside him. Thinking about his son, perhaps, lost in grief. After his shoes were on he must have stood, and opened the doors, taking pleasure in the solidity of the wood, then closed the doors behind him. Keiko opens the box and looks inside. Three rice balls, some pickled cabbage and radish, and a small piece of last night's eel. It is a bad lunch, but better by far than anything Keiko's mother or Yoshiko pack for themselves, or for her. War rations. Once, Keiko complained to her mother and she went to the cupboard and slid it open. "Make meat appear," she said, "and I'll pack your lunch full of it." Keiko was ashamed to have complained. But even now she is hungry.

Briefly Keiko imagines taking her grandfather's lunch to him. She could tell her mother she was well enough after all and get dressed quickly, then run to the bus stop beside the bridge, take the next bus downtown. She imagines him looking up, hot and hungry, a shovel in his hand, as she clambers over the firebreak, the lacquered box shining in her hand. He smiles—not the open-mouthed smile he used to use with her father, but a smile with closed lips, as though he were smiling and sad at the same time. He thanks her formally, because other men are nearby, some of whom may not have granddaughters who are so devoted. He does not wish to shame them. But some of the other men whisper that she is Kitigawa-san's granddaughter. *Look, she is only ten, but she has come all the way downtown on the bus, alone, to deliver his lunch.*

The brass clock in the alcove strikes the hour. Eight is when the schoolgirls are supposed to gather in the playing field. After that they are given their shovels and burlap bags. Some of them, to impress the teachers, talk loudly about what they would do to defend their homes against attackers, how they would use their father's swords, or sharpened bamboo poles, thrusting them through the hearts of the enemy. In Okinawa, the American soldiers picked up babies and threw them from the cliffs, this is what a girl told her. To be safe, Keiko came home from school and cut down a piece of bamboo, using her father's knife, then sharpened herself a bamboo spear. Grandfather found her in the garden, and he was not happy, not because they might be attacked by Americans, but because she had cut down his twenty-year-old bamboo. He looked as though she had done it to hurt him, but not wanting her to see how upset he was, he went inside and closed the screen. Keiko could only stand there, holding her father's pearl-covered knife in her hand.

Her mother moves in the next room; she is folding up Grandfather's mattress and opening the screens to air the room. She comes into the front hallway, dressed in her government-issued khaki blouse and trousers. This is not what her mother likes to wear. She has always been a fashionable woman. When they lived in Tokyo, when Father was alive, she wore western hats and pretty gloves. In Ojii-chan's house, her summer *yukata* is always ironed and she bathes every day at the bathhouse, taking Keiko with her. A pleasant outing, over the bridge, down several close streets to a door hung over with noren, the indigo curtains with white characters for "bathing house." They come home in the dark, over the bridge, seeing lights on the water, stars above, papery whispers from the shrine.

Her mother opens the front doors to create a cross breeze, then sits down on the foyer step beside her daughter. She takes her government-issued canvas shoes from the low cupboard and pulls them on.

"I hope you will feel better by the afternoon."

"Thank you, Mama."

"Please give me Grandfather's lunch box now."

Keiko does.

Her mother goes quickly out the front doors, leaving them open, not looking back. Keiko feels it in her heart: that sticky-sweet badness that will be her undoing. To take her mind off what she has done, she looks at the view of the hills, which she can see above the wall from this side of the house. The sun has risen a notch farther into the sky. It picks out the needles of the pines on the hillside, then slides into the cleavage between the hills. How long does she sit there? Ten minutes at most. The rash behind her knees has started to feel better. Then she unfolds her hand and looks down at the rice ball she has stolen from her grandfather's box. She pops it in her mouth. It is sticky and warm.

IV   GHOST

28.

DAISY AND WALTER WAITED for the news of Keiko's operation, and as they waited spring shook itself all over and became summer. The corn near Strickland's Grocery had grown to ankle height, and then all at once it was as tall as Daisy's waist. It became too warm for jackets or even sweaters. A breeze blew along Linden Street and Daisy opened the front and back doors to let it circulate through the house. She could hear children playing in the evenings: Kick the Can, Blind Man's Buff, Red Rover. Sitting on the front steps smoking, she heard their voices calling from the fields.

Red Rover, Red Rover, we call Joey over.

As though to herald the arrival of summer, the government detonated three new atomic weapons. They had the explosive power of seventeen, twenty-three and twenty-five Hiroshima bombs. Walking down Linden Street one evening, Daisy saw, through the Palmers' front window, the bomb exploding on television. She caught a glimpse of the black weight falling through the air, followed by the heated flash, then the mushroom cloud billowing upwards, sucking at the wind. She stood transfixed, thinking of the girl in the hospital, remembering her stiff body leaning towards Daisy, not quite submitting to an embrace; the small hand in Daisy's pocket, grazing last year's chestnut.

I don't remember what happened, Mrs. Lawrence.

Already Daisy had replayed the scene a dozen times, recalling how they had leaned over the bridge, looking down at the muddy stalks of grass, the girl's head strangely illuminated by the plastic rain cap.

There was a bright light, and then I don't remember.

But you must.

I'm sorry, Mrs. Lawrence. I am ashamed. I didn't tell the truth.

They waited for Irene to call, as she had promised she would the minute she knew how the operation had gone. There was no point going to the hospital: the nurses had strict orders that nobody was allowed to see Keiko. After all of Irene's wooing of the press, there was a surprising amount of secrecy about the operation. It was as though Dr. Carney, in the final moment, didn't quite trust himself to do the job perfectly and didn't want the glare of publicity.

Daisy heard nothing for twenty-four hours, then thirty-six, then forty-eight. It wasn't hard to picture the operation; this was what she discovered. It came to her at odd moments, as she crossed the field to Strickland's, or polished Walter's oxblood shoes, or washed the rim of the toilet—there it was again, the gas mask slipped onto the girl's face, then the counting backwards into darkness. Then they would go at her. Against her will Daisy saw this part—how they cut into the tender skin around the tough edge of the scar, severing the bubbled tissue from the underlying fat and muscle, clipping the delicate web of capillaries. She saw a flash of instruments, and Keiko prone, unconscious. It was a blessing she was out cold, because it was clear to

Daisy that having the effects of the bomb shaved from one's skin required bravery. She was glad there would be American painkillers. She tried not to picture every detail, but once her brain got going, it couldn't stop: she saw the scalpel, felt the massy weight of the scar on her own cheek. She saw it as a shadow image as she washed the dishes or made the bed. Again and again it peeled away, like a pancake from a hot griddle, as Dr. Carney slid a spatula beneath it, though sometimes it wouldn't come loose—it stuck to Keiko's tissues and muscle with a thousand connecting filaments, burrowing into her jawbone, sinus cavities, the gristle of her nose.

And what would they do with the scar tissue once they'd excised it? Would they scurry away with it, so that they could cut it open, study it—only to throw it in a pail when they were done and incinerate it? That was what they must have done the first time Daisy miscarried. As soon as it came from her body, the doctor had signalled for the nurse to take it away, and Daisy had sat up in the hospital bed saying, *Please don't. Please*. But the nurse had moved so swiftly, almost at a run, out the door, down the hall. It must have been part of her training—this prompt removal of the thing, against the protests of a mother. They did this because it was for the best, the doctor told her later, nothing cruel about it, indeed it was a kindness—and afterwards she told herself that this must be true, because who could bear to see the deformed thing the size of a grapefruit, translucent lids over bulging, milky eyes?

But she would have liked to have seen it.

Even the malformed spine, the soft, dwarfed head—everything wrong with it—she could have borne it. The nurses had been wrong. They had been wrong, and her doctor too, he had been wrong, telling her that it had been done for the best. If they had just let her hold her baby for five minutes, or one minute would have known what to do. She would have picked gingerly, taking care with the broken delicate body, and ld have cradled the baby against her chest. Daisy would have rucked her, spoken to her with silent thoughts, and when it was really time, she would have covered her baby's mottled face with a handkerchief and held her out for the waiting nurses.

Here, she might have said. *I am done now.*

We are done.

29.

THE PHONE RANG ACROSS THE GRASS as Daisy hung the laundry. She ran for it—knowing it must be news. It was Irene, calling to let her know that the operation had been a success.

"The girl is fine," Irene said. "The scar is gone."

The scar is gone. What strange words those were.

"What does she look like?" Daisy whispered.

"Ah well," Irene told her, "her face is utterly bandaged—has to be for ninety days. But after that, we'll unwind the bandages and show her face to the world. Raymond thinks she'll be completely scar-free."

"How is she?"

"She's fine. Naturally somewhat shaken. And tired. But fine."

Irene elaborated on the operation. It had been more complicated than expected because of the unusual nature of the tissue. A difficult thing, requiring all of Dr. Carney's skills, to excise the scar, then stretch and utilize adjacent skin, while sewing in a patch of grafted skin as well. Not to mention the stanching of the blood, the reconnecting of a hundred tiny capillaries.

"Can I see her?"

"Nobody can see her."

"But why not?"

"Doctor's orders."

A pause.

"Irene," Daisy said slowly. "She told me she doesn't remember. About Hiroshima, I mean. The bombing."

Irene laughed. "Is that what she told you? She's a tricky one, isn't she? I'll mention that to Raymond. He'll be interested."

"No don't. Please."

"Why ever not?"

"I just don't think you should."

At this Irene sounded irritated. "Raymond has to know," she said flatly. "But don't worry, Daisy. Whatever he does with what you've told us will be for the best."

Irene hung up, promising to telephone in a week, when the girl was receiving visitors.

In the kitchen Daisy set the kettle on the stove for tea, then she went out front to fetch the milk bottles. She had just bent to gather them when she glanced up, alerted by a black slash of movement in the corner of her eye. A furtive glee attached itself to that movement—something malignant, something from a fairy tale. Fran Warburgh, Evelyn Lithgow and Joan Palmer were descending on her down Linden Street, looking determined and excited. Evelyn and Joan had dressed carefully, in going-to-town skirts and nylon stockings, while Fran wore a blouse with pink rosebuds on it and a pair of toreador pants.

They came up the brick walk and stopped in an informal tableau at the base of the steps: three furies resting before bloodshed. Daisy pulled the housecoat around her as best she could, holding two milk bottles.

"What can I do for you ladies?" she asked.

"It has come to the attention of the Residents' Committee that—until three days ago—you've been acting host to an unusual house guest." It was Joan who spoke. Joan with the thumbprint-shaped birthmark on her cheek, hairy and soft. Oh, Daisy could see she was enjoying herself, they all were. Evelyn Lithgow's eyes were beady with adventure—the perfect follower. If someone had told her to round up suspects and stand over them with a rifle, she probably would have done it, delighting not just in taking orders but in the misfortune of her captives. Her expression made Daisy angry.

"You ought to have informed the Residents' Committee right away," Joan said.

"If you knew someone was here, which you obviously did, you could have informed the Residents' Committee yourselves."

"Well, we did, as a matter of fact. Though it wasn't our job to do so."

"It wasn't mine either. Besides, as you know, I've had a house guest staying, I've been busy."

"So have we!" Evelyn blurted out. "I have three children to look after."

Joan laid a calming hand on her arm. "As I said, we did inform the Residents' Committee, and a meeting was held. Now we're here to represent their interests."

Oh God, Daisy thought. Here it comes.

"It is our understanding that Miss Kitigawa is at the hospital." Joan opened her purse and took out a clipping, which she handed to Daisy: Keiko standing beside a broadly smiling Eleanor Roosevelt. Irene had squeezed herself into the photo as well, throwing a possessive arm around Keiko's shoulders. Below was a paragraph describing the meeting, and Keiko's scheduled operation. Daisy nodded warily, then handed the clipping back.

"We wish you'd informed us earlier," Joan said. "Luckily, Walter and Gordon rode to work together last week, and he took the time to describe the Project."

Several streets away a car backfired, making them all jump. Nervous laughter passed through the three women.

Joan folded the article and dropped it into her purse. "We have a message to deliver on behalf of the residents. May we come in? It's an official message—I'd rather not deliver it on your doorstep."

What could Daisy do? She beckoned for them to follow. As they trooped down the hallway, she saw Evelyn glance into the master bedroom. She loved to prattle on to Joan about the state of beds, made and unmade, in Riverside Meadows, though Joan was after something altogether darker. Evelyn was not a real connoisseur of what Joan Palmer found either titillating or damnable, Daisy thought, placing her milk bottles on the kitchen counter and turning to face them. It wasn't the unmade bed; it was the scent of neurosis, colourless as a gas; it was the air of panic secreted into the wallpaper. How did Daisy know all this about Joan? She just did. Suddenly she felt she knew Joan Palmer quite well indeed.

The women stood in the kitchen, looking about with interest. Even the yellowed crack in the linoleum seemed important. The gingham curtains moved in the breeze. Daisy saw Evelyn sniff, a professional housewife's snuffle used to check if pillowcases smelled of bleach, or whether the basement was free of mildew. This time, though, she was checking for the bat-screech of radioactivity caught in the folds of the curtains.

Then Joan began to speak, as though addressing not just Daisy, or Fran or Evelyn, but the crows on the clothesline, the greenhouse roof glinting in the morning sun.

"The Residents' Committee met last Monday."

"We all fought terribly," Fran blurted.

Joan gave Fran a look, and she hushed. Then she continued her recitation; her skin looked heavy, full of blood. "My husband, Sergeant Gordon Palmer, fought in the Philippines. He won a medal. Evelyn's husband, Eugene, served as a radio broadcaster and signalman——"

"He saw action twice."

"Ed Warburgh, as you know, was imprisoned for six months in a POW camp. Now, without discussing your plans with these men, whose knowledge of war is first-hand, you invited Miss Keiko Kitigawa to our neighbourhood. She is a Hiroshima victim. A victim of the bomb."

"I know who she is." Daisy's voice was tart.

Joan raised her hand—a gesture from the college debating club? From another lifetime anyway. "Daisy Lawrence," she said, "I am not here to condemn you. On the contrary, only to deliver a message. You might think that these brave men would not want to welcome Miss Kitigawa. You might think that the scars of war hadn't healed, that your actions would open wounds——"

Daisy sighed.

"But a Residents' Committee meeting was convened, chaired by my husband, Gordon. And it was agreed, almost unanimously, and with a great deal of feeling, that Miss Kitigawa should be welcomed to Riverside Meadows." As she said this, her face turned an even darker red. She stopped and looked down at the crack in the linoleum.

The other women watched her, silenced: none of them had seen Joan express anything genuine before. She took a deep breath, clearly to stop tears, and it was impossible not to think of the dead brother, the one Joan missed every day, limp body carried home by the school principal. A twin brother. A counterweight to the moody Joan. But as quickly as this image formed,

Joan regained her composure. "We've talked it over. We're glad you've done it," she said simply.

Daisy looked from face to face. Evelyn was staring at the cracked floor, but Fran was beaming at her. "When can we meet her?" she said. "I've never met an A-bomb victim before. Ed would kill me."

The kettle began to sing.

30.

THAT EVENING Walter and Daisy sat on the back steps listening to the Jack Benny show. Daisy had told him about Keiko as soon as he got home from work.

"She's going to be fine," she had said, sounding like Irene.

"When can we see her?"

"Not yet. She's not seeing anyone."

"Why is that?"

"Too weak, I think."

Walter had nodded, accepting this.

Now they were listening to the radio together, as he and Keiko had done every night since she'd came. In this episode, Jack and his wife, Mary Livingstone, rode a team of horses into a movie theatre, a ploy to get people to go see Jack Benny's new movie. "Now there's a notion," Walter laughed. "There's something you can only get with radio. Horses in a theatre."

Though Daisy knew this was a dig at her for wanting a television, she found herself laughing at the program, and she could tell he was pleased. And it *was* funny to picture them— all those invisible horses, white and piebald and ebony, crossing the carpeted lobby, clipping down the sticky aisles, taking seats around Jack and Mary, snorting softly through dappled noses. Eating popcorn. Watching the show. That was the fun of radio, Walter said. That was its genius.

When it was done, Daisy told Walter about the visit from the Riverside Meadows women. "A delegation," she said, "and not a murderous posse, which was what I'd always imagined." He laughed as she described their desire to organize a pool party for the girl when she got back.

"They knew every detail," Daisy said. "They could pro-nounce 'hypertrophic.' I mean, they sounded like they'd rehearsed it beforehand, but they knew the word." She was silent for a moment. A bat flew close to them; she felt its wings near her face.

We wouldn't want to tire her, Joan had said. *But everybody wants to meet her, and so some kind of party is in order, isn't it, girls?* She had said this as Daisy saw them out.

On parting, Joan had glanced back. *You've positively outdone yourself, I hope you know. You really are the talk of Riverside Meadows.* Then a rakish smile unexpectedly lit up her eyes.

Walter stood and stretched, his fingertips grazing the eaves. Now he would leave her, as he always did.

"You go for these walks. You walk for miles. But you come back empty-handed."

"I'll bring you a fish."

"Willard's Creek has nothing but guppies."

"You don't like guppy?"

"How do you think she's managing?" Again that squiggle of guilt, worming through her.

"They say she's recovering."

Daisy nodded. "She's a strange one, though, isn't she, Walter?"

"Don't know about that."

"Hard to get to know, at least at first. Don't you think?"

He shrugged. "Everyone's hard to know."

"I'm not."

He laughed. "Oh now—you're the hardest of them all."

"But *you* think you know me."

"Like the back of my hand. It's taken years of close study."

"I know you pretty well too, you know."

"So you think."

Later that night she woke to Walter typing. He had carried his machine into the kitchen so as not to disturb her. She lay in bed, listening: he was typing too fast to be working on a radio script, and the lines were too long; they seemed to go on for ages, and when he reached the end, he gave the carriage a hard slap with the back of his hand, and Daisy heard the satisfying ring. Again and again she heard the carriage ring. This wasn't the hedging and despair of his usual work, the careful accrual of damning facts. He must have found a thread, and it was pulling him into his story. As she drifted in and out of sleep she wondered what he was writing. She saw molls, like the ones who turned up in *The Whistler,* wearing tight-fitting satin dresses, the green of insect wings; she saw gangs of stevedores on the wooden docks of Puget Sound, unloading their holds of brown sugar, reams of orange silk; she saw David Greenberg standing in an immense Ukrainian field—the doomed and hungry faces of children raised to him, asking for food.

She woke right up and stared at the ceiling. The clatter of the keys had shaken loose a memory. It was of the first time they had slept together, at Walter's apartment on the West Side—how he had pounded at her with a dry need, a reckless concentration that seemed to have nothing to do with her. How exhilarating to feel him on top of her, fierce but disconnected. Afterwards he had kissed the top of her head. The whole experience could have made her feel ashamed, but it hadn't. She had been taken—that was how it felt—and it had left her smudged and chafed and far more worldly wise than she had been two hours before, crossing Columbus Circle in the wind, still a virgin.

She had gone to the apartment window and looked through the grating at the garbage cans and wild sumac and dilapidated fencing that filled the connected backyards. Something fierce moved beneath the surface of her skin, telling her that she had to hold on to this man, make him want her. She wanted to possess him. Funny to look back, to remember how she had felt impelled, like a salmon swimming up a stream. She had stood at the window and plotted Walter's capture; not overtly, but still.

After she was done looking out the window, she had come back to bed and lain on her side, looking at Walter's naked stomach, the shelf of his ribs. The vulnerability of the skin below his ribs had struck her as revealing, almost terrible. The wrinkled skin around his eyes, the stringy folds of his neck, the cracks in his heels, the shiny purple scar under his arm where a bullet had grazed him in the forest, near a place in the Netherlands called Hoogerhide—these broken, scarred and aged patches Daisy felt she could understand. But the skin below his ribs filled her with yearning and sadness. There was something childlike in that part of him, something unformed, and it seemed to indicate, in a way that she couldn't altogether fathom, that with a different twist in the road here or there he might have turned into another sort of man altogether.

Why was this coming back to her? It just was, in waves, as Walter pounded fiercely in the kitchen under the fluorescent lights. He typed, no doubt, the way he had typed *Fall from Grace,* which he maintained he had written in just fourteen days, writing as though words were something he had to expel, something physical in his stomach, his fingers.

What was this story burning a hole in him?

The Dark Night of David Greenberg.

And how did that story go? Could Daisy even say? She always assumed that she knew, but really she hadn't bothered to think about it for years. Besides, he kept it so private, next to his heart, in threads of handwriting she couldn't decipher, reams of typed pages—a rat's nest, with a rat's nest's grey stink: that was how she thought of it sometimes. Often Daisy had found herself wondering if Walter was, in fact, equipped to write a magnum opus, a treasonous thought for a writer's wife. Still, the thought had appeared so often in her mind, arriving each time all on its own, that it had become, by increments, a conviction, a certainty, perhaps the truest thing she knew about Walter.

Bit by bit he had added so many soft layers, so much stuff to the central story that it had become unbearable—to himself and to everyone. But now something seemed to have shifted. Perhaps he had found the thin line of truth, cold as a wire, running through it all. Lying in bed, remembering Walter moving on top of her, his face buried in the pillow, Daisy began to tell herself Walter's story, as he had told it to her once, at the beginning of their relationship. She remembered how intense Walter had been, sitting on a park bench beside her, chewing gum, staring at the East River.

Imagine a man lit up by conviction.

Imagine a man with a rake's smile and a way with women. That was David Greenberg—youngest prodigal son of a Bronx rabbi.

Walter heard him speak for the first time at a John Reed Society meeting, where David had been sent to explain the new United Front Against Fascism. In that meeting room, where people droned on using wooden, arcane meaningless words—*functionary, bureaucratic, left-wing deviationalism*—David lit up the place with a sense of power and chanciness. When he talked about injustice, you could practically hear the storm of Cossack hooves through his father's village. It seemed to Walter that something might even be wrong with a fellow who could talk so well. Something suspect. Something that might get him into trouble.

Brotherhood. He talked a lot about brotherhood.

Watch out, Daisy thought, lying in bed, remembering the sexy photograph of David Greenberg—brown hair swept off his forehead, a hand raised to block the sun, a stocky body, rather thick, chapped-looking lips. Watch out for a man who can talk about brotherhood like that: pretty soon he will light you on fire.

After meetings, women who were very used to scowling would go home with David, strip off their shapeless skirts and lisle stockings, and stand naked, while he traced their skin with his index fingers. Lots of them were Communist Party girls. Walter, who had a prudish streak in him, chided David, but he merely quoted from his rabbi father. More life, he said, that was the one edict given to the Jews, and David planned to follow that edict.

More life. David's father never dreamt his words would be used in this way by his atheist son—the son who had shamed him by striding hatless past his synagogue on Yom Kippur, whistling songs from vaudeville. *More life.* That was the promise passed from God to Abraham, the awful gift given to His people. You will suffer, but you will always know what it is to be alive.

After the meetings they went out for beer and talked for hours. Walter quoted Shakespeare, and David quoted the Torah and the

Zohar, and they both quoted Lenin. They both had liked Trotsky, and been surprised by his betrayals. They both had ideas about how to create a new society.

One afternoon Walter made the mistake of showing David some of his writing. David criticized it so severely they almost got into a fist fight. "You've been creating a golem," David said. "You haven't written a single thing that's alive. You have to find what's meaningful to you, puncture a vein in your arm and then write with your own blood." Walter stormed off, but that night he wrote the first scene of *Fall from Grace*. He thought it was a short story.

Now imagine this man, David, getting drunk—six months later—with his taller, less talkative friend at the White Horse tavern. David reaches into his corduroy jacket, brings out a ticket for the SS *Batory*. He grins.

"No more shitting our time away on the sidelines," he says. "No more Whistling Dixie. I know the Soviet Union won't be the worker's paradise, but it's the closest thing we have, and I want to be part of building it."

Come with me, David says.

Now they are really drunk, standing under a street lamp, the base moulded with black swirls, hard and sharp. David says he might end up meeting the genius Meyerhold, or driving a tractor on a collective farm, it doesn't matter.

Come with me, he says again, but Walter distrusts David's vision of the Soviet Union, which all night he has been likening, in his erratic way, to a fiery chariot—surely from one of his father's rabbinical visions. No, he will not go. He refuses the call. Maybe he tells David that he will come later; Daisy doesn't know this part. She does know that Walter feels furious that David takes such chances, seizes life so crazily, madly in love with it. If David punctured his arm, what would pour out? Chariots and rings of heaven, an ancient struggle with a beetling old man, Rabbi Greenberg. Utopia. But what would bleed out of Walter? So far, not much.

They walk eighteen blocks to the apartment of Trixie Baxter— a girl with coarse brown hair, stubbly legs, the smell of cumin to her underarms. The skin of her cheeks is ruddy, strangely thick, though her face itself is thin. Still, she's a sexy girl, Trixie Baxter, despite, or maybe because of, all those conflicting earthy qualities. Besides, how can you fault a girl with two *x*'s in her name? They throw rocks at her window, they howl, they jump at the fire-escape ladder, until at last she comes to the window, winding the belt of her satin night gown around her waist.

Come to Moscow, David calls up. *Trixie. I love you. Come to Moscow with me.*

It seems impossible, yet it is true. The next morning, in the pre-dawn light, Trixie and David stand awkwardly together on the deck of the *Stefan Batory,* arms not quite touching, David still drunk but beginning to feel his hangover, Trixie unable to conceal the bare, humiliating sheen of love on her face. They call down fond curses at Walter, which are lost in the crying of the seagulls, then off they go, up the Hudson, accompanied by the sad booming whistle of the SS *Batory,* which shakes the dock.

Off to find more life.

31.

THERE WAS A FINAL VISITOR that week. A knock on the door, and standing there, beaming, was the photographer from the wire services. He looked like an illustration from a Mabel

Lucie Attwell book Daisy had been given as a child—children feeding ducks with plump, dimpled hands, apple cheeks so rosy they seemed almost offensive.

"Hello, ma'am," he said gently, taking off his hat.

The man was about thirty, Daisy supposed, not so boyish up close, fine pale lines radiating from the corners of his brown eyes. His skin, too, had lost the gloss of youth. Still, his open manner made him seem boyish. He took a blue airmail envelope from his inside breast pocket. "You're Mrs. Lawrence, aren't you?"

"Yes, I am."

"I'm Tom Orley."

"I know who you are—you're the man who gave Keiko that watch."

"Yes," he said. "You're right about that."

Daisy took a hard look at his round face, his ridiculous, springy red hair. "What do you want?"

The man took a while to respond, clearly thinking this over. "Guess you could think of me as a well-wisher."

Daisy snorted.

But he shook his head, carried on. "You see, I've been writing to her, sending my letters to *The Sunday Review*. But I'm not so sure she's been getting them, so I thought I'd deliver this one myself—for when she gets out of the hospital."

"Why do you think she wants a letter from you?" It felt good, Daisy realized, to say something cruel to this cheerful, freckle-faced man. "You don't even know her."

"That's true, ma'am." He still smiled. "Though I did see her at the hospital, two days ago."

"You saw her?"

"I did, ma'am."

"Nobody's supposed to."

"I know that. Nurse chased me off. Still I saw her, and we sat together, maybe twenty minutes, all told."

Daisy shook her head. "That's against every regulation."

"Reckon it is." There was a pause. "Anyway," he continued, "after they chased me off, I decided I'd come to see you."

"Why?"

Again he seemed perplexed by the question. An easily perplexed man. He sighed. "To tell you the truth," he said, "I've not been too clear about why I do any of what I do lately." He smiled at her. He was used to winning women over, you could see that. Used to giving a little smile, having them melt. Daisy imagined a doting mother, perhaps a doting aunt as well. People who had listened to his every word indulgently. This irritated her.

"I'm sorry, Mr.—"

"Orley. Tom Orley."

"You've come a long way for nothing. As far as I'm concerned you have nothing to do with this project, and if I see you skulking around here I'll call the police."

He shrugged and looked at his feet. "I don't think you'd do that to me," he said.

"And why wouldn't I?"

"Because you seem like a nice person."

For Christ's sake, Daisy thought. Why did everyone assume she was nice? How had this happened? What simple benignity was stamped on her face?

"I have to go," she said. "Good day," and she closed the door in his face.

She went into the kitchen, began to clear away the dishes. Through the back window she saw the top of Ed's greenhouse roof. Beside it, hidden by the fence, was the fallout shelter, deeper by the day.

There was another knock.

"Go away," Daisy called out, but then she answered the door anyway. The man was still holding the letter, his hand raised to knock again. Two doors down, Daisy saw Joan watching, a dust shammy in her hand. Oh God, Daisy thought, I don't need this Midwestern well-wisher standing at my door, one more thing for the neighbours to gawk at. The shiny pleasantness of his face, bright and seemingly devoid of ill intention, struck her as deeply perverse. Wasn't he just like the others—the men who crept close to Keiko in the subway, on the street, wanting to be inside the magic circle of her affliction?

"Look," he said, "I'm sorry—Mrs. Lawrence. Maybe I didn't introduce myself right."

"How did you even get here?"

He scratched his forehead. "I took the train—"

"There is no train to Riverside Meadows."

"I took the train to Stoney Creek. Then I walked across the fields. I can't get the cab on Fridays. They don't let me." He was silent. Obviously this encounter was not going as he'd planned. He looked like a child who tries to do right but finds himself blamed by adults. "At least could you give her the letter? I mean, when she gets back?" Again he gave her his open smile. So hopeful. In truth he wasn't much like those other men, Daisy had to admit it. Something different was lighting him up. His mouth was a bit fleshy, lips loose, but overall he didn't seem like a bad person. His shirt smelled of Ivory Snow.

"All right," she said. "Give it to me."

He handed it over and even gave her a little bow. "You won't regret it," he said.

"I'm regretting it already," Daisy said.

He wiped his hands on his jacket. "Thank you," he said.

"It's all right. Goodbye."

He turned and walked down the steps, then crossed the lawn and continued up the street. Daisy watched him, and Joan from her side of the street watched too. When he reached the bend in the crescent he raised his hat and saluted Daisy with it.

When he was gone, she tore open the envelope and skimmed the contents. The first part seemed to be about a Mrs. Gordienko and the Dial-a-Cab Company. The second was all about his sister, Emmy, who wore her hair in braids and seemed to have died of polio. Last years of her life in an iron lung. (How dreadful!) A long paragraph described how she had trained her chickens to jump from hand to hand. Another described a rabbit, Clover, that had been her favourite, before she got sick. . . . *At first I thought you were a lot like Emmy,* he wrote. *But now I'm thinking you're probably different in a thousand and one ways. It's just you kind of hit me that way at first.*

Already he seemed to treat Keiko—a near stranger—as a willing recipient of rambling stories. So like a man, Daisy thought. The next part was about his mother, who lived with a Mrs. Cullard, above the dress shop in town.

She flipped over the page, read the end of the letter.

> *Please let me know if you need help. I saw you at the hospital. You can trust me to help you.*
>
> *Your loving friend,*
> *Tom Orley.*

Daisy dropped the letter into the trash can, pushed it deep down, beneath the shells of Walter's egg, some scraps of toast. It was just so strange, this man—freckle-faced but quite good-looking—taking one look at Keiko and deciding—deciding what? That he could help her. That she was like his sister, Emmy.

Emmy—a trainer of chickens, a keeper of a white rabbit. Emmy—the sister he couldn't help. An image formed in Daisy's mind of this girl, with two stiff braids, a pale know-it-all face, skinny arms. And then that awful end, trapped in the iron lung. Tom, her older brother, looking through the glass at her inert body. Like the prince staring down at Snow White in her glass coffin.

32.

"HAVE YOU HEARD ANYTHING about when she's coming home?" Fran leaned over the back fence. She was slower than she had been a month ago, and bigger too, but Daisy found that her eyes could go to Fran's belly. She even let herself imagine the sensations: by now the baby must be kicking—delicate kicks like bubbles escaping from a bottle.

"I'm expecting a call soon." This wasn't true. But Fran didn't need to know.

Ed's bomb shelter was five feet wide now and as deep as a man. "I don't know why he had to dig his hole directly under the clothesline," Fran said. It was true: Fran had only a small patch of grass near the back porch from which to launch her clothes. She pulled a pair of Ed's underwear from the enamel pail she used for wet laundry, pinned them on one side, then the other, then gave the line a hard yank, sending the underwear to drip into the fallout hole.

"How's Ed doing?" Daisy asked.

"Same as ever. He's so crabby. He keeps acting as though she—you know—Keiko," she said the word gently, as though it were valuable, "as though Keiko is his number-one enemy."

"Maybe he'll settle down after he meets her."

"I doubt it. He never does settle down about things—just gets worse and worse until he explodes."

Fran took another pair of underwear and wrung them out, then hung them with pegs and launched them over the hole. "You know what it is, Daisy?" she said. "He's afraid. I've seen it on his face. He watches the television, he sees that stuff, you know the stuff, the stuff from the bomb—"

"Radiation."

"And he gets frightened."

Like me, Daisy thought. That was how I was at first. And she felt a pang of sympathy for Ed Warburgh.

Fran frowned. "I just wish he'd stop being so moody. When do you think she's coming home?"

Daisy shook her head. "You asked me that already."

"I did, didn't I? I can't think any more. Listen, it said in the paper that she used to work in a hair salon. I have about a million copies of *American Hair*. Do you suppose she'd like them? I mean, to read at the hospital."

"Sure. That would be nice."

"I just hope Ed doesn't notice they're gone. But if he does, I'll just say they're mine. I have a right."

Daisy smiled. "Does he keep close track of your hair magazines?"

"Oh well, you know. There's nothing I wouldn't put past him." Fran knelt down and pulled up a sheet. It was sopping—her wringer was clearly not working. She hung it doubled over the line, but it was so waterlogged it touched the edges of the hole, picking up dirt. Daisy could see Fran moving around behind the sheet, a watery shadow with two edges. Daisy walked quickly to the end of the fence, slipped through the gap and crossed the Warburghs' lawn. Fran had her face against the sheet, cooling her cheeks.

"I get so hot," Fran said. "And look at my feet." They were badly swollen. "I don't know why that's happening."

"It's just the pregnancy."

"He doesn't ever hurt me, Daisy, if that's what you're thinking. He's just trying to do what's right."

"But *you* don't think he's right."

"That doesn't matter."

"Yes it does."

"I don't see how."

"It just does, Fran."

"How do you know?"

Daisy shook her head. "I don't know. I just do."

Fran looked at her through watery eyes, then she gave Daisy a quick hug. It was a feathery gesture, done quickly, regretted instantly. She picked up the enamel bucket and turned to go inside, but then stopped when she reached the porch steps.

"I'll leave the magazines at your back door."

"Put them on the chair."

"Ed will have no idea."

33·

DAISY STOOD INSIDE KEIKO'S BEDROOM. What was she looking for? Clues, that was all: she wanted clues to what this girl was. The anger, the malevolency that poured so potently from the top of her head, the small but perfectly constructed lie she had told on the bridge. *I can't remember a thing about the bombing. Help me, Mrs. Lawrence.*

No, the girl had not said *help me.* That was something Daisy

had added, going back over the memory. The movement of the
stalks of muddy grass, the girl's head, luminous in the plastic
bonnet. *Help me.* Then that unexpected gesture, the one that
seemed destined to undo Daisy, the small hand clutching the
chestnut in her pocket.

Her chest of drawers was littered with gifts: presents from
the Atchitys, from Dr. Carney, from Irene, even, foolishly,
from Daisy. So many gifts from so many well-wishers. People
trying to right the infernal balance. There were gifts from all of
the Project members, but also from total strangers: handkerchiefs, cards, pen and pencil sets—all sent through the mail,
and from whom? From old ladies in the suburbs of Palm Beach,
or housewives in the badlands of Alberta; from handsome men
who'd seen the wire-service photo of her getting off the plane;
from schoolchildren prompted by their excitable teachers.
Gifts of goodwill, items Keiko had stacked on her desk, some
of them still in their wrapping. Daisy picked up a set of three
cotton handkerchiefs, still in their gold box, folded between
pieces of white tissue. A note was attached:

> *Dear Miss Kitigawa,*
>
> *I bought these at a white sale for my daughter-in-law's
> birthday, but when I heard about you on the radio, I decided
> you needed them more. I hope the operation on your face goes
> smoothly.*
>
> *Blessings,*
> *Dagmar Palme, Witchita, Kansas.*

Beside the handkerchiefs was a Hiroshima Project folder.
Daisy undid the elastic string. Inside were a dozen children's

drawings sent by a Mrs. Cora Wysebrook, from Mt. Holly Elementary School, Georgia. Children with faces zealously coloured yellow, pink, brown, holding hands, circling a globe; children dancing; children in a playground, swinging on swings. Mrs. Cora Wysebrook had obviously edited the drawings: there were no crayoned pictures of bombs falling, no rivers clotted with corpses—just children, dancing their dance of reconciliation.

This made Daisy angry. *Don't throw your sweet, syrupy emotions all over her. At least get it right.*

Not that she had got things right. She'd been as crazy as everyone else, turning Keiko into—into what? Someone through whom she could prove herself. Irene had once said that Daisy needed to be the nicest person in the room. Wanting to be good, now that was a murky desire if you saw it in a certain way; especially if it meant force-feeding Keiko with that goodness.

Daisy pulled open Keiko's top drawer and reached in. Oh, that felt strangely erotic, to touch her slips and undergarments, fingertips brushing satin and silk. She pulled out a peach nightgown and then a chiffon scarf with a hand-rolled hem. Where had all this come from? Dr. Carney, of course. Or Bertha Atchity. She rubbed the fabric between her fingers, the rainbow chiffon turning them yellow, then violet, then red. She pushed her hands into the drawer again. Had she ever felt such creamy satin, such gorgeous watermarked silks? And such colours: cloud white, mimosa, petal pink. And stockings—such stockings. Daisy dug her hands into the pile and her knuckles grazed something hard, which she pulled from among the creamy negligees.

It was a simple box, about ten inches long by three inches wide, unvarnished but prettily made, with dovetailed joints. Its wooden lid could slide off, like a pencil case. The faded letters on top read, *Burns Goldenloaf Cheese. Burns and Co., Ltd., Toronto,*

Canada. Beside these words was a black line drawing of a wind-mill with a maiden waving beside it. She wore a polka-dotted dress and a Dutch-girl cap.

This was a treasure box brought from Hiroshima. Daisy's heart beat harder at the sight of it, and when she slipped it open—this was strange—she saw a tiny brooch inside. It was not just any brooch: it was Stacey Atchity's butterfly brooch. She picked it up. It was cold and heavy between her fingers, its back gold. When she turned it over she saw the enamelled wings painted a dusty purple, like pansies, the jewelled antennae made of golden wire, the faceted garnet body.

Oh, this was duplicity. This was rare. So rare it felt scalding. At last, this was something Daisy could understand. Who wouldn't want to steal from the Atchity family, with their perfect house and their lovely sweaters and their good-as-gold World Federalism? Their wholesome luck. Their delightful children.

Keiko must have taken it the week they showed her around Manhattan. Stacey had noticed it was missing on the ferry ride to Staten Island and had whispered as much to her mother, who searched for it desperately. The butterfly had been a gift from Dean's mother. In the end, Bertha reprimanded Stacey so severely she burst into tears; while Keiko, sitting on the ferry bench in the cold sunshine, must have known where it was the whole time, on the ground by the smokestack, perhaps, or beside the lifeboats. And when the others moved off, she must have scooped it up, placed it in her pocket.

What else was in that box?

An ebony elephant with ivory tusks. It fitted neatly into Daisy's palm, and must have fitted neatly into Keiko's when she snitched it from wherever she snitched it from. Maybe from Eleanor Roosevelt's desk. It looked valuable, with its ropelike tail, bony haunches, glowing belly of black wood.

Also in the box: A pair of calfskin gloves, trimmed in black. Irene's probably. A king cob marble. Walter's lighter. Two photographs. These last were in sepia shades, dog-eared. Daisy carried them to the bed, where it was brighter. The way the light fell on them, the white parts jumped out and the blacks became opaque and dull.

The first photo was clearly of Keiko's mother. Now this was a surprise. Everybody knew that the child was beautiful. But that the mother was beautiful too, that was a secret that Keiko had kept to herself, a knot, a seed at her core. She looked so quietly elegant and well put together in her coat of Persian lamb, her small, slightly military hat cocked to one side. Her eyes were large, and probably the same startling colour as Keiko's. They held a look of sorrow, as though she could already see into the future and knew what to expect.

The other photograph was of a little girl. It was Keiko— Daisy could tell from the wary, intelligent gaze, the slight frown. But it wasn't the Keiko who had come to them, thin and scarred and determined to survive, but a pudgy girl of perhaps five. Her hair was cut just above the ears, and she wore a ceremonial kimono of such a small size! Daisy could picture how Keiko's mother must have delighted in dressing her for this photograph, having her hold out her arms for the embroidered sleeves, then turn and turn so that the *obi* could be wrapped around her tiny waist, telling her not to cry when she found the layers of padded material itchy and hot.

Keiko's mother must have touched Keiko a hundred times, just in this one act of dressing her. Perhaps the aunt, Yoshiko, had helped as well, the two women bent over the girl. *Be patient, don't fidget. We'll be done soon.* But they weren't done soon; it seemed to go on and on forever: there were those toe socks, *tabi,* to place on her feet, and pretty wooden sandals, and three or four or even five layers of silk and embroidered satin weighing down the girl's shoulders. The scarf was tied with an enormous bow, as though it wasn't made for a child's kimono at all, as though this were dress-up. Then her smooth cheeks had to be painted white, and perhaps powdered too, so that the paint wouldn't smudge, and lipstick needed to be applied, and black eyeliner. Oh, how these women must have delighted in it all, dressing Keiko like a little doll. Perhaps they had cried for joy when they were finished: she was so small and lovely, with the headdress tinkling, the lotus flowers around her ears and that lily clutched in her dimpled hands.

34.

DAISY TELEPHONED IRENE, but there was no answer. She phoned the hospital but wasn't allowed to speak to Dr. Carney. In a fit of desperation, she telephoned Dean Atchity and spoke to his secretary: "I'm the host mother of Keiko Kitigawa. I need to speak to Mr. Atchity immediately."

Surprisingly, the secretary put her through.

"Mrs. Lawrence." Dean Atchity's voice, as usual, carried a bounty of good things, like a well-laden merchant ship—green lawns, humanitarian intentions, the World Court, support for Negro desegregation, a bust of Whitman (which Daisy had seen on his desk).

"I want to visit Keiko," Daisy said. "But they say I'm not allowed."

"Really? How strange."

"Have *you* seen her?"

He had—though not often, as Dr. Carney kept a close watch over her. But he believed she was recovering nicely. Stronger by the day. He would have Irene ring Daisy immediately. As host mother, he said, she must have access. Daisy hung up, not minding at all about getting Irene into trouble.

A few minutes later Irene telephoned.

"So," she said. "You've spoken to Atchity. No need, I was about to ring anyway, to let you know the girl can go home."

"When?"

"Soon. Day after tomorrow."

"When can I see her?"

Daisy could see Irene's shrug, even through the telephone. "Any time. Come in today if you want. Suit yourself." When Irene hung up, Daisy went quickly to Walter's study. He had the boxes of *Dark Night* open, and he was bent over one of them, reading through an earlier draft.

"We can see her, Walter."

He put down the file and sighed. At first he seemed disoriented, like a deep-sea diver breaching the surface. Then he smiled.

"How's she doing?"

"Recovering—that's what Atchity says."

She switched on the overhead light—Walter had been working in near darkness—and then went into the kitchen and telephoned Joan Palmer.

"We have good news," she said simply. "Keiko is coming home."

She did this knowing that Joan would phone Evelyn, and Evelyn would phone Fran, and that by the end of the day they'd know in the teachers' lounge and in the drugstore, that Mr. Strickland would congratulate her when she crossed the fields to pick up milk.

Let the news be spread. And what was odd—considering how much hate she had felt for these women—was how good it felt to pick up the telephone, to dial Joan's number, to pass the news along.

35.

YOU DO SOMETHING. And then you do something else. And before you know it, the universe shifts in your favour.

Little acts. It is always little acts in fairy tales. It is a heel of bread given to an old woman at the crossroads, the releasing of a mouse from a trap. Daisy's thoughts moved gently but relentlessly in this direction. She took the train into town, six copies of *American Hair* resting on her lap.

At Mount Sinai Hospital, Keiko lay in bed on her back, eyes closed, face bandaged. The room smelled of disinfectant and something else, something unmistakably putrid beneath the higher smell. Daisy wondered if it was the edges of the graft beneath the bandages. She wanted to open the window, get a cross breeze blowing, but no, she forced herself to breathe it in, whatever it was, the scent of radioactivity, the scent of death— breathe it in, then breathe it out again. Keiko opened her eyes.

She didn't acknowledge Daisy in any way. She seemed to be looking inside as much as out, and her eyes had a film over them. The bandage on her face had a patch of yellow ooze in the area where the scar had been. Daisy wondered what the graft looked like: if it was holding on, adhering, as it should, through hundreds of small capillaries, or if it was refusing to attach itself to Keiko's tissue. When she looked into Keiko's eyes, the girl was studying her, but not as though she expected a thing from her. More as though Daisy was a stranger.

A copy of a Mary Marvel comic book lay beside Keiko on the bed. Daisy opened it and asked Keiko if she wanted to hear the story. Keiko nodded. Daisy pulled her chair close. She read the balloons of dialogue and pointed to each picture: Mary Marvel holding a car in one hand; Mary Marvel apprehending criminals, one of whom had a mottled, deformed face with cauliflower bumps for ears. Daisy shot a glance at Keiko, but she registered nothing.

"You'll come home soon," she told her.

After a while Keiko fell asleep.

36.

IT WAS KEIKO'S MOTHER who told her what to do.

This was on the thirteenth day after the operation, as she lay in bed, a stack of hair magazines beside her. Already she was beginning to mend, at least on the surface, though the nurse who brought her food reported a high fever. When she opened her eyes, Mrs. Lawrence was studying her.

"Keiko," she said. "I'm hoping that from now on we can be good friends."

That was when she heard the swish of the animal's tail. Not a heavy drag, a dry whisper on the linoleum.

The next day Keiko was sitting up, waiting for her dressing to be changed, when Mrs. Lawrence arrived. She read to Keiko from a Mary Marvel comic book. "What do you think of this picture?" Mrs. Lawrence asked, but Keiko said nothing. After a while she turned the page.

When Mrs. Lawrence left, Keiko closed her eyes. She could

feel the ghost of the scar on her face. There had been red blood on the bandages at first, then black blood and now, finally, the flow had stopped, except for occasional ooze. On the surface she was healing. On the surface she must be grateful.

At first she thought the scaly tail must belong to a rat, but then she remembered her grandfather saying that the foxes on Shikoku had ugly thin tails. It would not speak to her. Instead, it slipped under the chair by the door, then disappeared down the hallway, its rough tail dragging across the floor.

She slept soundly, and the nurse brought her a cup of tomato soup and some cottage cheese and Jell-O, which she left on the bedside table. After a while, Keiko heard the rustling of papers and opened her eyes. Mama sat at the end of the bed.

"I came back," she said.

She had the same tiny birthmark under her right eye, the elegant curled hair, the sorrowful eyes and bitten fingernails. Keiko tried to explain that she was sorry for having the scar removed, sorry, too, for what happened on the bridge—the bridge that spanned the river near their house. Hiss of paper above the hospital bed. Her mother pressed her hand to Keiko's forehead.

"Don't speak," she said. "Just listen."

"They want to know so much. They keep asking questions."

"What about the others—Mrs. Lawrence and her husband. And that red-haired boy?"

"That boy is in love with me."

Her mother tilted her head. A boy in love is useful. She sat at the end of the bed. Rather than speak, she gestured in a wild but precise calligraphy. This. She drew in air. And this. And this— this is how you flee from a burning city.

"But I can't."

"You must." After a while she added, "Have I shown you my back?"

She turned. Her clothing had been burnt away, and her skin was marked; not as the skin of a *hibakusha* is burnt, with charred ridges and crusty edges, but in shades of bruised purple and inky green, like a blurry tattoo, forming a pattern of leaves and flowers.

37.

SHE CAME BACK to Walter and Daisy on June 1. The fields had erupted in buttercups. Daisy would always remember that because, exhausted and bandaged as Keiko was, sitting between them in the front seat, she had turned to look out at the shock of yellow fields.

That was on the drive home. But first they picked her up at Mount Sinai.

When the Lawrences arrived at the hospital, Irene was waiting in the lobby, wearing a black and white outfit. No kiss on the cheek this time, no whispered questions as to whether her nylons were straight. "Wait here," she said severely. "Keiko will be down in an instant." And in an instant the elevator doors opened and there she was, flanked by Dr. Carney and Dean Atchity. Bandages covered her, eyebrows to chin, so that only her eyes, forehead and lips were visible. Coming towards them, the effect was different from Keiko's face on the pillow, white on white. We've erased her, Daisy thought. The girl looked just like the Invisible Man. He wore bandages too—over his invisible body, invisible face—but when he unwound them at the end of the day, there was nothing there.

That was the first thought Daisy had, seeing Keiko bandaged.

They came forward slowly. Atchity's and Carney's shoes rang on the tiles, magnified by the acoustics, but Keiko's made no sound. The whole procession seemed to take forever, and to have a formal significance, as though Keiko was being led from her bridal chamber; but because of the wavering light in the lobby, it might have been a bridal chamber at the bottom of the sea.

In the car Keiko put her head to one side and closed her eyes until they had left the city behind. Only then did she open them again.

"Are you all right?"

"Yes, Mrs. Lawrence."

She turned to face the buttercups in the field outside the window, pure and bright in the afternoon sun, as though painted by children. And all the while, Walter held on to the leather steering wheel with both hands and drove as though chased, his hat low on his brow. They sped along the Northern State Parkway towards Riverside Meadows, Linden Street, their house, their neighbours, the bedroom where Daisy would help Keiko take off her jacket, unbutton her dress—all those tiny pearly buttons—and slip it from her frame.

Then Keiko would unwrap the soft pink nightgown Daisy had bought for her, and Daisy would help her put it on.

38.

CHILDREN RAN OUTSIDE THE WINDOW, through the wild grass, the timothy, in a place that looked like the Russian steppes. The train rumbled and shook. All at once Daisy was afraid, knowing she had been afraid before, but still hoping that if she alerted the authorities, she could make things right. "We've got to stop now," she shouted, but her voice came out low, a whimper that made her need to pee. A mother kept reading quite tenderly to her pale son, and there were soldiers bent over a table, playing cards. She looked out the window: all the colour had leached from the grass blades and the air had filled with silver dots. When she thrust open the window her scarf billowed into the poisoned air and her skin prickled and grew hot, as though hundreds of pins had been inserted beneath the surface.

She must have heard the door close in her sleep, the faintest click, and yet it woke her. She looked down the hallway. Keiko's bedroom door was open. Daisy went towards it, feeling that she had walked down this hallway many times, and each time she had found the covers rumpled, the bed empty. Her head jangled with déjà vu.

Keiko's blue blanket was folded back neatly. She was gone.

Daisy heard Walter hacking behind her. He appeared at the bedroom door, pulling up his pyjama bottoms. The string was broken.

"She's gone out," Daisy said.

"Why?"

"I don't know. She can't have gone far—" Daisy ran for her shoes, but Walter stopped her.

"I'll go. You stay here."

"I'm worried."

"That's why I should go. I'll be quicker." He slipped on his boots and sweater and was gone, out the back door.

Later he told her that as soon as he reached the back alley he saw her ahead of him, wearing her pale pink nightgown, moving with surprising swiftness. He did not call out. She crossed Old

Middle Road and passed quickly through the playground, taking the path leading to Willard's Creek, moving sure-footedly. She zigzagged down the trail, stepping with such purpose Walter began to think that she was off to meet someone. (Tom, Daisy thought. Tom, her red-haired Romeo.) But that wasn't it, because when she came to the stone bridge, she stopped, leaning over, looking at the water.

Walter watched her. Being out in the night, surrounded by unlit, rustling fields, didn't seem to frighten her. She leant against the bridge, hands on the parapet, looking with patience at the trickle of water.

When Walter said her name she turned. Her eyes were blank, dark. Her lips looked strikingly dark too, surrounded by the bandages, as though she had been sucking on licorice. Somewhere off in Stoney Creek a dog howled.

"She told me to wait here." Keiko's voice was clear, a tone or two heavier than he had heard it before. She turned back to the water.

Walter took a step, another step, until he was near enough to touch her. She was shaking her head, a tiny automatic quiver, as though refusing to believe something.

"You'll need this." He took off his sweater and draped it around her shoulders.

She looked at him and smiled. "Thank you," she said.

"Who told you to wait here?" he asked. "Did Daisy say something?"

A troubled look passed over her face, his question forcing ripples. He was afraid that she would wake up and find herself alone with him, on a bridge, in the darkness. "I think it's time to head home." He said this firmly but lightly.

Keiko looked towards the pathway, trying to remember something.

He put his arm around her and led her from the bridge.

Daisy saw them from the kitchen window as they crossed the back lawn: Walter's arm was slung protectively over Keiko's shoulder, his sweater sleeves hanging far past her hands. She threw the back door open, but Walter motioned for silence. Keiko came up the back steps easily, a bounce in her step they had never seen before, but her eyes were opaque and dull. As soon as she had stepped inside, Walter reached behind and bolted the door, then Daisy led her by the arm to the bedroom. She sat her on the bed, then knelt and took off her muddy slippers.

"Lie down," Daisy said, and Keiko did as she was told. Daisy adjusted the pillow beneath her head, then tucked the edges of the coverlet between the mattress and box spring, sealing her in place.

"Stay in bed now."

"I will," the girl said in a bright, clear voice.

Walter sat at the kitchen table, breathing heavily from his walk.

"Eyes open, but senses shut," he said.

"Frightened."

He nodded. He felt for his rolling papers, but of course they weren't in his pyjama pocket. "She said someone told her to go there. To the bridge. Did you say that?"

"Of course not."

"She's remembering."

"It's the pressure."

"I think you'd better sit up with her tonight."

Daisy nodded.

"I'm going to stay up for a while," he said. "I'll be here if you need me."

"Thanks. I mean, for finding her so fast."

He shrugged and turned back to finding his tobacco. "You're all right, Daisy Lawrence," was all he said.

❈

When Daisy entered Keiko's room, she was sitting up in bed, fumbling at the window latch. "I'm letting them in," she said.

Daisy sprang for the window, yanking it shut. The girl turned blank eyes on her. "No use letting them in tonight," Daisy said briskly. "Not when everyone needs their sleep." The no-nonsense voice did the trick. Keiko stopped fumbling for the catch.

Daisy gave her some water and she drank deeply, holding the glass with two hands. She handed it back and lay down. Daisy sat in the chair and watched her. Eventually a shiver ran through her body. Her eyes were closed now; she had slipped back into sleep. Or a deeper sleep. Daisy switched off the bedside lamp, but she didn't leave. She sat in the chair by the light of the moon, which was waning slightly, though its face was still intact.

After another few minutes Keiko shivered again, but rather than falling into a deeper sleep, she seemed to be emerging, like a swimmer from the bottom of a pool, up and up, into the room again. She kicked the blankets away, rolled to her side. Gently, Daisy placed the covers back over her. But her small feet were untucked. Daisy knelt and began to tuck Keiko's feet beneath the blanket. She touched the girl's heel and then, for some reason she could not explain, she cradled it in her palm. It fitted exactly. Oh, this reminded Daisy of the dream, all those children, the livid stalks of grass, and she felt her scalp grow hot from the effort of not crying. It wasn't just losing the babies, or being with Keiko—this girl with her small feet that she had never touched until now—it was the other children too: Emmy-Mae, in her glass coffin, and Joan's brother, falling from the monkey bars, and the others too, too many to think of, at Babi Yar and in the ghettos and raising their hands to stop the blinding flash. Daisy didn't know why she hadn't seen them before, but the room was thick with them now; they pressed in on her, imploring her to notice, to feel them there, as she bent to that soft foot and held her breath to stop herself from making any noise.

A twitch ran through Keiko's body. Her legs were covered in goosebumps. Then she sat bolt upright, eyes wide open, and stared at Daisy, who knelt at the end of the bed holding her foot. Keiko drew her knees to her chest.

"What are you doing?" Her voice was full of accusation.

"You were—" Daisy stopped. It was too awful a thing to say: *You walked a quarter-mile, unconscious; you stared into the water, asking for someone; you returned. Look, here are your muddy slippers to prove it.* Daisy couldn't say any of it. Nor could she say why she had been crying.

"I just came to check on you. Look, I brought you water." She pointed to the glass. "Perhaps you'd like some now?"

Keiko put her knees down, but kept clutching the blanket. "I'm fine," she said.

"I'm going now. You sleep tight." Daisy took the glass from the bedside table and left. But when the girl was fast asleep again, Daisy returned to sit by her bed.

39.

THERE IS ONE MORE THING TO DESCRIBE from that night.

At 4:00 a.m., Keiko sat up in bed, startled out of sleep, startling Daisy as well.

"It grew back," she whispered, touching her ear. "It grew back."

Daisy took her hands and gently laid them at her sides. "It was a nightmare."

"I can feel it." Keiko covered her face.

"Shh," Daisy whispered. "Don't be afraid." And then some instinct made her add: "I won't let them hurt you."

Later, when Daisy remembered that night, she could smell the scent of honeysuckle at the window and see the moon on the floorboards. But in her memories Keiko wasn't bandaged: her face was broken down the middle, just like the moon. One half was pure and white, the other half mottled and porous. The unbroken side was as smooth as porcelain, terrifying in its brightness, but in every memory it was the pocked side that drew Daisy in.

V INTERPRETER

40.

THE METHODS OF TORTURE AMAZE: the ad hoc embellishments, the precise and careful attention to detail, the creative variations on a single theme. Who knew that causing pain could take so many forms? But human beings are nothing if not inventive.

Men sick with dysentery are forced to crouch beside the open hatches of the ship that bears them to Shamshuipo; semiconscious, dizzy with fever, one by one they pitch into the sea. Men stand in the scorching compound, arms outstretched, holding buckets filled to the very brim. For two days and two nights they struggle to keep the buckets upright. When one man drops his bucket, all the men are beaten senseless. Then there's the water torture: a man is forced to drink water until his stomach bulges, then he's ordered to lie on the floor. The guard places a board on his stomach and jumps onto it, pressing the water into the man's heart and kidneys and lungs.

These are things Ed Warburgh has seen.

These are things he knows intimately.

More intimately than the number of teeth that have cut through his daughter Patti's gums, more intimately than the feel of his wife's pregnant belly in her flannel nightgown, printed with yellow flowers.

He digs his hole in the backyard, levels the ground by stomping back and forth and thinks about what he knows.

One morning Ed sees two prison guards arrest a Chinese woman. She is gathering seaweed on the beach below the compound. They wave their guns at her, ordering her to leave her straw basket where it lies, then escort her across the white compound, sand fine as talcum, where the prisoners stand for roll call—*tenko*—morning, noon and night. She hurries between the two guards at a jog, as though by rapid compliance she will show that she means no harm at all, that she will do whatever they say. Standing in the shade of the prison barracks, Ed cannot see the woman's features clearly. The sharp sun casts a shadow down her face, making her eyes appear like a jack-o'-lantern's.

With formal politeness now, they gesture for her to stand on the wall at the north end of the compound. Below is a forty-foot drop, then the sea. She does not understand. One of them bounds onto the wall, demonstrating, standing with his back to the compound, signalling for her to join him. She clambers up—a tiny figure on the white wall—while the guard climbs down. Ed wonders what she is thinking, looking at the fishing boat near the horizon. He knows what will happen next, but he doesn't stop watching. He takes in the black figures of the guards against the scorching sand, the sea in the distance, a seagull above them, stationary, flying against the wind. This is how he will remember it later. The guards talk for some time. Something is decided between them, because the taller one goes and leans against the compound wall, in the shade, while the shorter one raises his pistol. He does this without sound, or at least Ed can hear nothing, a hundred yards away. Then he shoots. There is no cry from the woman. She sags at the knees. The impact of the second shot pitches her forward, out of view.

Ed follows the wall of the compound, staying in the shade, until he reaches the north wall, which on the prisoners' side is covered in high barbed wire. Leaning forward he sees the woman's body face down in the sea.

Ed's neighbours in Riverside Meadows know about the tingling in his feet, shooting pains that he relieves by soaking them in seltzer. They know he has nightmares. But none of them know that he can sit on the back porch steps, or dig his hole in the yard, or walk home up Linden Street, any time of the day or night, and see a woman's body floating in the waves, shirt blackening as it takes in water.

The next day the interpreter comes to Shamshuipo.

She makes her first appearance at afternoon *tenko*. How many men line up in the sun? Eighteen Americans, seventy-six Canadians, two British. For a while there were a couple of Dutch men, but they died of dysentery. The prisoners are called to muster. Standing still causes shooting pains, like having pins buried in the soles of your feet; all through the lines there is the shuffle of men shifting their weight.

Ed stands at attention, yellow-skinned from dysentery. The rice has given him diarrhea. A trickle of bright orange rust burns his anus, and runs down the back of his leg.

The chief officer of the *Kempetai* has barked out an order. The men all call him Monkey Face, though sometimes they call him Tojo's chimp. It is true that he looks like a monkey— scruffy chin, wrinkled brow, long arms, big lower lip: a monkey on a mission.

The young woman repeats the order. This is something new. The men listen to the bark of the officer translated into a feminine register. Her voice is clear and cold. Heavily accented. She wears a belted tunic of dun-coloured cotton with two breast pockets, over shapeless trousers. She stands stiff and stern beside the chief. Perhaps she feels that she must not show compassion—for her own protection, this must be so. But how can she look on them and be unmoved? Ninety-six starved men standing under the burning sun, some with bellies fat with beriberi, one with a goitre as big as a grapefruit dangling under his chin, men shifting from foot to foot, the restive stirring of chickens, a smell of rotting flesh. In the front row an open wound forces one man to lean on another. Within the pink flesh, watermelon-coloured, the girl can see bone.

Their eyes are on her now. Something new to look at: a woman's face. They see her cheekbones, her dark eyes in which they search for an acknowledgment of what they have become. She sends her gaze to the corrugated roofs of the huts, before glancing back again at the goitres and bones, the swelling and thinning of flesh. She finds the courage to look at faces: faces of men whose souls have been swallowed by their bodies, pain forcing them to focus on nothing but the soft sand at their feet. Faces of the ages, showing no surprise.

She hears a slurping sound to her left. A man falls forward. The *Kempetai* chief calls out an order for hospitalization. She translates. *Attention. This man is sick. You men to the right, to the left, take him away.*

The guards shove two other men with the end of their bayonets. They are released from the line to drag away the fallen man, his feet pigeon-toed in the sand.

Tell them they are cowards who allowed themselves to be taken prisoner.

She hears the chief officer say this and she nods, translates his words. That this suffering might have been brought about by some fault of their own sends breath back into her lungs: they are so terrible in their suffering, covered in running sores, and yet they still cling to life. This itself must be cause for punishment. She tries, under the burning sun of the compound, which has given her a headache, she tries to believe they deserve to suffer, through faults of the worst cowardice and depravity. She tries to tell herself that they are less than human; otherwise they would have killed themselves long ago. It is a trick of thought: it goes through her head faster than she can control it—because humans who get treated in this way must be criminals, or belong to sicker, weaker sub-species.

Now the chief officer says that there has been a theft of vitamins from the medical hut. Boxes have been broken into and five bottles have been stolen. She knows this means the Red Cross bottles that belong to the prisoners. She was told about Red Cross supplies by a male interpreter who received his training, as she did, at Tokyo-2D. She pauses only an instant, then she translates clearly, staring between the faces of the men, feeling the sweat between her breasts, running down to her stomach, tickling like a fly.

There has been a theft of vitamins that were to be evenly distributed in due course to all the men in the camp. But a coward took them for himself. A man was seen pocketing bottles. Call out your name.

The chief officer's voice is very loud, as though he were bellowing orders at troops, not ghosts. He stands with his legs apart, his long, curved sword in its sheath, wearing shorts and a dun shirt.

Call out your name.

Why does he care so much who stole the vitamins? Who is he?

He is a man with a large moustache. He is short with a wrinkled brow. Often she has seen him scratching his scalp furiously, when he thinks he is not being observed. But now he plans to make something happen. He is calling up his *bushido*, his fighting spirit. Honour is at stake in this courtyard. These men are half-dead and should be finished, but still they cling to life like leeches. They steal vitamins. Now he, the chief officer of the *Kempetai*, unbuttons the leather sheath and draws out his sword.

The magic of weapons. The interpreter feels what he has done—how he has made himself invincible, drawn a circle around himself, protecting his body from the shambles, the smell and the animal shifting of feet. He alone believes in something noble. He believes in the fighting spirit, he believes in killing those who do not have the dignity to die. He believes, most ardently, in the blade of his father's sword.

Coward. It will be better for you if you step forward.

His words, so loud, are like muskets fired above their heads. They are followed by the words of the interpreter, but they do not carry well; they barely rise above the heated sand. By now the men understand that her little voice is just as merciless as the chief officer's. His brutality is bad and full, a parody of cruelty, but it gives them something real in their ears. The interpreter's voice is precise. She does not look again at their faces, but she does not falter.

The sun is directly above their heads now. Shadows smaller than tombstones at their feet. Heads without hats suffer in heat like this.

You. Stand forward.

The sand is not white. Close up it is grey, the same colour as the gravel in the compound at Tokyo 2-D. An old man used to go out in the late afternoon and rake the gravel in swirls.

A man has been pushed forward from the second line.

The interpreter looks at the sand, imagining swirls. She hears a sound that is loud, a crack to the head, perhaps, then another sound, which is a boot on a body. Thuds. Very bad thuds such as she has always known. Cries of pain, a high-pitched cry, a groan. She glances to her left to see jumping up and down. The guard is jumping on the man's back. She studies the ground again. In the patch ahead of her it is worn through the sand to the dirt, and covered in a talcum-like dust. More thuds. Boots against his back. She hears another groan; leather boots against what must be spine.

It is then that she looks up and meets the eyes of the prisoner standing directly in front of her. He has seen her flinch. Just that, nothing more. She lets herself look into the eyes that have seen her flinch. They hear another groan, and then she looks beyond his head.

For a long time the sounds go on. She notices that the light on the wall behind is very bright, the cleanest white, like porcelain. Beyond that far wall is the sea. It cannot be seen, but it is there. She realizes she can hear seagulls crying. For too long there has been thudding, kicking. Sweat has run down her stomach, into her belly button, soaking the belted area of her waist.

At last the chief officer calls out: *March.*

The interpreter's voice, a refrain: *March.*

The men move out of the compound, a band of ghosts dispersed. In the sun a body, knees bent, an angle of awkward prostration; blood pooled like a shadow around his head.

Dead bodies, she will learn, look like sacks stuffed full of nothing. Shit and blood. They are the worst thing. A man who is dead is less than nothing. And this man is dead. He has been kicked to death for stealing vitamins.

That was the interpreter's first day at the Shamshuipo prison camp for men.

41.

The Women's Circle
by Irene Day

AUGUST 1, 1952—Two months have passed since our Hiroshima Maiden returned to Riverside Meadows, post-surgery, and there can no longer be any question: Keiko Kitigawa is having a marvellous time. You have read in this column about her visits to the Norwegian ambassador's residence, her wonderful conversation with Mrs. Eleanor Roosevelt and of the banquets and luncheons she has graced with her presence. What may be less well known is the way she has adapted to life in a Long Island suburb. Dr. Raymond Carney operated on Keiko Kitigawa's face in mid-May. Plastic surgery, our latest science, has advanced greatly in recent years, and Dr. Carney is optimistic that Keiko's skin will show no trace of its former disfigurement. To heal properly, her face has had to remain swathed in compression bandages for a period of ninety days. This period is soon to be over, at which point the bandages will be removed. As you may imagine, Keiko and the Project organizers are on tenterhooks awaiting the final outcome.

Soon after her return to Riverside Meadows (See "Around the Clock Care, June 3"), Miss Kitigawa quickly began to regain her strength. Before the second week was out, Keiko was gossiping over the fence with the young mother next door. It helps that Frances Warburgh is only a few years older than Keiko herself, and that both love to pore over magazines about fashion and hair, discussing the latest "do's."

While Keiko's surgeries are famous, less well known are the small obstacles she faces daily. All the timesaving gadgets

American women take for granted have been a puzzlement to Miss Kitigawa. There are no big refrigerators in Japan, nor are there those basic necessities in a woman's kitchen: the electric toaster and automatic can opener. Yet Keiko mastered both appliances and even prepared Japanese teriyaki for the Lawrences (see photo facing page).

Her neighbours confessed that they were surprised to see an "atomic maiden" walking to the grocery store or waiting for the train. "I never dreamed I'd see such a thing," said Mrs. Evelyn Lithgow, a mother of three. "Initially, I had no idea how to react." Luckily, she did what comes naturally, extending a neighbourly hand. It wasn't long before Keiko found herself overwhelmed with invitations to picnics and backyard parties.

Mrs. Daisy Lawrence, a charming plump woman with a huge smile, has taken every step to make Keiko feel at home. Mr. Lawrence, our equally charming resident host, is a radio writer, though presently he's hard at work on a novel. I asked him if the new work was to do with the Hiroshima Project, to which he replied, "Not likely." One can hear the sound of Mr. Lawrence typing whenever one visits Riverside Meadows. "How often does he work like this?" I asked. To which his cheery wife replied, "He stops to sleep." Clearly, however, he stops to make himself amusing to his young guest. He can be seen often in her company, fanning the coals in the barbecue for an outdoor picnic, or escorting Keiko and Daisy to the drive-in theatre in neighbouring Nassau County.

But these easy pleasures will—to everyone's regret—be suspended when Keiko's bandages are removed. As soon as Dr. Carney unveils the affects of his surgery, Miss Kitigawa will begin a series of engagements, starting with a nationally televised appearance on *Ask a Doctor*, Dr. Carney's own program. With the hydrogen bomb daily rumoured to be close to completion, Miss Kitigawa's voice has never been more needed.

As for ending her summer of relaxed suburban pleasures in order to speak out against the hydrogen bomb, I recently asked Keiko how she felt about making such a sacrifice. We were lounging on the front steps of the Lawrences' bungalow while the afternoon sun filtered through the linden trees. At that very moment a red-haired boy of seven sped by on his bicycle, streamers flying, bell ringing—a real summer spectacle. He waved to Keiko, just as though she were part of the neighbourhood gang, and she waved back, before a shadow touched her face. I knew she was remembering her own childhood, which, too, had been free from care, until that fateful moment seven years ago.

"I do not want any more children to suffer," she said to me quietly. "Not American children, not Japanese children, not Russian children."

These words, spoken with such gentle conviction, moved me indescribably.

42.

IRENE PAUSED IN HER TYPING and read over what she'd written. Marvellous time. Backyard picnics. She had been composing her article to take her mind off what had happened last night in bed, her conversation with Raymond, but what she'd written wasn't so bad: it had the lilting cadence her readership asked for, the feminine touch. The reality didn't completely match her description, but that was often the unfortunate case with articles for "The Women's Circle."

In truth, Keiko's success—the way she seemed to fit into that suburb; her interest in the newest fashions, which she lisped to

Daisy's neighbour, that appalling, pregnant redhead; even the arrival, out of nowhere, of a beau—all this success, this talent at being precisely what everyone wanted her to be, struck Irene as perverse. But she couldn't write that.

As for Riverside Meadows itself, there were at least a thousand neuroses skittering like mice through the streets of that suburb. More than one woman looked like she drank heavily; while the men, pressing their wan, middle-aged faces to the windows of the train, haggard from nights out on the town, might be dreaming of anything, death even, as an escape from their wives. That was Riverside Meadows: a scream of despair, which nobody could hear above the grind and shake of the train.

People were talking about such a thing: how the incessant rocking of the train could affect a man's brain waves, his libido even. Meanwhile, the women were all quietly going mad behind their gingham curtains. And so last week, wearing a gorgeous black hat and matching waffle-weave skirt, cut on the bias, Irene had knocked on Dean's office door and suggested that she write her next column on that phenomenon, from a woman's perspective, of course.

"Everybody knows about the malaise of the suburban man, but what about the college-educated suburban woman, wiping Jell-O from her baby's face and quietly contemplating suicide? What about pill popping? Drunkenness? Promiscuity?"

It was as though she'd let out a massive burp across his desk, spraying the bust of Whitman. Dean even took out a handkerchief and wiped his hands. Then he told her gently, and paternally (that fatherly part of him never wavered), that the readers of the *Sunday Review* would never be interested in such issues. He didn't say that she was imagining things, but he somehow managed to imply that her vision of the world was skewed, warped by the dizzying vertical of her twice-divorced state.

And so she had written yet another column about Keiko.

She placed a hand on the telephone, willing it to ring, willing it to be Raymond on the other end. She held her palm against the cold curve of the receiver, but no: nothing. He had pulled back over the last month, giving no reasons. The things that had held them together—the pleasures of sex, and of planning the Project—had been put on hold while the girl lolled around Riverside Meadows and healed.

It was Keiko's fault that Irene no longer understood Raymond. He was obsessed, and the form his obsession had taken was of a patient suitor, arriving at Daisy's house with flowers, speaking of a thousand things, but never of the bomb. He wasn't recording her story, or recording how she avoided telling her story—he was enjoying her company, changing her bandages. When she had asked him, he had said that he was waiting, but she wasn't so sure.

"What on earth are you up to?" she had said to him last night, after a week of not seeing him, not sleeping with him. They were in his bed. He'd been silent, quite unlike the old Raymond, until at last she pestered a reply from him.

"I'm not up to anything."

"You've changed."

"Have I?"

She felt like kicking him. "You know you have."

"If you say so." After a while, he added: "If we proceed with care, I believe Keiko will give us what we want. I'm putting my trust in your gentle friend." That was what he had said: *Your gentle friend.* Her gentle friend. The words fell like burning shards of stone. She stood up and went to the bathroom, looked at herself in the mirror and saw Irene Podborsky. All the effort, the voice she used these days, that sounded, even to herself, faintly British, not to mention the pinching shoes, the fine vertical lines between her eyebrows—all for what? So that Raymond Carney could put

his trust in Daisy Lawrence. Oh, she should never have brougı
Daisy into the Project. She went back and sat at the end of the
bed, putting on her shoes. She couldn't say another thing or she'd
show how much she cared, and that wasn't part of their bargain.

After a while he spoke again. "Keiko's tremendously complex."

"I know."

"I've realized that we can't force her, Irene. She needs to come
to us on her own."

A pause.

"I suppose Keiko has a soul," Irene added. That old game.

He'd looked surprised, as though she'd asked him a question he
had been brooding about. "Several," he answered after a pause.

"Oh, she's got me beat then. I can't compete with that."

Several.

A world of souls.

It was then, standing at the end of the bed, fastening her shoe,
as Raymond lay in bed looking out the window, that Irene had
realized she hated Keiko. She hated her slender wrists and her
tiny feet and her smooth voice. She hated her way of listening as
though she understood. She hated the burning city that drew
them all in, like moths. But what she hated most were the happy
pleasures everyone had managed to find in one another's company, midsummer, in the suburb of Riverside Meadows.

43.

THE POOL WAS THE PALEST TURQUOISE: the turquoise
of oceans in Bermuda, the turquoise of the sky over the Gulf
Coast, the turquoise of chlorinated water at its very best. Just

ald Strickland was mixing drinks while flirting
w. One of his concoctions rested beside Daisy
patio table. The smell of charred steak swept
m the brick outdoor barbecue. True to tribal
tradition, all the other men had gathered around the flames,
preparing to give Gerald advice on his technique. Walter had on a
new short-sleeved shirt, covered in thick red and white vertical
stripes, like a barber's pole. He glanced across the Stricklands'
pool to where Keiko sat on a deck chair with the women.

"On the hottest days," Keiko was saying, "you could smell
snow. This is what my grandfather said."

The women leaned in, mesmerized by the city Keiko could
conjure up, the delta carved by seven rivers, the sacred shrine of
Miyajima with its *torii* gate floating in the water. All obliterated—
all gone.

"When you hear the word *Hiroshima*—you always think of
the bombing," Joan said. "You never think of what was there,
before."

"How tall was the bamboo?" Fran asked. "The bamboo you
saw from the train window." She already knew the answer.

"Taller than an elephant. Taller than this house. It was the
old bamboo of Hiroshima Prefecture. It got cut down to feed
the boilers during the war. Women and schoolchildren were
sent out to cut it down, then to cut the pieces into lengths to
be shipped north." She got up and went to the edge of the pool
and put her foot in the water. "Excuse me," Keiko said. "I would
like to swim now."

The Stricklands lived in Stoney Creek, where the yards were
much bigger than in Riverside Meadows. Gerald and Ella had a
vegetable garden in the bottom left corner of the backyard:
there was corn and lettuce, radishes and carrots, yellow beans
and scarlet runners. Along the east wall, near the garage, Gerald

had espaliered three pear trees. They looked splayed and captured, a few green pears dangling from thin limbs. Artie Shaw
was on the record player, mellow arcs of clarinet.

"You won't mind visiting the neighbours?" Daisy had asked
Keiko. Every day Keiko seemed to grow more talkative, lighter.
Now it was a week until the bandages were to be removed, and
she seemed almost buoyant. Less like her real self, Daisy
thought, then stopped herself, wondering why she felt she knew
that self so deeply.

"I don't mind going," Keiko had said. "I like to swim." As
though the issue at stake was merely whether, like any teenager,
she would look good in a bathing suit.

"You'll have to make sure your bandages don't get wet."

"You're a long way from home," Gerald had said to Keiko,
greeting them at the front door, then added, "Just how old are
you?" When Keiko had told him her age, he said, "You come on
back and meet my girls."

Now Keiko was sitting a stone's throw from these girls at the
edge of the pool. Joey Palmer floated on his back. He was a
plump, dark-haired boy of seven, with overlapping front teeth,
and skin that tanned rather than burnt. He kicked water at the
girls and then went under. When he came up he was a foot from
Keiko. "What's that on your face?" he said.

"Bandages."

"Joey," the Strickland girl said. "That's rude. I'm telling
Mom."

"That's okay," Keiko said. "It's to cover my skin graft."

Joey thought this over. "My mom says you're an A-bomb
victim," he said. "We're supposed to feel sorry for you."

"Joey Palmer!" Joan sprang up from her chair, reached the
pool in two steps and yanked her son from the water by one
arm, scraping his side against the concrete edge. His whining

was drowned by her staccato bark: "You! Joey Palmer! You'll get a hiding!"

"No I won't!"

"And a bad one!"

She dragged him around the side of the house and everyone could hear the hiding going on: Joey's cries, and then the hard *flack, flack, flack* of her palm against bare skin. Soon Joan emerged, leaving the humiliated Joey at the side of the house.

"I'm so sorry," she said to Keiko.

"Oh, I don't mind him asking, Mrs. Palmer."

"Joan. Call me Joan."

"I don't mind."

One of the Strickland girls felt moved to add, "We're real sorry about what happened to you."

And Keiko smiled. "That's okay," she said, as though it were a little thing, done yesterday, a slight that was already forgotten.

The hospital had changed Keiko. Daisy had felt this before, but seeing her in Stoney Creek, alien territory, brought the changes home. How altered the girl was now, how light—as though, by making herself the currency of air, she could become what every person wanted, and thus escape them. It made Daisy want to weep to think of it—how faceless the girl could make herself, like the fox in the fairy tale. The bakemono. Keiko had told that story to Daisy one night, while Daisy sat at the foot of her bed, rubbing her feet.

Keiko talked a lot now—that was the other change: she talked about Hiroshima, though never about the bombing. She talked beneath the bombing, around the bombing, describing the city as it had been to a child of ten. She told Daisy of the shadow-dappled hallway leading to the kitchen of her grandfather's house, the shrines he recorded, in minute writing, in his black leather notebook—a tracery of notes to describe a tracery of secret places. She spoke often of her grandfather, and Daisy imagined his gentle, wizened face, substituting the bespectacled, mustached face of her own dead father.

Near midnight, at the Stricklands', there were only a few people left—Keiko, Joan, Ella and Gerald (asleep in his chaise lounge) and Walter and Daisy. Walter sat quietly smoking. It must, Daisy thought, be a nice relief for him to be away from his typewriter; to let whatever he thought float away, unrecorded, like smoke from his cigarette. Keiko sat between him and Daisy. We'll need to get her home soon, Daisy thought. It's long past bedtime.

Joan said something about mosquitoes coming out, and for some reason this made Gerald sit up on the chaise lounge and shout, "Fuck it!" Then he lay back down and everyone laughed. But Ella didn't like it—it interfered with her sense of decorum. "Stop it, Gerald," she said severely. "You're having a nightmare." And then to the rest of them, " He thinks he's back at Omaha Beach."

He must have heard through his sleep because he shook all over like a dog. Ella went inside and fetched a blanket, then spread it over him.

"He'll sleep out here till dawn. There's no moving him."

"Lucky it's warm out," Joan said.

Ella lit a mosquito coil. The scent filtered through the air. Daisy watched the ash forming at the end of the coil, growing longer every minute. They sat breathing in the dusty, sweet smell, hearing traffic on the turnpike, just a car every two minutes or so. The smell of cut grass filled the night air. The sprinklers were on, and every now and then Daisy felt a faint mist against her face.

Later Daisy was not able to remember how the story began, or to understand why Joan chose to tell it. The pool lights were off, and they might have been sitting beside any body of water, in ancient Egypt or Israel perhaps, any place where people gathered to tell stories in low voices, while drunken soldiers like Gerald snored in nearby tents. Daisy never remembered afterwards what got Joan started, perhaps it was because earlier that afternoon Joey had put his head too close to the chlorine filter, but all at once she was in the middle of it, describing how she and her brother had loved to synchronize their movements under water. A game they had. "He'd do a back somersault," she said, "and I would do the exact mirror, all of this at the lake. We thought we were bloody magnificent. We thought we should run away and join the circus—only they don't have water acts in circuses, not something we spent a lot of time thinking about. The details, I mean. Course it was all my idea—synchronized swimming! What boy would think of that?" On she went, directing her comments to Keiko's bandaged profile. She told about how she had stayed home sick from school one day and seen, through the front window, Mr. Wren, the principal, carrying her twin brother down the street, cradling his head. The principal was dressed in black like a preacher, and behind him came a procession of children. "Mr. Wren was too distraught to tell them to get back to school, so they just followed behind." A dozen children, looking important and full of harm, and almost out of control, though they were silent. Some of them, as is the way with children, almost dancing with the terribleness of it. They came down the street, beneath the orange leaves, figures in a silent film.

She told this story, and everyone pictured it exactly: the limp boy in the man's arms, the procession of children, the mother throwing down her rake, not running, just standing on the lawn, while inside Joan peered through the picture window angry, because she thought her brother had hurt himself, and she was supposed to be the sick one that day. It was just like him to steal the attention.

❄

Afterwards Walter, Keiko and Daisy walked home from Stoney Creek along the silent turnpike, shoes crunching on the gravel verge. Every now and then a car came by, dimming its headlights. Keiko walked between them, her face glowing and bobbing in the darkness. In the grocery store parking lot Daisy saw their three shadows—courtly, tall man, slight girl, rounded woman—stretch across the asphalt. They found the pathway, then followed it in silence. Around them the corn sheaths spoke in their native tongue—spoke and spoke—while Daisy thought of Joan's story, the swimming brother, the twin. Then she thought of Tom Orley, the photographer, who came often now, in the afternoons, and she thought of Walter, sitting each night on the back porch, speaking in a low whisper, while Keiko listened—all of them finding something in the whiteness of that face that suggested absolution. And yet still, the crafty side of Keiko moved and breathed beneath the bandages, and thought of what to do next, and planned her escape.

They crossed the bridge over dried-up Willard's Creek and then walked up the slope, past the old farm foundations, towards the school, while around them the crickets sang wildly—not caring the least that any of them existed—and above, the night sky burnt with a million cold stars.

44.

THEY CAME TO HER.

The neighbours came, bearing platters of lemon tarts and angel-food cake and a wobbling green-and-red tomato asparagus aspic. Dr. Carney came, clutching, with each visit, a bouquet of pink roses, or daisies, laced with baby's breath, his notepad tucked securely in his inside jacket pocket. Tom Orley came too, and this time Daisy asked Keiko if she cared to see him. She did care to see him. She cared quite a bit. After a long fifteen minutes, she emerged at the front door wearing a red-and-white gingham dress, holding her shell-encrusted purse.

"Oh my," he said, unable to look.

He dropped his hat and it rolled down all three steps.

They sat out front, unsure of what to say to each other—the late sun behind the house no longer warming them. Daisy could hear Junie bouncing her ball in the Warburghs' car port and the sound of the Good Humor Man ringing his bell. As the big white truck rounded the crescent, Jimmy Jr. and Joey Palmer came tearing from the direction of the fields, waving at the driver to stop.

"Would you like a Fudgsicle?"

Tom came back with two, the outer paper covered in shards of ice, then showed Keiko how to balloon the paper cover by breathing into it so that it slipped off easily.

After a while he spoke haltingly but eagerly about his family's farm. He compared the fields around Riverside Meadows to the fields of Iowa, the Long Island potatoes to Iowa potatoes. There was a silence, during which he must have looked at the cloudless sky, the sun hitting the edge of the neighbour's rain gutter, because after a while he compared the sky to the one back home, how it felt standing in a field as though on a tabletop, looking in every direction to see the sky so near the ground. "Like a huge bowl," he said.

Walter came home to find the two of them still sitting on the front steps, Tom chewing his Fudgsicle stick. Daisy rushed out to introduce them. Walter shook hands calmly enough, though

Daisy noticed a small vein ticking in his right temple. "A friend of Keiko's. You don't say. Come on in then. Stay for supper—you've made enough, haven't you, Daisy?"

At the table Tom caught Keiko's eye, pointed to the blue Pyrex bowl piled high with steaming white potatoes. Potatoes—his special interest, Daisy thought. Oh, dear. But then he reached out his fingers to touch the deep blue of the bowl. "That's the colour of the Iowa sky at dusk," he said softly.

He smiled at her.

And through the thick mask of bandages she smiled back.

Often Keiko rested in the afternoon—lying on her made bed, or on the couch, while Daisy brought her Jell-O or soup. If she was sleeping, the neighbourhood wives gathered on the front steps, not wanting to disturb her. They whispered about her condition—was she healing, under those thick bandages? They asked about the exact status of the graft, the catgut sutures, but there was little Daisy could tell them. She had never seen beneath the bandages. It was, she told the women, a surgical task to unroll those layers of cotton gauze, open Keiko's face to the light, wipe away the peroxide cream, clean the sutures with a Q-tip. It required Dr. Carney. The women nodded. Dr. Carney came three times a week, and the women became used to seeing his mushroom-coloured coupe driving down Linden Street.

"You'd better get Fran a chair," Joan said one afternoon as they sat on the steps. "She doesn't fit there any more."

Daisy sprang up to fetch a deck chair from behind the house, but Fran reached up and squeezed her hand. "Don't bother, I can't stay. Ed's expected. Ooh!" She squirmed and held her belly.

Joan looked at Daisy. "The baby's kicking," she said, holding Daisy's eyes a fraction longer than necessary, those eyes of Joan's, with their violent flecks of black against the blue. Daisy had read in a magazine that dark flecks in an iris showed trauma, each spot marking a time of pain.

"I felt my baby kick once," Daisy said. "Just once. I think it was the baby anyway. It felt like champagne fizzing in my stomach."

"That's what it feels like at first," Joan said.

"Here—feel now." Fran leant back, elbows propped on the step and pulled up her checked shirt. Daisy put her palm to the taut skin, covered in tiny pale hairs, while Joan watched proprietarily. The movement was sudden and sharp against her palm and Daisy jumped. Joan laughed.

"That was his heel," Fran said.

45.

LATE AFTERNOON. Late summer. Fran wrapped a strand of Keiko's hair onto one of the foam rollers from her home permanent set, clipping a strand of it in place. She worked slowly. Keiko's hair was fine, and though it had grown since she had arrived, it only brushed her shoulders.

They had just heard on the radio that a group of housewives outside Chicago had begun to collect children's teeth to protest atomic testing. So far they had collected a hundred. They planned to get them tested for strontium-90.

Slowly, carefully, Fran wrapped another strand of Keiko's wet hair around a roller.

"And what is the Hiroshima Project doing?" Irene's voice speaking to Daisy on the telephone had been squeaky, out of control. "They're collecting teeth and we're doing nothing. Am I the only one who notices any more? You know," Irene added, musingly,

"I've never heard Keiko say an actual word about the bomb. Not once in all this time. How do we even know it was the bomb that damaged her face? Maybe she was caught in the firebombing in Tokyo. You know it caused more destruction than Hiroshima? Maybe she's not a war victim at all. Maybe she burnt herself with a pot of soup." There was a pause. Irene was probably searching for her cigarettes. Daisy heard the click of Irene's lighter. She was high up in her *Sunday Review* office, probably standing by the window, looking out at the people far below on the street. They'd be small—not the size of ants, but miniature people nonetheless.

"Maybe she never planned to speak, have you thought of that? Maybe she always planned just to come here, get her face fixed—an operation costing us, what? Thousands of dollars— and then leave. Go back to Japan. Go to hairdressing school." Irene laughed.

"You're not being fair."

Again Daisy heard her drag on her cigarette. "She's a sly one."

"I have to go," Daisy said.

"Yes, you go—but make sure she knows she'll be speaking at any number of public venues soon. And remind her about the H-bomb, will you? It can kill three hundred times more people than the bomb dropped on Hiroshima. Shouldn't that mean something to her?"

In the kitchen, Keiko was standing behind Fran now. On the table they had laid out the things they needed to do each other's hair: rollers, bobby pins, hairspray, setting lotion, barrettes. Daisy watched as Keiko parted Fran's hair down the centre, then parted it again, from the centre to the ear, rolling the strand in a sponge. She wore Walter's pale blue cardigan, the one with leather patches at the elbows. Under the sweater she had on a loose housedress that Joan Palmer had given to her—rayon, with forget-me-nots in blurry bunches.

"That was Irene."

Daisy waited, but neither Fran nor Keiko said a thing. Keiko squeezed some blue setting solution onto a plate, and then combed it through Fran's red hair. She wrapped a strand in a foam curler and clipped it. Daisy could imagine the pleasant weight of it on Fran's scalp.

Daisy looked hard at Keiko, but she was studying the sponge on one of the rollers. She's sly, Irene had said. A word that sounded like what it meant: thin and wily, able to change shape according to what was called for. Daisy watched Keiko's fingers on the sponge-roller, her soft nails, almost like a baby's. She remembered Fran saying that the best way to cut a baby's nails was to bite them off as the baby slept, rather than using scissors.

46.

THE DAYS WERE LONG NOW. Pale light streamed through the window at 4:00 a.m., followed by bursts of robin song. Night didn't fall until after nine. On days Walter went to town, Daisy would ask if Keiko wanted to walk to the store, or drive to the beach. But as often as not Keiko declined, saying she was tired. She would have one of her long showers, then the rounds of visitors began. Fran, with Patti under her arm. (*Can Keiko come out to play?* That was what Fran's visits were like.) Then Joan and Evelyn, carrying platters of squares or brownies, wanting the strange taste of Daisy's house, which was better than a lunchtime gin and tonic. Then along sauntered Tom, strolling up Linden Street from the train station.

Daisy watched Keiko, noticing how easy she was with them all. There was something missing in her during these daylight hours. Then, when Walter arrived home, Keiko's orbit again subtly switched, as they talked in low voices on the back porch, or in the living room.

"Will you work on your book tonight?" Keiko's voice.

Daisy was in the kitchen, whisking lemon and eggs for a mayonnaise. She couldn't hear Walter's reply for the life of her, though she strained to hear. Anyway, he wasn't writing any more. He must have hit a snag, or he just preferred this—to laugh quietly, out of her hearing, to speak quietly, letting his words form as they would. Any shape acceptable. Daisy thought of the invisible horses moving steadily into the movie theatre—how hard he had laughed at that simple idea.

More whispering. More.

Daisy put down the bowl, spilling mayonnaise on her dress, and went to the living room. They were sitting on the couch, a magazine spread on their laps. It showed a picture of a television set—a ruby console, burnished cherrywood. He looked shyly at Daisy, as though caught in an act he couldn't altogether explain.

Cherrywood, the ad said, real veneer.

"A television!" she said, as though it was the first time such an idea had ever occurred to her. "But you're a radio man, aren't you, Walter?"

He shrugged, sheepish, but full of sly mischief too, as he must have been in the days before she knew him, out on the town with David Greenberg, throwing rocks at Trixie Baxter's window.

After dinner Walter walked, as he always did, out the door, past the turnpike. She imagined territory more alien than anything in the triangle of Riverside Meadows, Stoney Creek and the Parkway. She imagined pine forests, the earth covered in thick layers of needles.

✻

That was how their days went, but nighttime was different. More than once, at midnight, or one in the morning, Daisy would be woken by Keiko calling out, fumbling at the window latch. Daisy went to her. Because of the sleepwalking she had to go. She sat beside the girl and spoke to her softly, lulling her back to sleep. Once, while Daisy sat at the end of the bed, rubbing Keiko's feet, the girl said, *You are like my mother.* But, of course, Daisy knew better, because of the photograph: such a pretty mother, and so slender. Still, she liked the idea.

"How so?" she asked. "Is my face like hers?"

"Your expression. It is your expression."

There were other conversations too. At night, her bandaged face turned to the wall, Keiko said all sorts of things she didn't say in the daytime, as though night had erased the distinction between them. Perhaps Dr. Carney had been right about one thing, even as he was wrong about most: the pressure to tell her story seemed to have started a flow in her. There was so little time left now, before the bandages would come off and the speaking tour would begin—and Keiko seemed, almost, to be rehearsing what she might say, lightly circling closer to the unthinkable.

She had come all the way to Manhattan to erase the scar, but there were things, after all, that couldn't be left behind. She had stolen a lipstick. She had lied to get out of school. Later, she had walked to the bridge—the bridge near the Inari shrine. When people asked for water, she had said sorry, no, I am looking for my mother. Forgive me, I can't. The bridge was at the centre of the worst memories—that much was clear.

"You're young," Daisy said. "You don't realize that now, but you are." She wanted Keiko to understand that things can be left behind, no matter how terrible. To illustrate what she meant, she described her miscarriages. She didn't go into detail: it wasn't to expiate her own sorrow that she spoke, but only to help the girl see how the healing could happen. She described the baby—how something had been wrong with it, which she was sure she herself must have caused. How it was taken from her before she could hold it, or cover its face with a handkerchief.

Keiko was silent a long time.

"Did you say a prayer?" she asked at last.

"There wasn't time. But if I could have, I would have said a prayer."

"Tell me what you would have said."

"I'm not sure. Something from chapel."

Again she was silent, absorbing every word. Then she said, "You would have covered its face with a handkerchief?"

"Yes, Keiko. That is what I would have done."

She lay down beside Keiko in the bed, Keiko making room for her, their two heads on the same pillow.

Her speech must have had its effect, because Keiko began to speak about what Dr. Carney and the others had done to her at the hospital. Done or not done. From one angle it was all quite normal, just the sort of treatment any medical establishment would give a Hiroshima survivor in a hospital. From another angle, it was darker. Everything was like that now: carrying a double shadow, so that you could never be sure if what you saw was strange or natural.

That first day in hospital the nurses had had her take her clothes off: a perfectly normal preliminary. She had stripped, folding her clothes neatly, placing them on the orange chair. Then she had lain on the table, covering herself with a sheet. The table was cold and gave her goosebumps.

When Dr. Carney came in, he told her to put her feet in the stirrups. "It's routine," he smiled, but Keiko had never heard of this routine before. "This will only take a minute," he said, and then he lifted the sheet and she could feel one of his hands, surprisingly warm, palpitating her stomach, while the other found the mouth of her opening. While she stared at the wall, something cold slipped deep inside, pressing against interior walls. She spoke in Japanese, forgetting her English: *Why are you doing this?*

He breathed hard through his nose and mouth. She had stared at the ceiling, counting, as the doctor pushed open her legs and felt inside with his hard, despotic hands, searching for whatever he was searching for. After a while he had left, with his metal shoehorn and his scrapings. The nurse came back and told her to get dressed.

That was what Dr. Carney had done to her: a routine physical exam.

Daisy tried to explain that such things were standard in America, but Keiko did not reply. Instead she said, "After the operation, he asked me questions."

She paused, took a breath, and then continued.

"It was Dr. Carney. And sometimes he brought two other men. They started with questions about me," she said. "About how I felt. I said I felt fine. I was in my bed, and they sat in chairs, facing me. They wanted me to talk about how it was—on the day. They asked me, Do I think about it all the time or just sometimes?"

In fits and starts she told Daisy what had happened.

There were three of them: Carney and two men connected with the Atomic Energy Commission. They told her that if she co-operated it would be easy, the session didn't need to take long, it depended on her. When she was silent, Dr. Carney reminded her that recounting her experiences was part of her signed contract with the Project. Didn't she remember?

And she did. She did remember.

At first she was reluctant. She closed her eyes. It seemed impossible, but for a long period of time she fell asleep. This had to do with the painkillers, she thought, but she wasn't sure. Then her mother whispered that she must save herself—as she had several times, pinching her lips, counselling her, when Keiko couldn't go on. Without even willing it, she began to talk about her grandfather, about standing on the bridge, about the shrine, the words coming easily, flowing and roaming and sliding from their hidden thickets.

After a while they asked how she felt.

"I feel bad," she said.

"Why bad?"

She told them about the many bad things she had done and they wrote them down. They seemed to like it when she said that—that was the kind of thing they were looking for. So she told them about the seeds.

"What kind of seeds?" they asked.

"Black seeds."

"What are they like?"

"Bad."

"Describe."

"*Shi no hai.*"

And when they asked what that meant, she said, *Ashes of death.* All three of them wrote that down.

They questioned her for a long time. Keiko was not sure how long. They asked what she felt about herself. She said she felt as though she was not there any more.

"Invisible?"

This she could not answer.

"Tell us about the seeds again," they said.

"I have bad seeds in me."

Someone noted that the play *The Bad Seed* was playing on Broadway. Dr. Carney frowned.

Describe the seeds, he said.

ark, "she said. "All inside my skin. They make me a

_b victim," Dr. Carney explained to the others.

"Why do you call them the bad seeds?"

"Because I didn't take Ojii-chan his lunch box. Because I lived when they died. Because of the fox woman on the bridge."

"What woman?"

"The woman who sat at the end of the bridge."

Dr. Carney wrote this down.

"Was it your mother?" he asked softly. "Did you find your mother at the end of the bridge?"

Keiko shook her head. Not answering.

When she had spoken for a long time, the men left. She woke to a nurse yanking open the blinds. She took Keiko's pulse, then told her it was time for her medication. "You're a lucky girl," she said, "coming here for surgery."

When Keiko was done telling Daisy this, Daisy sat up and looked down at the girl's face lit by the porch light, the ribs of the coverlet palely glowing.

> *Describe the burns on this woman's back.*
> *What does it feel like to carry these seeds in you?*
> *Tell us why you are bad, Keiko. Tell us, we want to understand.*
> *Why did you say that a fox woman waited for you? What does this refer to?*
> *Tell us.*

Daisy caught hold of Keiko's hands. She told her that Walter and she would stop anyone from asking her another question. And Joan and Fran and the others—they would stop Dr. Carney and the men from the Atomic Energy Commission. In fact, Daisy said, all she had to do was talk to Dean Atchity. "He can't possibly know what Dr. Carney is doing."

The back porch light was on, and it poured through the bedroom window, so that she could see Keiko's eyes, quite clearly, turned towards her. Her irises looked empty, like mirrors.

"As long as you're here with us," Daisy whispered, "you'll be safe."

"Thank you, Mrs. Lawrence."

47.

TOM WALKED KEIKO down Linden Street. It was still light out, the end of a long summer afternoon, five days until the bandages would be removed. Jimmy Jr. ran by. "Hey, Tom!" he called out.

"Where you off to?"

"Joey's place. Look it." The boy took a red baseball card from his pocket. It showed Mickey Mantle holding his bat. Over his shoulder was the broad blue sky. Tom whistled.

"I traded three Mayses for it."

"You reckon Mantle is three times as good?"

"Naw, I just didn't have his card yet. Now I've got everyone but Campanella, Mathews and Jackie Robinson."

Tom could have stayed and talked about baseball, but he saw that Keiko wasn't interested, and so he said goodbye and they walked on. People called to them from their houses. An old couple who lived halfway down the block waved to them. A dog barked. The three-legged cat crossed a lawn. No longer lit directly by the sun, the grass had taken on a rich, cold colour.

At the corner where Linden Street met the crescent, Evelyn Lithgow was out front potting a geranium.

"Evening, ma'am," Tom said.

She came towards them, wiping dirt on her black-and-green tartan apron.

"Where you off to?"

"Creek."

"Not much good walking around here. It's more fun in the city, I guess."

They walked on. Tom thought of it as a ceremony: tipping his hat every third house or so, saluting the neighbours, whose names he was beginning to know; the sound of the sprinklers optimistically ticking; the ringing of the Good Humor bell several streets away. At the school some teenagers were smoking in the basketball court. The girls wore dungarees rolled up at the cuff, tight blouses accentuating their pointy breasts, high ponytails. One of the boys took out his comb and pulled it through his hair, before slipping it into the front pocket of his jeans, a provocative gesture. He said something mocking, and the girls laughed. Yes, that was there too: laughter ringing off the bricks, and the sound of Keiko's feet as they stayed their course, stepping across the gravel, veering away from these children. He took her arm and felt her wince.

"Does it hurt today?"

"Only a little."

It wasn't because her face hurt that she had flinched. She saw herself in her skirt and cashmere sweater, clothing donated by the Atchitys, and she saw them in their rolled jeans and sleeveless blouses and sneakers, teenager clothes, and she thought about how she must look, face outlandishly wrapped, walking with her arm in the arm of her suitor.

American kids. She had seen them from the train, and in the

lineup for Frank Sinatra, and pushing each other in the shadow of the El, the boys with cigarette packages rolled in their T-shirt sleeves. It was hard to look at them; if they noticed her she averted her gaze or they would laugh, or stare, or—worst of all—look alarmed, as though she were a monster, wrapped in her bandages.

She was a teenager too. As she grew stronger, this fact seemed to have grown in importance. She read the copies of *Seventeen Magazine* Mrs. Lawrence had left in her bedroom. In one of them there was a picture of a girl sitting on a bed, wearing rolled jeans, a striped shirt, painting her toenails red while laughing into the telephone. Her lips formed an ooh of surprise, as though some-body had said something shocking and funny. Kissable lips, that was what they called lips like that. The girl had taken long-playing records out of their slipcovers and strewn them all around her bed.

Keiko stepped along the path that led to the creek, through the yellow grass, towards the old bridge so like the bridge from home. She was imagining the duck-tailed boy holding her face, kissing her the way they did in the movies, thoroughly, taking his time.

At the creek Tom told her about the barn silvered with age, the chickens, Emmy's effort, for a full summer, to train Clover to roll over. As he spoke she glanced back, past the marsh, towards the embankment. Twilight had opened the fields and grasses, and she wondered if the duck-tailed boy had come to the edge of the playing field, if he was looking down at her, even now.

48.

DAISY STOOD AT THE WINDOW, staring out on the street even after Tom and Keiko had rounded the crescent. Tom wasn't so bad to have around. In fact, Daisy liked him. He was kind and easy, and he accepted, in a way Fran and Joan didn't, that she was the one who knew Keiko best. He would sidle up to her quietly while Keiko was in the bathroom and ask if she supposed Keiko might like to go to the movies, or if she might prefer just to go for a walk. As though Daisy had the puzzle pieces in her hand. It was too bad that Keiko seemed, at least on the surface, interested only in the novelty of him. There was no drawing together—not that Daisy had seen.

"You talk too much about your sister," Daisy had said once. Jabbing at him a bit, to see what would happen.

"Oh, I know. I can see it ain't a good topic. Nor the farm either. I'm still trying to figure out what interests her."

"Why don't you talk about hair?" she had said. "It seems to work for Fran."

Each morning the girl was again dryly talkative and friendly and aloof—the shell of what she was at night. And so Daisy could not imagine grasping her hand, as she ate her eggs in the kitchen, bending down, swearing to keep her safe. She was afraid Keiko might look up at her, every part of her bandaged except her bright, incurious eyes, and say, "I'm sorry, Mrs. Lawrence. I don't know what you mean."

Or perhaps a frisson of alarm would pass over her—what had her Aunt Nancy called it?—as though a goose had walked over your grave: that might be how Keiko would look if Daisy were to bring up what transpired in that closed room, at night.

Tell me, she had said. She meant August 6, tell me about August 6. They went so far each night, not to the actual day itself, but around the dappled edges of it. Frogs call. Dripping stone. Then Keiko might turn her face to the wall, severely upset, and mention the seeds that, at least in this small bed, represented the very texture of her suffering. She told Daisy of her mother's name for her: Kitsune-chan, little fox child. She spoke of being bad for having stolen the lipstick. Daisy tried to soothe her. It was nothing, she would say. Something anyone would do. She told Keiko about finding the Goldenloaf Cheese box, just to show how these small thieveries, which seemed so wicked from the inside, meant nothing to Daisy. Keiko held her breath. Then her voice, just that once, came out coldly.

"You *looked* in my drawer?"

"I had to—but, you see, nobody blames you."

A pause. During which Keiko let this disturbance, this small revelation, sink back, disappear.

"Tell me again about your baby," Keiko had said then.

Daisy—moved—had told her story again: the dead child taken from her; the small handkerchief that she might have laid over its mottled face.

But in the morning Keiko came into the kitchen with her head down, avoiding Daisy's eyes, then made her way to the bathroom, where she washed for a long time, using all the hot water. It wasn't as though she didn't remember—no, no. She remembered. But it seemed to Daisy there were two sides to Keiko now: the side wandering down the street with Tom— the bright, shyly talkative, hair-curling girl; and the nighttime side. Both were using all their subtle strength to discover what to do next.

That night Daisy woke to voices, though at first she was sure she had been woken by the brightness of the moon. It had travelled around the house and now it poured through the window and onto the bed, a blind spray of light.

Then she heard it again: Keiko's voice flat, a counterpoint to his. His was a surprise: it went on and on; it rose and fell;

Daisy kept expecting the words to end, but they kept going. She listened—listened so acutely that her ear might have been a knot in the wall. The hum of their voices reminded her of her parents, many years before, their voices rising and falling in their bedroom.

She got up, her body hot, sweat between her breasts. She knew with the instinct of a survivor that Walter had always been kindest with the most broken, and that Keiko would use that knowledge, as skilfully as every night she drew Daisy in. Oh, she felt sick waves of knowing: they coursed through her body, black splotches of knowledge. What kind of a woman invited another woman into her house, a beautiful, vulnerable victim of the war, and left her alone with her husband for days? What had Daisy been doing? What had she been trying to prove? It was as though she had asked for this to happen.

They were not in the kitchen, though his many cigarette butts were in the Bakelite ashtray. Their voices came from out back. When Daisy thrust open the screen door, they were sitting a good two feet apart from one another. He was reading from a book on his lap, and she was listening. Daisy had seen that look on Walter's face before: a sheepish smile, a mouth not straight, an expression sliding towards innocence, but not there, not yet.

"What's going on?"

"I'm reading Keiko something."

He was reading a passage from Arthur Koestler's book *The God that Failed*. But now that Daisy was standing in the doorway in her nightgown, there seemed to be no point in continuing.

"It's all right," Daisy said. "I'm not staying."

She got a glass of water at the sink and went back to the bedroom. But once there she crept back along the hallway, kneeling, listening. She caught the smell of Walter's cigarette. He took a long drag, then butted it out on the stair and threw it into the backyard. The moon broke into pieces on the greenhouse roof; the dog in Stoney Creek howled; then the girl spoke, yes, that was the voice of Keiko, such a strange chill voice, so like the voice the moon might have had if it could speak: blue and white, liquid, without variation. "Yes," she said. "I understand what you are saying."

Daisy could see his darkened eye sockets. He snapped his jaw twice, blowing two perfect smoke rings. "I thought you'd get it," he said.

"I do."

"We were lit up," he said. *Lit up.* A pause.

"We burnt," he added, "with righteousness."

"Will you put these things in your book?"

He shook his head. "No, Keiko," he said gently. "I don't think so."

He was hunched forward now—doing what? Pressing his fingers to his forehead, digging the nails in hard. He spoke so softly Daisy could barely hear. Neither could Keiko, because a second later, he spoke again, more loudly.

"I knew I was lying." His mouth was turned down bitterly at the edges. "Some part of me always knew—but I told myself that lying was important, that twisting the truth was part of what we did, the price we paid—gladly, we paid it gladly. It was our biggest contribution, you might say. They were shooting our comrades by the thousands, in back alleys, while here in New York, I signed a letter, a letter published in *The New York Times,* condemning another fellow who had dared to say that the trials were a frame-up."

He reached into his back pocket, flipped open his wallet and took out the photograph. He handed it to Keiko the way, years before on the park bench, he had shown it to Daisy—David, a swath of brown hair across his forehead, a tight-lipped grin, sleek eyes, almost like slits.

"Your friend."

"They said he was a Trotskyite ring leader. *Zhid. Zhid.* They kept saying that, over and over, as they beat him with rifles."

"How do you know these things?"

He smiled, close-lipped. "Girl we knew, Trixie Baxter, was with him. She wasn't killed—she hid on the fire escape."

"I am so sorry."

"They made him confess first."

He looked at the stars, holding his breath, and the girl, who had listened in such a calm way, like a slice of the moon, leaned forward, put out her hand, touched his knee.

"Had him kneel on the floor. Confess he had exhibited individualistic tendencies. That he was a Trotskyite, an enemy of the working class, a foreign spy. He had to repent every crazy fool idea that had sprung from that mouth of his.

"David was always a good talker, I can only imagine how he must have talked that night—trying to save his life."

At four o'clock in the morning, Daisy was woken by Walter moving around in the backyard. He was making a lot of noise. She knew he must have been drinking, just by the number of crashes and bangs of garbage lids or other things with percussive metal sides. Daisy put on her quilted housecoat and went to the back door and looked out. He had a stack of his papers in a wheelbarrow, and he was throwing pages into the incinerator—a metal can by the back fence—pouring a bottle of rum on the contents, watching them burn. He was laughing and talking to himself and whistling too: the five piercing notes of *The Whistler*. Then he started to sing, "*Mairzy doats and dozy doats and liddle lamzy-divey.*" Daisy knew the song. It sounded like nonsense, but slowed down it was:

Mares eat oats
And does eat oats
And little lambs eat ivy

Daisy grabbed a bucket from under the sink, filled it half full, then ran with it down the steps and across the lawn, flinging water into the incinerator, which made the manuscript both burnt and sodden. Still, she tried, while he stepped back grog-gily and looked at her, tsk-tsking, as though she didn't under-stand what was happening, but give her time and the truth was bound to hit. Then he lay down on the lawn.

Daisy stood looking at him. The moon poured down, full as anything. "You're going to regret this," she said at last, hating the parsimonious tone in her voice.

Walter appeared not to be breathing.

"You told the girl things you never told me."

Again no response.

"I'm sorry he's dead."

"You knew."

"Not everything."

"Enough."

He stopped looking at the stars and looked at her face. His was lit by the moon, but hers was in shadow.

"Was it every page?" she whispered. "Every page in the incin-erator?"

"Think so."

"Because you told it to the girl—and that was enough."

He laughed, a sharp bark. Then he made a grab for her ankle. But she dodged away.

His face, lit by the moon, looked both old and young—his eyes were young, but his chin was covered in a glint of salt-and-pepper bristles. He wore a small, goofy smile, which Daisy remembered from way back. Always pleasant when drunk, that was Walter. He wasn't one of those angry drunks.

"I'll tell you everything," Walter said. "Just come over here."

She knelt beside him.

"C'mon."

She sat. The lawn felt surprisingly warm against her legs and buttocks, in her light cotton nightgown.

He pulled her down next to him, head to his chest, then stroked her hair. They lay in silence for a while. A few orange sparks floated up from the incinerator.

"You know," he said, "I knew a playwright once who had the misfortune of also being a teacher. A student came into his class one morning, said he'd burnt his novel—all three hundred pages. So his teacher said, 'That's the best bit of work you've done all year.'"

He gave her a dry kiss on the top of her head. "I've missed you," he whispered. "Miss Daisy, I've missed you something fearful."

49.

THREE DAYS UNTIL THE BANDAGES WERE REMOVED.

Walter prepared for work—pale, sober, smelling of hair tonic and last night's debauch. As he ate his poached egg, Daisy asked how he felt.

"Never better." He pushed back his chair. She thought he looked raw, unprotected, without the massive buttress of his manuscript holding him up. What must it feel like, nothing but air all around him? She would have liked to tell him he was brave, but she was afraid to focus his mind on the enormity of what he'd done.

At the door she stood on her toes and kissed him hard. He looked at her like she was kidding, a twisted smile on his mouth.

"What's that for?"

"Don't know. Just felt like it." She kissed him again, too hard, feeling her teeth against his. "There's more where that came from," she said, knowing it was a corny line, something from *The Whistler*. He seemed to think so too, because he lifted his eyebrows and gave a low whistle between his teeth. Then he raised his hat, stepped out the door and was gone.

Daisy knocked on the girl's bedroom door. Keiko had had her shower and was lying on her neatly made bed, leafing through the Mary Marvel comic book Daisy had given her at the hospital. She looked up at Daisy. Such pretty fragile fingers, holding the comic book. Those were the fingers, the parched little palms, that had reached out to touch Walter's knee as he confessed, his face contorted, grim and miserable.

"You were up late."

"Yes." She sat up and placed the comic book neatly on top of the lace doily on the bedside table. "I was talking to Mr. Lawrence."

There—she had said it plain as plain.

"You like him, don't you?"

"Oh, yes."

Daisy couldn't really read her expression, because of the bandages. All she could do was guess, based on her eyes.

"He's a good man," Daisy said.

"Oh yes. I think he is very good."

A pause. There seemed to be nothing more to say. She was a child. He had confessed to a child—and now that child sat looking up at Daisy, wanting, no doubt, to be left alone.

"Would you like to come to the store with me?"

"Thank you, Mrs. Lawrence, but I am tired."

Please, she wanted to say. *Please come. We can lean over the bridge. You can tell me about being like your mother.* "Are you sure? We could pick up Popsicles."

"Thank you, Mrs. Lawrence, I will stay. I will do the dishes."

"Don't worry about them."

"I would like to."

After all this time, they were still so formal. Now Daisy had to go to the store alone, knowing that Keiko was avoiding her.

"You'll be all right on your own?"

"Yes, Mrs. Lawrence, thank you."

Daisy came close to her, to remove the water glass from beside the bed. Keiko smelled of the sandalwood soap that Daisy kept in the medicine cabinet. A gift from her mother, sent from California. For a second this small betrayal shocked Daisy. Keiko must have taken that soap from its box, a long box with a picture of a steamboat on the outside, removed the paper seal, unwrapped the tissue from a virgin bar, seeing, as she did this, the imprint of the honeycomb perfectly etched on the face of the soap. Then she must have rubbed the bar all over her skin, on her hands, under her arms. *Daisy's* sandalwood. Perhaps she had had that gentle fragrance on her skin the night before, talking to Walter. Daisy had been saving that soap! She left the girl alone.

As she walked down the path to the store, she thought about Keiko. She could still smell the bitter, slightly powdery scent of the soap in her nostrils, and wished she had checked, before she left, how much of the pattern had been washed away. But the soap wasn't important. Nor, in the end, was Keiko's closeness to Walter. Daisy remembered how he had lain on the grass, drunk, then reached for her ankle and pulled her down beside him. No, what mattered was something deeper, to do with the three of them. That by doing the right thing, again and again and again— tiny acts of love or belief or contrition—they seemed able to reach towards each other. Daisy was definitely closer to the girl than ever, though their communication, at least in the daytime, was based more on how they stood, heads inclining towards each other when they were in a group, or how Keiko's light fingers might touch Daisy's as she handed her a dish she had dried. It was, Daisy thought, as though people's souls had shadows, and Daisy had slipped inside of Keiko's, or perhaps Keiko had slipped inside of Daisy's—neither of them meaning to, both of them fighting it, especially at first.

As Daisy walked, a bubble of an idea came to her, though in truth it had been there for some time. Why not have Keiko stay with them, not just for this short time, but actually stay, settle in Riverside Meadows, go to college even? She could take the commuter train in the morning. Daisy imagined saying goodbye to both Keiko and Walter at the front door, wiping her hands on her apron, bustling off to clean up after breakfast. Neither of them were particularly neat. She would talk to Walter about this, but already she was sure he would agree. He was, as she had said to the girl, a good man.

The plum leaves hissed as the wind passed through their branches. They seemed to be speaking an alien and interesting language, echoed by the murmur of the poplar windbreak on the other side of Old Middle Road. She saw the stark image of three crows on the line. Joan waved from her window, and her face seemed alive, the pores of her skin made of something shiny. Not that her skin wasn't pouched and reddened: it was aging and prone to wrinkles, as everyone's was; but it looked radiant too, in its way, as she raised her feather duster and waved it at Daisy.

At Strickland's, Daisy leaned over the freezer, trying to decide between lime- or grape-flavoured Popsicles. Lime seemed the best choice. As she straightened up, clutching the Popsicles, she glimpsed a streak of white in the parking lot. It was Fran, scuttling crabwise between the parked cars, past buggies, slapping the door open with the palm of her hand. It rang violently, startling Gerald Strickland from his crossword. "Easy on my door, Mrs. Warburgh," he said.

"Have you seen Daisy Lawrence?"

Fran's pregnant belly stuck out in her red stretch pants and short white blouse. She saw Daisy and rushed down the aisle. "Come right away," she gasped, taking her arm. "It's Ed—Ed and Keiko."

They tore out of the store, through the parking lot, and they were on the corn path before they slowed down and Fran spoke again. "He says he's had enough of our highjinks. He's gone to talk with Keiko. I said no, he couldn't, but he said he wasn't going to stand for her being here any more. It's because of the sickness."

"What sickness?"

"Oh God." Her face was red from the running. She bent over, hands on her knees, panting.

"Tell me."

"I'm so sorry, Daisy."

"For what?"

"It's just a misunderstanding," she said. She was a hundred per cent to blame. "I ought to have stood up to him—but I was scared."

Ed had stayed home from work because he felt sick. He was lying on the sofa when Junie came out of her bedroom, where she had been playing with cutouts from the Sear's catalogue. "Look at my feet," she had screamed. "Look at my feet!" She pointed to a slough of red dots between her first and second toes. "I have what Keiko has," Junie shrieked, "I have the A-bomb disease!" Then she doubled over, squirming as though something live were wriggling through her guts. A stream of yellow vomit forced itself from her lips.

"Like pee," Fran said to Daisy. "That colour."

Fran ran to call the doctor, but she couldn't find the number. Jimmy Jr., eating Shreddies in the kitchen, began to search the backs of his arms for red dots and knocked his bowl to the floor. Then Junie threw up again. Fran rushed to Patti in her playpen. Her forehead was burning. Fran stripped off her bibbed rompers and discovered a mass of red pustules on her bottom. Ed thundered about quarantine, A-bomb disease and then Patti threw up too—a real projectile vomit, hitting the fridge with a splat.

"Not regular throw up—it was corn-coloured. Well, I took a hard look at Patti's rear end, and then I said to Ed, 'They're chicken pox, that's all. Look,' I said to him, 'the only person who has to be scared of chicken pox is me, cause I'm pregnant, but I've had them before. So there's no risk.' But Ed wasn't listening any more. He said it was time he and the Jap girl next door had a conversation. I couldn't stop him, Daisy, I'm so sorry."

Later Daisy will not remember crossing the second field, only the sound of her feet on the bridge, three hard steps. She easily outdistanced Fran, sprinting up the embankment and through the playground, where some teenaged girls were lighting bits of grass on fire. A premonition was pumping through her blood, as though beneath all her good plans, she had been waiting for this moment. She ran up the front path, threw open the door, calling out for Keiko.

She stopped to listen.

Voices came from the back porch, steady and cool. Daisy went through to the kitchen. Ed was standing beside a deck chair, looking down at Keiko. Two glasses of ice water sat beside the chairs, at their feet. Ed's face, that big pumpkin head of his, was pink, and his neck was pink, and his throat was red, wattled and textured from the sun. Daisy could smell his sweat: like old potatoes and something crisp, oniony. The scent of his adrenalin.

When he saw Daisy he muttered, "I'm going to go now," then he walked down the porch steps two at a time and crossed the lawn. He closed the back gate with a yank that made it spring back open.

Keiko sat looking at her hands, bandages shining in the morning sunlight.

"I couldn't find anything to offer but water."

"What did he say to you?" Daisy knelt and took her hands. She called her my dear, and my darling, and other things, which later she would not remember having said—only the string of words, coming from deep within her. "He doesn't know you," Daisy whispered. "Ignore him."

"No," Keiko said in a clear, low voice. "I didn't mind what he said."

This was what had happened:

Ed had flung himself across the front lawn, leaving Fran terrified, with no recourse but to run and get Daisy. He knocked at the door, ready to see for himself this girl whose presence caused him such grief. He would tell her she was a source of disease in his community, although he knew full well that his kids had the chicken pox. Still, there she was, trailing her mortality like a curse through Riverside Meadows, and he planned to tell her what was on his mind. Or perhaps that was all just bluster and show; perhaps he only thought he would say such things, and underneath another tide was taking him towards a different place.

Keiko was still in her bedroom. When she heard the knock, she got up and pulled on her robe, thinking, perhaps, that it was Tom. She fiddled at the latch, then opened the door.

Ed looked at her bandaged face, her frightened eyes, the pretty hand that held the door. He hesitated, the bluster receding from him like a dank tide. She let him in, telling him that Mrs. Lawrence had gone to the store, but that she'd be back soon if he cared to wait. She knew that he wanted something from her, she could see it in his eyes, but she pretended he had simply come to call. He followed her down the hallway to the kitchen, his big hands dangling at his sides, while she opened the fridge and, finding nothing to give him, poured water into two tumblers, then cracked open the ice tray, placing two cubes in each glass, as she had seen Daisy do. She opened the door to the back porch, praying that Daisy would come home soon, and she and Ed Warburgh went out to sit on the chairs.

After a while Ed mentioned the fine weather.

She said yes, it was fine.

"You're lucky to see the place when it's so fine. It rained all last summer. Rained terrible."

"I have been lucky in the weather."

He had only a brief amount of time to say what he had to say. He looked away from her to the fence, his greenhouse roof, the hidden fallout shelter, deep now, with a floor of hard dirt, a few nasty roots poking from the sides, which he would have to cut out with a saw.

"You've been doing pretty good here, haven't you?" he said.

"I beg your pardon?"

"You've had it pretty good."

She didn't know what he meant so she said nothing, sitting still, mostly invisible—she knew that—because of the bandages. He didn't say much after that, just a few words to paint the picture. The sandy compound. A girl interpreter, real pretty, who watched a man die at roll call. Quite a thing. Quite a thing. His voice was low and confiding as he warmed to his point. Yes, quite a thing it was. Shocked a few of the men, to have such a pretty young thing around, watching men shot or kicked to death, or what have you. Kind of thing gets stuck in your brain afterwards.

"But do you know what I think?" He turned to her now, his face amiable. "I think you could have done that. Yep——" He nodded sagely. "If you had to. What do you think? I bet you could have."

She could not answer, and in the stillness that followed there was birdsong, a child screaming in a nearby house.

"All summer," Ed said, "I've been seeing you come and go. And I've thought that every single time—bet she could have. Bet she could have. And now I'm here, telling you all this—and you know what I'm thinking? This'll interest you, miss." He scratched his head, as though perplexed but pleased. "I probably could have done it too. I mean, if I had to. So there you are, miss. We ain't unalike at all. Probably the whole lot of us could have done it."

Keiko still said nothing, and Ed stood up in a leisurely sort of way, stretched his big arms over his head, then turned to face her, his body blocking the sun. He stood a while looking down at her, but she would not raise her eyes, nor show a touch of that humanity—or inhumanity for that matter—which he so craved. How long they were like that, she couldn't say. Then, strangely lithe for a stocky man, Ed bent, quick as quick, to take a sip from his water glass. His face came close to the girl's, his eyes met hers—and there it was, before she could stop herself. A flinch.

"Don't be startled," he whispered, unable to conceal a note of triumph in his voice. "Don't be startled, miss, I'm just like you."

And that was how Daisy found them—Ed standing over Keiko, who sat very still, and who said, when he was gone, quite gone: *I could only find water to serve him.*

Later that afternoon, while Keiko was resting, Fran came to the back door.

"She's not like he thought. He says she's just like everyone else. 'Well, if she's just like everyone else, why have you been giving us grief all summer?' I didn't say that, but I might have. I swear he makes me mad sometimes. Him and that place."

"Shamshuipo."

"Now he's gone to town. But tell me what happened—he won't say anything, except that they talked."

"I don't know."

"He must have scared her. I tell you, I've really had it. You want to know where he is now? He's watching girlie shows. And I bet he'll come home drunk. I think this may be the last straw, Daisy. I said to him, 'Why do you have to go running at people like that?' He just told me to shut up. Said he and the girl understood each other—which I doubt severely, he hardly knows a thing about her. He's telling me to shut up, but I'm not going to—not any more. If Keiko weren't here, I'd go to Tulsa, where my sister lives. I would."

"We should be quiet. She's resting."

It was just like Ed, she said, to panic on account of the chicken pox. "A-bomb disease! I don't know where he got a notion like that."

"But, Fran," Daisy felt moved to say. "You panicked too, you told me so. You thought it was something—just for a second." And so had Daisy, at least for a second, hearing about that spire of vomit shooting from Junie's lips.

"You're right," Fran said, and she began to blame herself, apologizing for having let herself think such a thing about Keiko, even for a moment. Not wanting to seem like Ed, who was, even that moment, drowning his memories at a strip show, in a bar with sawdust on the floor. "He thought Keiko was contagious," she snorted, shaking her head, reverting to ridicule.

Daisy shook her head too. Still, she thought, Ed may have been right about one thing, even as he was mostly wrong: there was something contagious about Keiko's presence. And for an instant she let herself imagine those tiny motes of radioactive dust—breathed in by Ed, by Fran, by Walter—mixing with each cargo of human frailties.

50.

MIREN-WO NOKORAZU. MIREN-WO NOKORAZU.

She had lit the wick of rush pith floating in the rapeseed oil. She had prayed to the *ihai* of Ojii-chan and Mama, at the ancestor shrine in Yoshiko's ugly hallway, covered in grey wall-paper. Suffer no regret for this world to linger with you. Do not go astray.

But the spirits had followed her here. They arrived in full force the night after the neighbour man bent so suddenly to look into her eyes, trying to see what was inside her: *Shi no hai,* ashes of death—what she carried inside her despite the surgery cutting away the scar, despite every attempt to leave the past behind.

How had he known?

Keiko imagined the ghosts floating across the icy Siberian Sea, following the misty clouds above lakes, making their way up tiny shrunken waterways, ditches, creeks, going through cis-terns to get past the highway, until at last they rubbed their invisible fingers against the window.

First there was Mama and Ojii-chan, pressing their palms against the pane, finding their way inside, trying out the metal pedal of the garbage can, wafting from room to room alarmed by the unfamiliar odours. But then there were the others, too many to count, clustered at the window or pushing under the door. There was the faceless woman on the bridge, whose skin hung from her wrists like empty gloves. She wanted water, but Keiko would have had to climb down under the bridge, near the grotto and the shrine. The faceless woman had clutched a dead child.

Mizu, she had said. Water.

Mizu is the cry on everyone's lips. But there is no water.

And then there were the new ones, who came because she dared to believe she could cross the world, escape: there was Emmy-Mae with her wheezing breath, and Joan's twin brother, whirling in the water like a black top, and now there was the interpreter, watching men die. *Bet you could do that*, he had said to her. The smell of the neighbour man, dank and bathroomy. The ghost of that woman was in the room now. And the babies were there too. They were the worst. Keiko could feel their fingers on the bedcovers.

She had said to Mrs. Lawrence that she would pray for the soul of her babies. *Suffer not the soul of the dead to linger near us.* When she said that, Mrs. Lawrence had started to cry. Not as film stars do in the movies, dignified tears falling down polished cheeks, but in gasps, like a fish coming out of the water. She had knelt by the bed and hugged Keiko so hard it had hurt.

"Nobody but you has offered to pray for them."

Suffer not thy souls to linger near me. She had said it to make them go away, but the ghosts, sitting at the end of the bed, had only gathered closer.

That evening Daisy came to Keiko's room. "Nothing Ed Warburgh said can mean anything," Daisy said. "He doesn't know you." Keiko leaned her head briefly against the older woman's collarbone. She asked Daisy to stay with her, and so Daisy sat on the floor beside

the bed and rubbed the girl's calves, which had cramps in them.
Then Keiko turned her face to the wall and began to speak. If
Daisy had chosen to write it all down, there would have been
much to record. Daisy asked her not to—she was sure, later, that
she had done this. Please, she had murmured. Don't. But Keiko
shook her head. And so Daisy rubbed her legs and listened.

Hiroshima is a city of many stories—that was how her grandfather
always started.

Keiko could have told Daisy a story about the shadowy world
before the bombing. She could have told about her mother and
grandfather; the garden full of frogs, or the green snakes along
the riverbank that ate the frogs at night. She could have told
about the path of uneven pebbles that ran past three large,
crooked stones, two of them moss-covered. She had heard
Mama teasing Grandfather one morning:

*Now tell me, Ojii-san, how is it you have this gift to encourage moss
to grow? What do you do?*

*My dear Sumiko, you ask a question to which I'm sure you know the
answer.*

Indeed, I do not.

*Ah well. I speak to the moss gently, and I rake leaves from its hair, and
I occasionally admonish it, much as you encourage your Kitsune-chan.
And after all that, it grows in spite of me.*

Yes, she laughed. That is like Keiko. She grows in spite of me too.

She could have told Daisy stories from that world. Hiroshima
was a city of many stories, that was what her grandfather had
believed, seeking in his quiet way to preserve the places that
existed below and beyond the Imperial dictates of official
Shintoism, with its massive new shrines.

But there is only one story left.

In the dark, with Daisy beside her, Keiko begins to rehearse it.

VI   BAKEMONO

51.

KEIKO SITS ON THE LOW STEP in the foyer. She can hear their neighbour, Takahura-san, in his front garden, trimming his azalea bushes. She licks the palm of her hand, sticky from the rice ball, and then steps out the door through which Mama disappeared only moments before. She climbs a rock she knows well, fat and moss-covered at the base, thinning to a ridge of granite at the top. Balancing on the ridge, she can lean against the wall, peer over the tiles and spy on Takahura-san. His back is to her, and he is trimming green sprigs from the limbs of an azalea. When he turns, he spots the top of her head outlined in shadow on the gravel. He bows elaborately.

"You are late, Keiko-san. School must have started by now."

"I don't have to go to school today, Mama said."

He raises his eyebrow, then takes off his cap and wipes his brow with the back of his hand.

"Hot already. Today will be scorching."

"I smell snow."

"Do you? You've got a keen nose then. Why are you home? Don't they need you girls moving rubble downtown?"

"I've been given a different job." She switches feet. It is difficult to balance and talk.

"Something top secret. A government job?"

"Mr. Takahura, why do you spend so much time on your bushes?"

He laughs.

"Does your daughter ask you to?"

"My daughter may be no lover of beauty, perhaps that is what you mean. But these azaleas must be trimmed, even in wartime. Otherwise when the war is over, nothing will be as it was."

He says this and then he looks troubled, and Keiko knows he wishes he had not spoken. Keiko has lost a father, albeit a father she hardly thinks of, but Mr. Takahura has lost nobody, having only one daughter. Yesterday she heard that daughter saying she wanted to go to Shikoku to stay with her aunt until she gives birth, to get away from the city and the heat. But Mr. Takahura told her there were no good doctors left on Shikoku, and besides—this he asserted strongly—Hiroshima was a safer place to be than an island.

"Why is Hiroshima safe?" Keiko says now.

Takahura-san pauses, the scissors raised in his right hand. "Hiroshima is like Kyoto," he says. "A city with a great history and an ancient castle. Throughout the world people recognize that it would be uncivilized to bomb such a place."

"That is not what you told me last time, Mr. Takahura."

Last time he had told her that Hiroshima would not be bombed because so many of its citizens had emigrated to America. They sent a special delegation from California to speak to Mr. Truman, he had said.

High above, over Keiko's left eyebrow, something glints in the sky. She turns to look, craning her neck, raising one hand to block the sun. A small silver airplane buzzes into view, flying towards downtown. She sees planes every day here, and sometimes she is afraid, especially when a formation of airplanes flies low over their house. Then Mama gets her to dive beneath the table. But there is nothing in this plane to frighten Keiko. The all-clear has sounded; this plane is a Japanese aircraft going to refuel or, at worst, an American reconnaissance plane. It is all alone, flying high, off to somewhere else.

As she watches, a spot the size of a fly drops from the plane, a single blemish against the whiteness of sky, then needles blind her eyeballs and she is knocked sideways through the air. The moss-covered stones hurl themselves at Mr. Takahura, smashing the wall between them.

52.

IRENE FLEW THROUGH THE BRONZE DOORS of the *Sunday Review* building, which wheeled and spat her out. She adjusted the veiling of her hat, then clicked her way over to Daisy. Her raglan sleeves billowed open, offering glimpses of red satin. Satin buttons adorned the wrists of her gloves. Without waiting to hear why Daisy had summoned her, she took her friend by the arm, led her across the street, holding up a hand to stop traffic, then thrust open the door of a café. They sat in a booth and ordered coffees. Perhaps to stop Daisy from speaking first, Irene began to talk—though it was less talk than free-form recitation. She held her coffee cup in one hand, gloves in the other, and beat time with them as she talked, flicking them nervously at the table. "Here," she said, "are the components of an anti–hydrogen bomb tour." Podiums had been rented, train berths booked. *Ask a Doctor* had advertised its TV debut. The volume of detail that poured from Irene's mouth left Daisy itchy all over, but still Irene continued, from the rental of coffee urns to the securing of Robert J. Oppenheimer, from promotional posters featuring Keiko against a background of a mushroom cloud to dealing with Quaker organizers in Pittsburgh who wanted to start their event with fifteen minutes of complete silence.

Irene tucked a curl behind her ear. "Now," she said, "enough about this." She laid her gloves on the table, pressed them flat. "Tell me why you needed to see me."

Daisy's heart was beating fast. She reached into her purse for her cigarettes and her hands shook. Irene was watching her, half smiling. "You seem upset," she said.

"I am upset."

Irene raised an eyebrow at this, then twisted and picked up a bit of gum wrap from the heel of her shoe, disposing of it in the ashtray.

"Go on."

Daisy took a long drag on her cigarette, then sipped her coffee. "Irene," she began. "I've searched my heart."

"I like that expression. It makes it sound as though the heart has compartments. And what did you find?"

"I've searched my heart." Daisy spoke more firmly. "I was up all night, and when it was day, I telephoned."

"Damned early too, but never mind. Who needs sleep? It's overrated." Irene stopped: Daisy's face had not a trace of her usual social smile. "Go on, then," she said.

It was true what Daisy had said—she had been up all night. In the early morning she had spoken to Walter, charging him to look after the girl. Then Daisy had dressed, choosing her clothes with exaggerated carefulness, and Walter had driven her to the train station.

"Look after her."

"I'll try."

He had sat in the car, watching her stout, muscled buttocks crossing the platform, then he had driven away.

"Go on," Irene said now.

"Tomorrow the bandages come off."

"Finally."

"Yes, finally." Daisy waited, Irene watching her. "I am sure you know my feelings in the matter. And Walter's too. We don't think she should go on tour. Or appear on *Ask a Doctor,* or talk to the press. It's all a ghastly mistake, and we mustn't do it to her."

Irene's nose twitched, that tick Daisy knew so well. "I can see you feel this deeply."

"Yes I do. She could get citizenship, go to college. We don't have much money, but Walter and I could save."

"That's a sweet idea."

"No, it's not. It's not sweet. You always say that about me, but I'm not sweet at all."

"My mistake."

"I just happen to know what Keiko needs."

"And what's that?"

"To start over without people peering at her all the time, or pointing, or saying, 'There's the girl with the blasted face.' She told me her story last night, Irene."

"Really?" Irene leaned forward with large eyes.

Daisy nodded.

"Tell me."

"She told me the whole thing. It was—" Daisy stopped.

"As bad as that?"

"It was awful—it was—I begged her not to speak."

Irene bit her fingernail. "It was riveting then?"

"Don't." Daisy sat back.

"Don't what?"

"Don't do that. The look on your face—as though she's your prey!"

"Quite a choice of words."

"Irene, please." Daisy tried again. The girl was, she said, a remarkable child, and yes, she was a child: a girl on the edge of adulthood but not yet grown. She was not merely an A-bomb victim, or a story, or the best weapon the Project had against the H-bomb; she was a girl. She had come to America to escape the ravages of the bomb. But if Irene and the others made her relive her experiences again and again, they ran the risk of destroying her, turning her into a person with only one experience, one reason to exist, to say, *This is what it was like—the blast, the heat, searching for water.*

"Don't you see, Irene?" Daisy leaned across the table. "She will never be able to escape." She closed her eyes and saw the sickening pins of light, the blast tearing the air with a crack of thunder. *Pika-don,* Keiko had called it, a name children used to describe the bomb. It meant, "the big flash-boom."

Irene shook her head. "Your compassion does you credit, Daisy," she said, "but it's too late. If Keiko had wanted peace, she should have stayed home, not come to America to have expensive surgery on her face. It's cost us tens of thousands of dollars."

"I don't think she knew what it entailed."

"There was a lineup of Hiroshima Maidens, all with scarred faces, all ready and waiting to condemn the H-bomb. Girls who needed this surgery more than Keiko. But she convinced us to choose her. She decided to be best."

"The best what? The best scarred maiden anyone could wish for?"

"Yes, if you want to put it that way."

"But that's not who she is!" Again Daisy saw the girl spinning on one foot on a rock, holding up her fingers. "Don't make her into that!"

"I'm not doing anything—this *is* who she is—or who she sold herself as, and that's what counts. We've built an entire campaign around her."

"I don't care about the campaign. I want you to leave her alone."

Irene laughed—one short bark. "Alone in Riverside Meadows, with you and Walter and the rest of your neighbours? What makes you so sure that Keiko wants that?"

"She needs to rest."

"I'd double-check that, Daisy. I had a talk with Keiko this morning, after you'd left the house, and she said something entirely different."

"You telephoned her?"

"Why not?"

"You waited until I'd left?" Daisy stood up.

"Please, Daisy. Keep your shirt on. I didn't do anything under-handed. I'm still allowed to talk to her, I suppose. She isn't your exclusive property, is she?"

Daisy sat down again. That was true. What had she been thinking?

Irene reached into her bag for her cigarette case, offering one, which Daisy refused.

"We had a profitable talk. She said she had spoken to you. And as a matter of fact I suppose I ought to thank you: you seem to have jogged her memory."

"I did nothing of the kind. She told me she wanted me to hear the story. I begged her not to tell me."

"Yes, well, you're good at opening people up. I told you that."

"*I didn't open her up.*" But as Daisy cried this, she wasn't com-pletely sure. She *had* begged Keiko to stop, but underneath she had felt a furtive stirring—wanting to hear the worst, feeling that it was her right, at last, to know everything, so that there would be no more secret places between them. So that she could protect her.

"Regardless. She's ready to begin; her story's all there. It might have been an awkward conversation except that I'm rather good at these things. What she wanted, what it all came down to, was some financial remuneration."

"I don't believe you."

"I mentioned a fundraising component to the tour and she pricked up her ears and before you know it we'd agreed on a sum, a cut of each tour stop. It's not a lot, but it's enough to give her some independence."

Daisy took out some change and laid it on the table. "We're getting nowhere," she said. "I'm going to talk to Dr. Carney."

"Yes do, and congratulate Raymond, please, on solving the riddle of the girl's recalcitrance. He's the one who thought to offer a cut of the fundraising. Such a simple solution."

"You're bribing her, Irene—"

"Call it what you will."

"—and I don't believe a word you say."

"But you should believe me. And in fact, I think you do. You're the one who said the girl was cold. You pointed it out. You're the one who alerted us to her peculiarities. And now you're the one who's delivered her story. Well done."

For a second Daisy felt dizzy. She grabbed hold of the shiny aluminium edge of the tabletop. She was remembering the contents of the cheese box, the girl's look of hatred that first night; then she saw her crying out, standing in her underwear, legs covered in dust, blood pouring from her ear.

"Yes," Irene said, "go home and talk to her. You'll find that she's quite communicative, especially if there's something in it for her."

"This is your view of things." Daisy stood up. "Don't you see what you're doing?"

"What am I doing?"

"Everyone turns her into what they need her to be. And w. you see is a woman prepared to do anything to get her way. You've made her over in your own image." Daisy closed her eyes. She felt it again: the blast, the child running towards the bridge, hearing cries for water, all this pressed against the other pattern, where a clock chimed the quarter-hour and gradations of light played through the screens. There was a world in the shadows, but you could only see it if you squinted, let your eyes adjust to the half-light. But Irene didn't give a hoot about any of that. All she cared about was the blast, the flash, the damage.

Daisy opened her eyes. Irene was watching her, two lines of worry on the bridge of her nose.

"You've been awfully lonely out there, haven't you?" she said.

The change Daisy had placed on the table was insufficient. She threw down more, knocking her cup with her purse. Coffee spilled across the table and dripped onto Irene's lap. They both looked at it, then Irene reached for a serviette and began to blot it.

"It's not wash-and-wear, dear," she said.

Daisy turned on her heel and left the coffee shop.

53.

MAMA CANNOT HAVE GONE FAR. White dust falls like snow. She looks down to see that she is naked. Sticky blood pours from her ear.

These are details to remember, facts to tell herself and the others.

What happened first? Her own voice shouting as loud as she could, her mouth full of dust. She lies on her back covered in stones and wood and broken roof tiles. She spits, then shouts again, hardly any sound coming. She cannot move.

Takahura-san's voice above her: "Keiko. Say something."

"I'm here."

"You're alive."

"I can't move my legs."

She waits in darkness, something stuck in her ribs, until he moves the debris away and she can breathe. His face looming over her is a jammy pulp. His shirt hangs from him in strips of rag; the scissors are still attached to his thumb. He pulls tiles from her chest and legs, then lifts her up and sets her on an over-turned rock. Nothing looks right: the rocks have rolled every-where; the house—she turns to see Grandfather's house, but it has collapsed. Strips of Ojii-chan's cypress doors poke from the rock and tile. She will get in trouble for this, though it wasn't her fault. She didn't leave the hibachi on.

Mr. Takahura stands on the rubble of his own house, calling for his daughter, a long shard of glass embedded between his shoulder blades. He turns and holds up his hand, shouting at her not to go, but Keiko picks her way across the tile-strewn yard. All the houses in the street have been knocked down, plaster, stones and beams collapsed into heaps, except for one home, which stands like a doll house with the walls blown away, so that she can see every room. Wooden shelves hold pots and a wire egg basket.

Dust falls like snow. She feels it on the skin of her thighs. Looking down she sees that she is naked except for a black tracing of the waistband of her underwear. Something hangs from her cheek, a translucent sheet. She plucks away a piece of skin as large as her hand. This frightens her, and she calls out for Mama, run-ning now towards the bridge that spans the Ota River.

54.

Daisy got off the train at Stoney Creek, then hurried along the highway to the path by Strickland's. She traversed the two fields, corn reaching to her shoulders, crossed the bridge, then rushed up the trail to the schoolyard, empty of teenagers. It was just after one o'clock. They must have stopped smoking, burning bits of grass, necking, in order to go home, participate in family lunches. As Daisy crossed Old Middle Road, the suburb lay ahead of her, and she could hear sounds of dishes being cleared, a baby crying, the radio.

There was still time, she was thinking, still time to stop the Project in its tracks. It was all-out warfare now: Daisy had accused Irene of using the girl, then, to top it off, knocked coffee onto her skirt. This, Irene would not forgive. As for Irene using the girl, making her over into something sly, a fox woman— well, Irene was that voracious, that determined. I'll offer you a sum, she had said to the girl. A large sum. Yes, such a conversation seemed likely. Keiko might even, with her many-layered silences, have managed to negotiate a reasonable price. Daisy could imagine a small figure met by silence, a larger by silence, until the largest was met with that standard, indispensable phrase: "You are kind. Thank you."

Daisy had taken her hands in the darkness, cradling her. *You don't have to go on,* she had said, though a part of her had also thought, *Tell me everything, I need to know it all.* But Keiko hadn't listened, either to what the voice said or what it meant. She had only paid attention to what was ahead—the necessity to tell what had been hidden: by this step, and by this step, and by this, I fled from the burning city. As though that was what she was, after all.

A *hibakusha* and nothing else—oh, that strange word, which sounded like a radioactive wind moving through branches.

As Daisy rounded the crescent onto Linden Street she imagined the letter she would take to Dr. Carney. Yes, she would write a letter, and not just to Carney either: to the Project, to Dean Atchity and Bertha, to the press, if that was what it took. She would expose the lot of them. She began to write the letter in her head, describing the vulnerability of the girl, then the blast—a blast so terrible it burnt itself not just into the body but into the mind—then the girl's flight to America to escape. The sentences composed themselves in her head as she strode up Linden Street, white-hot words lighting up her skull.

55.

AS SHE RUNS THROUGH THE STREET the seasons change. Huge flakes fill the air and every landmark she has known is no longer there. She looks to her left, trying to locate Hiroshima Castle, but sees a blackened hill. This is terrible, like a dream: the castle has always been there. The noodle house by the river is gone too, collapsed: beneath a heavy beam she sees the stocking feet of the owner lady, dirty white *tabi*. A dead man lies in the road, a piece of wood sticking from his eye.

Ojii-chan, she calls, though he is miles away. Ojii-chan, she wails.

Now a line of people move out of the smoke like sleepwalkers, walking towards her from the direction of the bridge. She runs towards them, but stops, aghast, because they hold their hands in front of them, and the skin hangs from their wrists, ragged gloves.

Faces swollen red like pomegranate. They walk past Keiko. One bumps into her and says, *Excuse me.*

To her right a house catches on fire, all on its own.

56.

DAISY PAUSED IN FRONT OF HER HOUSE. Strange to hear noise drifting through the window: it sounded like a party. She went up the steps and opened the door.

It wasn't a party; it was a television set, shining at the end of the living room. A lustrous, purple-grained television—its cherrywood doors neatly retracted, exposing a black-and-white image of Lucille Ball dressed as a tramp, freckles the size of moles covering her cheeks, mascara-lashed eyes popped wide open. Canned laughter.

Keiko and Walter sat on the couch. Walter had his arm slung along the couch back, and he was chuckling; Keiko sat with ankles crossed, hands in her lap, wearing the outfit she had worn her first night at Riverside Meadows—a burgundy cotton dress, crunchy with hidden layers of tulle.

Daisy didn't say a word; she just stood at the door. Walter got up and turned off the set.

"A thing of beauty," he said gently. "Black-cherry veneer, heirloom quality." He used the words pointedly, knowing they sounded like ad copy, but with pride in his voice too. "Today was delivery day."

Keiko stood up, not meeting Daisy's eyes, and slipped down the hall, closing her bedroom door. "She's leaving in half an hour," Walter said.

"What?"

"Yes." He described what had happened. The telephone call from Irene, while he and Keiko were making breakfast. No, he hadn't heard what they said to each other. He'd gone outside, smoked a cigarette on the porch.

"I asked you to keep an eye on her."

"Well, that's what I did."

Later he had looked out the window and seen the top of the delivery van, over on Elm Street, and so he'd run after it, directing it to their house. In that time Keiko had put in a telephone call to Dr. Carney, requesting that he pick her up. "She's happy about the television set," he said. But still, she's decided she wants to spend her last night, before the bandage removal, in town. At your friend Irene's house."

"She must be so confused. I'll speak to her."

He took her arm. "She needs to finish packing," he said. "Better give her some privacy."

Daisy looked at him blankly. "I have to talk to her," she said.

"Let her pack first."

She shook him off. But she did as he said. Instead of going down the hall, she went into Walter's study and sat down. The room was an empty-looking place without the many *Dark Night* boxes, the mountain of Walter's past. Daisy rolled paper into the typewriter, then began to compose a letter. *Dear Mr. Atchity,* she wrote—then stopped, hardly knowing how to start. Angry phrases, like spasms, composed themselves in her mind.

This girl is not a guinea pig.

I won't let you hurt her.

Over my dead body.

She bent her head to the typewriter, resting her forehead against the keys. Nothing coherent or dignified came out. She ripped the paper out of the machine and threw it into the garbage, among the last remnants of David Greenberg notes, and then went through the kitchen and onto the back porch, letting the screen door hiss closed behind her. She looked out at Ed's greenhouse, the crazy monster of a hole, blocked by the fence. The door opened behind her, but when she turned she saw it was Walter, cigarette in his fingers, long, crooked body leaning against the doorframe. Daisy sat down with a groan and put her head in her hands. "They're going to hurt her. They're going to force her to speak—and this is your solution? Go along with everything she says. Buy her a television set, for Christ's sake!"

Walter sat down and put his arm around Daisy, but she shrugged it off. "A television set!" she repeated bitterly. "Did you think that would make a difference? That you could buy her?" Then she laughed. "Funny thing is, it's probably the best idea yet. Too bad you didn't think of it sooner."

They sat in silence for a while, her words soaking the air. Then he said quietly, "Nobody can decide what's right for another person."

"I can."

He shook his head, a quaver of motion.

"Walter, please." Daisy turned to him. "I need you to help me. I can't fight this alone."

"She's got to make up her own mind."

"But she's so upset—don't you see? She doesn't know what her own mind is!"

He looked at her shrewdly, then butted his cigarette out on the underside of the porch banister. "I'm going in." She heard him in the kitchen, mixing a drink. Keiko came out of her bedroom and stood beside Walter, as she had the first night, cutting a lime into thin, precise slices. After a while Daisy heard the screen door open again.

Keiko stood on the porch.

"So off you go," Daisy said.

"Mrs. Lawrence—"

This made Daisy want to cry. "And why am I *always* Mrs. Lawrence? I asked you ages ago to call me Daisy."

"Daisy."

"You're safe here, you know that. Nobody can touch you."

"I am sorry, Mrs. Lawrence."

"There you are again. *Mrs. Lawrence.*"

"Forgive me." A small bow.

"You won't be able to do what they want—it will hurt too much. I know you, Keiko. *I know you.*" She felt the force of those words slip through her. Yes, it was true: she knew the girl through and through, better than Keiko knew herself even. She turned to see how that felt, her face full of reproach, but Keiko had slipped back inside, moving so softly that Daisy had not heard the door close.

57.

THE RIVER TO HER LEFT IS FULL of rowboats on fire, but then she realizes they are people, bodies charred, some still burning. The fire eats the wooden houses, leaps the walls of rubble meant to act as firebreaks. Now she has reached the bridge. She hears a blasting noise, the booming of flame. Looking into the grotto she sees strings of shrine papers in flames.

A woman sits at the other end of the bridge, cradling something in her lap, her back to Keiko. It is burnt. Keiko sees a pattern, leaves of bamboo from a summer kimono, printed there, like a tattoo.

Mama, Keiko calls.

Mama.

A little boy runs past them screaming, his padded headcovering in flames.

She is in hell, this is true, because when she looks again at the woman, she sees her face. She is not Mama, she is the faceless woman of her nightmares, crouched beside the stone parapet, clutching a baby that does not move.

58.

AS SOON AS DR. CARNEY PARKED in the driveway, Daisy ran across the lawn and leaned down to speak to him through his window, even as he opened the car door.

"Dr. Carney—"

"Nice afternoon," he said, ignoring her panic. He got out of the car, holding his medical bag. It smelled of disinfectant and leather. Next door the Warburghs had had their driveway repaved; what Daisy remembered later was facing off with Dr. Carney against the smell of chewy tar.

"I don't want her hurt!" Daisy's voice was louder and lower than she meant it to be.

"What on earth do you mean?"

"She says she wants to go, but I don't believe it—"

"She's opening up. That's good."

"It's not good! It's wrong!"

He was walking up the path towards the house and she caught at his sleeve, a rough gesture. He stopped in his tracks. "She won't be made into your puppet," Daisy said. "If you want to photograph her, you have to talk to me first. If you want people to interview her, you come to me. And don't you dare have her appear on your show."

Dr. Carney looked at Daisy's hot face and he laughed. "I think you're out of your depth, Mrs. Lawrence." He turned again and walked up the steps.

"If you exploit her," Daisy hissed, "I'll go to the press. I'll tell them that you're using her to advance your career. Using her like a guinea pig. I'll talk to the State Department."

He took a step towards her, and for a moment Daisy thought he was going to hit her, but instead he merely patted her on the shoulder. "She will speak out, Mrs. Lawrence."

"Not if I can help it. It's the worst thing for her."

"You're the expert, are you?" He went up the steps and put his hand on the doorknob. "She's in here, I take it. You haven't spir- ited her away to some hiding place. Taken her underground?" Dr. Carney's eyes, which often looked blurry, were sharp now, studying Daisy.

The door opened. Keiko stood in front of them, clutching her shell-encrusted purse. Walter stood beside Keiko, skeletal and sardonic and handsome as ever, holding the girl's moon-shaped valise, greeting the doctor amiably, shaking his hand, man to man. *Don't bother with my wife, Doctor*—his handshake seemed to say—*she's given to hysterics. Mood swings. Bouts of fevered irrationality.*

Within moments Keiko was sitting in the front seat of the doctor's mushroom-coloured car. She would not look at Daisy, and Daisy for her part turned her face, but Walter smiled, closed-lipped, and waved. The car seemed to take a long time to drive down Linden Street and round the crescent, but in less than a minute it was out of view.

59.

AT DAWN, in a place called Yucca Flat, an atomic bomb thirty-three times more powerful than Hiroshima's bomb was to be detonated. "The self same morning," Irene had repeated in her telephone calls to the press, "that Keiko Kitigawa, our Hiroshima Maiden, enters the hospital for the removal of her bandages—one might say that destruction and redemption have been packed into a single American morning." The press had taken the bait. As Keiko and Irene stepped from their taxi in front of Mount Sinai Hospital, they were overwhelmed by photographers, reporters, even a newsman making a sound recording. They ran at Irene and Keiko, as they had at Mitchell Air Force Base. *Will you say a few words, Miss Kitigawa?* A flash went off and Keiko covered her face instinctively. But now a familiar large and freckled hand reached out, grasped the journalist's camera, held it lightly like a toy, then flung it to the ground. "Keiko," Tom Orley called out. "I'm over here, I won't leave—" but Irene pushed by him.

"Hold on, miss," Keiko heard a journalist say, close to her ear. "Tell us what you think of the H-bomb." She stepped into the revolving door, a triangle of muffled seclusion, and left them behind.

The seventh floor was clean and modern. The blue linoleum created the illusion of stepping across the sky. The walls smelled of bleach. Keiko had to fight off a sense of panic as Dr. Carney greeted her. "Your big day," he said jovially, handing her to a nurse. She helped Keiko change into a medical gown, then led her to the hospital room and told her to lie on the bed. Instruments sat at a table to her left: a roll of bandage, packet of gauze, sterile

cream, a beaver scalpel, tiny, sharp scissors, as well as a strange
metal scoop, like the ones they used at home to scoop rice.

Dr. Carney closed the door behind him

"You can go." That order puzzled the nurse, but he had to be
alone, no observers.

"Now," he said, when the nurse had left. "How are you feeling?"

"I am fine, Dr. Carney."

"Up to snuff, eh? Good for you. Still, we must take your temperature." He took the thermometer from the side table and
gave it a shake. "Open up, Keiko."

As soon as he spoke he saw her spirit desert her body, go into
retreat, while she opened her mouth passively, a hole surrounded by the white bandages. She closed her lips around the
thermometer.

"Under your tongue," Dr. Carney said. "Right under," and he
pushed it into the soft cavity beneath her tongue. He saw her
flinch, but never mind, it must be done. He counted out the seconds on his watch. After a minute he asked her to open and she
let her lips go slack.

"A slight temperature. Nothing to worry about. Now let's
look at your face."

He said it routinely, as though it were one of a number of small
requests. He asked her to turn to one side, exposing the bandaging
on her unscarred cheek. It was safer to begin snipping here.
With one hand he pressed lightly against her forehead, balancing himself, and then he began to snip. He knew what he was
doing—this diminutive, bulky-shouldered doctor, with his fingers
smelling of soap. Scissors nipped the layer of tensile bandaging
first, three snips and it sprang loose. "Easy now," he spoke abruptly
as she winced. *Easy now.* He placed the scissors under the next
layer, an eighth of an inch of gauze, and snipped. The humming
and ticking of the clock on the wall was the loudest noise.

He could tell she was frightened. Frightened by the lightening
of weight on her face. It had all been coming to this. She closed
her eyes, seeing—once again—the march of the dead, the blast
of light that sent the mossy stones flying. *Shi no hai,* that was
what she had carried all this time, until this very second:
twirling, spinning, trying to shake the black seeds from her body.
Telling lies, when it was necessary, telling the truth.

Please let it be all right, Daisy prayed, waking early, standing
alone in the kitchen, the curtains in her hand, holding her breath.

Tom in the lobby, having agreed to pay for the damage to the
camera, prayed too. And so did Joan and Fran and Walter. Even
Ed Warburgh was thinking of Keiko. Only Evelyn Lithgow had
forgotten, and was smoking a cigarette in the bathroom while
taking curlers from her hair.

With tweezers Dr. Carney pulled away tissue-thin strips of
gauze. He drew them back one by one. He was reminded of
the slow disinterring of a mummy. Though her eyes were to the
ceiling, Keiko moved her hand and fumbled for the edge of the
steel bed. She flinched, shaking her head. Something had gone
wrong. She could feel it.

"Please," she said to the doctor. "This is hurting. Can we do it
tomorrow?"

"Tomorrow?" He laughed. "After all this wait?"

"I think I might be stronger tomorrow."

"You don't know yourself, Keiko. You are strong enough now."

But what hurt? He was surprised. Was it the air touching her
skin through the last layer of bandage? Was it the tip of his scissors?

"It has to be done. Keiko. You know it has to be done."

For two minutes he snipped, bent over, pulling back the last
layer of custard-stained gauze. Keiko tried not to wince. He
drew it back inch by inch, away from her undamaged cheek,
away from her nose, from the indentation above her lip, which

he knew was called the philtrum; the moist gauze stuck to her cheek but then—with a tug of the hook—away it came, revealing her face.

It was a trick of light that made her scar show like a slick of oil. As Dr. Carney stood back, the better to gaze at her, he saw that her skin was shiny and taut, yes, but except for that tautness, her skin, her cheek, her face were perfect.

He shook his head. Took out a handkerchief, wiped his face, the palms of his hands: grinning, disbelieving—then he reached out and hugged her gently. "Too much," he whispered. "A wonder to behold."

A miracle, in other words.

"Keiko," he said. "You're beautiful." She continued to stare at the ceiling, her self submerged beneath the surface of her intact, perfect skin, concentrating on something only she could see.

"Do you have a mirror, Dr. Carney?"

"A mirror, of course—how foolish!" He rushed to the door, called for the nurse. There was bustle and noise, and then he returned with an opened powder compact. Not perfect, he thought, but it would have to do.

"Look."

He held up the thing. She fixed her gaze on it, saw the skin taut across her gorgeous cheekbone. Saw herself unscarred, no longer wearing the face of a survivor.

Carney reached into the mouth of the medical bag at his feet, never taking his eyes from her face, his fingers finding his Brownie camera. He unsnapped the case, adjusted the lens, held it to his eye, and she watched him, not protesting. Just as he found the focus, she spoke, in her pure, sweet uninflected voice.

"Please," she said. "I need you to look behind my ear."

Dr. Carney lowered the camera. She turned to show him what she meant. Behind her left ear, in that secret crease, a new keloid had bubbled up from the pearly line of the incision—hot purple flesh mushrooming between the stitches.

60.

DAISY WOKE BEFORE DAWN, thinking about Keiko, never letting her out of her thoughts. She imagined the drive to the hospital, the reporters, the rush of silence as Keiko stepped through the revolving doors. She didn't let her thoughts slip, even as she put on the coffee and laid the table for breakfast. When she stepped outside to hang dishcloths, Fran was out already, pinning up diapers.

"Nothing yet," Daisy said, turning to go back in.

"You'll tell me when you hear."

"I promise."

Inside, Daisy picked up the phone and called Irene at home. No answer. She tried Mount Sinai. Seventh floor. Dr. Carney's office. Irene answered.

"Daisy—I can't speak."

"Why did you pick up the phone then?"

Irene sighed. "What can I do for you?"

"Are the bandages off?"

"Can I ring you back?"

"Irene, please."

There was a long pause.

"I'm sorry, Irene," Daisy whispered. "I need to know. I'm worried."

Daisy could hear Irene rearranging her skirt. Then she said, "I suppose I'm the one who's going to have to tell you." Her voice became cold, no-nonsense. "Everything was just fine," she said. "The skin graft on her cheek was a good match, the sutures hardly showed."

"Thank God."

"That's not all."

She described the keloid behind Keiko's ear, how it had sprouted between the stitches——hard, bubbled flesh with a mind of its own. Well, it was a most delicate thing, it turned out, to get blood to pump through new skin in an area of keloid growth: you couldn't force it. And so keloids often did grow back on burn victims—and A-bomb victims must, Carney thought, be particularly prone. Something in the skin itself.

"Seeds," whispered Daisy.

"I beg your pardon."

"*Shi no hai.*"

Anyway, Irene continued, that was the terror of the thing, the fundamental risk—there was always the danger that the new skin around a keloid simply would not be as powerful as the old, bubbled flesh and would get pushed aside in time. They had known this from the beginning, Irene said, though it was the first time Daisy had ever heard of it.

"We'll have to cut it away immediately."

Daisy closed her eyes. She imagined Dr. Carney explaining all this to Keiko. He must have taken refuge behind scientific and medical explanations, words like *contusion* and *malformation*.

"When can I see her?"

A pause. Daisy imagined Irene searching for her cigarettes.

"I'll ring you."

"Did she ask for me?"

"As far as I know, Keiko never asked for you once. Far from it. As for your seeing her, we'll have to wait: there are only three days until *Ask a Doctor* and Keiko is, as you yourself know, very eager to make herself useful."

"You're lying to me, Irene."

Irene hung up.

Daisy stood in the hallway, holding the telephone until it began to buzz, then she replaced it in its cradle. *It grew back,* Keiko had whispered as she woke one night, palm pressed to her bandaged ear. Daisy had pulled the hand away, telling her it was a nightmare.

Daisy imagined her small body covered by a sheet. She saw the girl's knobbly knees, finely boned feet, stretched out before the doctor. A massive steel-necked lamp would be rolled into place and then, in an instant, the fluorescent glare would illuminate the new bad skin, hidden in its secret crevice. Daisy could feel the fug of fear Keiko gave off as the big light seared her eyes. When Keiko shut them, the light would be so bright it would cut through her eyelids, making things red.

Daisy closed her eyes.

Save yourself, the woman on the bridge had whispered.

The feeling came to Daisy—and later she could not explain it, not to Walter or to anyone, because it didn't come from her brain but rushed up through her body, radiating from the ache between her breasts. She could hear the rustle of the shrine papers. Tears burnt her swollen eyes. She was praying to gods whose names she did not know, and at the base of her skull she felt the first of them arriving behind her in the hallway—a gust of old meat on its breath.

She didn't faint.

She didn't fall to the ground and jerk like a chicken with its head cut off (something a girl at Sacred Heart once did). She opened her eyes and saw the phone still in its place, beside the china shepherdess in its murky mirrored alcove. Yet the thing stood behind her, of this she was sure. Freezing water poured down her arms, just below the surface of her skin.

She turned.

Walter stood at the doorway to the bedroom, face groggy, cheeks unshaved. He looked frightened.

"It's Keiko," Daisy whispered. She took a step towards him and he took a step back. Her voice, Walter told her later, was not her own. But Daisy didn't care—she was only thinking that she must rush to Mount Sinai, through the brass door, up the seven flights, to find Keiko where she lay, under the terrible glare of operating-room lights; that if she could unstrap her, lift her, hold her body close—burnt and terrified, full of dark seeds—she might still save her.

61.

IN HER DREAM, the city has just been struck or is about to be struck. Either way it is eerily quiet, smoke and ash consuming the sky. Urgency stirs in the pit of Daisy's stomach: miles separate her from the city, miles of countryside full of animals with yellow eyes. Sometimes she travels with Fran, sometimes with Walter. Once, she sat on the train with an entire delegation of Riverside women. Ella Strickland wore a hat the size of Tokyo, layered like a wedding cake.

Always she is trying to get to Mount Sinai.

To travel from Riverside Meadows to the hospital was a trip of one hour and seventeen minutes. This included the transfer at Penn Station, and took in every stop dotting the length of

western Long Island, a series of names like beads on a rosary—
Hicksville, Carle Place, Mineola, New Hyde Park, Jamaica.
However, the trip took Walter and Daisy longer than an hour and
seventeen minutes, because they had to debate whether it was
faster to take the train or drive—it was faster to take the train in
rush hour—and they had to dress and search for Daisy's purse.

Daisy has dreamt this trip so many times that she has trouble
distinguishing actuality from fantasy. She can imagine Manhattan
ahead, its gaunt towers, the perfect spire of the Chrysler
Building bisecting the sky, but she cannot see the city, not for
hours and hours. The train takes a minute and a half at each station, then lurches and heaves, picking up speed. She is no longer
in her seat; she is in a boxcar, the doors of which have slid open.
Children run beside the train, and everything is green: the legs
of the children and their feet and the grass. As Daisy watches,
rain begins to fall. "Black rain," an ancient man beside her says. A
voice of calm acceptance. The next moment the boxcar doors
slam shut and the children are left behind.

Though she had taken the train a thousand times, she never
realized that the countryside around the city went on for so long,
that there were so many water towers, cement foundries, church
spires, rusted cars, graveyards. She glimpsed a basketball court,
boys playing beside a pile of wooden ties. They had to wait forever
at Jamaica, where the conductors called out for other stations,
then at last they gained speed, rushing past a broken billboard for
Shredded Wheat, past a shed covered in Virginia creeper, and at
last the city was glimpsed, misty and pale, before being obliterated by the boiler-room blackness of the East River. In the tunnel,
Walter squeezed Daisy's hand: *Steady on, girl,* that pressure
seemed to say. *It's going to be all right.*

If they had travelled more swiftly, would things have been different? It felt like that afterwards—hence the dreams, not just of

the city, unreachable and green with ash, but of failing to find her purse, searching for change, looking for her gloves or a hand mirror or a hat with a pink bird nesting in the rim.

At Penn Station they raced through the station and up the steps, feet ringing on the diamond patterns, hands on the cold rail. Outside, Macy's towered above them, flying its flags. Walter waved down a cab. "Mount Sinai," he said curtly and the cab took them past Broadway, crowded with shoppers, then up Madison, past the Whitney, past the black canopy of the Carlyle, past a string of boys in yarmulkes and forest-green knee socks. The street hulked up and down as they crested the hill, making Daisy nauseated.

Stepping from the cab at Mount Sinai, an updraft of warm air caught Walter's hat. They watched it swirl upwards, then come down not five feet from where they stood. Walter scooped it up and smiled at Daisy for the first time that morning: surely this must be a good omen.

Tom Orley stood in front of the hospital, smoking, agitated, his cheeks ashen. He flicked his cigarette into the gutter when he saw them.

"Is she all right? What's happened?"

Daisy heard his voice but didn't stop to answer.

62.

DAISY WAS AWARE that no two human faces could be identical, but when she and Walt came out on the seventh floor and saw the nurse filling out forms at her station, she could have sworn that the woman was her Aunt Nancy from Seneca Falls, an old battle-axe who used to pinch Daisy's cheeks, comment on her plumpness and who once told Daisy's mother that her daughter's looks were common. Now Aunt Nancy's dead ringer looked Daisy and Walter up and down. She had broken capillaries in her cheeks; her nostrils were alarmingly hairy. Even before a word came out of Daisy's mouth, this woman began to shake her head.

"Today there's followup surgery. She's not allowed visitors."

"But we need to see her."

"Nobody is permitted."

"I'm permitted."

"And who are you?"

"I'm her homestay mother."

"We're members of the committee that runs this project." Walter kept his voice amiable.

"I've been told that nobody is to be admitted."

"Then you've been told wrong," Daisy said. "If you give me the room number—"

"I certainly can't do that—not unless Dr. Carney himself says so."

"Then call him, please."

The nurse glanced down at the telephone as though Daisy had suggested something vile. Daisy gave Walter a beseeching look, and he took off his hat, swept it to his breast. "Miss." His voice was low and courtly. "I guess you might say we're like family members. The kind of people somebody might want to see before a major event of this nature."

"Well—" A flicker of a smile, then she opened a folder on her desk. "What did you say your name was?"

Daisy repeated it, and the nurse leafed through the file, before snapping it closed with a smirk. "You've been prohibited access," she said.

Walter shook his head.

"You've made a mistake," Daisy whispered. "Get Dr. Carney on the telephone. He'll tell you we can see her." She must have looked quite wild because the nurse dialed zero and asked to be put through, then pressed the receiver to her small, pointed earlobe. Down the hall beyond the steel door, Daisy heard the faint sound of ringing. After five rings, it stopped.

"Dr. Carney, there's a couple here to see Miss Kitigawa. A"—again she consulted the file— "Mr. and Mrs. Lawrence." She paused. She nodded. She nodded again. "Yes, sir. Absolutely, sir. Yes, of course. But I thought—Yes, I—of course, sir." She hung up, sniffed, then looked at the two of them with pursed lips. "Dr. Carney has informed me that he wishes to see you in his office. Follow me, please."

"Ma'am," Walter said, lifting his hat, "you've been most helpful." He gave her a small bow, and she narrowed her eyes, then smiled despite herself. Walter took Daisy's arm and they followed the nurse past her station, down the hallway and through the steel door.

Dr. Carney's desk was strewn with papers and tissues, a pair of reading glasses, several cups of cold coffee and a plate holding some half-eaten sandwich crusts. Several withered aspidistra plants sat on his radiator. Carney himself looked dishevelled. He leapt up when he saw them, led Daisy to a chair, then pulled up another one for Walter.

"Forgive the clutter. A room says so much about a personality, and I'm sure mine says I have a series of disgusting fixations." He made a show of tidying up some papers on his desk, then gathered up the plate and cups, put them on the counter beside the small sink. "What I need is for the good nurses to see my mess for what it is—a repressed infantile obsession. Then perhaps they would take pity on me and tidy up more than once every twenty-four hours. But they won't. When I tell them I'm hopelessly dependent, they just smile, pat me on my head."

Walter laughed.

"You understand? I'm glad. As for the nurses—they don't give a hoot about psychological urges and needs. As far as they are concerned, we are all the horrible creatures we were born to be. A refreshing outlook."

Daisy straightened her back, clenched her purse strap. Her palms felt sweaty. "Dr. Carney," she said, "we need to talk about Keiko."

"Yes, beautiful Keiko. The scar is quite gone."

"But the keloid."

"That's unfortunate. Still, we'll have her fixed in no time. I'm going to operate"—he checked his watch— "in twenty minutes. The nurses are prepping her now."

"I need to see her."

"I want you to make yourselves comfortable. We only have to wait for Dean. Yes, Dean Atchity is coming up to see you too. He was in the conference room. I buzzed him the moment I heard you had arrived. Mrs. Lawrence, your cheeks are quite rosy. Let's take off that little jacket, shall we, and make sure you're comfortable." As he came close, she could smell the Brylcreem in his hair. She handed him her jacket, and he hung it with ostentatious precision from the back of his chair.

Then he started to pace: "Mrs. Lawrence, Mr. Lawrence, the mind is powerful. You think so too, I am sure?"

"I don't know." Daisy had rushed here determined to stop the madness of the Project, to throw herself between it and Keiko. Instead she felt as though she had plunged though a rabbit hole, and Dr. Carney, a joker affixed to his front, was the first person she'd met.

"You are a typical American husband and wife, am I correct?

That's why you were chosen to host Keiko. And yet, beneath the surface, there are depths, are there not? What do you think, Mr. Lawrence?" He turned to Walter, who was rolling a cigarette.

Walter shrugged. "Usually are."

"Usually are." This made Carney chuckle. "A man of few words. I like that. Usually are." There was a flutter of nails on the door. Daisy recognized that signature knock; it showcased a manicure without causing damage. Irene entered, a black silk jacket slung about her shoulders, raglan sleeves flopping like minor characters in themselves. Her face was excessively powdered, her hair bound tight, pinned beneath a black cap decked with two crow's feathers. She looked like a figure from kabuki theatre.

"Nobody stand," she said by way of greeting. "Just find me a chair, Raymond, and I'll flop. Can someone explain why I bought these shoes?"

Irene sat down, nodding to Walter.

Daisy straightened. "Irene," she said. "Dr. Carney. We exchanged words. I was, perhaps, rash. I regret it now. I regret it."

Irene tilted her head like a bird and smiled.

"All I care about—all we care about—is Keiko's welfare. I'm worried, knowing her as I do. I can't see how she can bear this latest setback."

"She'll be all right," Irene said.

"She ought to come home, regain her strength. Rest."

"She's beautiful, you know," Dr. Carney said.

"Beautiful," Irene echoed.

"One more operation—that's all it takes—Mrs. Lawrence, and she can do what she came here for."

Daisy glanced at Walter for support, but he was looking at the laces of his shoes, as though her intensity were distressing him. Well, never mind. "That's why we came," Daisy said. "We believe it will be psychologically disastrous to make her speak, especially in light of this new surgery. We have—we have terrible fears—"

"Fears." Dr. Carney smiled as though at a joke only he could get. Daisy glanced at Walter, full of apprehension, but he was lighting his cigarette now, face turned away.

"She's sensitive," Daisy said. "Just a child."

Dr. Carney went to the window and adjusted the blinds. He seemed on the verge of shaking all over, like a dog after a swim. "A child."

"Yes, that's what I said."

"Raymond," Irene said suddenly, "I hate it when you're like this."

"Like what?"

"Leaping around the room, taking *pleasure* in your devices."

At which point there was another knock on the door, and Dean Atchity entered.

He said hello, then perched on a corner of the desk and looked down at the floor, then at Walter and Daisy in turn. He cleared his throat. When he spoke, it was to the others.

"If you don't mind terribly, Dr. Carney, Miss Day, I'd like to be alone with Mrs. Lawrence."

They got up, and then, to Daisy's surprise, Walter stood up too. Daisy reached for his hand, but Dean Atchity intervened. "I think it's better, perhaps, if your husband waits outside. There are a few things I'd like to say to you privately."

All three departed quickly, like children dismissed from a difficult class.

When they were alone, Atchity sat down heavily behind the desk.

"Mrs. Lawrence," he began. "It pains me to say what I am about to say. I believe you are a good woman, and that you have been an asset to this project." He was trying, Daisy could see, even through the scrim of her apprehension, to word things kindly.

"It is tempting," he said, "to love those who have suffered. To love them with every ounce of love we have, whether this love is misplaced or not. I am sure," he added, "that in years to come, Keiko will feel enriched by your kindness." He spoke so calmly, so caressingly, that Daisy was temporarily disarmed.

"But in the end, we need to do what is best for Keiko."

"I've been trying to do what's best."

"Ah, well, there you are."

"And I'm concerned by the plans that have been made: the national tour, the television interviews. I know this girl, Mr. Atchity. I can't tell you strongly enough what a terrible mistake these things are."

Even as she spoke, Atchity shook his head. "I don't want to make things harder than they already are. But let me say this clearly. I am afraid we can no longer have you or your husband in the Project."

Daisy felt his words as a blow to her stomach. Still, she kept her voice calm. "This is Irene's doing."

He shrugged. "Irene has alerted me to a certain situation, yes."

"Tell me what she said."

"She mentioned that your husband has, in his past, had some unfortunate associations. It is unclear whether those associations have continued."

Daisy stared at him, not understanding the words.

"We felt it best not to alert the authorities. It would only compromise the Hiroshima Project. But we have taken steps to separate you from the Project. It is the only wise course to take, Mrs. Lawrence. I'm sorry."

"But you know he isn't a Red. It's *Walter.* He hates everything to do with Communism."

Dean looked embarrassed, as though her protestations only caused some kind of shame, a smell of bathroom odours. "I'm not sure that's entirely true, Mrs. Lawrence." His eyes, in that gaunt, well-scrubbed face, bored into her. "Yes," he said gently. "We asked the girl and she told us. He still speaks warmly of his experiences."

"Oh God."

"Her words corroborated Miss Day's own fears."

"And you've removed Keiko because of this?"

"Keiko has decided herself that she would prefer to live elsewhere. She has asked to be transferred to another family, but we think it best that she stay with Miss Day. You must honour her wishes. Mrs. Lawrence, you and your husband must never contact her. Your proximity jeopardizes this project. If you do see her, I will have no recourse but to inform the FBI of your husband's past connections."

"But everyone used to have connections. I know you did. And Irene did. And Keiko—I mean, she didn't have connections, but I can't believe she would say such a thing."

"She has asked to be removed permanently."

"I don't believe it."

"You will need to believe it, because it is true and she has told me."

"What did she say?"

"Mrs. Lawrence."

"Go on. Tell me."

He paused, looking—looking what?—looking as though he wished to spare her. At last he spoke: "I'm afraid that in the end, her wish to be removed had less to do with your husband than with you. She said that in your house she is frightened."

"She *is* frightened," Daisy said, standing now. "She's frightened of the committee and all of your horrible plans for her, and of the operations, which hurt horribly, and aren't successful—"

"No, Daisy."

Somewhere high above them an airplane was passing over Manhattan. Daisy could hear it. She thought of the girl's soft hair, which she had touched.

"She says that you watch her as she sleeps—is that true?"

Daisy thought of her cries in the night, and how she had comforted her.

"She says that your house is full of ghosts."

Daisy breathed out.

"I cannot tell you how this pains me." Atchity took a deep breath and reached across the desk for Daisy's hand, but she pulled it away. "Dr. Carney calls it transference. It's a form of dependency."

"Don't—"

"You've had a hard time of it. Irene tells me that you wanted to have children." Daisy raised a hand to object, but no words came.

"In the end, we put too much responsibility on your shoulders. Do not blame yourself for anything."

"Does she really not want to be with me?"

Again Atchity reached for her hand. She let him take it. "It's what she has requested. She wants to start over when the bandages come off. And she feels, well, I think she feels that things have, perhaps, been slightly overwhelming in your home."

Daisy shook her head. How could she explain? There was no explanation. She could not argue with Dean Atchity's reasonableness. There was nothing to say. She felt riddled by darkness, by shame, by what he described as perfectly normal transference, by her unspeakable needs.

"I would like to see her," Daisy said. "I'd like to speak with her one last time."

"Please understand—she does not wish to see you. And with your husband's connections, it's no longer advisable."

"But what did I *do?*" Daisy's voice leapt out in lament. "You can't trust what she's saying. She must be so confused. Let me see her. I can't believe she's frightened of me!"

"As you say, as you say." Dean stood up. "I'll talk to her in the morning. I'll do what I can do," he said, meaning he would do nothing. Meaning she was dismissed.

The summer sky was bright when Daisy emerged onto Fifth Avenue. The leaves above her head were fat and full of spores. Walter wasn't there, and she couldn't bear the idea of looking for him, so she began to walk: it was all she could do. She couldn't bear the idea of flagging a cab to the station either, or of locating Walter in some coffee shop and taking the train home together, to their ugly haunted house. She felt ashamed, but underneath, like the mother that she was, she was thinking about Keiko.

She didn't know if it was true, or if they had made Keiko say it, terrorizing her with lights and questions. She might have cried out for Daisy, in the car, in her hospital room, as she was wheeled down the corridor, until Dr. Carney and Irene and Dean concocted this story and twisted it into Keiko's mind. She imagined Keiko sitting up, calling from her hospital bed, and Daisy felt panicked, as though Keiko were a defenceless child shut up in her room on the seventh floor. She imagined bending over that hospital bed to look as deeply as she could into Keiko's eyes. *Are you afraid of me? Are you, are you? Or have they done this?*

She imagined Keiko holding up her hand to block Daisy's gaze, then turning away towards the wall. Daisy could only see half of her face, the scarred half, the half illuminated by her stare: the other half, deceptive and slippery, was blotted out by shadows.

VII   FIREBIRD

63.

PEOPLE WHO SAW KEIKO KITIGAWA on television in the fall of 1952—and there were many of them—noticed several things immediately. First, they noticed her clear skin, which on television showed not a hint of a scar. Then they noticed her eyes. Always remarkable, they were especially startling on television. They might also have noticed her clothes. She dressed like Irene Day, skirts and jackets in the height of fashion and beautifully cut, often belted or flared to show her small waist, or cut dashingly at the neck to reveal her delicate collarbone. Lastly, they might have been struck by her poise: she was at ease in front of the camera, or had the ability to seem at ease. She had the winsome charm of a quiz-show participant; in fact, she reminded many viewers of the returning champion from *Winner Takes All.*

The interviews began with *Ask a Doctor,* an enormous cross-country success, launching Dr. Carney on his television career, and launching Keiko as an anti-bomb spokeswoman. But there were many appearances that fall and winter, and each followed the same pattern. The interviewer would ask if Keiko was comfortable.

"Oh, quite, thank you," she would say in what sounded to Daisy like a new, trained voice. It had a bit of the Eastern Seaboard in the vowels.

"Now tell us, Miss Kitigawa, if you would, about the events that changed your life. I'm speaking, of course, of the events of August 6, 1945."

Keiko spoke deliberately, looking either at the interviewer or directly into the camera, depending on what she had been told to do. When she reached the part about the flash— "*pika-don*, the children called it"—the interviewer invariably stopped her.

"Can you describe it in more detail?"

"It was brighter than the sun," she said. "And it seemed to turn everything white. I heard a terrible roar, and then I felt pain, like pins inserted in my skin."

"And then you turned?"

"I raised my hand to block my eyes, and my palm covered one cheek, which is why only one-half of my face was scarred."

"Remarkable. Now tell us, Keiko, in vain you searched for your grandfather in the rubble. He was close to the centre of the bomb and died instantly. Your mother also died in the bombing. Now I understand that you, too, had intended to go downtown, in which case you would have been instantly vaporized when the bomb exploded."

"Yes I did. But we schoolgirls had to work hard, doing physical labour, creating firebreaks in the downtown. I was tired and so I told a fib to my mother, said I felt sick, and so she let me stay home."

"A fib that saved your life, as it turned out. Do you remember other details of the bombing?"

"Indeed, I do." Staring into the camera, she told details that scorched the imagination. She told of looking down at the city a week after the bombing, and seeing plumes of smoke rising along the riverbanks where bodies were being burnt, and how the scent was still in her nostrils. She told of looking for Mama's bones downtown near the Aioi Bridge, finding three buttons and a burnt collarbone, which she and Yoshiko brought home in a box, and how they never found Ojii-chan's bones, though they looked for weeks. She told of the child with his head on fire and of the burning corpses in the river. She described the injured woman clutching her baby at the end of the bridge, begging for water. As the firestorm swept towards them, this woman, face-less and terrible, beckoned to Keiko.

Daisy, standing with a duster in her hand, watching the television, felt a chill run through her. Surely Keiko would not tell this last story.

"And what did you do, Miss Kitigawa?"

"I was frightened," she said. "You see, at first I thought the woman was my mother, but then I realized that she couldn't be. My mother had been wearing a civilian outfit, trousers and a cotton shirt, the kind the government issued, but this woman had been wearing a kimono. I could see its pattern burnt onto her back."

"Now tell us what you did."

Don't, Daisy thought, sitting on the couch.

"A firestorm was nearing—all the wooden houses burning."

"You had only minutes to escape."

"I saw that the woman held a child, a baby—it was dying, or perhaps even dead. Blood ran from its ear. Its body was burnt. The woman was bent over, weeping. But when she saw me she gestured for me to come close."

"Did you?"

"As I say, I was frightened. But yes, I did as she asked."

"And then what?"

Keiko had stood in front of the woman, who raised her

face—it was pink, skinless. "The woman said, 'Please. Take my baby. Take my baby. Run.' Because of the firestorm."

"She wanted you to carry her baby to safety?"

"Yes, she did."

"And what did you think then, Keiko."

"I thought the woman was from a nightmare."

"But you took the baby?"

"Yes, I took the little thing in my arms—as I say, it was dying—I saw that, but I took it, and I was about to run towards the city, but the woman—the faceless woman—she held out her hand, the skin hung from her wrist like a glove, and she said, 'No—go back.' Because of the fire, you see. So I ran. I ran and ran until I got to the park near the military grounds."

But this wasn't how it went. Daisy shook her head, hardly believing what she heard. Keiko had told her—bandaged face turned to the wall—that she had run from the woman and her burnt child, too terrified to stay another second, to heed the woman's pleading request. "Forgive me," Keiko had whispered. "I can't. I must find my mother."

Forgive me.

"And what did you do then?"

"I undid the bundle, and I saw that the little thing was dead. So gently, I covered its face with the cloth it had been wrapped in. And I said a ritual prayer."

Here Daisy shook her head in disbelief. That's my story, she thought. That's my secret. My baby. My ritual prayer! She watched Keiko's face for some sign—some signal that she knew she had slipped Daisy's story in—right there—at the heart—but the girl continued bravely on, answering the interviewer's questions.

Ever excellent in what she did, Keiko closed each interview by thanking the Hiroshima Project for her surgery, turning her face from side to side, to show the lack of scarring. Then she urged the American people to give their generous support to the next group of Hiroshima Maidens, who even now were readying themselves for the voyage to New York.

"And what is your hope for the future, Keiko—you who have seen so much?"

"I hope we can raise our voices—all of us—to stop the madness of the hydrogen bomb." She said this lightly, like a chant, her voice pure and clear. Watching television, you would have to know this girl very well to see, as she glanced away from the camera, her milky eyes betraying the smallest hint of contempt. It was on her face an instant only, and then it was gone.

64.

INDIAN SUMMER GRIPPED the Five Boroughs that fall. Fran, waddling and huge now, set out her sprinkler and Junie and Jimmy Jr. and the other neighbour children ran through it, slipping on the grass. Daisy watched through her window, a feeling of betrayal moving, anew, at the sight of them. She walked away, down the hall, but caught a glimpse of herself in the smoky mirror, hungry and overwhelming, just as Keiko had said. Her massive needs, her frightening desires. She felt a furtive presence behind her down the hall, which, when she turned, was nothing at all.

She made tea and forgot to drink it. She ran a shower and washed herself with the sandalwood soap—Keiko's sandalwood—using all the water, as Keiko used to. She would have given Keiko the soap, if she had asked. All she had ever had to do was to ask.

That night Daisy found the Goldenloaf Cheese box, pushed far beneath Keiko's bed. Everything was still inside—the brooch, the lighter, the ebony elephant. Why leave it behind? Daisy sat on the ugly brown carpet, remembering Keiko's clear, urgent voice, telling her story on television: *Yes, indeed I did. I covered its face with a cloth. I said a ritual prayer, to ease the passing of its soul.* You would have had to listen so closely to hear—no, nobody could hear it, there were simply no seams to show where she had let drop her own, unimaginable, untellable story, and inserted Daisy's.

I covered the dead baby's face. Oh, it was coolly done. It was impeccable. I gave her that story, Daisy thought, staring at the tiny golden brooch, its perfect antennae, the dusty pansy markings on each wing. She listened and I told her. I wept! And then the girl told that story instead, because her own—her own was too awful. And why leave the Goldenloaf Cheese box behind? Because Daisy had told her she had seen it, of course. It was no longer secret.

When Walter came home, he found her sitting on the floor, holding Keiko's box. He asked what was in it and Daisy said a few things—a few things the girl had left behind. Then she burst into tears. Walter took Daisy in his arms, cradled her, which was awkward to do in that position. Eventually, he sat on the bed and patted it.

"Sit," he said, and she sat down obediently.

He traced the line of her nose with his finger, kissed her cheeks, one then the other. "You're a good woman, Daisy," he said.

"I'm not! I'm a monster."

"A good woman. Remember that."

He put his arms around her and comforted her as best he could.

In those days after Keiko left, Fran did not give up hoping for her return. She brought more magazines, and she kept asking questions. Did the skin match perfectly? Was Keiko happy?

Daisy dreaded hearing the phone ring, or seeing Fran at the back door, panting, red faced, knowing she would have questions that Daisy could not answer. Seven and a half months' pregnant, hips loose and wobbly, belly huge, it took a concerted effort for Fran to go through the back gate, up the steps. When would they see her again? When would she come to visit? Wasn't she wonderful on television? A celebrity! Who would have thought it.

It was not as it had been when Daisy had lost the baby. Then she had hated the women of Riverside Meadows and felt removed, sealed behind her piece of glass. Now she felt that all her limbs were heavy, filled with a bulky remorse. Sometimes, thinking about the pouches and aches and loneliness laced into her cells, she would shake her head, realizing that the person who would most understand these sensations would be Keiko. But Keiko had been ripped away from her. No, that wasn't right. She still had to correct herself, remember what had happened.

The girl had taken what she could and then fled.

65.

IN THE MOVIES, anti-Communist agents travel around in ominous-looking Oldsmobiles with big running boards and hoods shiny as black beetles, sinister and immediately identifiable. But, in fact, the cars agents drove in 1952 were undistinguished-looking vehicles, rusted and weather-beaten, with windows that didn't close all the way and milky stains on the leather seats. The agents were undistinguished too—a new breed of itinerant man hunter, Pinkerton detectives down on their luck, or veterans with shell shock and no job prospects. They were hired to gather information on suspects and then submit it to the FBI.

Daisy saw a car just like that, parked in front of their house, as she turned the corner onto Linden Street. She had come from the grocery store, taking the path through the fields. The corn leaves were sticky and huge, cobs frothing with hair, and she had been thinking about a story that she had heard, long ago, at Sacred Heart, about a corn blight. One of the older girls had told the story, trying to frighten the little ones. Farmers had peeled back the leaves of their cobs, one bad year, to find baby mice nested there, in purple-blue amniotic sacs. But some farmers hadn't realized, and had sold their cobs to the markets; some mothers hadn't realized, and had served the cobs steaming onto the table; some mice had been buttered; some had been eaten.

How did she recognize the car so quickly, when she had never seen one quite like it before? It was a station wagon, with corroded fenders, a dent in the door. Clever, she thought later, for them to enter the suburbs in a family car.

She didn't plan to mention the car to Walter when he got home from work, but he brought it up himself.

"Are you expecting a visitor?" he said as he took off his tie.

"I don't know—what do you mean?"

"Fellow outside. Lurking."

"Is he?"

He smiled, tight-lipped. "Reckon he is." He stopped to roll himself a cigarette, then walked out the front door, down the steps and across the road—observed by all the neighbourhood women. He knocked on the car's window. Told her later the fellow was reading the funnies. L'il Abner.

"Are you lost?"

The man, a stout fellow with boils on his neck, put his paper down and started the car in a real panic.

"Cause if you're lost, I can give you directions."

He bolted while Walter stood on the road and whistled under his breath—the notes that began *The Whistler*. He rubbed his palms on his trousers (the weather was still unseasonably warm), then bowed to Fran Warburgh, who let her curtain drop.

Inside, he asked Daisy questions. It was one thing to protect him when all it took was silence, but now he was after her, so she told him what Dean had said. He listened in silence, then went into the bedroom. She followed him and saw a vein moving in his temple as he undid his jacket. She thought he might go silent on her, but he hung up his jacket, then turned to her.

"Girl must be under a lot of pressure," he said.

Daisy nodded, though in fact neither of them knew this for certain. She had been under pressure in their home—so she said—but since? Who could say? Had it been hard for her to give Walter's name, had it come after hours of pressure, or had she sung it out brightly and blankly, as soon as she was asked? Daisy saw a cage. Inside that cage a furious animal, screaming betrayal. That was how Daisy felt. If she looked at Keiko one way, she saw a victim pushed into a corner, fighting to survive. But when she pressed the velvet nap the other way, she saw the girl giving up Walter's secrets, as she had taken Daisy's, without a qualm. Quite able to do what was necessary.

The agent turned out to be named Melville Shrank.

Most evenings Walter walked out to speak to him, to offer a drink or a smoke. And because Melville Shrank was a drinking man and his job was hard, he would, from time to time, accept a nip of whisky, especially after nightfall.

Once, Daisy brought out a bowl of stew.

"Thank you, ma'am," Shrank said. "That's right kind of you." He took the bowl and spoon and ate it right there.

"You would think they'd be warned not to eat the stew of Communist infiltrators," she said to Walter when she came in. But apparently not. Hunger had won out, at least for Melville Shrank. Later, she found the bowl resting on the front mat, licked clean.

He was an odd man, ugly but not unpleasant. When he sweated, his boils deepened in colour. As Indian summer progressed, they spread to the backs of his hands, and some of them developed scales.

His presence in Riverside Meadows changed everything. One morning Daisy knocked on Fran's door to see if she wanted anything at the store. She knocked again. Fran opened the door a tiny crack and thrust a piece of paper at Daisy. It had been recently gestetnered, the pale blue ink smelling of licorice: *For the sake of national security, can you take a few minutes to answer questions about your neighbour?*

"You've done it this time, Daisy Lawrence." A look of pure fear contorted her face. Beyond, at the bedroom door, Daisy saw Ed wearing his brown robe. He stared at her, cold and motionless, as Fran snatched back the paper and slammed the door.

That was the beginning of the worst time. Daisy knew what the women of Riverside Meadows would do with this information: a traitor in their coffee klatches; a spy sitting by the Stricklands' swimming pool! Imagine what the Lawrences must have done to Keiko, she pictured them saying: how they must have whispered incendiary messages in her sleep. And this time everything went the way she thought it would. The women of Riverside Meadows did not descend on her wielding golf clubs and barbecue forks, but they seemed quite ready to hate her, and as viciously as necessary. Someone left a scoop of dog shit on her doormat; a child pelted her front window with eggs. Keiko's stay had been, it seemed, a hiatus, a truce, like the one at Christmastime in World War One, when Germans and Canadians wandered into no man's land, leaning up against the barbed wire, exchanging greetings, smoking one another's cigarettes.

66.

DEAN ATCHITY HAD SAID that if Daisy and Walter were silent, and never tried to see Keiko, that the FBI would not be notified, and Daisy was never sure why things unfolded the way they did. Perhaps Atchity couldn't control the process. Or perhaps it had nothing to do with Atchity. Perhaps the FBI had managed to get hold of Walter's old writings, the signature on the letter sent to *The New York Times,* for instance, condemning those who condemned the Moscow Trials. Or perhaps Walter had tried to see Keiko a final time—slipping off, as Daisy herself had done, to stand below Irene's window, just to try to catch a glimpse of the girl coming or going. Perhaps Irene had looked out and seen him there, and her fury at Daisy had made her blow the whistle on Walter. For there could be no question that Irene had hated Daisy—not the lisping, insecure girl who had come to her from Sacred Heart. Not Margaret Mary—but the woman she had, briefly, become.

It was also possible, of course, that Keiko herself had done the final betraying. Certainly she had done enough of it to know how it was done. Perhaps she had stood at the window and pointed Walter out, negligently, with delicate cruelty. *Look, Miss Day, it's Mr. Lawrence standing across the street. I wonder if he wishes to visit you.*

The subpoena was brought to the house by a more official-looking fellow than Melville Shrank, a man with a fedora and polished shoes and a cream-coloured Studebaker: Shrank's more prosperous cousin. But it was still up to Shrank to see that Walter arrived at the hearing. That morning Daisy looked out the window and saw him sweating in his car, his neck red as a scarf from its mass of boils. She imagined ringing out a wash-cloth in cold water, pressing it to his skin.

Walter dressed carefully, slicking his hair so that it shone. As they left the house, he gave Melville a small salute, as though to say, *Here we go.* Shrank drove three car lengths behind them on the Northern State Parkway, close enough to pursue if they bolted. Daisy could have told him not to worry: Walter kept Shrank in his mirror the whole way, showing a gentlemanly care, even stopping midway through a yellow light and backing up so that Shrank and he wouldn't get separated.

It was not one of the major hearings the House Committee held, sandwiched as it was between exposing Reds in high schools and Reds in unions. Walter was part of the entertainment industry, but he was no Elia Kazan, no Lauren Bacall. His appearance did not even make the television news, though it was written up in some newspapers. In the end, his refusal to name the people he'd associated with in the old days made little difference: it certainly didn't affect national or international security. Walter Lawrence took a stand, but not every stand has an influence on history.

He stood with his back straight, hands clasped behind him, his salt-and-pepper hair dignified and sleek. The committee members tried to shame him and berate him about his radio work, his old comrades and why, as an ex–Communist Party member, he had insinuated himself into the Hiroshima Project. He was far too much of a gentleman to say that involvement in the Project had been his wife's brainchild.

He told Daisy afterwards that he had felt sick the whole

time: the fried-egg sandwich he had eaten that morning had not agreed with him. But that was not how he seemed. A weight was gone from Walter's body; the grey outer skin, that last self-punishing layer, was scrubbed clean. Or maybe he looked like a condemned man, the kind you see in cowboy movies: a posse had built a gallows and were about to hang him, but he stood there while they tied the rope around his neck and, for however many minutes were left to him, he yelled out every true thing he could think of.

He had a statement in his pocket, typed up on a piece of yellow foolscap. When the committee refused to have it read into the record, Walter began to read anyway, raising his voice above the banging of the gavel and the shouts of outrage.

"You can make people speak, Mr. Chairman. If you push them hard enough—you've shown that well enough. But you can't get at our insides. Inside we're all free. And the American people may go along with you now, but give them time and they'll rise up and find their voices. Because you can't silence the truth, Mr. Chairman. And the more you call black white, and darkness light, the more the truth just wiggles around and finds a way to get itself heard."

The committee members had no idea he had been trying for a long time—ten years, in fact—to be able to say these things; that these few words were, in fact, his magnum opus. Nor did they know that he was speaking both to the committee and past it, to another place, another trial—that this was his final answer to the gulags, the executions, the confessions exhorted at gunpoint.

Inside we're all free.

He was still telling the committee what he thought when they charged him with contempt and hauled him off to serve two months in jail.

67.

DAISY'S RETURN TO RIVERSIDE MEADOWS was to an ominous, perfect silence. The voices of the women had been stilled; the screaming of Fran's children had been stilled; even the howling dog in Stoney Creek had been silenced. Daisy parked the car in front of the house and walked up the brick path. Someone had thrown a rock at the window, but it had left only the smallest hole, like a puncture: the glass had not shattered. She heard the click as the door unlocked. This then was what she had feared, the whole drive home: the empty hall, the deepest quiet, how her face would look first in the telephone alcove mirror, then distorted and elongated in the toaster, then—as she prepared for bed—in the mirror above the bathroom sink.

She put on Walter's cardigan, then sat at the kitchen table, not turning on the lights, so that nobody could walk round to the alley, peer over the back fence and see her there. She listened to the ticking of the stove clock, the creaking of the walls expanding, stared at the wallpaper with its cherries and pale stripes. She heard a movement at the side of the house. Children, she thought: another rock thrower, or egg thrower, or someone with matches. She went to the door, listened, ear to the wood, before opening it.

Someone had left a squat box on the doormat, beside the empty bottles. She took it inside, unsure whether to throw it out or open it, but curiosity got the better of her and she pulled back the lid.

It was a rhubarb pie. Daisy put her nose down close and smelled the crust, wondering if it might be filled with shit. It was fragrant. She cut it open and ate a slice with her hands, sour and stringy and soft. It needed sugar. Whoever baked it didn't know the trick of setting the piecrust first, by baking on an egg-yolk glaze, so that the fruit juice didn't dampen the dough.

Next morning Daisy heard a soft knock at the door. It was Joan Palmer.

"For Christ's sakes, let me in."

"Do you *want* to come in?"

"Give me a goddamned break. Yes, I want to come in."

Daisy made coffee in the kitchen while Joan sat at the table. There had been a Residents' Committee meeting, she said abruptly. "A lot of loudmouths talking about stuff they don't know a thing about."

Daisy put the cream on the table.

"Don't worry, Daisy," Joan said. "I stood up for you. Practically got lynched." She grinned. "But there you go. There were others too. Gerald Strickland. He said you'd obviously had the wool pulled over your eyes by Walter: the little woman was confused, that sort of thing. But it worked: you can stay."

"And Fran?"

"She couldn't support you, you know her— 'Ed would kill me.' I mean, he *would,* but it's also an excuse for her, isn't it? For an extremely shallow woman, she does have her deep side. Anyway, Ed put his foot down and there was nothing I could do. I've always found her pliable, but I guess she's been plied enough. Fair-weather friends, Daisy—all except me."

Through Joan's visits, Daisy got a sense of what a stir she and Walter had caused. Most of their neighbours had voted to use the "grave misconduct clause" in the residents' agreement to kick them out of Riverside Meadows.

"Lock your door," Joan warned.

She kept Daisy abreast of other news, too. One morning in

mid-November, Joan told Daisy that Fran had had her baby: seven pounds, three ounces. "She said she's going to leave Ed, just as soon as the baby's weaned, but mark my words, it will never happen." They sat at the table, not even bothering with the formality of coffee. Joan's lips were chapped and raw: a virus she'd had for the past week, something nobody had ever heard of before.

"Lucky Keiko isn't here any more," Daisy said. "She would have been blamed for sure."

Joan snorted. "Those fools," she said, and Daisy felt a bit ashamed that it still felt so good to be inside the circle Joan cast.

They talked about other things as well. Joan talked about her twin brother and, increasingly, perhaps spurred by Joan's reminiscences, and how much solace she seemed to find in them, Daisy talked about her childhood in Syracuse. Mostly she talked about Sacred Heart, the rituals, for instance, curtsying in chapel when they sang Jesus' name, and making up sins in the confessional booth, because nothing she ever did seemed bad enough. She talked about the sugar lambs they got at festivals, how careful she had always been to eat the lamb's hindquarters first. All these memories came back to her, and she spoke of them to Joan, describing the solemn whispering of the girls, down on their knees on Lady Day, holding lilies in their sweating hands. Or on the Feast of the Sacred Heart, how they wore white and prayed to the actual heart of Jesus. *Heart of Jesus, desire of the everlasting hills. Heart of Jesus, burning furnace of charity.* This last was because Jesus had appeared to the founder of Sacred Heart in a vision. He took her heart and without a single word he placed it inside the furnace of his own chest. After a while, he had smiled at her, as if to say, *See how easy this is,* and he had taken out her burning heart and returned it to her.

When Daisy mentioned Jesus, Joan rolled her eyes.

Jesus! Now there was a name you didn't hear much these days. Joan looked like she'd rather Daisy confess she was a Red and had given away the secret of atomic weapons, as they said Ethel Rosenberg had done, then lisp on to her about Jesus—why him?

Daisy didn't consider herself to be brave. She didn't believe she could spend two months in jail, as Walter was doing. Nor did she believe she could have stood up to the mad howlings of the Residents' Committee, as Joan had done. The only real strength Daisy felt she exhibited in that bad period, when Walter was jailed, was to keep thinking about Jesus—like a zealot, Joan had hinted, but that wasn't right, more like a woman with a secret. Yes, with one small secret left. She was childless, and Walter was gone and Keiko had fled (she shook her head when she thought about Keiko), but the nice thing about Jesus was that you could believe he was made up—all that love he was supposed to have—just a beautiful made-up construction. So she could imagine him opening his flannel robes, pointing with his delicate, bloodied palms to his flaming heart. She could imagine him resting her head against the burning furnace, showing her how easily this was done. She could imagine him loving her.

Daisy and Joan talked about Keiko a lot, sharing news of her appearances on television. Daisy braced herself to hear about every new growth in the girl's abilities. Joan was able to discover, without probing too piercingly, that Keiko had told the Project about Walter, and that the Project, in turn, must have told the FBI.

"She fingered him," Joan summarized.

"I don't think she knew what she was doing," Daisy said.

"They forced her?"

Daisy shook her head, said nothing. Just to think of all the pain Keiko had caused had its bracing effect, like so much cold air blowing along the baseboards. The night before the pipes had frozen.

Sometimes, if Joan had news of Keiko, she started tentatively.

"Are you sure you want to hear?" she would say, though she knew Daisy wanted the news. One day she told her that Keiko had spoken to a gathering of eight hundred people at Carnegie Hall. Paul Robeson and she had sung a duet afterwards.

"Gordon and I tried to see her backstage. We waited for an hour. She wouldn't see us."

"Maybe she didn't know it was you."

"She knew all right. She trotted right by us on Dr. Carney's arm! I called out to her, and she just looked at me blankly."

"She may not have seen you properly."

"Daisy, she saw me. She snubbed me." Joan shook her head. "Oh, she isn't what she seemed," she said, marvelling. "I guess Riverside Meadows wasn't good enough for her."

Daisy shook her head too; not that she agreed with Joan's way of seeing things, but it felt good to sit with her, to bask in the comfort of their joint reproaches. They had given her everything, that was what Daisy and Joan were telling each other—everything!—and it hadn't been nearly enough.

"Walter bought her a TV, I guess you know that."

"That committee of yours is going to discover, sooner or later, that they can't trust her," Joan said. "Mark my words."

"I'm not so sure."

Joan asked how she could possibly say that, after all she and Walter had been though, but Daisy decided not to answer. What she was thinking lately was that Keiko's contract with the committee was different from the one she had with Daisy. The committee merely wanted her to speak, but Daisy had wanted to understand every silence, every moan, to follow her when she walked in the night, to stop her from crying. Daisy had felt

Keiko enter her heart's heart. And it was from this
place that Keiko had had to gnaw her way free—like
vivor, escaping from any trap.

68.

HYDROGEN TEST FLASH EQUALS LIGHT
OF "TEN SUNS"
3 ASSERT ATOLL VANISHED

WASHINGTON, NOVEMBER 2, 1952—The world's first
ever hydrogen bomb test explosion yesterday, at Eniwetok Atoll in
the Marshall Islands, was a devastating blast, with approximately
three hundred times the destructive force of the Hiroshima bomb,
according to reports by servicemen.

Vessels were scattered around the island about thirty miles
from the explosion. Aboard the ships men donned protective
clothing before the blast and were instructed to turn their
backs, close their eyes and cover their faces with their arms.

At 7:14. a.m. Eniwetok time, a voice over the loudspeaker of
each ship started counting the seconds. For six seconds after
zero there was silence.

The first sign of the explosion came to the men aboardship in
the form of a flash many times brighter than the sun, followed
by a wave of heat across their backs. It would take ten suns to
equal the light of the explosion from a distance of thirty-five
miles, a navigator said.

Ten seconds after zero the men on ship started turning
around to face the direction of the blast.

"I could hardly believe my eyes," one said. "A flame about two miles wide was shooting five miles into the air. Then we saw thousands of tons of earth being thrown straight into the sky. Then a cloud began to form. You could swear that the whole earth was on fire. It was really something."

At least three eyewitnesses reported that the island on which the bomb had been exploded disappeared after the blast.

"The whole island burned for about six hours. During this time it was gradually becoming smaller," one man said. "Within six hours a three-mile-wide island covered in palm trees and coconuts had disappeared."

69.

ONE MORNING IN DECEMBER, three weeks after Walter had returned from his stint in prison, the telephone rang, and when Daisy picked it up she knew who it was right away, even before Keiko had said a word: Daisy could tell by the breathy silence.

She told Daisy she wanted to see her, her voice tentative at first, then growing harder as she spoke, more distanced, so that as Daisy put the receiver down it seemed possible that Keiko might change her mind and not arrive for their meeting at all. Hearing Daisy's voice, hearing whatever she projected involuntarily (victimization? deep sighs of smothering love?), might have put her off entirely.

"I'm leaving on Tuesday, Mrs. Lawrence," Keiko said. "Now that the H-bomb has been exploded, I am to go on an international tour. I hoped we could meet again before I leave."

The idea of never seeing Keiko again ripped at Daisy's heart, the way that old word *banishment* must have ripped at the heart of medieval townspeople. Daisy had not seen Keiko or touched her since that night in August when she left Riverside Meadows.

"You go Tuesday," Daisy said, blank whiteness in her stomach.

"Tuesday, Mrs. Lawrence."

"Thank you for calling, Keiko. I would like to see you one last time."

Keiko suggested that they meet at a café not far from Irene's apartment. "If I'm there first," she said, "I will reserve a table. It can be crowded in the afternoons." She said this with Irene's exact intonation. When Daisy heard that, she felt something stir in her, an urge to reach across the distance, even after all that had happened, pin the girl down. She put down the receiver and began to wipe the counters, wondering what she could do to occupy herself until their meeting.

Walter had come home from prison looking grey and gaunt and with the beginnings, though they didn't know it yet, of emphysema in his chest. He coughed a lot at night. His name had been added to the blacklist of people in the entertainment industry. It was a bit of a who's who of political artists, and in later years it was considered an honour to have been on it, rather than the reverse, but it meant Walter couldn't do a stick of work in radio again.

As Daisy drove him home that first day, he kept commenting on the view outside the window, how the pumpkin crops had done, how children looked walking on the shoulder of the Parkway, how the cows back east sure weren't the cattle of Washington State. Near home, Daisy realized that he sounded like an old man enjoying a drive, just glad, in a simple way, to be taken around by someone charitable, shown the day. His edge was gone, that thorny side that made him hate everybody shamelessly. In the relief to have him with her again, Daisy didn't realize how much she would miss that caustic side—how much she had depended on that edge to point her in the right direction.

The evening following Keiko's phone call, Walter and Daisy had a celebration of sorts, because Walter had found a part-time job as a salesman for portable heaters and air conditioners. It was Murray Kesselman who offered him the job. Murray, Walt's old rival at *The Inner Sanctum,* had been put on the blacklist too. Always a mover and shaker, Murray had bounced back by starting a small business selling air conditioners door to door. When Walter went to see him, they had talked about all their years in the party, their old friends and enemies, and in the end Murray had offered Walter a job. He had also given Walter so many books to take home that Walter's briefcase had been hard to carry onto the train.

"It must have riled the FBI agent that was trailing me," Walter said elatedly when he got home. "He must have thought I had all the workings of a bomb in there." He was still being followed, though Melville Shrank had disappeared.

He opened his briefcase and took out a black box wrapped in a thick satin ribbon. He tossed the box on the bed, along with the jacket of his suit.

"That's for you," he said.

"Why me?"

"I don't know. Guess I must fancy you."

"Really? After all this time."

Daisy took the ribbon off and lifted the lid. There was peanut brittle inside, quite a bit of it, her favourite kind. He used to bring it to her in the early days: in some ways, she thought, she had been courted with peanut brittle. Then later, when she was pregnant, he brought it to her from town because she had cravings for it. Daisy was thinking that he'd forgotten that, but then he came around to where she sat on the bed and stroked her hair, then her cheek, in that way he had of touching her, which she had almost forgotten about, a sort of "pet owner to dog" touch, which Daisy had never minded. She closed her eyes, the better to feel what he was doing.

He rubbed her cheek with his thumb and the palm of his hand. Then he moved his hand down to the collar of her dress. His fingers lingered on the top button, and he coughed, a raspy hack. Daisy worried that he might get distracted, so she arched her back and led his palm to her breast, clamped beneath all of its wiring and cupping. She undid her dress, big buttons sliding easily through the holes, and slipped her breast from the cup. Now he could see it completely. He had always been rather taken by her breasts, way back when, fondling them and feeling their weight in his palms. There was little chance, she knew, now that he was concentrating in his new way, gently taking in whatever was placed in front of him, that he would turn down an offer like this one.

Later, over dinner, Daisy told him that she was going to see Keiko. He was quiet, holding his fork, which was loaded up with macaroni and cheese. She saw a muscle trembling in his jaw. Then he brought the forkful to his mouth and ate it slowly. She didn't actually know what was going through his head, what layers of feeling passed through him. Was he thinking of Keiko as the girl who landed him in jail, or as a confidante, a secret muse, a daughter—or just as Keiko—a girl with so many sides that nobody, as it turned out, could know her completely? Daisy looked at him, but she didn't ask.

That night in bed he lay beside her, reading one of Murray's books, sighing, laughing, groaning. Daisy looked at the title: Trotsky's *History of the Russian Revolution*. At one point he put down the book, astonished. "This man can really write," he said. Just as Daisy was falling asleep, she felt him curl up behind her, kneecaps brushing the inside of her knees, fingers cupping her breast. They fell asleep like that, with Trotsky on the nightstand.

My husband, Daisy thought, tasting the words in her mouth. My husband. Walter Lawrence. Air Conditioner Salesman.

He had five good years as a salesman before the emphysema forced him to quit work. After that, Daisy went to work in the cafeteria of the new Riverside Meadows high school. A year later he would get up one morning, shuffle to the front door for the newspaper, and read Harrison Salisbury's account of the Twentieth Congress of the Soviet Union, read, in all that tiny fine print covering two full pages, Khrushchev's revelations of the secret crimes Stalin had committed—the back-alley murders, the tortures, the confessions, the gulags, the mass starvations: massive amounts of text, detailing what Communist parties around the world were still denying. "Between 1930 and 1941, Stalin killed every single person who knew him from the past," Walter said to Daisy. "That's certainly one way to deal with your in-laws."

Daisy imagined steel bars lifted from Walter's chest. She imagined air circulating through his ruined lungs.

By the time he died, in 1968, everything had changed once again. For one thing, some fiery new couples had moved to Riverside Meadows and they'd voted to allow black families to buy houses there. Then they voted, at one exciting meeting, to get rid of the Residents' Committee altogether, and never to meet again. These couples set a new standard of conduct: jumping into one another's pools fully clothed, or naked, sleeping with one another's partners, holding consciousness-raising sessions, to which they dutifully and kindly invited Daisy and Joan. Around this time, too, there was the sudden resurgence in the left-wing theatre scene culminating, at least as far as Daisy was concerned, in the off-Broadway revival of Walter's old play, *Fall from Grace*. It got decent reviews, and earned the play its "seminal place" in American theatre, though Walter, who was in hospital by this time, could only read about it in the papers.

70.

You CANNOT SAY with certainty why things happen. If you have influence. If what you do alters a stone, a twig.

Save yourself, Daisy said—a final time—in a voice deeper than her own. And Keiko did in the end, Daisy will always believe that she did, though it was possible to read Keiko's disappearance as something different and far bleaker, a continuation of a pattern of terrified flight. Her story was always able to break into opposites. You could look at it one way, then surprise it, turning swiftly, to see a new visage on its changeable face.

In the years to come, Daisy would write about Keiko, pages and pages, in her journals. She wrote about Keiko's amber eyes, her interest in fashion, her feet, her delicate finger joints, her tiny knuckles, her soft hair. This was late at night, unable to sleep, after a day working at the high school cafeteria, the voices of the teenagers still in her ears, cacophonous and full of eager swear words. She had gotten the hang of who hated whom, and who was dating whom—it was amazing how much you could pick up across a counter. The kids all thought of her as the woman with the open, friendly smile who doled out the stew and meatballs. Mrs. Lawrence, they called her, though some liked to call her

Daisy—an aging woman with a warm, slightly stupefied look on her face. Though some of them knew about Walter, his imprisonment. One of them once said to her, *Mrs. L, you are cool, man.* Which pleased Daisy more than she felt inclined to admit.

Coming home from these long days she would get out her journal and write, amazed that out of these ordinary days there was so much to record, and so much to get down, too, of the old days. She was amazed at how, slowly and quietly at first, and then with increasing vigour and certainty, she could flip back over the pages, read what she had written and discover that she liked it.

She wrote everything she could remember.

And when she had written everything she knew, she wrote about what she didn't know. She wrote about Keiko's disappearance, the week after Daisy met her at the café. She imagined the pounding on the door, waking Daisy and Walter from their profound sleep. (Now that Walter was dead, in her imagination they always sleep folded together, legs entwined.)

Walter turns on the bedside lamp, surprised, then gropes his way to the front door, belting his old tartan robe. There Keiko stands, gleeful, draped in Irene's mink coat—because yes, wherever she disappeared to, she took that mink with her, that much has been established.

"Tom and I got married at seven," Keiko whispers, her eyes lit up like mirrors. "Nobody knows—it's a secret." Oh, the fox is in her for sure, the very devil of the bakemono. She asks Daisy for a cigarette, and lights it and blows out smoke—like one of the femme fatales from *The Whistler.*

Behind her, Tom's car is parked on the road, expelling plumes of exhaust into the freezing air.

"I just stopped by," she says. "Stopped by to say goodbye." She uses her new, Eastern Seaboard voice. But now Tom leans over, undoes the passenger window and calls out that they have to get moving. He has been keeping the engine revved, but now he gets out, stamping his feet on the packed snow, and grins up at them. "Can't come up, the car may stall out in this cold."

Daisy and Walter put on gumboots and sweaters, then walk down the frozen brick drive to wave the two of them goodbye. They stand in the middle of Linden Street as the car performs a three-point turn and drives away, past the snowbanks, leaving puffs of exhaust like a jet trail behind it.

And then?

And then?

Keiko would sleep and wake, warm in her purloined mink, and eventually, in the cold dawn—there it would be—plain and terrifying and utterly new: the blank Midwestern prairie, spread out on all sides, turning red in the morning sun.

And what do Keiko and Tom think, seeing each other plainly in that dawn? This is hard to imagine.

Still it might be true. They could have children by now. They could live in a house with a red door. When Daisy tries to picture this part, the images slow and become cloudy—Keiko in a station wagon, applying her makeup in the side-view mirror, wearing a scarf and dangling white earrings, Tom swatting his big hand into the back, telling the brood to be quiet. And if she tries to imagine further, the story slows to a creeping pace—becoming still, becoming frozen—until Daisy stands at the door, hand raised to knock, but never able to bring it down on the shining wood.

There are other possibilities: Keiko returning to Hiroshima to work in the back of Yoshiko's hair salon. On Sundays taking the bus to the Atomic Bomb Casualty Commission Office, grimly spouting medical facts: facts about her skin, her hair, the strange bruises behind the knees. Keiko in a high school auditorium, spotlit behind a podium, describing, once more, the details of that one morning, August 6.

But as Daisy grows older, she trusts her own version. It helps to remember what Keiko once told her about Hiroshima: how people believed nothing could grow again, yet how quickly the burnt areas burst forth with grass and weeds. And how terrible that was—to see the cherries bloom too, then the plums, the azaleas, peonies, lilies—the abandonment of it all, the wild and profligate blossoming, as though nature had no stake in human suffering.

But still at night sometimes—after a busy day at the cafeteria—Daisy wakes from dreams of children crying, trains swiftly passing through fields of long white grass. Sometimes the city in the distance was New York; sometimes Hiroshima, or sometimes a mixture of both: each laid out like a holy grid of roads and streetlamps.

And every August 6 since Walter has died, Daisy puts on her husband's old gumboots and takes up two tin cans, into which she has punched holes with a screwdriver. She picks up her matches and candles and she walks out the back door, the screen door hissing closed behind her. She crosses the backyard, the smell of cut grass in her nostrils, and slips through the end of the fence into the Warburghs' yard. The greenhouse is gone, and so is the fallout shelter—it's been replaced by a bed of orange daylilies and purple windflowers. Down the street, the Palmers are gone, and so are the Lithgows—they left after Evelyn killed herself. The Palmers' house was bought by a South African couple whose child is so blond that he burns in the morning sun. But Ed and Fran Warburgh still live next door.

Junie Warburgh waits on the back steps. When she sees Daisy, she stands up. She is rather burly, like her father, with stringy red hair held back by a red paisley bandana, low-slung corduroys, a jacket with the Union Jack sewn on the back. She is in her last year at Hofstra University, though it seems to Daisy that she spends far more time picketing the draft board and organizing alternative classes than attending college. Her brother, Jimmy Jr., is in Viet Nam. Ed and Fran have recieved letters from him. So far, he's doing fine. It makes Junie crazy that he enlisted, and she worries, Daisy can tell, though mostly she talks about "the fucking government," and "shutting down the system." Apparently that is what is needed: shutting down the system once and for all. Daisy listens as she describes the injustices— the body bags, the insanity of Kent State. In six months Junie's boyfriend will have to appear in front of the draft board and they are both thinking of heading to Canada.

They walk down the back alley, then turn onto the crescent. The trees, which were once stick figures, are huge now, a canopy of red-cabbage coloured leaves above their heads. The school has changed too: in the playground there are now a series of turquoise tunnels for kids to crawl through and a concrete bridge over a sandpit. The path is solid, covered in mulched bark; it leads past the school and down to the golf course. Riverside Meadows at last has a meadow at its centre, a nine-hole course that has doubled housing values. Almost every house backing onto the course has a swimming pool. Daisy opens the gate and the two of them go through onto the green. Junie talks non-stop as they walk, furious about the pictures of My Lai that have appeared that week in the news. As they walk closer to the old bridge that spans the verdant edges of the creek, they begin to hear the frogs. Only at the creek, when Daisy gets out her matches, does Junie stop talking, and this is because Daisy tells her to.

Daisy lights her candle.

Junie asks in a low voice when Keiko died, what year.

At first Daisy doesn't answer, she leaves everything to silence. But Junie Warburgh is a nice girl, despite what they all thought of her at the time, and so Daisy explains that she doesn't know what happened to Keiko and that the candles are not only for her but for other souls as well, other children.

"Yeah," Junie says. "There's so fucking many."

Junie takes the matches and lights a candle for herself, and they hold their candles tightly. They sputter, a faint breeze buckling the flames. Daisy lowers hers into the tin can, and Junie does the same, and they clamber down to the pristine verge and set the cans on the still water.

They watch the tin cans burn and bob in the golf-course creek, not speaking a word, which is hard for Junie.

71.

SHE WAS SITTING AT A BOOTH by the window, plucking her calfskin gloves from her fingers, looking poised. She wore a jacket with a Persian wool collar, and a hat with a bit of fishnet veiling, which obscured her face, while at the same time revealing it. The scar was gone—Daisy, sitting across from her, could see that much. She peered hard, but Keiko's skin looked perfect. Her beautiful strange eyes shone out from under the net, and Daisy felt her stomach tighten.

"I can't stay for long," Daisy said. "And I'm sure you must need to rush off to wherever you're going. Have you ordered?"

"Not yet."

Daisy could smell Keiko's perfume: Eau de Joy. Irene's scent. She imagined Keiko dabbing it on when Irene's back was turned, behind her ears, at the temple, and this made Daisy feel brighter. Around them she heard the sound of laughter. Someone at the next table pointed out the window at the snow—huge flakes, the size of ping-pong balls, landing on the sidewalk, the hoods of cars, the roofs of the carriages parked along Central Park South. A horse shook its feathered headdress. When the door jingled open, people came in rosy-cheeked, wiping snow from their shoulders.

Keiko ordered hot chocolate.

"So appropriate," Daisy said. "I'll have the same."

While they waited for their drinks to arrive, Daisy could have made ostentatious, bright—frighteningly bright—small talk: *I hope you're enjoying the winter pleasures of the city. Skating at the Rockefeller Center, or in the park. You must see all the sights, before you head away.* Words slipped into her mind, then slipped away. Why bother? She didn't have to speak, and neither it seemed did Keiko, who sat looking at the water glasses on the table, every now and then glancing up, trying to gauge, so Daisy suspected, the depth of the wound she had inflicted.

"So off you go, on your international tour."

"Yes."

"Everything arranged?"

"Everybody has been most kind."

"Yes, well that's everybody's specialty, isn't it? Ah, here are our drinks." The hot chocolate arrived with great sculptures of whipped cream on top, sprinkled with chocolate.

Daisy took a sip, delicately wiping her lips. Keiko watched her.

"So, my dear," Daisy said. "I suppose you have things to say."

"Can you tell me how things are in Riverside Meadows? How is Mr. Lawrence?"

Daisy pursed her lips. What could she say: *There were rats in prison, you know. And worse. A lot worse. And he coughs up blood.* She looked into Keiko's face. The girl was braced to hear the worst, *wanted* to hear it. Her chin was up, her eyes met Daisy's. Here I sit, that posture said. The unforgivable enemy. Unforgivable survivor.

Daisy turned away, took a sip of her hot chocolate. Finally, she spoke. "He's fine, Keiko," she said, which was also true. When Daisy looked up, Keiko's eyes were still on her.

"And Tom?" Keiko said.

"Have you not seen him?"

"He came at first—to Irene's apartment. He stood beneath the window, and I saw him at Carnegie Hall, where I spoke. But the Project—Miss Day and Dr. Carney, they thought it best if I didn't speak to him. He gave me his telephone number once. But that was many weeks ago now. I haven't seen him since."

She looked at Daisy. "And you—" she said. "How are you, Mrs. Lawrence?"

Daisy looked at the folds of whipped cream on her drink. "I'm sure you didn't arrange this meeting to find out how I was. It's a bit late for that, even you have to admit."

"I wanted to say goodbye," Keiko said simply.

"Ah."

Daisy waited, but nothing more came. Daisy would not volunteer to cover the empty waste with words; she took another sip of her hot chocolate.

Keiko said, "Goodbye, Mrs. Lawrence."

Daisy put her cup down in its saucer. "You never could get the hang of calling me Daisy."

"Goodbye, Daisy."

The word sounded unnatural from her mouth.

"So that's it, then. Goodbye, Keiko. Good luck."

Keiko had begun to put on her gloves, leaving her hot chocolate untouched. She looked down, and saw that she had not even taken a sip. But in order to drink, she had to lift her veil. She set aside her gloves and pushed back the netting—a casual yet perfectly contrived gesture. It was like watching a stripper drop a bit of clothing.

For a moment, Daisy thought, they did it: she's really fixed.

The bubbled scar was gone. Across the room it would have been perfect, or in front of a podium, or on black-and-white television. But sitting intimately at a table beside a window increasingly thick with snow, Daisy could see that every inch of her skin was covered in foundation. The scarred area itself was smooth, but along its edges, following the old outline of South America, a lip of new scar tissue protruded, requiring a deeper coating of foundation.

Keiko looked at her—as she had so often in the past—as though to say, There. Now you know.

"Keiko," Daisy whispered.

"It's better than before," Keiko said.

"Yes—yes, it is."

The skin graft was not quite the same colour as the surrounding skin. The affect in total was of a different, subtler kind of deformation.

"They keep trying," Keiko said. "But it seems that I am a difficult case after all. The skin along the edge of the graft keeps bubbling up, no matter how many times they cut it away."

"You've had more operations?"

Keiko took a delicate sip of her hot chocolate. "It doesn't take long. It doesn't hurt. Every three months or so—that's what Dr. Carney says."

"A new operation, every three months?"

"It doesn't hurt, Mrs. Lawrence. It's the only way I can do the international tour."

"But do you *want* to do the tour?"

"I think I should." Keiko looked away. Her eyes had begun to fill with tears. Was this real, or guile? It seemed impossible to say. The girl could always tug at her heartstrings. She glanced back at Daisy. "I think you understand," she said softly. She didn't say, You are like my mother, but Daisy heard the words floating there, unspoken, and she felt the bones in her legs go watery. I'm not at all like your mother, she wanted to say. I never have been. I was wrong. If she was anybody she was the faceless woman on the bridge, a stranger asking for water for her dead child. Holding it out to her. Frightening Keiko.

"This is who I am," Keiko said softly. "They can't get it to go away."

Shi no hai. That was what she had called it. Ashes of death, with a half-life of forever.

"No, Keiko," Daisy said forcefully, shaking her head. She leaned forward, grasped the girl's hand. "Listen to me. This is not who you are."

"And I know why. Because I ran away, and lied, and I took—"

"I know what you did. It doesn't matter."

"—I took the things you said—"

"None of that matters—"

"And I wouldn't help that baby—though she held it out to me. She begged me—"

"*Listen!*" There it was—her own voice, but deeper. "You don't have to be this person—you can change into something else. I've seen you do it—"

"How can I do that? I don't have money. I don't have anything!"

"We have some money, Keiko. You can have it. But you must make a plan, and you must get away."

"Oh, Mrs. Lawrence!"

Daisy got up and slid in beside Keiko, in the small booth with its leather seat the colour of dried blood. She put her arm around Keiko's shoulder, stroked the soft Persian wool of her collar. It felt like poodle. A low sob rose in Keiko's throat, but she pressed it down, and instead she held tightly to Daisy, buried her head in her coat.

Keiko might be thinking of Daisy as her mother, or as the faceless stranger she had wronged, but Daisy didn't care either way. She did not move a muscle. She did not stroke the girl's cheek or whisper kindnesses, or say, There, there. But she had never felt such compassion for another person, and she knew that this feeling was love. Other people walked past, glancing or not glancing, it didn't matter. Keiko smelled of wet wool, and far away Daisy heard voices ordering drinks, the clink of glasses, the scrape of a metal chair leg.

In her mind Daisy was picking Keiko up, slinging the girl across her back, bare feet dangling, small, scarred legs drumming against her sides. They rose and walked through the burning city—and the city, fuelled by Daisy's arrival, burnt more fiercely, as though to say, At last you have come to help carry this child.

ACKNOWLEDGEMENTS

MANY PEOPLE SUPPORTED ME through the writing of this book. I'd like to thank Bob Penner—as always—for his love and support. I'd like to thank my parents, Barbara and Douglas Lambert; my children, Peter and Lucy; my brothers, James and John Lambert, and their families; my parents-in-law, Norma and Norman Penner, and the extended Penner family; and my aunt, Lorna Schwenk. Thanks also to dear friends for their support—with special thanks to Colette and Wendy Wright, Karen Mahon, Debbie Field, David Kraft, Ann Rowan, David Smith, Mike Magee and Madeline Hope. Thanks to Eva Stachniak, Linda Solomon and Barbara Lambert for their critical advice on earlier drafts. I am very grateful to Mark Rothenberg, historian at the Patchogue-Medford Library, for valuable insights into Suffolk County in the 1950s, and to my brother and sister-in-law for hosting me so graciously while in Japan, and for arranging my trip to Hiroshima.

Huge thanks to Anne Collins, my editor at Random House of Canada: her belief, enthusiasm and editorial guidance carried me forward. Thanks as well to Lennie Goodings, my editor at Virago, for thoughtful insights and support. Many thanks to the people at Random House Canada—Scott Richardson, Janine Laporte, Pamela Murray, Kylie Barker, Sharon Klein— and to freelance editors Heather Sangster and Liba Berry. Huge thanks to my agent, Anne McDermid, for her encour- agement and advice, and to Martha Magor and Jane Warren at Anne McDermid's agency, for their involvement.

Many books influenced me during the writing of this novel. I am particularly indebted to Robert J. Lifton's *Death in Life: The Survivors of Hiroshima,* which first inspired me, and to Rodney Barker's book *The Hiroshima Maidens: A Story of Courage, Compassion and Survival.* I am also indebted to Arata Osada's com- pilation of oral histories, *Children of Hiroshima,* and Hideko Tamura Snider's book, *One Sunny Day: A Child's Memories of Hiroshima.* Lafcadio Hearn's work was inspirational, particularly *Glimpses of Unfamiliar Japan,* as was Jan Morris's wonderful book *Manhattan '45* and Eleanor Early's *New York Holiday.* I would also like to thank the Canada Council of the Arts for its generous assistance.

SHAENA LAMBERT is a novelist and short story writer. Her work has appeared in many periodicals and literary journals and her first book, a collection of short stories called *The Falling Woman*, was a *Globe and Mail* Best Book and a finalist for the Danuta Gleed Literary Award. She lives in Vancouver with her husband and two children.